THERE'S NOWHERE TO HIDE

A Novel By
Patricia Cormack

ISBN 978-0-9847993-1-2

Chapter One

I was first conscious of the gentle breeze that stirred the sheers on the bay window, then aware of the nearby warbling of a bird and the distant barking of a dog. As I looked about me, my eyes focused on a room that I loved. Hanging directly to my left was a painting by Degas entitled "Waiting," a canvas that I had discovered in a small discreet art shop in New York City. I probably identified the girl's expression of anxious anticipation because it mirrored my own feelings of frustrated hope and eager determination. After one last glance, I turned my gaze to the white, solid, marble fireplace that faithfully promised me warmth and comfort on cold winter nights. I was in the process of mulling over my plans for the day when my mind unintentionally shifted to previous disturbing times, memories that dragged with them both pain and regret. Feeling distressed, I threw off the top sheet and quickly slipped out of the bed.

After entering the adjoining en suite bathroom, I activated the flow of water by placing both hands under the faucet, and then leaning over, I splashed a generous amount of the cool liquid on my face. Just as I was about to squeeze some toothpaste onto the bristles of the brush, my hands froze in mid air. When unexpected memories flooded my mind, I snorted through my nose and gave myself a sarcastic defensive grin into the mirror.

Once in the shower, I savored the warm liquid as it therapeutically pelted against my body, and by the time I commanded the taps to deactivate, the entire room was completely filled with steam. Winding a towel around my hair and tucking the end in securely, I then removed my favorite well-worn terry robe from the hook on the back of the door. The instant I entered the living room I was welcomed by the brilliant sunlight streaking through the bay window, bringing with it a blanket of warmth and protection. Feeling somewhat better, I sank into the plush cushions of the sofa, tossed the towel aside, and commenced to dry my hair. At the same time, I attempted to push my most recent disturbing memories aside and to concentrate on more pleasant thoughts. Today was my day off.

Standing in a line-up at a pre-arranged location, I shelved all memories from the previous night for future consideration; however, they definitely were not forgotten. Almost immediately a pleasant middle-aged woman ushered me to a table, handed me a menu, and informed me that a server would be with me shortly. She was soon followed by a second younger girl who was leaning slightly to one side in order to balance the weight of an almost full pot of coffee. I had only taken a few sips when I spotted Lara awkwardly maneuvering in a zigzag pattern around the tables. After bending down and giving me a generous hug, she settled in the chair directly across from me.

"Hi sweetie, like I said earlier on the phone I've been meaning to call you but I've been so damn busy." In order to feel more comfortable, she wiggled her weight around in the seat, and then with a heavy sigh, she looked over at me. "How in the hell are you anyway? It's been a while. I think the last time that I saw you Becky and Bill were still in school."

Before I could answer her question, the waitress interrupted our conversation, and it wasn't until later that we once again focused on her children.

"By the way, I forgot to tell you that Becky has met a boy by the name of Don," there was a short pause, "something or other." She shook her head and looked confused. "Damn, I can never remember his last name. I think that it's Jones, or some other common name. Anyway, strangely he's from here. Don't you think that it's weird that she had to go halfway across the country in order to meet someone that lives practically next door? Evidently he's also in school in Toronto and is taking a course in aerospace engineering at Ryerson. Actually the two of them will be coming home for Thanksgiving, so thankfully I'll get a chance to meet Don."

"That's nice, but without meaning to change the subject, just think: when your son Bill graduates from medical school, you'll also have a doctor in the family." I gave her an all-important look. "Now that's what I call class!"

With a sarcastic frown, Lara aggressively leaned forward. "Hell, what you mean to say is that then we will be able to afford to get sick."

We both laughed at the humor.

Suddenly the smile vanished as Lara became very serious. "Isn't it funny how some people know from the very beginning what they want to be in life. It's almost as though their destiny has been carved out for them. I know that Bill has always wanted to become a doctor." She looked at me sideways. "What about you, Christine? Have you always known what you want to be?"

Feeling a little uneasy I began to toy with my cup, and it took me a few seconds to answer due to a slight lump that had formed in my throat. "Actually, I guess that I have always known what I want to be, and where I want to go." I paused and laughed nervously. "It's getting there that's the problem." Before Lara could make an attempt to analyze my comment, I quickly changed the subject. "Anyway, how's Tom?" Tom was her husband.

"Oh he's fine. His business is doing better than most."

Suddenly Lara sat up straight and dabbed the corners of her mouth with her napkin. "Well enough of my problems." There was an impish look on her face. "Chrissy, I really wanted to see you, but there is a special reason for asking you to meet me here for lunch."

I rolled my eyes. "Oh, no, where have I seen that look before?" With an expression of disapproval on my face, I sat back in my chair and waited.

Leaning forward, Lara enthusiastically informed me that she was having a few people over for dinner the following evening. "I know this is short notice, but I would really love it if you could come."

I gave her a painful look. "I don't know, Lara. I was just going to take it easy this weekend."

Lara glared at me. "God, you're becoming an old stick-in-the-mud."

I looked at her sideways. "As you said, it is short notice."

"Oh, come on. There's a chair at the table with your name on it. Please, Chrissy!"

Pursing my lips together, I looked at her suspiciously. "And who is the wonderful, fabulous, gorgeous gentleman that I am going to meet this time?"

Ignoring the sarcasm, Lara's eyes flashed with excitement. "Wait until you meet him. He is so handsome, very rich, and extremely smart."

My eyes narrowed in distrust. "But more importantly, is he totally unattached?"

"Weeell, he almost is. Actually, his divorce is to be finalized in the next few weeks." There was a pleading look on her face. "Christine, just come over and meet him. The worst you could have is a dull evening."

Reluctant and feeling that I had just been coerced, I succumbed. "Well, since my name is already on the chair…"

Lara's face lit up. "Great! Good choice! Dinner is at seven but come over at six for cocktails."

I motioned for the check and when it came we both scrambled for it. Lara won and gave the piece of paper a triumphant wave in the air while I scowled and said that the next time it was my turn. In the parking lot, we said our goodbyes, hugged each other, and went our separate ways.

I spent the rest of Friday doing some grocery shopping and making a few necessary purchases at one of my favorite boutiques. By seven p.m., attired in jeans and a sloppy bright red cotton shirt, I opened the refrigerator, stuck my head in, and after rummaging around, pulled out ingredients for a salad. First I cleaned and tore the lettuce into a bowl; then I added two kinds of cheese, some tomatoes, celery, almonds, raisins, and pieces of chicken that I had cooked the day before. After pouring some wine, I moved into the living room. Selecting a movie from the menu on the screen, and finding my favorite spot on the couch, I proceeded to enjoy both the story and the meal.

When the movie ended, I sat back on the cushions and slowly sipped my second glass of wine. The room had already darkened and the only illumination was coming from the distant street lamps outside. Tendrils of pale light shone through the windows and crept inquisitively across the room, poking and probing, producing eerie shadows and black foreboding spaces everywhere. Having a low tolerance for wine, as more than one drink always made me sleepy, it was not surprising that I was soon breathing deeply with my conscious mind shut down while the clock ticked away the hours.

Suddenly my eyes popped open as though I had been roughly shaken awake. Sitting bolt upright, I frantically grabbed the pillow beside me and hugged it to my bosom for protection. The air in the room seemed heavy, making breathing difficult, while tiny beads of perspiration covered my forehead. Looking around, I expected to find some alien person, or thing, lurking in the shadows, ready to pounce. After I was certain I was alone, my head snapped toward the clock. It was three a.m. Five hours had passed since I had fallen asleep.

Trembling and in need of support and comfort, I curled myself into a ball and wrapped my arms around my bent legs. At this point, all that I could remember were the eyes, the strange menacing eyes that were indelibly embedded in my memory. Rocking back and forth, I became disoriented as my perspective between reality and fiction was lost.

Having difficulty sleeping after the episode, I lay awake for the remaining few hours while trying to put the pieces together, and when I finally dozed off, I slept fitfully until ten. When I awoke, I suddenly remembered that I had agreed to go to Lara's for dinner that evening. "Oh no," I moaned as I shoved the pillow over my face. Dragging myself out of bed, I made a quick trip to the bathroom then wandered into the kitchen where I put on a pot of coffee. The apartment was soon permeated with its rich, succulent aroma.

Pouring myself a mug of the dark liquid I sat at the table in the adjoining eating area and gazed out through the bay window. As I stared down at a park that was quickly filling with weekend activity, my attention became focused on several joggers as well as on some young children with their nannies, or mothers. A few lovers were either stretched out on the grass or else strolling hand in hand seemingly oblivious to anything, or anyone around them.

After lethargically sipping on my coffee for perhaps fifteen or twenty minutes, an unexpected jolt went through my body almost causing me to drop my cup, while at the same time a sudden wave of nausea washed over me producing a loss of equilibrium. Without warning I had remembered more of the bizarre dream. Staring blankly ahead I saw nothing except the image that had menacingly flashed into my conscious mind.

My expression was grim, my eyes were hard and cold with determination as a lonely tear trickled down my left cheek. "It wasn't just a dream. I know. It wasn't just a dream."

Chapter Two

That evening when Lara's maid opened the door her face broke into a wide spontaneous smile. "Miss Anderson! How nice it is to see you again."

After stepping into the spacious entranceway I slipped my wrap over her outstretched arm, leaned slightly forward and asked in a lowered voice. "Is everyone here?"

"Yes, they're in the main room. Please go right in." Her lips suddenly broadened into a genuine smile. "And have a pleasant evening."

As I was passing an ornate mirror in the entranceway I paused briefly to rearrange a strand of hair that had fallen out of place, then moving closer to the glass surface I inspected my teeth for lipstick. Finding none I pulled my shoulders back and with a positive attitude crossed the span of black and white tiles to the formal living room.

Pausing under the archway I eagerly scanned the room for my hostess and when our eyes locked. Lara politely excused herself from two of her guests. After a quick wink and a smile in my direction she made her way towards me. Giving each other a careful hug, as well as a kiss that hung in the air, she affectionately linked her arm in mine. "Come on Sweetie, I'll introduce you to everyone."

I was already familiar with four of the people from previous occasions while the other two couples were business clients of Lara's with whom she was in the process of completing a substantial real estate transaction. After the usual salutations I turned my attention to the last individual who, up till now, had been partially obscured from my vision. I was totally unprepared for the encounter. He was tall, at least six-feet-three, or four, had a full head of medium brown hair and eyes that were fascinating as well as intense.

In the corner of my eye I could see Lara as she shrewdly scrutinized the two of us by quickly glancing from me to him then back to me again. "Christine I'd like you to meet Robert Power. Robert this is my dear friend Christine Anderson." There was a distinct promotional emphasis on the word dear.

The second our skin touched, and our eyes locked, I not only felt breathless I also felt slightly disorientated. When there was an obvious delay in relinquishing of hands Lara of course immediately noticed.

"I'll leave the two of you to get acquainted." With a mischievous grin she reached over and brushed my arm up and down a few times with her hand then apparently satisfied turned her attention to some of the other guests.

After an awkward silence Robert politely asked me what I would like to drink. By the time he returned with two glasses I had already made myself comfortable in one of the two soft cushioned chairs that were conveniently arranged at the far side of the room for conversational purposes. After handing me the glass, then sitting beside me, there was another uncomfortable moment while we took a few sips of the dark red liquid.

I broke the silence. "So, Lara mentioned that you are a lawyer. Do you have a specialty Robert?"

When he responded his voice had a matter-of-fact tone to it. "Yes, actually I'm a criminal lawyer."

I raised my eyebrows in surprise. "Hmm, that's very interesting but I do hope that I will never need your services." Since I was teasing him there was a slight twinkle in my eyes, however when I looked into his they had narrowed defensively and his lips were pursed firmly together.

"What line of work are you in Christine?"

Quickly without giving it a thought I answered, "I'm a nurse." The words were hardly out of my mouth when I realized that I had walked into this one.

With a smile of satisfaction he responded, "Likewise, I'm sure."

With the color on my face darkening slightly I conceded, touché.

For the next forty-five minutes we chatted as though we were old friends. I was genuinely impressed when I realized that Robert was not only intelligent but that he also possessed a good sense of humor. As well as being an attentive listener he had a knack of extracting information from me, perhaps an ability that was a prerequisite to his profession. We were so absorbed in our conversation that it seemed premature when Lara announced that dinner was to be served.

It was Lara's custom to assign the seats, a practice that she always found created a more interesting and enjoyable evening. She would split the couples up while at the same time she would ensure that the sexes alternated around the table. Since Robert was assigned a seat directly across from me I was periodically aware of his intense gaze throughout the meal. Each time I looked over and was confronted by a serious penetrating appraisal our eyes would lock as though a magnet was drawing us together. Pleased with the apparent success of her matchmaking Lara would, from time to time, give me that 'I told you so' smile.

After the dessert we withdrew to the family room where the atmosphere was warm and cozy. The area was filled with soft cushioned couches and green leafy plants. The walls were adorned with oil and water paintings, and the shiny hardwood floor was partially covered with a large colorful Persian rug. Flames danced erratically on the grate of a stone fireplace thus giving the room a life of its own, while the melodic tones of one of Mozart's symphonies, played by Vladamir Ashkenazy, could be discreetly heard above the hum of conversation. Sitting together on a love seat pleasurable feelings rippled through me whenever we accidentally touched, and when he turned his body in my direction his weight shifted slightly on the couch.

"Have you known Lara for a long time Christine?"

"For the last fifteen years but we have been very close friends for the last ten." I raised my eyebrows. "How long have you known her?"

"Tom and I met through a mutual friend about a year ago".

I cocked my head as I looked at him quizzically. "It's strange that we haven't connected until now because I usually attend most of their parties."

His smile was rather uncomfortable. "Well I haven't been socializing too much lately. I don't know if Lara told you but I'm in the process of getting a divorce."

"Yes, she did mention it. Still you know what they say about all work and no play...."

Robert suddenly looked tired as his eyes darted to the far side of the room and when he spoke his words had a hard ring to them. "It's not the first time that I've been accused of being a workaholic." By the long uncomfortable silence that followed I could see that my comment really bothered him. Suddenly he turned to me with a quizzical look on his face. "Christine, how did you come here tonight? Did you take your car?"

"No, I came by cab. Why?"

"I was wondering if perhaps you would allow me to drive you home, that is if you don't have any other plans."

I could feel my color deepen as the corners of my mouth tipped upwards. "Actually I was hoping that you would ask me."

At the door Lara gave me an extra long hug in order to whisper a message. "You guys look great together," then pulling away she said in a louder voice, "thanks for coming Chrissy." With a conquering smile she looked up at Robert. "And you too Robert. I'm pleased that you finally tore yourself away from that dreary office. I hope that we will see you again, and soon." She turned and gave me a rather obvious look of expectation.

Feeling somewhat embarrassed I apologized to Robert while walking down the sidewalk. "Sorry, I wish she wouldn't do that. I think that she thinks that I'm unhappy and is determined to get me married."

He smiled as he gave my hand a squeeze. "She means well."

On the way to my condo we were fairly silent. When we were approaching the building I rotated my head slightly to glance at his profile, at his almost perfect features. In the dim glow of the streetlights I had to admit that he certainly was a very attractive man.

"Would you like to come up for a nightcap Robert?"

He turned and looked at me for a second then quickly resumed his vision in front of him. "Now it's my turn to say that I was hoping that you would ask me. I'd love to."

Filled with contentment I sunk further into the seat.

After Robert parked his car in my extra slot in the parkade we took the elevator up to my private lobby, a small room that was approximately eight feet square, where I used my pass card to let us into the suite. While walking across the living room floor towards the fireplace I casually removed my shoes, then after bending down to make sure that the damper was open I lit the fire-log starter. Almost immediately the flames began licking at the three logs that were already in the grate. After I voice-activated a C.D. by Barry Mallow I asked him if he cared for a drink.

Placing his hand uncomfortably on his midriff he let out a soft moan. "No I don't think so Christine. I'm still stuffed from the meal". While I was curling my legs under me Robert was scanning the room with a look of approval. "Your place is very nice."

"Thank you. When my parents passed away I sold the house and bought this condo. Most of the furniture that you see was theirs." I pointed to a painting that was hanging over the fireplace. "Actually those are my parents."

Because the subject made me feel somewhat melancholy I quickly changed it and we were soon immersed in a political, theological and cultural discussion. Since we both frequently attended the theater, and enjoyed all forms of the arts, we were amazed that we hadn't encountered each other earlier. We also both read by authors and shared some of our favorites. When I noticed that the fire was dying I placed three more logs into the grate. While I was moving them into a better position with the poker a cloud of sparks exploded from the wood and disappeared up the chimney. In the mean time Robert had changed his position and was resting one of his arms over the back of the couch.

"So you play squash? That's usually a man's game." He appeared to be impressed.

I carefully placed the poker back into its slot. "I know. If a man is my opponent it is necessary for me to resort to brain instead of brawn. Since I don't have a strong arm I have to compensate for it in other ways, such as by hitting a low corner ball. This of course irritates my opponents since, as you know, it's a very difficult even impossible line to return."

"Well maybe we could have a game sometime so that I could see just how good you really are."

When our eyes met there was a hint of a seductive challenge emanating from both of us. It was almost morning before we were standing awkwardly in front of the elevator saying goodnight. "I had a wonderful evening. Actually it's been a long time since I enjoyed myself so much. Do you mind if I call you some time?"

"No. In fact that would be very nice. I want you to know that it has been a long time since I have enjoyed myself as well."

We stared at each other until the elevator arrived and when it did Robert stepped into it, turned, and held the door open with his hand. His gaze was open and sincere.

"You are a very beautiful woman Christine."

As the door closed I felt beautiful.

Chapter Three

When I checked into nursing office on Monday morning at 0710 hours Ronda was busy on one of the units making arrangements for a staffing problem. After acknowledging me with a smile and a nod of the head she covered the mouthpiece with her hand and indicated that she would be with me in a moment. As the secretary in the Nursing office Ronda was responsible for coordinating the float team for the units. She also had the undesirable duty of calling in nurses to replace those who, at the last moment, had canceled their shift due to illness. Because she treated people fairly and had a diplomatic way of handling flack I always admired and respected her. When the arrangements were completed Ronda turned her attention to me and asked me how my weekend had been.

"Great! And yours?"

Ronda rolled her eyes. "Busy. I had loads of company from out of town so it's nice to get back to work where I can get some rest." After pressing a few buttons on her computer she looked over at me with an apologetic smile. "Sorry you're to go to 4A."

I closed my eyes and groaned. '4A' was the neurosurgical unit in the hospital. The area was always extremely busy, as well as being a very sad floor to work on. Ronda looked at me with genuine concern.

"I'll try to give you a break tomorrow but I can't promise you anything".

"That's okay. The staff is nice to work with on that unit."

After signing in on the nursing office log I went up to 4A where I checked the assignment sheet and obtained a printout of the nursing care plan for my patients. At 0730 sharp I carefully listened to the report that was given by the night staff then I made a brief round to ensure that there was no critical problem that had to be dealt with immediately. Due to the workload on this unit there was no time for casual conversation and every minute was precious and not to be wasted.

I carefully poured my 0800 medications, picked up the tray and carried it to the first room where four young gentlemen, all between the ages of eighteen and twenty-five, had suffered head and/or spinal injuries. The tragic result of their traumas was that two of the four would never function fully as human beings again. I introduced myself to the two patients who were able to comprehend informing them that I was to be their nurse for the next twelve hours then I walked over to the bed by the door where the first semi-comatose patient was and began the standard patient check system. First I noted all of his in-going and out-going tubing: a central line intravenous that was used to instill fluids and medications, a Foley catheter to collect his urine, and a Keofeed tube for nutrition. Next I did a Glascow scale to assess his vital signs, such as his pulse and blood pressure. Satisfied I instilled a medication into the Keofeed tube then flushed it with water.

Pausing for a moment I sadly looked down at the patient. He was an eighteen-year-old man who was in a vegetative state consequently he would be institutionalized for the remainder of his life. I knew that he would never be married and that his parents would never again experience a response to the love and affection that they had showered on their first born son. The patient would never know what it would be like to father a child of his own, nor to see that child produce a grandchild for him---and so on and so on. He had been drinking and driving and was totally inebriated when his car crashed into a rock-cut. I felt overwhelmed with sadness. It was such a senseless waste of life.

Moving to the second patient the injuries were also alcohol-related but this time the victim was completely innocent. He had been walking down a busy thoroughfare at night keeping well on the shoulder facing traffic, when a drunk driver had veered off the road hitting and throwing the twenty-five-year-old-man one hundred feet into a field. Even though a quick-thinking witness had immediately summoned for help, and the medical team had arrived within minutes, the injuries were severe and now the prognosis was poor. He would function with few physical deficits but mentally he was at an infant level---having to be fed, washed and dressed. His wife had tragically lost a husband, and sadly gained a son.

The third patient, who had suffered an industrial accident falling twenty feet from a scaffold, would fully recover. The fourth man had lost control of his motorcycle and slid through asphalt and gravel ending up in the ditch. Luckily the latter patient had only suffered a slight concussion but there were severe skin burns and lacerations over his legs and arms. You see, he hadn't been wearing protective clothing.

After checking my watch I quickly moved to the second room where two women had been admitted in order to have some tests and monitoring done. They would be discharged either that day or the next. The older of the two had just received the sad and unbearable news that she had an inoperable aneurysm. Since she was only forty-six years old she would possibly, prematurely, leave a loving husband and three beautiful children behind. Life was just not fair.

The remainder of the morning was hectic. I passed up my coffee break due to an emergency that had developed on the unit. For the remainder of the morning my own load of medications, IVs, analgesics, and treatments kept me busy. The only time that I had a chance to talk to my patients was while I was giving them their baths. Even though two of them appeared to be unable to hear or comprehend I always treated them as though they could by chatting lightly while doing their care. I had just completed pouring my noon medications when Anne, one of my co-workers, came into the small room and asked if I was ready to go to lunch.

"The first group has just come back and the rest of us should be ready to go in about ten minutes. How are you doing?"

"Fine," I answered. "I should have these passed out by then."

After I had dispensed the contents to the appropriate patients I informed one of the other nurses that I was going to lunch and gave her a brief status report. I washed my hands, grabbed my lunch bag and purse, and in a group the four of us went down to the cafeteria.

Since it was Monday and all of the departments back to full power the place was buzzing. Students were doing their stints on the units and every doctor was making his, or her, round. It took ten minutes from the time we left the floor to the time that we sat down exhausted at a table.

"Oh it feels so good to take the weight off of my feet," one of the nurses groaned as she wiggled into her chair then therapeutically arched her back and moved her shoulders and head. "I think that I'm going to be late getting off today because one of my patients is going sour. Her blood gases are the pits."

"Which one is that?" Bill mumbled through a mouthful of food.

"It's the one in 416, the M.V.A. (motor vehicle accident). We might have to transfer her to I.C.U. (intensive care unit) in order to vent (ventilate} her. It's really sad because she is only eighteen years old and," she looked at her co-workers with that 'life is unbearable' look, "she is also an only child." She then took a large bite from her sandwich.

Across from her the color on Bill's face darkened as he began to fume. "Yeah!" he snorted in disgust. "I heard a drunk driver hit her car and all he got was bruised up." By now his hands were shaking from his anger. "Fuck! We should take those assholes and make them look at the misery they have caused." He shook his head in exasperation. "Why are people so stupid that they think they can drink and drive?" He exhaled a long breath as he looked down at the table. "Excuse me but I get so angry when I get on this topic."

"Ditto," we answered in unison. We all understood his intense feelings. It was two years ago that a drunk driver had killed his younger sister.

Due to the fact that we had to head back to the floor in twenty minutes the four of us silently attacked our food. I had just finished eating and was sipping on my coffee when I was suddenly overcome with a strange, uncomfortable feeling. Puzzled I quickly looked up to where my attention had been drawn, to a man standing by the cashier. I found it extremely curious that I was unable to divert my eyes away from him but I was even more surprised when I realized that there was a second man who was already seated in the room. After they gave each other a look of acknowledgement I watched in fascination as the man who was paying for his bill picked up his tray, walked to a table a few rows away from me then sat down facing in my direction. After getting himself comfortable in the chair he slowly looked up and our eyes instantly met and locked.

Suddenly all the noise and chatter faded away, as did the people, and it felt as though the man and I were the only ones present in the room. My throat tightened making it difficult to breathe and I could feel my heart pounding in my chest. I could never, ever, forget those strange oddly shaped intense eyes.

Aware that I had recognized him the first man looked bewildered then he quickly glanced in disbelief at a second man two tables over who sarcastically gave him a smirk and slowly nodded his head. 'Well, what did you expect? Of course she remembers you.' His mouth didn't move but I could clearly comprehend his thoughts.

For some reason it didn't surprise me that I could hear them.

Filled with curiosity the perpetrator and I scrutinized each other for only a few minutes, however since my mind was racing with confusion it seemed to take an eternity.

'Yes, I remember you,' I thought, emphasizing each word as though answering a question.

When a look of fear spread over his face a peculiar reaction took place within me. It was as though there was a sudden shift of power, as though in that specific moment I had regained a semblance of control that had been denied to me in the past. Suddenly I was aware that my friends had been trying to get my attention.

"Hello, hello. Are you there? Yoo-hoo."

I turned my head with a jerk. "Wha...? Oh, I must have been thinking of something else. Wha..., what did you say?"

"My God, you look as though you've just seen a ghost."

Glancing back in the direction where the man had been sitting I realized that the seat was now unoccupied. Filled with relief, but at the same time disappointment, I searched around the room but he was nowhere to be found.

"I just feel a little queasy. I think I'll go back to the floor." In a last hopeless attempt to clarify my reality I once more stared at the empty seat then I quickly scanned the room for the other man. He was also gone.

"Chrissy, are you sure that you're all right?" They were all quite concerned for me.

Making a valiant attempt to appear okay I glanced back at them. "Yes, please don't worry." Pushing my chair back and depositing my tray on the rack I walked out of the cafeteria in a daze. Going directly to the nearest washroom I entered one of the cubicles, sat on the toilet seat and wept.

It seemed to take forever for my shift to come to an end during which time I had great difficulty concentrating on what I was doing. In the nursing profession a lack of concentration is very dangerous because a mistake could threaten the life of one of the patients so I triple checked everything I did.

Finally at 1930 hours I gave my report to the night nurse, grabbed my purse and gratefully went home. But before I left I called the nursing office in order to book off sick for the next day. I couldn't trust how I would be feeling by then.

"Oh, I'm sorry to hear that you're ill, Christine. You never book off. Do you think that you'll be able to do your Wednesday shift?"

"I'll have to let you know tomorrow. It depends how I feel but I'll call your office by 1200 hours on Tuesday."

I was totally preoccupied on my drive home as well as when I entered my apartment. On the way to the en suite bathroom I shed my clothes and carelessly dropped the apparel on the floor. Reaching down I turned on the tap of the Jacuzzi then I went to the bar and poured myself a glass of wine. After returning to the bathroom and dimming the lights I placed the glass on the marble ledge then slipped into the hot steamy liquid. Lying back with my eyes closed I allowed the angry water to lash at my body.

As I slowly sipped on my wine my mind and muscles began to relax and with the sedative effect of the alcohol my thoughts soon became less acute. My left arm dangled over the side of the tub and I spread my legs slightly so that the water could caress all of the skin surfaces.

When I climbed out half an hour later I was no further ahead than I had been when I first stepped in. Towel drying myself while walking over to the bed I lay down on my back with my hands tucked under my head. Finally making a decision I activated the audio portion on the phone only.

"Hello, Johnson residence." A hesitant voice came over the phone.

"Hi Lara it's me, Christine."

"Yes, I can see your name. But why in the hell is your video turned off?"

"Because I'm naked and I didn't know who would answer."

"I guess that's a good enough reason." There was a pause before she spoke again.

"This is a surprise because you don't usually call me when you're working."

"I know but I'd really like to talk to you." I attempted to keep the anxiety out of my voice.

"You know I'm kind of tied up this evening. I would suggest tomorrow but you're working then."

"No I'm not. I booked it off."

"Now it really sounds serious. You're not sick, are you?"

"No, but I prefer to talk to you about the subject when I see you."

"Okay. Would you like me to come over tomorrow, oh say around, seven, seven thirty?"

"I would really appreciate it."

"I'll see you then."

At nine p.m. I took one milligram of Ativan, an anti-anxiety medication, and slipped between the sheets of my bed. I flicked the screen of the television on for distraction and within twenty minutes turned it off. I tossed and moaned occasionally throughout the night while my unconscious mind refused to sleep, or to forget.

Chapter Four

While I was lying in bed the following morning I repeatedly rehearsed several similar and related experiences from my past. Giving up on the chance of getting a little more shut-eye I stumbled through my necessary toilet routine then wandered into the kitchen where I made myself a pot of coffee. When the dark aromatic liquid was ready I poured myself a mug full, shuffled into the living room and curled up in a ball on the couch.

I attempted to orient myself to the most recent disturbing episode---my dream, but more shattering to my spirit was the moment when I recognized the man in the cafeteria. With fact becoming confused with fiction I became lost in an empty existence. Up to now I had dealt with it on my own but tonight I was going to share my thoughts with a friend. Perhaps I was making a big mistake. Would Lara accept my theory or would she think that I was confused, or even worse psychotic, because I know that if someone bounced the story off of me I would find it almost impossible to believe. I called the hospital to confirm that I was also booking off the Wednesday shift resulting in me feeling a little less stressed after being relieved of my obligation to work. The monitor buzzed at seven thirty.

The moment Lara saw me she reached over and gave me a long close hug. "God, you look awful. And you feel warm. Are you sure that you're not sick?" She stood back at arm's length and scrutinized me again. "Oh honey, I am so glad that you called me."

I gave her a weak smile. "Thanks for coming." "Would you like a drink of tea, coffee…?" "Hell I think something stronger is in order".

After settling into our favorite spots I sheepishly looked over to my friend. "I hope Tom wasn't upset that I yanked you away for the evening."

"Oh hell no, in the real estate business one's out more evenings than one's in." Lara studied me for a moment then said with concern. "What's the problem, Hon?"

Unable to find the strength to speak I simply stared painfully at the portrait of my mother that was hanging on the opposite wall. Finally taking in a deep breath I turned and looked directly at my friend.

"What I have to tell you is weird, I mean really weird, like, let-me-get-my-screw-driver-for-you weird, so perhaps you won't believe me. On the other hand I want you to understand that to me it's true because it happened to me." I picked up my glass, took two generous mouthfuls for courage then placed it back on the coffee table. After taking in a deep breath I began.

"I had a dream a few days ago, at least for now we will call it a dream. In my dream I was with a man, an ordinary man with no particularly unusual features except for his eyes. He had strange dark eyes." I looked pensively across the room. "I don't know why they were so different. Perhaps it was the shape of them, perhaps the colour, or the intensity, or even all of the above." I shook my head in confusion. "I really don't know." I glanced back at Lara. "Anyway, when I stared at him he scolded me saying, "Don't focus. I told you not to focus." That was all that I could remember at that time."

"Later that day when I was having a cup of coffee in my kitchen I remembered more of the dream." When a sudden uncontrollable shudder convulsed through my body I looked apologetically at my friend. "Sorry but this is very difficult so you will have to bear with me."

As I gazed across the room I felt as though I was focusing a million miles away.

"In my memory I was in a building or a large complex but I was not alone. Instead there were other people present. The man with the eyes took me by the hand and led me into a hallway. Turning to me he said, 'this is a good place,' then he told me to lie down and when I did he lay down on top of me and entered me. He had sex with me."

As I desperately attempted to accept the memory I placed my fingertips on my forehead and covered my face with the rest of my hands. "I don't remember having to take my clothes off which led me to believe that I was naked, and in the middle of the sexual act another man, who was wearing a uniform, came down the hall. It wasn't the type of uniform that we are used to but was more like the ones that you would see in one of the famous TV series----close fitting and dark in color. Because we were in the way he ordered the man to go somewhere else saying that it wasn't the proper place to do it. Since the second man seemed quite upset the first one quickly took me by my hand and brought me down the hall. At that point I lost my recall."

I paused for a moment and took in a few deep breaths.

"I know that you are probably asking yourself why I'm over-reacting. You're probably thinking that it was just a nightmare. Well, I wish that it was just a dream."

After taking another generous mouthful of my drink I placed the glass on the coffee table then settled back against the cushions.

"Lara, what upsets me the most about the incident is that it feels so much more than just a dream." There was a pause while I attempted to bring it into focus by concentrating on the memory. "It's difficult to explain but everyone seemed so intelligent and the sequence-of-events were so logical. Secondly, I almost felt that I was in a trance which necessitated that I had to be led by the hand. I was also totally compliant because I gave no resistance even though I did not want to be there and I did not want to do the things that I was doing. I remember that I was in such distress that all I could do was whimper.

Stunned by my story Lara said nothing but waited for me to continue.

My expression slowly changed to one of hopelessness. "Lara, yesterday I saw that man in the cafeteria at the hospital." With this memory my body shuddered in a post- traumatic response. With difficulty I continued. "When he saw me, when he looked at me and realized that I recognized him, he was totally surprised." I quickly glanced at Lara. "I know because his reaction was so obvious."

Filled with concern I leaned forward. "Lara, if two plus two equals four then this event really did happen; and if this event did really happen then I have totally lost control of my life." At the mere thought of this prospect I covered my face with my hands and broke down sobbing. Overwhelmed Lara moved towards me taking me in her arms, stroking my hair and back, all the while whispering soft reassurances until my tears subsided.

Finally I dabbed my eyes, blew my nose, and sat up straight on the couch. After regaining some of my composure I continued. "I know that my reaction might appear to be a little melodramatic. After all I could be wrong and it could have been just a dream. Let's just say that it didn't really happen. Let's say that it was just a nightmare." I turned and looked at Lara with sad eyes. "The frightening part of it is that it isn't just this one isolated incident. It's not the first time that something like this has happened to me."

We sat staring silently at each other neither one knowing what to say. To me time and my existence no longer had any meaning, while, as if with an ironic sense of humor the clock on the wall ticked away the seconds. We talked into the wee hours of the morning. At times I lost control and cried while Lara, feeling helpless and sorry for her friend also cried. The whole story was so bizarre and far from the reality that we know concerning our existence on this planet. Lara was also frightened at the possibility that I could be imagining or inventing the strange scenario in which case the tragedy would be that I was suffering from a deep psychotic illness. Either way was not a pleasant thought.

I was completely exhausted when Lara led me down the hall to my bedroom. Helping me into bed she tucked the covers over my fetal positioned body then sat in a chair beside me until she heard the regular, deep breathing of sleep. As she crept softly from the room and left the building she had already rejected any possibility of the validity of such a frightening revelation.

Chapter Five

Due to the fact that the drapes hadn't been closed during the previous evening the following day my eyes opened to a brightly-lit room. As the memories came flooding back they brought with them a wave of regret and embarrassment. I contemplated why it is that when one bares one's soul to another there is always a feeling of self-reproach and awkwardness afterward. A concerned Lara called me shortly at which time I assured her that everything was all right and that I was feeling much better.

"Thanks for being there and for listening to me without criticism, or ridicule. Also thanks for tucking me into bed. I think the last time anyone did that for me was when I was a little girl."

We both gave a dry laugh easing the tension somewhat. Before we hung up she made me promise that if I needed someone to talk to at any time, day or night, I would call her, and that I would also let her know if there was a repeat episode.

Robert also called.

"Hi Christine, I was wondering if you were free to go out with me on Friday night."

"Actually I have nothing planned."

Robert looked pleased. "Good! I have two tickets for the dinner theater at the Inn. Dinner is at six so I thought that I would pick you up at five thirty."

"It sounds wonderful. Just have the security buzz me and I'll meet you down in the lobby."

He stared at me for a few seconds with concern. "Is there something wrong? You look a little under the weather. If you want to change your mind I'll understand."

I answered with a forced smile. "No, no I'm just a little tired. Actually, as I said, I'm looking forward to seeing you again and the plans that you've made sounds great."

"Good. I'll see you on Friday. Take care." We disconnected.

For the next two days I lounged around the apartment, read a book, and took long walks. At night I curled up in front of the television screen watching one program after another not really caring about them or absorbing their content. At bedtime I slept undisturbed for seven, or eight, hours.

When I awoke on Friday morning I immediately anticipated my date with Robert. The nice thing about living alone was that any mess is your own mess. There was also no one to pick up after and no need to re-arrange one's schedule in order to accommodate someone else. However at the same time I realized that there was the other side of the coin. There were things that were sacrificed, such as having a lover to snuggle up to each night. Things like knowing that in the morning your daily hug was only an arms-length away.

I called Lara giving her an update of my plans then checked my closet in order to decide what to wear that evening. I was on time for my appointment at the salon where I was scheduled for the works: a hair wash and styling, a facial, a manicure and a body rub. By the time I left the building I was feeling relaxed and beautiful. At home I soaked in the tub for half an hour and by five thirty I was standing in front of the full-length mirror studying myself, first with scrutiny and then with a sense of satisfaction.

I had chosen a simple pale blue silk suit styled with a neckline low enough to expose the antique lace of a French camisole. A slit in the skirt bared part of a shapely leg when I moved and my accessories were the same creamy white color matching my lingerie. My hair was swept up in soft wispy curls and several strands cascaded around my face. Genuine pearl earrings dotted each ear and a matching necklace hung around my neck.

The security guard called up at precisely five thirty.

Standing in the middle of the lobby in his black tux Robert turned at the sound of the elevator door opening. As I walked up to him we both raised our eyebrows and smiled with approval then arm-in-arm we left the building.

At the Inn we were ushered to a table that had an excellent view of the stage. The maître'd politely pulled my chair out then with a flourish he spread my napkin on my lap. "Enjoy the meal and the play Mademoiselle et Monsieur." He bowed slightly to both of us.

"Merci, Jacques." Steven picked up the wine list.

Even though the meal was superb the taste didn't really register due to my trance-like state of mind. At one point Robert impulsively reached over taking one of my hands in both of his.

"Christine, you are so beautiful."

Now in the past I had always accepted compliments lightly but this time I was surprised how beautiful his words actually made me feel.

At eight sharp the lights dimmed and the play began. When the lights turned back on and the last curtain call was over, we slowly moved with the crowd to the lobby where several curious friends and business acquaintances of Roberts stopped us and introductions were made. Finally escaping the noise and bustle of the theater we climbed into the Mercedes, turned on one of the local FM easy-listening stations, and drove in silence. We were each filled with the anticipation of what lay ahead for us in the next few hours.

When we entered the apartment there was only one soft light on in the hallway. As I removed my shoes at the door I turned to Robert and asked him if he cared for something to drink.

"Perhaps some coffee would be nice." He later said that he felt rather foolish because in reality he really didn't want anything but was simply using it as a good stalling tactic. It had surprised him just how nervous he was.

In the kitchen Robert leaned against the counter taking pleasure in the way I moved about while I was making the coffee. Once it was perked I poured some into two cups then each of us picked up our own mug and carried it into the living room. After placing mine on the coffee table I voice activated some background music by Van Cliburn then started the fire. With only one lamp on ghostly shadows danced randomly throughout the area giving it a life of its own while the music soothed and stimulated the senses. As I walked over to the couch and sat down close to him I could feel his eyes scrutinizing every inch of my body. The only sound other than the music was the quiet ticking of the antique clock and the snapping of the firewood in the hearth.

Reaching over and taking one of my hands in his he slowly brought it up to his lips and kissed the tip of each finger one at a time. As my breathing became heavier I felt dizzy and a warm feeling flowed through me. Reaching over with my other hand I sensuously ran my fingers through his thick hair. Suddenly, as though spontaneously inflamed, we were in each other's arms, kissing passionately, frantically removing each piece of clothing.

With my jacket off his hands cupped my breasts, his mouth moved eagerly down to the fullness of my flesh. I had yanked off his jacket and was madly attempting to undo the buttons on his shirt when a few of them popped off and flew across the room. Pulling the garment aside I exposed his chest and eagerly ran my hands over his muscles feeling the firmness of his physique, caressing his taut nipples with my finger tips then nibbling at them with my mouth. We continued to urgently remove the remainder of our clothing until we were both naked. Picking me up in his arms he carried me to the open area in front of the hearth while the feeling of flesh on flesh was almost climactic. Slowly moving our bodies down to the carpet we lay consuming each other with our eyes as the light from the fire reflected off of our glistening bodies.

When we climaxed he placed one arm across his forehead and quickly gulped in some air. His voice was raspy from spent passions. "God that was fantastic."

I could only manage a whisper. "It was good for me, too."

Shortly we moved to the bedroom where we brought each other to greater heights of pleasure over and over again until the night turned from black to gray.

When I awoke the sudden awareness of his presence generated a contented smile as well as a peaceful feeling of belonging. Turning my head I found myself facing Robert whom was lying on his side and gazing at me with a satisfied look. Feeling at a disadvantage I wondered how long he had been awake.

"Good morning, Princess." He kissed me lightly on the tip of my nose. "How are you feeling this morning? Or should I say this afternoon?"

Comfortably snuggling against his chest I groaned. "My goodness, what time is it anyway?"

As he nuzzled his face into my neck he answered. "Almost one but who cares." At first we began kissing each other gently but with our bodies pressed together our passions began increasing in intensity. Unfortunately we were suddenly interrupted by the rude ringing of the phone.

"Oh no, excuse me," I moaned then voice activated the audio only.

"Hello Ms. Anderson. This is Larry. I'm sorry to bother you but I thought you would like to know that your apartment complex on the West Side has a problem."

Suddenly feeling wide-awake I sat up. "What is it Larry?"

His voice had a slight John Wayne drawl to it. "Well, there's a broken water main on the road. I thought you might want to take a look at it because I think that there is going to be some damage to your front yard. The city is already on the job and fixing the break."

"Thanks for calling, Larry. I'll be right over."

Disconnecting I turned apologetically to Robert. "I'm so sorry but I really have to go and check this out."

There was a shocked look on his face. "You own an apartment building?"

Just as we were getting out of bed Robert's cell phone rang. It was his answering service informing him that they had a call for him and that they were transferring it to him. After a brief conversation he announced that he would have to go to the office for a few hours.

In the parking lot we gave each other a long hug.

"Would you like to have dinner with me tonight, Christine? I don't know how long it will take you to check the problem at your apartment building but I should be free by five or five-thirty at the latest."

"It shouldn't take me too long so why don't you come here for dinner. I'll grill a couple of steaks and toss together a Caesar salad."

"It sounds great." We decided on a time and parted company.

As I rounded the corner the problem that was in front of my building was obvious. Partially blocking the road was a vacuum truck, a front-end loader, and a van housing a mechanical company. They had already dug a large hole and were using a hose to suck up the water that had resulted from the break. As I pulled up to the curb Larry ran across the yard towards me. When he reached the car he bent down to the window level.

"Part of the lawn was damaged when they were digging Ms. Anderson but the water doesn't seem to have gone as far as the building."

"Thank God," I muttered. Climbing out of the car I walked over to the supervisor who was wearing the typical white hard hat. I had to yell to be heard above the noise of the machines.
"Hello. My name is Christine Anderson and I'm the owner of the building." Turning in the direction of the huge, obvious, hole that was in front of us I made a generous sweep with my arm. "That's quite a mess."

"Yes, but we've found the break and hope to have everything back in shape 'tout suite." Distracted by the working performance of his men he barked out a few orders then excusing himself walked towards them.

Before leaving the area I checked the building inside and inspected the foundation outside to ensure that no water damage had been done. After I was satisfied I walked back to the car to call the insurance company on my car phone. When I had them on the line I made sure that there would be a reimbursement for any damage to the grounds.

As I turned the key in the ignition I suddenly realized that it was the first of October and the rents were due which meant that I would have to work at my computer tomorrow. Cruising down the freeway on my way home I was pre-occupied with thoughts of the previous evening with Robert while Natalie Cole sang the sweet strains of Unforgettable.

Chapter Six

While I was tending to my apartment building Robert was busy hashing over a case with a detective that worked in his law firm, Sam Spade. It always puzzled Robert why anyone who had a last name of Spade would ever call one of his sons Sam. He came to the conclusion that his parents had a fascination with detective stories.

In one of his cases Robert was defending a woman who had shot her husband six times thus totally emptying the gun. One of the bullets had entered directly into the heart, which of course killed him instantly. Allegedly, she had been a battered wife for years and had shot her spouse in self-defense. Through the six years that they had lived together her late husband had not only beaten her continuously he had also consistently, viciously, raped her and forced her to do what to her were gross unnatural acts.

Robert had Sam do the usual investigation, that of interviewing family members, friends and neighbors, some of whom would later be subpoenaed as character witnesses to appear in court in his client's defense. Sam was a very colorful character who was efficient at his job. As a master of disguises he had a flare for drama and theatrics which opened doors that would have remained closed to others. In this case dressed as a wino he had befriended a man in a local bar, the same bar that had been frequented by the dead husband. Evidently, one night the husband had had too much to drink and began bragging how he planned to kill his wife and make it look like a suicide. Because of his client's state of mind at the time of the crime, along with the testimony of several witnesses, he was confident of his client's release.

After discussing the details for approximately two hours Robert informed Sam that he had another appointment but that they would discuss the case further at another time. As Robert was sorting through some papers and stuffing them into a file folder the phone rang. It was his soon-to-be ex wife, Hillary.

"I've been trying to find you all day. I should have known that on Saturday afternoon you would be in the office," she snapped sarcastically.

One of the chief complaints during their marriage had been that he was hardly ever home. He leaned back in his chair and ran his hands through his hair. "What is it Hillary?"

"It's Sara! She's becoming uncontrollable. I gave her a curfew last night and she came home two hours late with her face loaded with makeup. When I questioned her where she had been and why she was late she became insolent."

Feeling weary Robert closed his eyes. "What would you like me to do about it?"

"I would like you to have a talk with her." As she glared at him through the screen her face took on a look of satisfaction, and when she spoke to him the tone in her voice became quite sarcastic. "I think she is doing this because she is upset that you have left us."

Leaning back further in his chair Robert focused on the ceiling. "All right Hillary I'll drop over tomorrow afternoon. What time would be convenient for you?"

"Why can't you come over now?" She pouted.

"Because I prefer tomorrow as it will give Sara time to cool off and me time to think about it."

"Well I can't stand another night like last night. She'll be here this evening because she's grounded." Her expression suddenly changed to one of disdain. "Of course if you have something more important to do...!"

He perfectly understood the innuendo.

"All right I'll be over by eight, or eight-thirty." He reached across the desk, switched off the phone then voice activated my number.

"Christine I'm calling about our dinner arrangement. I just want you to know that if I come over I'll have to eat and run. If you prefer to cancel I'll understand."

"Why the hurry, is there something wrong?"

"Hillary called to say that she's having a problem with Sara. She wants me to go over and talk to her, which would mean that I would have to leave your place around eight."

"I certainly agree that if there's a problem with your daughter you should definitely clear it up now but it doesn't change the fact that you still have to eat. I also have the steaks thawing so why don't you come over anyway."

"Thanks for understanding. I'll be right there."

When he arrived at the apartment Robert was in a mood to ventilate his feelings. He spoke about his courtship with Hillary and their marriage of eighteen years. They had met in high school when it was stylish to go steady which resulted in him having very little contact with other women. Even with the extra-curricular activities of being a star on the basketball team and a quarterback in football he managed to maintain an honor standing academically. After graduating the two had attended the same university. He had chosen law, and she had chosen accounting. When her course at school had finished she had accepted a position with an accounting firm and a year later they were married. Along with a subsidy from her parents, who happened to be fairly well off, she had worked to support them for the next three years until Robert graduated.

When their daughter was born they both felt that it was more advantageous to have Hillary at home rather than working, especially after she gave birth to a second child, a son. Actually she welcomed the rest. After graduating Robert received an invitation to join one of the leading firms in the city. He worked for them five years then he branched out and opened an office of his own becoming very successful, very quickly. Hillary on the other hand became resentful, unhappy, and soon dissatisfied with her lot in life. He had encouraged her to return to work but without success so he suggested that she go back to school. She resisted and always seemed to have an excuse. When he attempted to reason with her by saying that she could do anything that she wanted to do since they could afford a Nanny she reacted with anger, ranting on and on about how she had given up everything for the marriage.

Eventually Hillary went into counseling but little seemed to be gained. Instead she became more despondent and unhappy, berating him constantly and becoming resentful of any time that he spent away from the house. In retrospect he wondered if she had ever been happy. After thinking about it he made a firm decision that he would not allow her to drag him down with her so from that moment on he focused his attention on his commitment to his work, and to his career.

Robert and I became so involved in our conversation that we lost track of time causing Robert to make a hasty departure. Wrapping his arms around me and pressing his body against mine at the door our lips met in a familiar, electrifying kiss.

Pulling back I said in a rather formal voice. "Robert, I don't want to interfere with your plans but at the same time I would like to suggest that perhaps you could come back here after you speak to your daughter. As I said if it isn't convenient I certainly don't want to coerce you into sleeping here." I looked at him with what I felt was a very serious expression about a very serious topic.

With a quizzical look on his face he held me back at arm's length then burst into laughter. Taking me into his arms he squeezed me lovingly. "Sweetheart, you never have to coerce me to go to bed with you. I'll be back as soon as I can."

After he left I leaned against the closed door and paused to reflect for a moment. "I think that I'm in love," I murmured to an empty room. With a contented smile I went to clean up the kitchen.

When he returned later that evening the strain on his face was evident the moment I opened the door. After accepting a drink from me he sat staring into the fire. I waited until he was ready to talk.

"My only regret, as far as my marriage is concerned, is in regard to my children. You see, since Hillary is a very nervous person she is not always the best role model for the kids. Not only that, she has also hated to be the disciplinarian. When I was around I could always smooth out any problem that arose by taking Sara and Johnny aside and speaking to them on a one-on-one basis, but with me gone they both seem to be at loose ends. Sometimes it frightens me."

"Does it upset you so much that you might want to reconcile?"

"No, definitely not it's so unbearable living with her. Besides, by not having to listen to the constant bickering between the two of us the children should feel a little more harmony in their lives." He sighed. "I think that it will just take a little time."

"How's Sara? How did she react when you spoke to her?"

"Oh she regretted what she did and promised not to break her curfew again. As far as the makeup was concerned I suggested that we make an appointment with a cosmetologist so that she will learn how to apply it properly. I told her that since she had so much natural beauty there was no need for her to 'guild the lily', so to speak."

Moving over beside his slumped body I held his face between my two hands and leaning over I kissed his lips. "I love you Robert."

He returned my look and said with deep affection. "I love you too, Christine."

At breakfast the next morning Robert informed me that he had to go to the office in order to catch up on some work. I told him that I too would be busy with my accounting.

After he left I showered, threw on a pair of jeans and a baggy shirt and then wound my hair into a French-braid. As I sat at the kitchen table with a cup of coffee the sun cast its rays into the room filling it with warmth and rejuvenating energy. Shortly I retired to the den and to my computer.

With the sizable estate that my parents had left me I had traded our home for the condo that I now lived in. With the significant remaining assets I had purchased two, sixteen unit, upper-middle-class complexes, and since then I had added a third similar building to my investments. I had been fortunate to find an excellent superintendent to oversee the group of buildings---Larry. He was honest as well as competent and had a wide range of knowledge in the electrical, plumbing and carpentry trades. He not only kept the building and grounds clean and well manicured; he also settled any problems that arose with the tenants.

I did my own bookkeeping. By pouring all of the revenue from the apartments back into the investment the balance on the principle had decreased considerably. Since I always allotted a sufficient amount of money in the budget for upkeep and repair the buildings were in an excellent condition resulting in the vacancy rate always being low to nil. My financial picture was very secure.

It took me most of the afternoon to get my books in order at which time I noticed that all rents had gone through the system, except one. If a deposit were not made by the following day the tenant would receive a notice. Also one of the apartments had been vacated therefore it required a general cleanup as well as a complete paint job. Larry and I had checked the unit the moment it was empty and arrangements had been made for the work to begin first thing Monday morning. It was already rented for the fifteenth of the month.

I had two phone calls that evening. The first one was from Lara who was pleased to see that I was feeling well, and the second call was from Robert.

"Princess I was thinking of you on my way home and I suddenly thought how nice it would be to spend a weekend with you in the mountains. That way I would have you all to myself."

"Mmmm, it sounds wonderful."

"Good then I'll make arrangements right away. By the way, do you have any preference?"

"No, it doesn't really matter. Why don't you make the choice?"

He answered in a low sensual voice. "Talk to you later."

We disconnected.

Chapter Seven

My so-called abductions usually happened without any warning just as it did on a particular Wednesday night. The moment I opened my eyes the following morning I was instantly aware of that unique and bizarre encounter. Physically I was experiencing a sick feeling in the pit of my stomach; mentally I was feeling myself withdrawing into that dimension of denial. As I desperately grabbed at a fistful of sheet while staring vacantly at the ceiling, it was as though I was suddenly being confronted with an excruciating pain. The image of the room disappeared and in its place another scene materialized, one that had been enacted within the span of the last six hours: in other words since I had fallen asleep the previous evening. As it became clearer I began to feel fear, then panic, and finally helplessness. This time the memory was crystal clear akin to total recall.

I was standing in a room with three men who I gauged to be in their middle to late thirties. Two were fairly nondescript with unremarkable facial features. They had average bodies, being neither thin, nor fat, and wearing the typical type of uniforms that I had seen in my previous dreams. The third man wore street clothes and seemed to have a unique status.

Displaying obvious signs of hostility and anger I moved erratically about the room while muttering to myself. They watched my unpredictable and uncontrollable behavior for awhile then the leader told the two men to transfer me below for safety reasons and to leave me there until I became more relaxed.

Escorting me through a doorway and down a ladder-like set of stairs that was firmly secured to the wall, they took me into a small chamber which was completely void of furniture except for two lonely cots, each one positioned against opposite walls. Moving me to the one on the near side of the room they ordered me to remain there until I was ready to return to the control room. As I slumped down on the side of the bed I was overwhelmed with a frightening fear that I had been abandoned, that I was to be left there forever. Lying with my head resting on the pillow I began to sob bitterly. "I don't want to be here. I don't want to be here," I kept moaning. At first I felt as though I was protesting to an empty room but I quickly changed my mind when one of the operators entered at the exact moment that my crying ceased. It made me wondered whether they had been listening to me, or even worse watching me.

"Well I see that you're feeling better."
His smile was sincere and could even be described as being beautiful. Now under normal circumstances I probably would have reacted differently however under these horrific conditions his compassion only angered me. "Would you like something to eat or would you like to go to the bathroom?"

The look on his face was caring, almost serene, but with such a gamut of emotions coursing through me at that time my reaction was quite spontaneous. I screamed at him."I don't want any food and I don't want to be here. I just want to go home. You have no right to do this to me."

For several seconds he stood in the middle of the room as though assessing me then apparently disappointed he turned and left. The moment that I watched his back disappear through the doorway I was immediately overwhelmed with the realization that once more I was alone---so alone. Devastated I lay down and curled up in a fetal position.

I wasn't sure how long I remained feeling sorry for myself but all of a sudden I sat bolt upright and stared across the room in disbelief. Nothing was making sense to my so-called logical mind. Why hadn't I noticed it before! There was no door, just an empty doorway? Suddenly having hopes of finding a means of escape the corners of my mouth curled up creating a sly look on my face.

How stupid those men are and how cunning I am, I thought. I am going to get out of here. Once again my thought-processes only seemed to operate to a limited degree. Slowly creeping out of the bed and cautiously tiptoeing across the room I turned to the right and carefully climbed up the seven or eight steps of the ladder. As my hand grasped at the top rung I anxiously peered out at the main floor level. There, no more than ten feet away were the three men. As they turned and smiled I was instantly filled with disappointment, disillusionment, and defeat. I firmly realized that any furtive behavior, or clever thoughts of escape on my part, had been futile. My abductors were definitely not threatened by my presence.

"Well hello," the leader said affectionately. "Are you feeling better?"

Again his compassion only created anger within me.

"No," I pouted.

"Well feel free to look around but do not touch anything. If you do it could prove to be very dangerous."

Disarmed by their non-intimidating attitude I slowly began investigating the totally alien environment. The room was circular in shape with a diameter of approximately thirty or forty feet. Ergonomically designed instrument panels circumvented the room at waist height, and an uninterrupted line of clear windows occupied the space between the top of the panels and the ceiling giving its occupants a birds-eye view of the space beyond. At one point a section was cut off of the circle by a partition. Against this wall there was a table and bench similar to that found in a breakfast nook. To the left there was a doorway, the one that I had just passed through a few minutes ago, the same doorway that led down to the sleeping area. Although it wasn't totally clear in my mind I thought that there was a similar doorway to the right of the table. Where it went I did not know.

The room was spotless, not a speck of dust anywhere. The lighting was clear and bright however its source was ambiguous since there was no sign of hardware to be seen. There was also no sensation of movement; in fact I assumed that we were stationary. As I walked about the room I foolishly ignored the previous warning and deliberately extended my hand with the intention of touching a part of the panel. Since I was being monitored closely by the three men I was instantly observed.

"Stop, don't touch that."

Startled I jumped back.

"We have already told you that it could prove to be extremely dangerous." The man's voice was stern and there was no room for compromise. With a grim face he gave me a second warning indicating that he would place me below if I tried it again.

When the three men returned their attention to the instrument panel I once more began to browse around the room. Filled with my usual curiosity I casually scrutinized the remainder of the panel. Since all intellectual thoughts were blocked in my controlled state of mind there was very little that interested me therefore I soon became very bored. Aimlessly I walked up to a portion of the windows and bending forward I inquisitively looked through it.

Suddenly I stood very still, very confused, and very frightened. Baffled I leaned even further forward and looked closer. At first my eyes squinted with curiosity and then they opened wide in horror. There was nothing out there. It was a void.

"W-where is the water?" My voice was strained and barely above a whisper.

One of the men turned to me. "What did you say?"

"Where is the water?" I repeated in a louder voice as my anxiety escalated.

By this time all three men were staring at me. "What do you mean, where is the water?"

I could feel insanity slowly creeping through me. "You said we were going on a ship. Well, where is the water?" I began to tremble.

Immediately aware of the misunderstanding the three men quickly exchanged glances. Slowly and cautiously the leader walked up to me and placed his body directly in front while the other two stood protectively, one on each side."We are not in a ship that travels on the water; we are on a ship that travels through the air. We are in space."

Overload! Overload! My mind felt like an overcharged circuit. "What do you mean we are in space? You said that it was a ship." In desperation I repeated myself, only this time it was almost a whine. "You said that it was a ship."

In order to escape insanity, but unsure as to which direction to go, I senselessly began to move in circles pivoting on the spot. There was definitely the danger of a breakdown occurring.

Suddenly without a warning, without a spoken word or a physical action being performed, I was unexplainably calm. I strangely felt quite detached from the situation although I was still aware of where I was and I still comprehended what they were saying. What happened? What did they do to me?

One of the workers walked up to the leader. "I told you that you can't take her with you. She won't fit in." The tone of his voice displayed compassion as well as frustration.

"I don't see why not? There are only a few changes to make and we can accomplish it as soon as we arrive."

As I listened to their conversation I naturally assumed that he wanted to take me with him so badly that he was grasping at straws.

"But will they accept her," the other asked. "You know the regulations."

"I still want to try," he stubbornly insisted. "I love her so much. I can't tolerate being away from her."

The other two men shook their heads in disbelief. "With all the women that are in the universe, why her?"

The third man looked tormented. "I don't know why. I only know that the other women mean nothing to me. I only want Christine. I can't stop thinking about her."

With an array of emotions, including confusion, curiosity, and even flattery, I stared at him. I knew that I had never seen him before, at least as far as I could remember, so how could he possibly love me? The whole episode was so mind-boggling.

There was a long silent pause while the leader walked over to the window and stood gazing pensively out into space. I became quite confused and upset when I realized that he was profoundly affected by my lack of affection. In an unbelievable quick period of time he realized the futility of his plans. Walking up and positioned himself directly in front of me he informed me that he decided to put me back into my home.

At that point I focused, an act that I was always warned not to do. It was an indiscretion that I frequently exhibited while in these dream-like states causing a photographic impression to be immediately imprinted in my conscious mind.

He was approximately six-feet-three, or four, inches tall, with dark, almost black hair and eyes. His nose was just a tad Grecian in shape and he had what I considered to be a very sensual mouth. Actually he was a very handsome man but unfortunately due to my situation I was in no mood to admit it to myself. It was all too soon for me to assimilate all of the colossal, unimaginable data that had been fed into my simple, primordial, non-evolved mind. Still filled with anger my reaction was spontaneous. I screamed at him.

"I hate you! I hate you! I think that you are ugly."

"Do not focus," he said firmly. "I told you not to focus."

"How in the hell did he know that?"

Before he sent me back a lingering message was imprinted on my unconscious mind. He took both of my hands in his and with genuine open sincerity said."I love you more than you can understand right now and I will always love you Christine."

Somewhere in the far recesses of my mind I knew that the day would come when I would love him too.

I lay in my bed for a long time trying to digest this new experience with a million questions racing through my brain.

"I have been in bed all evening; I have been sleeping since midnight; so how could this have happened? **When** could it have happened, and **why** did it happen?" The 'where', I did not question.

Suddenly a thought came to me. Quickly jumping out of bed I dashed to the door and tried it. It was locked. Not once but twice, by a dead bolt and a combination. The only way that one could gain entry to my flat was with a card or by being admitted by the custodian in the lobby. I turned on the security communication.

"Yes ma'am, Gerald speaking".

"Gerald this is Christine on the fifth floor. When did you start your shift?"

"My shift started yesterday evening at eight p.m., ma'am."

"Did anyone ask to see or speak to me since midnight last night?"

"Well no ma'am, is there a problem?"

Ignoring the question I continued, "Are you sure that no one could have eluded you and gained access to the elevator?"

"No ma'am. I'm positive. If there is a problem please tell me. You sound upset."

In order to appease Gerald I attempted to sound calmer.

"I realize that the question is strange but I just wanted something confirmed. Thank you, Gerald." I switched off.

I then went to each window systematically checking the locks. It would have been an impossible feat to climb up five stories and then to leave by the same way.

Convincing me to follow them was out of the question since I suffered from acrophobia thus necessitating a state of unconsciousness to even get me near the windowsill. There was no possible way that anyone could have entered my apartment, taken me out, and then returned me without someone noticing.

I began pacing through my apartment all the while talking to myself. "Why is this happening to me? What have I ever done to deserve this? Why is it happening over and over and over again?"

Leaning against the wall in the hallway I slid like a rag doll down to the floor then stared dry-eyed in hopeless despair. I uttered no sound. I was too weak and drained to cry.

Later in bed I curled my body up into a ball and wrapped my arms around me for protection. Feeling a depth of sadness that I had never experienced before, I wept until I ran out of tears. It is only then that I dragged myself out of bed, showered and made a full pot of coffee. After pouring a cup I moved into the living room where I sat curled up in the chair in front of the bay window contemplating this new experience.

I kept remembering the room and attempted to reinforce the imprint of it in my mind, anxious that it might fade away into oblivion: but I need not have feared as I had no difficulty in recalling it at any time. It would appear in full color with the characters moving about as though I was looking at a replay on a television screen. I was surprised when I identified the residual feeling that the experience had left me with----loneliness. It was the stranger.

Because of the intense sentiments of fear and anger as well as the loss of control that I had been experiencing at the time I had expressed revulsion and hate towards him. Now these sentiments had changed leaving me with feelings of regret. I was still horrified at the thought of being kidnapped and taken somewhere without my consent. I was still numbed at the thought of being projected into a technology of the future. I was still paralyzed at the idea of a sudden transition into outer space, but time allowed me to assimilate and constructively compute the events of this bizarre scenario.

He had, after all, been kind to me. He was definitely handsome but more important he did love me. He was also offering me the chance of a lifetime: the opportunity to travel in space. The whole episode left me with an overwhelming feeling of sadness, sadness that I was not yet ready.

A hundred questions bombarded my thought processes. Why had my mind been submerged and useless? How did I get there? Where were they from? How did he know that he loved me? Had I known him from somewhere else before? All of these questions were exposed then left dangling unanswered in mid-air.

These creatures were not like the specimens that had been recorded time and time again by people who claimed to have had encounters of the third kind. Unlike the gray, large-eyed aliens with sizable, hairless heads and long, spindly extremities, my encounters were with people like myself. They resembled the man next door, the gentleman who excused himself after he bumped into me on the street, or perhaps held the door open for me.

It was all so alarming, so menacing. I had never felt so helpless in my life.

Later that evening I sat in front of the window that looked out over the park. The room was pitch-black, while outside millions of stars were visible in the clear night. My mind kept mulling over a world that only I was allowed to see. It was all so very lonely. As I was gazing out into the void I remembered the days when I had scanned the Internet looking for some pertinent information, news that might help me to understand my situation a little more clearly. There was none. I was alone. Disappointed and exhausted I slowly moved down the hall to my bedroom.

Chapter Eight

When I spoke to Lara during the next two days I neglected to inform her of my last episode, partially because I did not have the energy to do so, and partially because I had changed my mind about taking my friend in as a confidante.

When Robert picked me up for our weekend in Banff the sky was clear and sunny. With the unseasonably warm temperatures as well as with the October sun streaming through the window there was an illusion that it was a summer day. Tears formed in my eyes as I looked up and surrendered to the ominous mountains. No matter how many times I was confronted with this scene it never failed to have a tremendous effect on my feeling of mortality. Each time it reminded me of how infinitesimally small each human being is, and how unbelievably endless the universe is.

When we arrived at the scenic village we immediately booked into a quaint rustic chalet, one that Robert had reserved for us before we left. The main floor consisted of a cozy living room, a versatile kitchen and a small dinette area as well as a bathroom containing a shower stall and a hot tub for four. A beautifully sculptured stone fireplace occupied the greater part of one of the walls in the living room, and two loose-cushioned couches, that was separated by a traditional bear skin rug, was strategically placed in front of the hearth. From the main room a cathedral ceiling reached up into a loft, where, lying on the king size bed one could look up through a skylight and fall asleep under the stars.

Longing to feel my warm flesh against his Robert took me in his arms and slipping his hands under my sweater caressed the smooth surface of my back.

"I missed you so much this last week," he murmured in my ear.

"I missed you too." Smiling innocently I suggested that we take our suitcases upstairs and unpack.

"Good idea." His voice was husky.

We carried our luggage up the stairs but that was as far as we got with our unpacking.

Dressed in slacks and warm sweaters we left the chalet. Choosing a charming restaurant that was located on the premises I gazed around the room while eating my salmon in puff pastry. Now the following episode might seem insignificant to others but to me it had a profuse impact. It was one of the many incidents that would pave a path for me throughout my lifetime by acting as a building block, an instrument for desensitization, and a process for conditioning and learning.

While sipping on a coffee I spotted a gentleman sitting two tables away that I had previously failed to notice. In every sense he seemed inconspicuous therefore I wondered why my curiosity had been so stimulated by him. Suddenly I realized that he reminded me of an anachronism: that he belonged to another time, or place. There was nothing unusual about him, nothing that would spark one's curiosity so I questioned why I had been so drawn to him. Why did I see the oddity when no one else did? Whatever it was I knew that the recognition was nothing that I could share with others but was purely an incident that benefited my own personal gratification.

It was now essential for me to keep my mind in two modes, one on Robert and one on this traveler. Drifting in and out of Robert's conversation I only picked up a sufficient number of words that would allow me to follow his flow of thoughts. Somehow I knew that the man was conscious of my awareness of him however he politely tolerated my curiosity. When I sensed extreme love and understanding, emotions that seemed to emanate from his gentle aura, I felt akin to him.

Suddenly I was aware that Robert was preparing to leave. As I reluctantly rose from my chair I looked back to the table one more time. At that instant the traveler slowly looked up and gazed deeply into my eyes. His smile was warm and loving but oddly it possessed a strange touch of sadness. Hardly discernible I recognized a discreet nod of his head. Filled with contentment, but deeply confused about his sadness, I left with Robert. Why the sadness? Was there something that he knew that I wasn't aware of? The thought was to plague me many times throughout my life.

Since the sun had already set the evening was cool. The air around us was filled with static energy as well as a collective feeling of togetherness and congeniality. The streets were crowded with many people all of them strangers, travelers who had come from all parts of the world. With my spirits heightened from my last experience in the restaurant the world suddenly appeared more beautiful to my senses than it had been before.

"My, you have a very happy and contented look on your face Princess," Robert said, squeezing my hand.

"I do?" I asked.

"Yes, but you also seem to be miles away."

"Oh, I'm just enjoying the beauty." I smiled and sighed. "I'm just enjoying the beauty."

When we stopped in at one of the many boutiques I was immediately fascinated with the articles of couturier clothing, especially with a coat that was designed and manufactured by a company in Toronto. I carefully picked it up and tried it on.

"Oh Robert it's beautiful." I glanced at the price tag. "And it's expensive."

Robert raised his eyebrows with a look of admiration then gave the saleswoman a nod. She promptly responded by ringing it up on the cash register.

"Robert it costs too much money," I protested.

"And you wear it so well so please don't argue."

Reaching up I gave him a kiss. "Thank you. I love it."

Later in one of the hotel's lounges we enjoyed a nightcap while a vocalist crooned nostalgic lyrics as her fingers moved effortlessly over the keys of the piano. Feeling light-headed and happy we walked arm in arm back to our chalet then much later we fell asleep under a blanket of stars.

After leisurely showering and dressing we threw our luggage into the trunk of the car and checked out of the hotel the next morning.

"Where would you like to go to for brunch, Christine?"

Hesitating for a moment I suggested the dining lounge on top of Sulfur Mountain. "I haven't been up there for awhile and I have always loved the view. It would be nice to see it with you."

After driving up the winding road to the Sulfur Mountain Gondola Robert found a space for his car close to the small building that served as an entrance and access to the cable cars. As we stood on the pavement and looked up I felt intimidated by the constant line of cars that were dangled precariously on a seemingly endless line of cable that ran up the side of the mountain to a dizzying height. Influenced by the wind, or any slight movement inside the car it moved freely. After any ascent, or descent, I always had an urge to bend down and kiss the ground thanking the gods for another safe arrival.

Once safely inside the car with the door securely hinged it took off with a jar. As it ascended the view was breathtaking. The village below grew smaller and smaller until it resembled a child's miniature collection and one could still make out the famous Banff Springs Hotel on the East Side. The river wound through the valley while range after range of mountains, blanketed with a marble-like covering of snow, filled the horizon   First we enjoyed a tasty breakfast in the circular shaped dining lounge then we decided to trek up the final spike of the mountain bringing us to a height of 7667 feet above sea level. When we had completed our ascent we moved closer to the rock's edge. While drinking in the majestic view of the endless peaks I was overwhelmed with the sense of appreciation for nature's power and glory.

Chapter nine

That evening when I returned to my apartment the light on my answering machine was flashing. After giving the usual verbal command I continued to walk with my suitcase toward the bedroom but stopped in mid-stride when the message blurted out through the apparatus. Dropping my bag I quickly returned to the machine and demanded a replay.

"Chrissy." Sob! "Oh Chrissy where are you?" There was more weeping. "It's Becky! Oh my God, she sobbed." When I was finally able to decipher what she was saying her words cut through me like a knife. "She's been raped. My Becky's been raped." Then, as though she was unable to talk any further Lara disconnected.

Stunned by the news it took me a few seconds before I could verbally request Lara's number, and when I did my voice was so shaky that it took a second effort before the machine could compute the order. Lara's distraught voice finally came over the audio however the video was blocked.

"Lara! I just got home. I just played the recording. Oh Lara, I'm so sorry. I'm so sorry that I wasn't here for you when you needed me."The only sound on her end was her subdued sobbing.

"What can I do, Honey? How can I help you?"

"Chrissy, I'm so glad that you're back. Do you think that perhaps you could come over for a while?"

There was no hesitation in my answer. "Of course I'll be right there."

After hanging up I immediately dialed the hospital and informed them that I wouldn't be in on the next day. They argued that they were desperate but I only retorted. "I'm sorry but it's a serious family matter."

Grabbing my coat and purse I hurried to my car.

Lara looked ten years older when she opened the door. After we were settled in the living room she filled me in with the details, which were a little sketchy at this point of time, but later with these facts plus the result that took place at the trial this is what had transpired that night.

As planned Becky and her boyfriend Don had both come home for the Thanksgiving weekend. Since both of his parents were away he had arranged to have a party at his place where there had been dancing, dips in the heated pool, and the hot tub, and a constant flow of alcohol. Several couples had gone off to secluded areas for sexual encounters however Don and Becky, being the host and hostess, had conducted themselves with propriety.

At one point during the evening Becky noticed that Don had consumed several bottles of beer but after she pointed it out to him he had agreed, without any argument, to switch to coffee. He kept his promise and the only other thing that he consumed were three, or four sodas, and several chocolates from a box that was sitting on one of the tables.

After the guests left, around three a.m., Becky offered to help to clean up the place however Don insisted that the maid would take care of it in the morning. As Becky collected her purse and jacket and headed for the front door he naturally followed her. She had her hand on the doorknob and was about to turn it when he reached over and grabbed her roughly from behind.

"Where are you going?" His voice was slurred. At first she attempted to discourage him by pushing his hands off and politely asking him to stop however he ignored her demands and became more and more aggressive. It didn't take her long to realize that he had no intention of stopping. That was when she experienced her first real taste of fear. The sensation of being trapped and helpless was terrifying.

First rule; yell, make a lot of noise, but here in the middle of nowhere there was no one to hear her. Second rule; fight, do not give up. However her five-feet-two inch frame was much too delicate for this six-foot football player, especially with the booze and the hormones flooding through his system.

As he grabbed her by the arms and pulled her up the stairs she let her body go limp, in hopes that her full weight would inhibit his progress. Attempting to reason with him she reminded him that he would be committing a criminal act but he simply ignored her. When she began screaming he hit her several times with his fist causing her to see stars and to black out.

Much later when Becky's eyes fluttered open a searing pain coursed through her body whenever she attempted to move. As the grotesque and loathsome memories flooded her mind she desperately hoped that it was all just a nightmare, however the second she turned her head to the right and saw Don lying on his back snoring heavily, in what seemed to be a deep alcoholic sleep, she was filled with nausea and revulsion.

Fear was now her friend as it cautioned her to creep quietly out of the bed and to get out of the house as quickly as possible. Standing in the middle of the room she stared down at her clothes that were torn and scattered all over the floor. The paralyzing fear of possibly waking Don up sent her exiting quickly through the bedroom's entranceway. When she stopped for a second in the open doorway she tilted her head thinking. 'This is strange. He must have left the room to use the bathroom before he collapsed on the bed'. She found it odd how her mind was able to focus on such a trivial detail when her spirit had been so traumatized.

As quickly as possible, using the banister to support her, she hobbled down the stairs and turned on the system by pushing the emergency 911 button. The vision of her bruised and bleeding body on the screen immediately alarmed the dispatcher while at the same time the system automatically computed in the address. After she gave a brief description of what had happened she was instructed to conceal herself until the police arrived---just in case the rapist woke up and came looking for her.

Filled with horror and revulsion at the thought of being in the same house as Don, Becky grabbed one of the pillows on the chesterfield and hastily exited through the front door. Finding some heavy shrubbery and crawling into it, insensitive to the added scratches that were being inflicted to her face and body, she grabbed the pillow to her chest then curled up into a protective ball. It seemed like an eternity before she heard the blessed sound of police and ambulance sirens, and within seconds she saw them moving through the gate and up the driveway.

As she emerged from her hiding place the paramedics and police rushed over to her and quickly threw a blanket around her bruised body. When she collapsed an attendant caught her and gently lowered her to the waiting stretcher. Through choking sobs she gave the police the location of her assailant and then she was quickly whisked away via ambulance to the nearest hospital.

With all of the noise there was no stirring upstairs. The police entered the building and stealthily made their way into the bedroom, where, amidst the obvious signs of the tragic scenario Don continued to sleep. He was wakened, handcuffed, and read his rights, then transported via police car to the nearest station where he was charged with aggravated assault, holding, and rape.

The whole event was horrible beyond belief and the result would be devastating and leave emotional scars on Becky for the rest of her life. Lara still found a few tears as she sagged like a limp rag and stared off into space.

"Where is Becky now?"

"She's upstairs sleeping. Her father is with her. We haven't left her side since it happened. At least one of us has been there at all times."

"What about Bill?"

"He left the University immediately after we called him. He came here to give us some support but there was really nothing that he could do. He also has his studies to worry about so we convinced him to return to residence. We promised to let him know if there was any change."

As the memory flooded Lara's thoughts, it brought with it fresh grief and pain.

"Oh, Becky, my poor little baby. I wish that it had happened to me and not to her. I would give anything if I could change places with her." The pain on her face was unbearable to watch.

"I know, I know." I put my arms around my friend. "I'm so sorry. I want you to know that I'm here for all of you. Please don't hesitate----about anything."

Looking closer at Lara I noticed that she appeared to be alarmingly exhausted.

"Did the doctor give you something to help you, like a tranquilizer?"

"Yes, but I don't want to take too much medication because I want to be there for her when she wakes up."

I reached over and took one of Lara's hands. "Honey I'll stay with her for the night."

Lara tried to object but I insisted that she and Tom go to bed and get a good night's sleep. "And take the pills." I looked at her sternly. Lara went to speak with her husband and returned shortly stating that he had agreed to the arrangement. The two of us went up the stairs together. Tom was sitting in a chair beside the bed looking like a defeated man. As I approached him he rose up and embraced me tighter than usual.

"I'm so sorry Tom."

"I know." He looked down at his daughter. "My poor, little, baby." He sobbed openly.

After checking Becky and giving her a kiss on the cheek and forehead they left the room with their arms around each other for support, as well as for comfort.

I stood over the bed and looked down at the tiny figure that was lying under the blankets. Right now she was sleeping peacefully with her memories blocked from her conscious mind thus allowing it to mend, but soon she would be awake and the whole devastating ordeal would have to be faced. I was well acquainted with the prognosis as well as the lingering effect that would always stay with the victim for the rest of her life. I sat in the chair feeling ill, my heart aching for this shy sensitive girl who would never be the same again. She would never regain what she had lost.

As I attempted to find an answer to this crazy illogical world I had no difficulty keeping awake through the night. They must have given Becky a heavy dose of sedation because she was still sleeping when Lara and Tom came in to relieve me at eight a.m. Once at home, exhausted from both the physically active weekend and the emotionally draining ordeal of last night, I gratefully sank between the sheets and quickly drifted into a dreamless sleep.

Since it was already morning when I climbed into bed I allowed myself only four hours of sleep. Later in the day I called Lara.

"Hi Hon, how are you feeling today?" I asked anxiously.

"A bit better, thanks to you."

"How is Becky?"

"She's sleeping right now."

"Would you like me to come over? I feel so helpless. I don't know what to do."

"I know but don't worry. Tom and I have hired a nurse to stay with Becky until she is out of the woods and feeling better. Also I have taken a leave of absence but Tom had to go back to work. After all it is his business." She sighed again. "I think that I'd like to be alone for awhile. I hope you understand."

"Of course and I'm really glad that you have help"

There was a brief silence.

I looked at her anxiously. "You will call me if you need me?"

"Of course"

After Lara's face disappeared from the screen I slumped back into the chair and wept.

Chapter Ten

There were two people in my life that was not just an acquaintance but instead was a true friend. Lara of course was one of them while the other woman was Crystal. I had met Lara almost fifteen years ago during a social function at the country club, and it was my mother and father who introduced me to her. It was that same tragic summer that I lost my parents, and it was Lara who came to my rescue giving me the solace and the support that I so desperately needed. Lara was ten years my senior, married, with two lovely children of her own and I often wondered whether I had unconsciously replaced my mother with this new kind friend. During the next four years while I was in school our relationship was often put on hold but we never failed to rekindle it each time we met.

I first came in contact with Crystal while attending the University; in fact we were in the same course and took the same classes. She had recently moved up from Alabama bringing with her that sensual southern drawl along with the most seductive body and beautiful face that I had ever seen. Her hair was fair and thick and fell gracefully to her shoulders, while every feature on her face was flawless, from her alluring green eyes and her high cheekbones, to the graceful lines of her chin. Not only was she aesthetically alluring she was also an outgoing person, had a pleasing personality, and a cheerful sense of humor.

Since God had so graciously endowed her with these enviable qualities one would expect that she would naturally be one of the more happy women in the world however beauty and happiness are not necessity synonymous. Many times the more exquisite that the beauty is, the more difficult is the path in life. At the mere sight of unusual beauty most men immediately become mesmerized thus entertaining phantom illusions of exploitation, while women, automatically threatened by her beauty, desire to put as much space as they can between this mutant of nature and themselves. When I looked at Crystal I saw a struggling and sometimes sad spirit.

During the next four years while we were in school I got to know her well. The moment that my classmates saw us together they discreetly took me aside and confidentially warned me about my new-found-friend. Evidently there was a consensus among them in regard to the girl's morality. Allegedly, she was excessively promiscuous, devoid of morals, and generally a dangerous woman to be around. I was always shocked, or at least surprised, because whenever I was in Crystal's company I had never seen any evidence to back up these allegations. I had decided to see for myself and to waive any preconceived judgments.

We continued to see each other as much as our conflicting schedules permitted. Interacting well we formed a strong bond of friendship displaying attitudes that were void of control or manipulative gestures. However, one day well into the fourth year I had to reassess the belief that I had in my friend, or perhaps I had to realize that I myself had a preconceived opinion. It happened quite unexpectedly and without warning. We were leisurely enjoying lunch in a rather classy restaurant whose clientele was primarily made up of members of the business and professional community. As we were eating our meal I became fascinated with a well-groomed executive type gentleman who was having a rather intense conversation with a couple of his colleagues. It didn't take Crystal long to notice.

"Well, I do declare," she emphasized in her southern drawl. "I do see that someone has caught your little ol' eye".

"Mmmm, not bad," I said as I raised my eyebrows in a gesture of admiration.

Now I was always aware that Crystal knew a countless number of people, a generous number of them being men, but I always attributed it to the fact that she was a lovely dynamic woman. However her next few statements took me completely off guard.

At first Crystal paused as though she was making a serious decision then she nonchalantly said. "Would you like me to introduce you to him?"

Totally surprised I peered over at her. "Why, do you know him?"

"Yes, I went out with him a few times. Actually he has a fair sized penis and he is quite a good lover." Her demeanor was very casual and the words flowed naturally from her lips.

In an attempt to recover from the shock and confusion I sat mute, my face expressionless. Finally I asked "You had sex with him?"

"Yes. If you aren't interested in him the man in the gray suit in the corner is extremely good in bed although his penis isn't quite as large. That man in the brown suit," she motioned with her fork. "Don't waste your time with him." She then sat back sipping on her coffee as though she had been commenting on the selection of foods they were eating.

I quickly realized that I was required to say something so I mumbled that I wasn't interested in any of them. We finished our food and the subject never came up again.

On Wednesday that week I bumped into Crystal in the hospital cafeteria. She still retained a fair amount of her southern drawl.

"Goodness Christine. I haven't seen you for at least two months. Where have you been hiding yourself?"

"Oh working and having a little social life," I answered with a satisfactory twinkle in my eyes.

Crystal opened hers wide with surprise. "I don't believe it! I do declare that you have found yourself a little ol' man. My, my, I'm dying of curiosity. Why don't we get a table for ourselves so that you can fill me in on all the delicious details?"

We paid for our meals at the cash register then finding a rather secluded table we were soon having a rather intimate conversation. I proudly and boastfully described Robert along with the relationship that we had up to that point.

"He sounds delightful." Crystal reached across the table. Touching my forearm she looked directly into my eyes. "Are you happy, Sweetie?"

"Yes, very happy."

"Good". She sat back with a satisfied look on her face. It seemed to me that if I was happy then she was happy too. "I know let's celebrate. Let's go out. I'm off Thursday and Friday as well, so why don't we go somewhere on Thursday evening."

We made arrangements to meet, picked up our trays and headed back to our individual units.

I was already seated when Crystal entered the restaurant. Once again all eyes were focused on the exceptional woman that was slowly weaving in and out around the tables as she made her way across the room. As usual the men smiled eagerly and the women looked guarded. After greeting each other warmly we checked the menu then ordered.

We were in a Hungarian restaurant where the waitresses were attired in the appropriate ethnic costumes while an accordion player was setting the mood by squeezing out native songs as he slowly made his way around the room. I loved the atmosphere as well as the tasty food. I added some sour cream to an appetizer of hot borsch then to a large cabbage role. It was followed by the entrée, a Hungarian platter for two; a dish that consisted of several of their ethnic foods.

Just as the accordion player was completing one of the lyrics I held up my hand to get his attention. Nodding in a gesture of acknowledgment he slowly began to move in our direction while his fingers continuously caressed the keyboard in non-specific runs and chords. When the musician reached our table I looked up and politely asked, "Would you please play Golden Earrings for me. It's my favorite song."

His eyes twinkled as he gave me a slight bow. "Certainly I will."

When the room was filled with the plaintive sad melody I became spiritually carried to another place, another time, and a million light years away. Crystal watched me with curiosity.

"My, my, where are you Sweetie?"

Suddenly snapping back to the room I gave a dry laugh. "I'm coming back down to earth." I sighed. "That song has a very special meaning to me."

"Ah, it must be a gentleman."

"Why do you say that?"

"Only a man can evoke such an expression of love, pain, and sadness all at the same time."

With a slight look of despair I admitted that it was. "Do I know him?"

My eyes went out of focus. "No, I doubt it."

When I didn't elaborate Crystal was unable to contain her curiosity. "Come on Christine. You have sparked my interest. Who is he?"

I deliberated for a few seconds then looked at my friend. "I must warn you. You may not believe this."

Crystal eagerly leaned forward. "Tell me anyway."

I was still hesitant when I began to tell my story.

"I have a memory of another life time." I raised my eyebrows. "In fact, I have memories of many lifetimes but for now I am referring specifically to one in particular."

Crystal was intrigued. "How interesting that is."

"Well, this one took place in a gypsy camp somewhere in Europe. I was a young vivacious woman, very spirited, very fresh, and full of life and vitality. My eyes always sparkled with enthusiasm and adventure, and I loved to tease. In the evening the men would build a fire and bring out their instruments. At the sound of their music I would dance around the flames, my skirt swirling with the motion of my body as I danced faster and faster to the pulsating tempo. I was well liked by all."

"One day a man, a stranger, came into the camp. He had pitch-black hair and flashing dark eyes. He was so handsome, so much so that I instantly fell in love with him.

Since he had fallen in love with me as well, and desired me as much as I wanted him, the fact that I was married didn't stop us. We gave ourselves to each other in wanton abandonment." I paused as I smiled at Crystal over my dramatic choice of words

"Tragically my husband discovered our indiscretion and in a frenzy of fury took a knife and killed my lover in front of me. The moment that the knife entered his body, and his soul took flight, a part of me also died while the part of me that remained wanted to perish also. My husband, feeling dishonored and betrayed, grabbed me and threw me on a grassy bank. When he threatened my life with the same knife that he had used to kill my handsome suitor I lay back welcoming my death, but to my surprise and dismay, instead of doing so, he viciously raped me. When he was finished with me he passed me over to another, then another, and another, until all of the men in the camp had diabolically had their way with me. I remember that after the first man entered me I went numb, feeling nothing, hearing nothing, floating in a void."

I stopped to take a sip of my coffee. Crystal was silent as she waited in anticipation for the rest of the story.

"They didn't kill me, but instead they allowed me to live within their community, however they never let me forget. I became the butt of their hate and ridicule."

"One day, a few years later, another stranger visited the camp. He was a tall man in his mid-forties with a gentle and caring nature. Somehow knowing of my plight, the moment he had me alone away from prying eyes and ears he offered to take me away with him, away from the cruel treatment that I had been enduring. Afraid to move into the unknown I refused. He attempted several times to discourage me from staying however I was adamant in my decision. When he realized that I would not change my mind, filled with disappointment he left me to my destiny."

Before I finished the story the song had already ended. Not wanting to break the spell that had been created by this compelling tale Crystal stared at me for a long time.

"How beautiful but how sad your story is!"

I sighed. "I still feel very lonely and melancholy when I think of him or when I hear that song and I often wonder where he is and whether he ever thinks of me."

Crystal sat there in awe. "And you say that you also remember other lifetimes?" She narrowed her eyes. "That's quite unique don't you think?"

"As a matter of fact I don't. I guess that the memories crept upon me insidiously from the time that I was a child. I just naturally accepted it and assumed that everyone had similar experiences."

"Well I certainly haven't." Crystal looked at me with curiosity. "You really are a very unusual person Chrissy. At least I have never met anyone like you before."

I simply shrugged my shoulders and we continued to finish our coffee.

Chapter Eleven

When we left the restaurant we were in time for the last show at the cinema, a mystery story that was filled with intrigue and suspense. As we were on our way after the movie to our cars I made an emotional grimace.

"It was a great story but it was a little too violent for me."

Instead of agreeing with me Crystal wrapped her arms around herself in a dramatic gesture. "You know I always have a lingering effect from any movie that I see." She threw her head back in a theatrical movement. "Right now I wish that I was wearing a raincoat with the collar pulled up, as well as a hat with its brim pulled down."

Glancing at her enthusiastic behavior I chucked. "It's a good thing that the movie wasn't about a psychopathic killer or else I would have to worry about my life."

Crystal simply sighed while gazing up into the blackness of the night. "Life feels so good right now, don't you agree Chrissy?"

Immersed in my own thoughts I merely nodded my head in agreement.

Crystal reached over and linked her arm in mine. "Well, where would you like to go for a drink?"

"I don't know Crystal. I haven't been bar hopping in quite a while so why don't you choose".

After thinking it over for a few seconds, she said. "At one of the hotels there is a four-piece-band that I think you'll probably love. They are playing songs from the fifties and sixties."

When we entered into the crowded room a group-of-four was pumping out the swinging rhythm of rock and roll from a modest stage that was squeezed against one of the walls. The room was jam-packed with people and on the dance floor young adults were closing the generation gap by swinging their bodies to the beat of the jive.

Within five minutes of our arrival we were ushered to a table where a waitress took our order. Instantly various gentlemen, all filled with great expectations, sent beverages over, and in each case the girl would indicate the source of our benefactors. The men grinned and nodded while hopefully waiting for our approval but we consistently declined with a smile and a shaking of our head. We felt that the act of accepting even one drink would generate certain obligations on our part and we wanted to maintain our independence. We did, however, accept invitations to dance. Two hours later when we stepped outside onto the sidewalk the silence was deafening.

"I think I'm getting too old for noisy bars," I sighed then grinned while reminiscing over the past. "Remember the days when we thought it was really cool to dance all night, go home, change into our uniforms, then go to work."

Crystal smiled and nodded. There was a pause.

"Why don't you stay at my place tonight, Crystal? We haven't had much of a chance to talk lately." Crystal quickly accepted.

Back in the condo I made us both a cup of tea then we settled into our favorite spots. Crystal stretched out in the leather chair with her feet supported on the footstool while I curled up at the end of the couch. Resting her head on the back of the chair, and closing her eyes in relaxation, she smiled contentedly.

"That was really enjoyable. But then I always have a good time when I'm with you." There was a long silence before she made the next comment. "You know Chrissy I feel that you have always accepted me at face value." She awkwardly glanced sideways at me. "Not everyone does that you know."

"Yes, I know," I answered sadly.

She closed her eyes again and gave a crooked smile. "Do you ever wonder about me, I mean all the rumors?"

Since the conversation was beginning to make me feel somewhat uncomfortable I squirmed slightly on the couch. "I guess I do wonder, whenever I think about it, which by the way is very infrequent. I think that what you do on your own private time is exactly that---private. After all you don't question me about my activities."

Crystal opened her eyes but instead of looking at me she stared straight ahead. Her voice lowered slightly changing it to a more serious and cautious tone. "Would you like me to tell you a little about myself?"

I really wasn't sure that I wanted to hear what Crystal was about to tell me, in fact I **know** that I didn't want to hear what she was about to tell me, but I felt awkward refusing. "If you would like to," I answered.

She then shifted her position so that she could have better eye contact with me. "Chrissy, you and I have been good friends for over ten years now. We have a lot in common and I really like you, in fact I love you. When we are together we really enjoy each other's company."

"And I feel the same way towards you," I quickly added.

"There are many ways that the two of us are alike but there are also many ways that we are different. I'm referring to life styles."

For a moment I thought that Crystal was about to inform me that she was a lesbian but when I considered all of the evidence that proved otherwise the thought was quickly dispelled. It was as though Crystal had read my mind.

"Oh don't worry I'm not a lesbian, at least not in the true sense of the word." She pursed her lips slightly. "What I'm trying to tell you is that I have had a variety of sexual relationships."

I suddenly wished that the conversation had never started.

"I've had sex with a woman, I've had sex with two people at one time, and I've taken part in an orgy." She blurted it out then carefully scrutinized me. As I quickly took a couple of long drinks from my glass I could feel my face turning red. Crystal smiled at my reaction. "Chrissy, if you would like me to leave I'll understand."

"No, no, it's nothing like that." I vigorously shook my head in denial, perhaps a little too much because of my embarrassment. "You just took me off guard." I began fidgeting with my glass. "I guess that I always suspected something like that but I felt that it was none of my business. You never flaunted your exploits in front of me when we were out, so," I grinned, "I never asked."

There was a long silence while I frantically attempted to assimilate what I'd just been told. "Have you always been that pro---that sexually active?" I flushed at my first choice of words.

Crystal smiled, "No, not really." I guess that at first I was what most people would call normal. She mocked the word. "Even though my behavior was the same as most people my attitudes were always different. You see I've never felt that sex was a gender thing. I could never see anything wrong with any variety of intimate activities. I realize that my feelings weren't the normally accepted ones in society but at the same time they weren't anything that had been taught to me. The whole concept seemed to come to me naturally."

I stared into the fire's fascinating erratic flames. "I really don't judge you, or anyone else. Not only do I not judge you, I do not find it offensive. Perhaps that's why we get along so well."

Crystal looked at me inquisitively. "Have you ever tried anything out of the usual?"

I quickly shook my head. "No," then I smiled sheepishly. "But I have to admit that I have thought about it."

"You know Christine I always had a fear that you would totally reject me if you knew."

"Then why are you telling me now, Crystal?"

Crystal looked perplexed. "I really don't know why."

Feeling very tired I inhaled as I held my glass towards my friend. "Here's to a long and true friendship."

Crystal extended her hand and our glasses touched.

Our conversation then turned to a lighter vein, until, with both of us yawning, we decided to call it a night. Lending Crystal one of my long T-shirts we both settled into my bed. Almost instantly Crystal was sound asleep but for a long time I lay on my back staring at the ceiling with a multitude of thoughts flashing through my mind. So many new ideas had opened up to me in the past few months. I felt as though I was standing in a pitch-black, empty room, where, in several directions, one by one a door began opening. Through the doors I could make out long, unrevealing hallways, where at the end, barely visible, was a pinpoint of light. Suddenly I realized just how far I had to go. The image left me feeling slightly disoriented and weakened with exhaustion. I finally drifted off, moaning occasionally in an unsettled sleep.

The two of us woke almost simultaneously the next morning. We immediately realized that not only was the sun up but by the obvious commotion that was coming from somewhere in the front yard the occupants of the building were also awake.

"Who is that yelling?" Crystal groaned as she rolled over on her stomach and shoved the pillow over her head in a futile attempt to drown out the noise.

Jumping out of bed I ran to the window. Carefully separating the drapes with one hand I peered down below.

"Oh my goodness I don't believe it. Two people are having a fight on the front lawn. Come here Crystal." I motioned with one hand. "Look at them." Becoming much less discreet I spread the curtains wider.

When Crystal's curiosity got the better of her she moaned in defeat then rolled out of bed.

Two people, a man and a woman, appearing to be somewhere in the forties, were having a terrible altercation. The woman was definitely the aggressor, yelling out obscenities and attempting to physically harm the man, who in turn was protecting himself from her flailing arms by defensively holding his upper limbs out in front of him.

"You bastard, you lousy bastard, go back to her then. I never want to see you again. I hate you! I hate you!" She was straining her voice so much that it was becoming raspy.

Furious and anxious to get away from the distasteful scene he turned abruptly and headed for the parkade, while she, as though unable to support the weight of her body folded to her knees. At this point a couple of concerned tenants rushed across the lawn to give her assistance. Withdrawing my hand, thus allowing the curtain to fall back, I turned to Crystal.

"I'm sorry about this. It has always been a quiet area."

There was a look of resigned sadness on Crystal's face. "Oh it happens," Glancing at her watch she commented that it was time to get up anyway.

Still attired in our nightwear we sat at the breakfast nook enjoying our first coffee of the day while the sun streamed pleasantly through the bay window. Crystal leaned back with her feet extended and elevated on the chair in front of her while I sat across from her in a forward position with my elbows leaning on the table, my face resting on the back of my hands.

"Boy I hope that I never get myself in a situation like that. It's so sad to lose sight of one's self-value and to surrender to the control of another person."

"I know what you mean. It is really very sad." Crystal stared pensively at the ceiling. "I gather from her words that he was seeing another woman."

"What would you do if you found out that Armand was cheating on you?"

It was a few seconds before I realized that Crystal was smiling, even chuckling in reaction to my question. I gave her an indignant look. "Did I say something funny?"

"I'm sorry Christine. Honey, at times Armand and I do have sex with other people."

I pulled back in horror. "You mean to tell me that you swap?"

Crystal made a face and slowly shook her head. "Chrissy, that word has such a horrible connotation to it. I would rather say that we have the right to have sex with other individuals. After all we do not own each other."

The fact that I was having a bit of difficulty in accepting the whole concept must have been obvious on my face.

"Look, I realize that what I am describing to you is a totally different philosophy with a totally different social-sexual structure. It is not something that you can just jump into without the appropriate setting otherwise you could end up with some deviant individuals with even more deviant minds. You must have friends that not only share your feelings but who also understand the idea. You see sex is not the be-all and end-all of a relationship. One does not harness or control the natural flow of feelings between men and women."

"But when you fool around," not the best words to use, "with other people doesn't it destroy the feelings that you have for your partner?" I was desperately trying to understand where she was coming from.

"No." Her compassionate smile told me that this wasn't the first time that she had found it necessary to explain her philosophy. "Actually, believe it or not, after an interaction with another person our relationship became even closer. When someone truly loves another one there are no chains, there are no restrictions of feelings, and above all there is no control. The so called straight people call it vulgar but we definitely don't view it that way."

I took a few sips of my coffee and at one point looked out through the window.

"You know this whole philosophy that you have just described brings to mind a book that I once read. In fact I thought of the same book when I was sitting beside Becky's bed after she had been raped."

Crystal's eyes suddenly widened.

"Oh, I'm sorry. I guess that I didn't mention it to you."

Crystal responded by slowly shaking her head. "No you didn't."

"Well to make it brief the daughter of my friend Lara was horribly date raped recently. The sad part of it is that she was still a virgin and rather naive when it came to sex. Anyway, the book that came into my mind was called The Harrad Experiment written by Robert Rimmer. The Harrad College, which is in Cambridge, Massachusetts, had set up a specifically structured social-sexual environment within the dormitories. They carefully selected a group of students and paired them off in compatible combinations placing two in each room."

"I don't understand." Crystal was confused.

"Each couple was of the opposite sex, that is a young man and a young woman were placed together in the same room."

Crystal raised her eyebrows. "That's very interesting. How did it turn out?"

"I thought very well. There was a lot of previous conditioning that had to be modified. It was necessary to rid them of old beliefs that had created fears, insecurities, and inhibitions. Individual beds were assigned and any cohabiting was left up to the discretion of the couples. One by one they became intimate, but more important they learned to live with each other, to understand each other, and to realize the everyday problems that can interfere with a workable relationship."

"One girl however held out. She was determined that she was going to wait for Mr. Wonderful to come along before giving up her virginity. One night she was abducted and thrown into the back of a van by a group of hoodlums whose intent, of course, was to gang rape her. Luckily she escaped with her life as well as with her virginity. The result of this horrible experience was that she finally realized that she had been overlooking something that was right under her nose; a caring, loving, wonderful man who would help her to make her first time a joyous event. Anyway, she willingly gave herself to him, with good results I might add."

"So what happened to them after they left university?" Crystal was very entranced with the story.

"Actually while they were still in school they began socializing together as a group. Soon the love that they felt was not confined to their partners. It could be compared with loving all of your children, all in a different way. If I remember correctly I believe that some of them later lived in a commune for a while but slowly they dispersed going their separate ways."

"Anyway, Becky reminded me of that girl who had been saving it for that special person but instead a monster had stolen it from her. Maybe you have the better of the two ideologies after all."

We sat in silence for a long while. "You know what I feel the bottom line is Crystal?"

"No, what do you feel?"

"I feel that you can only tolerate and understand what you are prepared for. Anything outside of that destroys everything in its path. I know that I would be devastated if someone forced me to voluntarily do some of the things that you do. It's not that I think that it is wrong. I'm just not conditioned for it"

"Sounds like a good bottom line." Crystal looked at me affectionately.

Just then the phone rang breaking the spell. It was Robert.

"Good morning, Christine. I won't keep you. I was just wondering if you would like to join me for lunch today. I realize that it is such a short notice but I just had a cancellation and thought of you right away."

From where she was sitting Robert could not see Crystal. When I looked in her direction she was giving a definite 'yes' sign with her head.

"I would love to," I responded with a broad smile.

We decided on the time and place and disconnected.

I looked quizzically at Crystal. "Are you sure that you don't mind?" I didn't want her to feel that I was dismissing her.

"Not at all, in fact I really should be going. I have a few things that I have to get done today."

Hugging each other we promised to keep in touch.

Chapter Twelve

While I had been enjoying myself on Thursday evening with Crystal, Robert, on the other hand, was having a rather stressful time with his wife Hillary. He had paid her a visit in his former house to have what she had called 'a little chat'. As he sat with his wife in the living room he attempted to keep an open, unbiased mind.

"You haven't been spending enough time with the children lately," she scolded. "You have always devoted so much of your energy to your work, and now I hear that you have a girlfriend. It certainly didn't take you very long did it? But then you probably had her stashed away somewhere while you were still living with me."

"That's not true," he answered calmly.

She stared directly at him with hate and bitterness. "Well I don't want you sacrificing the time that you should be spending with the children by sleeping with that whore."

The lines of his lips went thin and his voice became cold." If you're going to use such abusive language I'll leave."

Hillary knew her husband's pressure points and was fully aware of just how far she could push him. Noting his reaction she stopped and attempted to take a step backward. "I'm worried about the children. I don't want to see them damaged because you can't keep your pants up."

Giving her a warning look he let out a sigh of frustration. "Hillary, after repeatedly going over the issue of time allotment with our lawyers we finally came to the agreement of having open visiting privileges. That way the children will have a choice as to where they would like to spend their free time. Would you now, after all the negotiating, like to be more specific about the terms?"

Hillary looked unhappy and discontented. "Well perhaps it would be better if we were more clear-cut about the weekends."

By this time Robert was totally frustrated. "Hillary when we went into all of that with Mr. Sloan and your lawyer you firmly wanted to leave the choice up to the children. I want them to come to see me because it is what they want and not because it's something that the courts have forced them to do."

Feeling exhausted from the years of bickering he glared at her from across the room. "Do you know what you want Hillary? Have you ever known what you want?"

Robert had decided from the very beginning that he preferred the open door policy. He realized that the children still had a lot of things to work out and that it would be cruel to uproot them from everything that they were familiar with. At the same time he secretly hoped that they would choose to spend more and more time with him, and that perhaps one day they might decide to move in with him permanently. Knowing how contrary Hillary was, always reciprocating with an equal and opposite force, he didn't want to push her too hard.

"What about this weekend," she persisted. "Why don't you let them spend it with you? Last weekend you didn't see them at all."

Robert immediately felt guilty and he knew that Hillary was aware of his feelings. Even though he was eager to see Christine he also realized that if they stayed at his place it would give him an excellent opportunity to approach the subject of his new relationship and perhaps even allow them to meet each other.

"Fine." he answered rather curtly. "Are they upstairs?"

"Yes. They are in their rooms studying. I'll go and tell them that you're here."

As she began to stand up he held up his hand. "If you don't mind I prefer to get them myself."

Taking the stairs two at a time he approached their rooms. From his sons he could hear the sound of a computer game, and from Sara's there was some loud music blaring out of her sound system. After knocking twice on each door the two children rushed over to give him a hug.

"We missed you Daddy. Where were you?"

"Sorry, I went out of town. I should have let you know. Anyway, I'd like to talk to you about this weekend."

Settling into Johnny's room the three of them sat down on the side of his bed. Staring at him with wide curious eyes the two children waited for their father to speak.

"I was just talking to your mother and we were wondering if you would like to spend Saturday and Sunday at my place?"

"Yes, yes." they both shouted throwing their arms around him.Noting a sudden sour look on Sara's face Robert tipped up her chin and asked with curiosity. "What is it, Sweetheart?"

"I've already made plans to see my friend Suzie on Saturday."

"That's all right. You can still see her. I want both of you to keep your original plans and I will drive you wherever you want to go."

His daughter still continued to look a little upset.

"Is something else bothering you Sara?"

"Well," she hesitated, "are you going to be alone?"

"Yes, as a matter of fact I will be." There was a slight pause. "Are you worried that Christine might be there?"

"Yes." The muscles on her face tightened.

"Maybe that is one of the things that we can talk about this weekend."

With Sara scowling, and Johnny looking frightened, the subject was quickly dropped. After chatting briefly they accompanied their father down to the front door.
"See you on Friday after dinner," they hollered as he climbed into the car.

Just as Robert turned on the motor and was being buckled into the seat there was a rap on the window. When he looked up he realized that Hillary had followed him out to the car so he gave the command and the window rolled down. "What is it, Hillary?"

With a scowl on her face, and bitterness in her voice, she demanded. "I don't want that woman there! Do you hear me! I don't want that woman near my children!" By now her face was contorted with hate and her eyes were dangerously brutal.

Robert was furious. He could feel his face flush with anger and his voice became cold and hard. "Hillary, you don't control me. Do you understand? She is a part of my life, not yours, and I would thank you to stay out of it."

She jumped back as he jammed down on the accelerator and drove away, burning rubber and sending a cloud of angry dust in his wake.

Chapter Thirteen

The next day when I arrived at the restaurant I was ushered to an empty table and fifteen minutes later a concerned Robert showed up.

"Sorry about that." he apologized while slipping into the seat across from me. "I tried to get away earlier but the meeting ran a little late." Still keyed up from the tensions in his office he reached over, took one of my hands in his and gave it a gentle squeeze. "I missed you, Princess."

"I missed you too. I haven't been able to stop thinking about the weekend. I really enjoyed myself"

"Excuse me. Would you like to order now?" By the twinkle in her eye we realized that the waitress had inadvertently overheard the conversation. Grinning sheepishly we ordered and were soon eating. While relaxing over our coffees Robert's mood seemed to suddenly change to a quieter and preoccupied one. When I called his name to get his attention his head snapped up in my direction.

"Sorry about that. Actually I just was thinking about this weekend." There was an uncomfortable hesitation. "I don't think that I will be able to see you, Christine."

His comment took me by surprise. "I see, and why not?"

"My children will be coming over to spend that time with me."

I slowly nodded my head and patiently waited for an explanation.

He looked down at his hands then chose his words carefully. "I don't think that it would be wise to expose you to the children before I have a chance to discuss our relationship with them."

Of course I realized that it was a good idea for him to speak to them first however I had a bad feeling in the pit of my stomach. I simply shrugged my shoulders. "Don't worry there's always next weekend." Even though I said it, and believed it, I was still concerned about my troubling vibes. "Have you spoken to them about the two of us?"

He hesitated for a moment as though deciding what to say. "I want you to know that Hillary doesn't have the kindest mouth at the best of times. Before you meet them I would like to reinforce my side of the story and this weekend might be the ideal time to do it."

It all seemed quite logical so why did I still feel so uneasy.

Desperately wanting to change the subject I sadly brought up the topic of Becky's rape. After enlightening him about the incident I expressed how horrified I was at Don's behavior and empathized with Becky for the trauma that had been inflicted on her sensitive nature. I expected an indignant reaction but instead Robert quickly changed the subject. Not thwarted by his attempt to evade the issue I directed the conversation back to the topic again however he once again attempted to avoid the discussion.

I stared at him in confusion. "Robert, what's wrong?"

His face flushed and he avoided my eyes. "I'm sorry Christine but I can't discuss the case with you."

I shook my head as though to clear the frequency. "What do you mean you can't discuss the case with me? What case?"

There was a slight hesitation. "I'm representing Don in the action." His voice was hard and professional.

My jaw literally dropped open. My eyes went wide in stunned surprise.

"But you can't!" I shook my head vehemently. "You can't defend a man like that, especially when Lara and Tom are your friends." I looked at him pleadingly. "But even more importantly because they are **my** friends."

He let out a heavy sigh. "Christine I'm a lawyer. I do not mix business with friendship. As you know even the worst criminal has a right to the due process of the law."

"But they are your friends," I repeated. My eyes were already stinging with tears.

He added softly. "And Don's parents are also very close friends of mine and have been for years."

Feeling sick to my stomach I slumped back in the chair. Wanting to blot out Robert and the whole picture I leaned forward covering my face with my hands. I remained like that for almost a minute before I looked up. "I think I would like to go home Robert." My voice was cold and void of emotion.

Robert looked miserable. "I'm really sorry about the weekend and also about the case, Christine."
Ignoring him I looked the other way. He called for the check and the two of us left the restaurant. In the parking lot I walked ahead of him in the direction of my car.

"I'll call you on Sunday evening after the children leave." There was a slight ring of desperation in his voice.

With tears blurring my vision I didn't answer but just kept on walking.

That evening I called Lara. She informed me that there had not been too much of a change in the internal healing process, but that Becky's external wounds were mending well. As Lara was speaking I felt so humiliated and torn with guilt so that I couldn't bring myself to mention Robert.

"I'm not feeling too well this weekend Lara so I think that I'll probably just stay in and rest."
"Oh, you won't be with Robert?"

"No. He's spending the two days with his children."

"Well take care of yourself, Chrissy. I love you."

"I love you too, Lara." When I disconnected there was a lump in my throat.

Chapter Fourteen

It was still early in the evening when I realized that my stock of wine had run out thus necessitating a quick trip to the liquor store since I was one hundred and one percent sure that I would need a drink before the night ended. I was in the process of reaching for a bottle from a counter that stood in the middle of a nearly empty room when my hand froze in mid-air and at the same time the hairs on the back of my neck stood up. Overwhelmed with a menacing and ominous awareness I knew without any doubt, or question, that a presence, an unknown entity was standing behind me. With alarming anticipation I slowly turned around.

There, standing directly in front of me, and approximately two feet away from me, was an extremely handsome young man. He had a full head of fair hair, deep azure blue eyes that shimmered with luminous energy and perfectly formed features on a round-to-oval shaped face. With my back meshed against the counter I was unable to move, not only because space prevented it, but also because of my paralyzing fear. He smiled and moved forward until his face was within inches of mine.

If I had to select one word to describe his countenance I would have to choose the word curious, in fact curiosity personified would be more appropriate. Cocking his head to one side he appeared to be probing almost becoming one with my confused petrified mind. Around him there was a beautiful aura an ethereal glow that could be seen with the naked eye. The two of us seemed to be suspended for an undetermined period as though time itself stood still. Suddenly I became worried about the other people in the room and what they were thinking about his strange unusual behavior. 'What are you doing?' my thought process screamed. 'Please. Don't do that to me. Please! What will people think! We don't do things like that here!

My request fell on deaf ears as he continued to study me with intense interest and it seemed like an eternity before the hold that he had on me was released. The instant that it was I rotated one hundred and eighty degrees in a quick reflex movement. Once again I was facing the counter. Swiftly and without hesitation I immediately revolved another one hundred and eighty degrees completing the circle. I stood perplexed and bewildered. The man was nowhere to be seen. He was gone.

Puzzled and unable to rationalize what all of my senses had just witnessed I frantically studied the room just in case he might be hiding somewhere. Since the counter that I had been leaning on stood in the middle of the area and was only slightly higher than my waist it would be physically impossible for him to vacate the room or to conceal his self. He had simply vanished into thin air.

It was a few moments before I could control my overcharged emotions. Taking in a few deep breaths I picked up the bottle with trembling hands and carried it to one of the cash registers. When the cashier noted my obvious nervousness and my sickly chalk-white face he undoubtedly came to the conclusion that this was definitely a woman with a drinking problem.

Once I was out in the parking lot and was heading for the car I hugged the bottle like a security blanket. Alarmed that I might have a reoccurrence of the experience that I had just had in the store I nervously looked around me in all directions. If he happened to be anywhere nearby I couldn't see him.

I was only vaguely aware of the signal lights as my unconscious mind guided me across town, and upon entering the safety of my home I closed the door heavily behind me. After carefully checking the locks to ensure that both the apartment and I were secure I leaned my forehead against the door and sobbed in anguish and despair.

Dressed in my old familiar terry robe and my oversized dinosaur slippers I anxiously shuffled through my apartment from one room to another. How could last weekend have been so exceptionally wonderful and this weekend so terribly miserable? I tried to read but couldn't concentrate. I thought of jogging through the park but the sun had already set. After flipping through the menus for available movies I punched in the appropriate numbers then sat back as the life sized three-dimensional-imagery appeared on the screen. Normally I would have been totally captivated by the plot but this evening I kept losing track of the story line.

After two glasses of wine and the completion of the movie I shuffled off to the bedroom but not before checking every window, every lock, and every possible source of entry. Satisfied I crept between the sheets and was soon fast asleep.

I was first conscious of the cold hard surface under my supine body, then of the narrowness of the structure beneath me. I felt as though I was lost in a soft white cloud far away from reality. Looking about with smoky eyes I perceived a small unfurnished room, unfurnished that is except for whatever I was lying on. Still vagueness; I couldn't move. When I lifted my head with a great deal of effort and peered down at my body I realized why. Both of my legs were elevated and widely separated and each foot was secured in a pair of gynecological stirrups. I was naked, which was humiliating, and I was alone, which was terrifying. My greatest fear at that moment was that I had been abandoned and would be left there forever. Time and logic was non-existent.

After an obscure interval I heard and felt some commotion at the foot of my bed. Again lifting my head and using all of my strength to focus I saw four young men engaged in the process of eagerly and thoroughly checking the anatomy and physiology of my pelvic area by poking and probing all four of them seemingly at the same time.

As they extended their faces toward the subject matter, sometimes tilting their heads as though they were picking up a different frequency, their intense bizarre curiosity once again fascinated me. But their mode of communication was the most peculiar thing of all. Instead of using characteristic words their conversation consisted of a constant sharp high-pitched humming sound, and they were all talking, so to speak, at the same time. Immediately I recognized one of them as being the 'entity' that I had seen in the liquor store but became confused when the other three seemed cloned from the first.

I wasn't sure whether it was my mind that continued to protest in thought waves or whether I was vocalizing my thinking however it was all redundant since they ignored me and continued with their examination leaving me with feelings of helplessness and degradation. I was totally left to their mercy, which they appeared to be void of.

Suddenly the atmosphere in the room changed as the air became static with their attention. Following their concentration towards the doorway I realized why. I later wondered why I kept calling it a doorway since there never was a door. Entering the room was an older more officious looking gentleman in a lab coat who was obviously their superior. He began discussing the most recent specimen--- me---then satisfied he turned to leave. Having a second thought he stopped at the entranceway and said. "If you want to do it to her, feel free to."

"Yuk!"

With very little hesitation they declined.

How mortifying!

I was surprised when they returned a little later and 'did it' to me.

I woke with a start in the morning. As the sun was streaming through the window the memory of the last episode was vivid inducing me to draw my knees to my chest in an attempt to retreat. How awful and how demoralizing it was to feel like a guinea pig. Where were we anyway in the evolutionary scale of man? Right now I felt no higher than the animals in a lab, no more sophisticated than the primordial member of a prehistoric clan, no more independent than a leach gluing itself to its host for its subsistence, and no wiser than a sheep following its leader over the deadly edge of a cliff. The experience had left me without a trace of dignity and had greatly damaged my feelings of self worth and self esteem.

It was awhile before I made any effort to get out of bed and when I did I staggered to the bathroom, sat on the toilet seat and closely examined my vaginal area. I really didn't know what I was looking for or what I expected to find but nothing had changed.

Going to the shower stall I commanded the temperature gage to go up a couple of degrees then I stepped inside welcoming the distraction of pain coming from the overly hot water. The steaming liquid lashed at my body but it failed to get deep enough to wipe away the ugliness that was consuming me. When I became weak and faint from the heat, almost causing me to lose my balance, I staggered to the bed and collapsed on top of the blankets. Panting for oxygen, my skin red with rage, I stared at the ceiling feeling temporary defeat.

That day I had lunch alone in my breakfast nook hardly tasting the food then in the afternoon I went shopping buying nothing. For the first time in my life I was showing signs of paranoia suspecting everyone, trusting no one. My eyes carefully scrutinized every individual as I looked for suspicious actions and motives. Finally stressed out with fear I headed back home.

Since the day was cool but overcast I donned my jogging clothes in order to get rid of some of my tension. I ran across the street dodging cars and then entered the park. I ran down the path ignoring the burning in my chest. I ran oblivious of the screaming muscles in my legs. I ran until, unable to take another step, I collapsed onto one of the park benches.

The weekend turned out to be one of the worst ones that I had ever had in my life. As the old saying goes, "it never rains but it pours." Well, it certainly was pouring. My once seemingly perfect relationship with Robert was now feeling threatened and I could foresee rocky days ahead as far as his wife and children were concerned. Becky's rape had shocked my senses but the greatest trauma had been inflicted when I discovered that the man that I loved would be defending the rapist therefore sending my sense of moral values into a spin. Of course the unexplained occurrences that I had been enduring for the last several years set my every nerve on edge and left me with absolutely no explanation. To make matters worse I received a call on Sunday morning from my superintendent Larry. The previous night one of the buildings had been broken into and the burglary had just been discovered. As he gave me a brief account of what had happened I interrupted him saying that I was leaving immediately and should arrive shortly.

After his face disappeared from the screen I muttered under my breath. "Damn! It's just what I need, another aggravation".

Larry was waiting for me at the curb when I drove up. He began explaining the situation the moment I opened the door informing me that the police were in the process of inspecting the damage down in the locker room. I gasped when we entered the area. Each locker had been systematically pried open and the contents that weren't taken were scattered all over the room. As requested by the police several distressed tenants were making a list of missing articles. I approached the two officers.

The policeman that spoke was polite but professional. "Good morning ma'am. Evidently the perpetrator, or perpetrators, had no problem getting into the building. I see that you have an adequate security system at both doors as well as an alert sound on the lower windows that is activated when they are tampered with. My guess is that they slipped in unnoticed while one of your tenants buzzed the door for one of their visitors or else they just walked in with one of the residents. They probably hid somewhere in the building until everyone settled down for the night and then did the looting. The only additional security that I could suggest would be to have some cameras installed."

"Thank you officer, I will take your suggestion under consideration. Have you noticed any damage to the building?"

"No. The only damage done was to the door to the locker room Ms. Anderson."

I thanked the two policemen then went over to the tenants, listened to their comments, and consoled the ones who carried no theft insurance. After having final words with Larry and discussing plans to install security cameras I left making a mental note to call my insurance company on Monday. I also planned to speak to the residents concerning the screening of unclassified people when using the doors. Sagging behind the wheel on my way home I remembered that tomorrow was Monday which meant that I was booked to work at the hospital. I was exhausted and the thought of it only tired me even more.

"Why am I working anyway?" I said out loud to an empty car. There was so much on my plate right now that work was becoming a punishment. Perhaps this was the time to make the decision to terminate my employment, or at least to take a leave of absence. The more I thought about it the more I liked the idea. Sometime during this next week I would make an appointment to speak to my director at the hospital. Having made the decision I instantly felt a weight lift off of my shoulder and my foot became heavier on the accelerator.

Chapter Fifteen

While my weekend had been a disaster Robert's had quite an element of stress as well. As was planned the children spent the two days with him at his apartment. When the subject of me came up the unexpected reaction was quite disturbing and it was only then that he fully witnessed the result from their mother's brain washing process. How can any parent be so selfish and unfeeling that they could even think of planting self-destructing ideas within their children's innocent minds in order to manipulate a relationship?

"No, I don't want to meet her! I hate her!" screamed Sara.

Johnny feeling frightened sat with his eyes downcast, his hands clutched together.

"But Sweetheart, just meet her. Don't judge her until you have had a chance to assess her for yourself. Daddy wouldn't care for her if she wasn't a nice lady."

"Yes you would." Her eyes were wild with fury and hatred. "She wants to take you away from us. She is an evil woman!"

"Oh my God", Robert whispered under his breath. Leaning forward he looked directly into his daughter's eyes. "No one could ever take me away from the two of you. I love you so much and I always will. Christine knows that I love you and she's happy that I do. She's not trying to take me away from you."

Tears were streaming down her face. "And what about how Mommy feels?" She was determined to discredit the stranger who had barged her way into their lives. "She's all alone after all the years that she spent with you." Her lips were trembling. "She still loves you very much and she's so lonely."

Robert's heart bled for his daughter. Even with all of his expertise and experience in his profession he still found it difficult to explain the situation without discrediting their mother. "Honey, different people have different definitions of what love is. You are still too young to understand. Your mother and I do not care for each other in a way that we should but both of our feelings have not changed towards you and Johnny and they never will. We love the two of you very, very much."

"Well I still don't want to meet her and I still think that she's a very horrible lady who is just going out with you because you are a lawyer."

"Is that what you think? Sweetheart, Christine isn't going out with me because I have money. She has all of the money that she will ever need. She is very comfortably well off."

By this point Johnny was also crying so Robert decided to give the whole subject a rest. He put his arms compassionately around his son. "Okay. We'll talk about it another time. Let's just enjoy the rest of the weekend."

With that said the subject was dropped and so were his hopes of easily forming a workable relationship between the people he loved most dearly in the world. When Robert called me on Sunday evening the two of us were completely exhausted. Our conversation was brief during which time he promised to call me on Wednesday evening after I got home from work.

"Christine, I do love you and I am so sorry for the distress that I caused you on Friday."

"I love you too Robert." We sat staring helplessly at each other. "It's only fair to tell you that I have other things on my mind as well."

He stared at me pursing his lips together. "Listen" he said firmly. "Why don't we spend this coming weekend together? We could relax, have a nice long talk and maybe sort out some of the problems."

"I think that is an excellent idea. We need to talk."

"I'll call you on Thursday.

Chapter Sixteen

MONDAY

I was feeling optimistic when I booked into nursing office on Monday morning but when I was informed that I had been assigned to the pediatric unit my positive mindset changed somewhat. It was not because I do not like children. It is because I love them too much.

I have always viewed them as being the innocent helpless products of creation so that when illness or disaster befell them I believed that they had not earned whatever cruel destiny lay ahead for them. However, most children appear to accept their fates more gracefully and are more resilient and capable of adjusting quicker to circumstances than adults do. Perhaps they aren't as sophisticated and bound to this earthly plane so that death does not present such an ominous ambiance. Illnesses in children invade their systems much quicker than illnesses do in grown-ups. However they also seem to recover much faster, sometimes at a remarkable rate. As a nurse it was always nice to be a part of the process.

Pediatric diseases are also seasonal. Spring brings with it the deadly meningitis and encephalitis sometimes claiming its victim within the first twenty-four hours. During winter with its cold damp weather U.R.I's, (upper respiratory infections) thrives, such as bronchitis, pneumonia, and croup. Other illnesses flourish all year long the most heart wrenching kind being the terminal variety.

Nurses who function well with this type of patient do so by keeping their own pain at arm's length. I always admired how they only focus on the satisfaction that they receive when giving comfort to their young charge rather than dwelling on the prognosis and the end result.

During the past two decades there had been great strides made in the advancement in the medical field, so much so that it had become difficult to keep up financially with the progress of all of the new technology. As quickly as one concept was discovered it became obsolete due to the confirmation of a new and more advanced hypothesis. As far as cures for destructive or fatal diseases were concerned no longer was one controlled when another even more bizarre organism or biological mutation, took its place.

While I was doing my block as a student on pediatrics I quickly discovered that this was not my field of work. It didn't take me long to painfully realize that I was unable to sufficiently disassociate myself from the emotional aspect of the job.

One day I was assigned to be the primary nurse to a dark haired black-eyed little boy of Indian ancestry, a child that had been diagnosed as having an incurable malignancy. I had nursed him for weeks giving love and comfort not only to the patient but to the mother as well. As the weeks went by my control began to slip until to my dismay the mother was giving me solace. As a student on that unit my last shift was on a Friday and tragically the little tot passed away on Saturday morning. I often sadly reflected on how death leaves in its wake such a trail of grief and empty spaces for those who are left behind.

My assignment this day wasn't any more pleasant than were my memories from the past. Once again my patient was a terminally ill five-year-old little girl, a lovely child with blond hair and blue eyes. To look at her one would never imagine that her life span had almost come to an end.

It was early morning when I first walked into her room. Even at that hour the mother was sitting quietly, almost invisibly in a chair by the window. I immediately sensed a certain feeling of tragedy in the room, like a heavy cloud making breathing an effort and happiness impossible. After introducing myself I handed a few pills to the child while the mother filled a glass with water then once the pills were swallowed I began taking the patient's vital signs. Just as I was placing the blood pressure cuff back on the stand the child in all of her simplicity and innocence said, "I am going to die you know."

The wave of pain that swept over the mother's already grief-stricken face was agonizing to watch. In order to conceal her sorrow she turned her back, inhaled quickly, then stared vacantly out through the window. I wanted to walk over to her and wrap my arms around her. I wanted to produce a magic wand and with its touch remove the hideous disease that was slowly but inevitably consuming her daughters weakened body.

"Is that right?" I responded cautiously.

"Yes." The response was simple then she moved across the room, sat on the floor directly in front of the television and continued to watch an old Walt Disney movie that was already in progress on the screen. The subject was dropped.

I did not have a child of my own so I could only imagine how devastating it must be to lose one of your offspring. Evidently there is no greater pain. It is an injustice to the evolutionary plan for a child to precede its parents and no matter what its age the pain is the same. When the victim is an adult he, or she, is immediately altered in the parent's mind to that of the innocent babe that was held with loving arms and nurtured with protective care.

The day demanded my complete attention. On a pediatric unit calculations are estimated on a much smaller scale so that when administering medications the decimal point on a milligram, and gram, is crucial. Although the pharmacist has dispensed the ordered dosage the nurse still has the responsibility to check and verify its accuracy because if an error should be made she would be partially responsible. I confirmed everything more than once and when in doubt I checked either the drug book or questioned one of the staff members who were more familiar with the area.

When I walked off of the ward at the end of the day I was emotionally and mentally exhausted. Arriving home at ten to eight I prepared for the next day and was in bed by nine. I was pleased that the shift was over but there was the realization that, on days like this, I took a little bit of my work home with me. I fell into a restless sleep with visions of a little blond blue eyed child flashing in my dreams.

TUESDAY

On Tuesday I was assigned to the Cardiovascular Unit where heart transplants by-pass surgery and valve replacements are performed. Other invasive procedures, such as heart catheterization and angiography, were carried out in a short stay area. I reminded myself that I had an appointment with my director at 1300 hours. With my back slightly crushed against the glass wall of the elevator and my head resting on the hard surface I closed my eyes and smiled to myself while remembering an episode that had happened a long time ago back in the days when I had been a student nurse.

Well into our course I along with five of my classmates was about to begin a short four-week assignment on the Cardiovascular Unit, an area where the patients were sent to after having open-heart operations. The mere thought of the severity of the surgery sent us into sweating episodes of anxiety and apprehension. We were expecting the worst, envisioning an array of high tech apparatus with several tubes and IV's coming and going from each patient.

That morning we approached the hallway that led down to the desk area with humble timidity. To our surprise the floor that stretched out in front of us was almost void of carts and equipment which was totally unlike any critical care units that we had previously witnessed. There were two or three male patients in the standard striped pajamas and blue housecoats walking aimlessly through the halls or else deep in conversation with one of the staff nurses

The desk area was already busy with activity. A member from the lab department was discussing some of the blood work with one of the nurses while a man, that appeared to be a doctor, was dictating into a handset that he was holding close to his lips. He was speaking in a low tone as though whispering secrets into a confidant's ear. Although there was a fair amount of activity the whole department exuded a feeling of quiet, compassionate placidity, probably a deliberate climate set for the patients.

"Good morning students. Welcome to the cardiovascular unit."

Our clinical teacher Sharon was a kind and patient woman in her mid thirties. She was also a lady to whom no question was too silly or unimportant to give one hundred percent of her attention, and when she talked she spoke in a soft voice.

"I know that you've just arrived here on the unit but I was wondering if there were any questions that you would like to ask me."

There was silence from her new offspring.

Looking from one to the other she smiled. "Okay, let me first give you a tour of the area." Starting at the desk she introduced us to the charge nurse and the other staff members and following that she acquainted us with the medication treatment and utility rooms. Lastly she showed us a small kitchen where cardiac diets were shoved into microwaves then served to the patients.

"Now let me show you some of the rooms and introduce you to the clients."

Before we had reached the first room one of the students spoke up. "Sharon, where are the people who have already had the heart operations. All I see are the new patients walking around in the hall."

Sharon smiled. "Those **are** the patients who have had the surgery."

"But they don't even look sick!" We all had a surprised look on our faces.

"No. You see people recover very quickly after bypass and heart valve surgery. They remain in the intensive care area for a day or two, but once the doctor and staff are convinced that they are stable they are transferred back to our unit."

"Does that include heart transplant clients?" One of the students asked.

"After surgery those patients are transferred to an intensive care unit where they remain for between one to three days. From there they go to a standard unit where their stay can be as long as from ten to fourteen days. "Does anyone know what medications these patients are put on?"

I quickly put up my hand. "Cyclosporine," I answered.

"That's correct. And what does this medication do?"

"It reduces the possibility of having a rejection of the new heart."

"How long are they kept on this medication?"

"They have to take it for the remainder of their life."

I loved the rhythm and general atmosphere of this unit. The patients received an excellent work-up to their surgery by enthusiastic nurses who gave them descriptive lectures on the anatomy and physiology of the heart and of the forthcoming operation. They were then given videos to watch which reinforces what the nurses had already told them. The staff worked well together with a calm co-operative team effort.

Suddenly my focus was back on the elevator. Startled, realizing that my daydreaming had almost caused me to miss my floor, I anxiously followed the few remaining people out and hurried to my assignment.

The morning went well. I had one patient going to the operating room that day who would require the usual pre-op care and medication. He was booked to go at noon which meant that I would be free at one for my appointment with my director, Margaret Winston. At two minutes to one I was announcing myself to the secretary and at one sharp I was sitting across from my superior presenting my request.

"I'm not sure if a leave of absence will be possible Christine. These days the only way to get one is for the purposes of furthering one's education." Margaret looked at me with curiosity. "Is there any specific reason for the request?"

I answered with a firm "yes," nodding my head at the same time. "However it is one that is very personal." After hesitating for a second I asked. "Margaret if I decided to hand in my resignation right now could you make it affective immediately without the usual two week notice?"

Margaret raised her eyebrows in surprise. "Isn't that a little drastic."

"Perhaps it is, but could it be done?"

"Well you have a lot of holiday time owing to you so I could work that in for you but are you sure that this is what you really want? I've known you for a long time and I have never seen you being so impetuous."

My expression became serious. "No. It's a decision that I've been giving a lot of thought to lately."

Margaret sat for a few minutes saying nothing, her expression void of emotion as she studied me intently. "Considering the type of position that you have it certainly will be possible to work around your absence. Also the line up of applicants is endless right now so that I'm sure that we could replace you immediately. If you are really serious and would like to terminate working this week I can see no problem."

"Thank you. I really appreciate it. I'll have my letter of resignation on your desk by Friday."

We stood up.

"We really valued your skills in the operation of the units. If you ever want to come back on a temporary basis please come to me personally and I'll see what I can do."

She extended her hand. Our handshake was firm. "I wish you well in whatever endeavors you pursue."

"Thank you. It's been very enjoyable working for this administration." Walking back to my unit there was a flash of hesitation, but it was only a flash!

The remainder of the day flew by with no problems. During a lull before the supper hour I had a conversation with one of the patients, an executive gentleman in his early fifties. He sat in a chair near the window while I casually leaned against the side of the bed.

"You know Christine this didn't have to happen to me. I did it to myself." There was a penitent look on his face. "I abused my body and scoffed at warnings from what I now realize to be concerned friends. They constantly cautioned me about my smoking and my consummation of copious amounts of coffee and rich foods," he rolled his eyes at me, "and especially about the stress that was job related."He turned his head and looked toward the window through the clear pane of glass to the white, puffy clouds that were slowly moving against the blue sky.

"I always thought that it couldn't happen to me." He shook his head. "If only I had listened. Now my heart is damaged and it will never be the same." He shrugged his shoulders. "Oh, the triple bypass that I just had will help me but I will never be as healthy as I was before. Not only was my heart damaged but other organs were as well." He turned his head and looked at me. "Do you know what I am going to do now?"

"No. What?"

"I am going to spend the rest of my life trying to impress on other people that which I refused to accept for me." When he looked into my eyes his face was tinted with sarcasm. "Do you think that they will listen?"

I looked at him sadly. "No, probably they won't." We stared at each other for a long moment before I said. "You know we can't undo what has been done or change what already is. We must accept our mistakes and focus on the future because concentrating and dwelling on the past only drags us down." One of the corners of my mouth curled upward as I sadly thought about my own life. "Who knows? What each of us has discovered from our own personal experiences may prove to be invaluable in our walk through life. Let's just hope that we don't waste it."

He stared deeply at me for a full moment then leaning over took both my hands in his. "How did you ever get to be so wise?"

There was a melancholy reminder in my voice and in my eyes. "It wasn't easy."

WEDNESDAY

On Wednesday morning I entered the nursing office where I received my assignment for my last day at work. From her chair Rhonda leaned back and gazed at me. "You've been such an essential part of this nursing office for so long that I can't imagine you not being here. We are really going to miss you Christine."

"Thanks. I'll miss you guys too." After a short pause I took in a deep breath. "Well, where do I go for my last shift?"

"Christine it's a one to one. I'm sorry honey but it's a ventilator. All of the skilled staff is assigned to other areas."

I shrugged my shoulders. "It's okay. I don't mind."

Rhonda came around the desk and we gave each other a farewell hug.

It is difficult for one to imagine being paralyzed from the neck down. The thought of being totally dependent on others for support is incomprehensible. It is hard to imagine having to be washed and fed along with the dozen other everyday routines however this was the case with my next charge. Under normal circumstances this patient would not need the intensive care that was being offered in our institution but at this moment she was quite ill. Surrounding her there were four infusion pumps all with computerized numbers flashing in bright red lights on the screens and at least six intravenous bags dangling on their hooks. The only sound was the constant 'woosh-woosh' noise made by the ventilator, a life saving devise, as it pumped with a very specific control what we all take for granted, air.

The night nurse looked up from her charting and smiled. "Hi. I'll be with you in a second."   Placing my purse in one of the drawers I washed my hands in the sink by the door then donned one of the large isolation gowns. As I was tying the belt behind my back I took a few steps toward the bed and glanced at each piece of equipment that surrounded the patient. The woman's eyes were closed apparently in sleep.

The nurse finished with her notes then pressing a key on the keyboard flashed up the nursing care plan. The patient had been a quadriplegic since her accident ten years ago, in other words she was paralyzed from the neck down. Due to the fact that she had developed a severe infection within her system she had been admitted to our hospital. Because she was a diabetic her blood sugars had also become very unstable. At this point the bacteria were pretty much under control due to the massive amounts of antibiotics that were being pumped into her system from two, and sometimes three, of the infusion pumps. With the assistance of an insulin drip the sugars were being held at the normal range which necessitated checking the patient's blood every two hours then adjusting the rate of flow according to the results.

The ventilator's entry was through a permanent tracheotomy, a hole made through the indentation in the front of the neck. When a tracheotomy is performed on an individual the passage of air over the larynx, or voice box, is interrupted making it impossible for the patient to speak. However in this case it was irrelevant since the woman had been born both deaf and dumb. Another tube entered the abdomen and went directly into the stomach, an access for nutrient feedings. Lastly due to the loss of control over urination a third tube was passed through the abdominal wall into her bladder.

Immediately after the night nurse left I checked the ventilator equipment then the infusion bags comparing all levels of liquid with the amounts that had been recorded. When they all tallied accurately I leaned over and noted that the urine bag had been correctly emptied. I was in the process of inspecting the insertion site on the abdomen when I stopped abruptly. Suddenly feeling that I was being intensely scrutinized I slowly and somewhat guardedly turned my head in the direction of the source of the energy flow. The patient was awake and was watching me closely studying my every move. Slightly shaken I introduced myself by untying the straps at the back of the neck and pulling my isolation gown down thus exposing my name-tag. Nervously I finished my initial check.

Having completed this I sat down at the computer to enter a few stats. I was in the process of making an adjustment in the IV flow when I felt a pressure surrounding me, closing in on me, thus making it difficult to concentrate. I also had a disturbing sensation that any protective shield around my mind had been invaded and every thought was being probed. Filled with curiosity I once more looked up into those strange charismatic eyes. Losing myself in their hypnotic spell I forced my gaze away and focused on the rest of the patient's face noting her irregular features. The nose was too large, the chin too pointed, the forehead too high, but the eyes were the most enchanting eyes that I could ever remember seeing.

Once again I was captivated and caught in their spell. When the initial fear that I had, had disappeared I suddenly realized that there was nothing threatening about this woman. For all the blows that nature and God had inflicted on this poor soul I saw only love in return. Instead of anger I saw tolerance; instead of frustration there was acceptance; instead of sadness serenity prevailed. I stood completely captivated for what seemed to be a long time while our thoughts and feelings flowed freely as though words weren't necessary. I felt a kinship as I had never felt with anyone before.

Through the day we often stared at each other, our eyes locked in a strange bond, in an unexplained connection. As I moved through the motions of her nursing care I unconsciously thought of Robert and some of the events from the past. I thought of my intense feelings for him, and of the problems that seemed to be marring our relationship.

A few hours before the end of my shift, while I was in the process of doing the afternoon care with the assistance of another nurse, we rolled the patient to one side, rubbed the skin with a body cream and supported the back and legs with pillows. After we placed the sheets neatly over her and re-arranged the pillow under the head I thanked the nurse for her assistance.

"No problem." The nurse smiled and then left the room.

I was tossing the dirty linen into the hamper when one of the housekeeping staff walked in. After we exchanged a few words about the weather and about some trivial things concerning the hospital she went into the adjoining bathroom. In the meantime I walked over to the window in order to close the venetian blinds. Reaching up and gazing at the rod in my hand I twisted it until the slates fell into place then I turned towards the bed. Walking directly around the end of it I moved over to the woman's side. Slowly I raised my arm with intentions of pushing back a lock of hair that had fallen on her face but my hand suddenly stopped in mid air when the patient unexpectedly flinched.

At first I was confused by her strange reaction but slowly my attention shifted to the appendages at the end of my wrists. My mind froze and my face became a mask of disbelief. As I held up both hands in front of me and slowly rotating them from front to back the housekeeper returned to the room. The instant she saw the strange anomaly on my skin her eyes became wide with astonishment and fear.

"What in heaven's name is that?"

Unable to remove my own eyes I slowly shook my head back and forth. "I don't know." Suddenly the room felt as though it had miraculously moved to another dimension, to the Twilight Zone. Both of my hands were inexplicably covered front and back with thick black grease. It was even embedded deeply under my fingernails.

"Where did it come from?"

"I don't know." My voice was just a whisper.

"It must have come from somewhere." An obvious trace of panic was beginning to creep into the other woman's voice.

I looked at her helplessly. "I don't know." Quickly regaining control we both said in unison. "Let's check the room."

Frantically and thoroughly we searched under the bed and even in areas that I never would have placed my hands. Not wanting to miss anything we checked the workings of the electric bed and under the mattress. After doing a thorough search we stood helplessly looking at each other, each of us realizing that we had no alternative but to accept the fact that there was no way that I could have inadvertently picked it up in the room. Goose bumps rose on our arms. Suddenly the housekeeper bolted from the room.

Slowly I turned to the woman that lay quietly on the bed and walked up to her. Filled with extraordinary curiosity and drawn like a magnet I looked down at the supine figure staring into the remarkable face. 'It was you, wasn't it?' Again the words were only thoughts. The woman smiled awkwardly then closed her eyes.

Letting out a frustrated sigh I stared down at my hands then I began searching the cupboards for an agent that would remove the grease. Unable to find any I attempted to wash it off with soap and water. Of course it did nothing. Then I took a bottle of alcohol however I had the same results. At first I thought of calling one of the other nurses for help but I quickly decided against that because I knew that I wouldn't be able to give a rational explanation, and I certainly didn't want to be the center of an unusual happening. Just then the housekeeper returned holding a bottle and a rag.

"Here, let me try this. In our job we use it to remove grease." Her hands were shaking slightly as she began rubbing the skin with the turpentine until she had successfully removed the black thick sticky substance. It was a few minutes before either one of us could speak.

"Sorry about that," I said. I really felt bad that she had to witness such a bizarre phenomenon.

She smiled weakly. "Oh that's all right."

"Has anything like that ever happened to you before?"

She gave me a feeble look and laughed nervously. "I've had a few things happen to me but nothing like this."

"Yeah me too," I answered, relieved that the woman hadn't panicked.

I walked over to the sink where I washed my hands thoroughly with soap and water then turned to her.

"Are you going to be all right?"

"Oh yes. Don't worry about me," she answered.

We chatted for a few more minutes about unimportant meaningless things then the housekeeper left.

I regretted when the end of my shift came. I wanted to stay with this amazing woman, to spiritually feed on her strength and wisdom. Knowing that at any moment my relief nurse would be coming through the door I took the last opportunity that I had to speak to her. As though sensing my intentions the woman looked up with compassion.

'You know what I am thinking don't you?' I only thought the words.

The woman slowly closed her eyes in a positive response.

'You know that strange things happen to me?' Again only thoughts and again there was the same answer.

There was one last question that I had and the answer meant more to me than anything else in the world. I held my breath as I thought as clearly as I could. 'Am I going to find answers? Will I understand why these things are happening to me?'

It's hard to explain to someone who hasn't experienced it but the inner voice within my head couldn't have been clearer. 'You will get what you ask for if that is what you truly want.' I could almost physically hear the words. The message made me feel as though a death penalty had been suddenly removed from my soul. At the same time I was overwhelmed with a sense of birth, freedom and gratitude.

"Thank you," I said reaching over and gently touching the side of the woman's face. This time I spoke the words. The woman smiled.
Just then the relief nurse walked through the door breaking the spell.

"Hi Christine, I didn't know that it would be you! How has your day been?"

Looking down with affection at the patient I answered. "It has been the nicest shift that I have ever spent."

"Oh that's right. Today is your last day in the hospital. Congratulations!"

The woman and I smiled a conspirator's smile.
I gave a report on my patient but before leaving I walked over and once more looked down into those beautiful eyes.

'I love you,' I thought. The feeling seemed to reach from the very depth of my soul.

'I love you too,' she responded.

Bending over I gave the woman a kiss on the cheek and with one last look left the room taking with me the most precious gift of all.

Standing in front of the elevator with purse in hand everything felt so surreal. Not only was I still wound up and excited over my last assignment, I felt a tinge of sadness when I realized that I was leaving the hospital for the last time. Suddenly one of the two doors opened revealing an elevator filled with cleaning staff. Standing smack in the middle was the woman that I had just shared a miracle with. We instantly made eye contact and smiled a conspirator's smile.

Holding my hands up together I began rotating them in a washing motion.

"Don't ever forget."

"I never will."

The door closed and I never saw her again.

As I sunk into my Jacuzzi I slipped my body down further until only my head was above the bubbly steaming liquid. With the lights dimmed the starkness of reality was softened thus allowing my mind to rest.

The episode with the grease continued to overwhelm me creating dozens of questions that plagued the intellectual part of my mind. What was the purpose in doing such a bizarre thing to me? There had to be a message. The symbol was not a pleasant one...dirt covering my hands. It felt as though it had a negative connotation.

What would it be in regard to? What had I been thinking about at the time?

Suddenly I gasped when I faced the horrible realization that most of the content during the day had been in regard to Robert. Could the message have anything to do with my relationship with him? The thought caused me to sink even further into the water until my whole head was submerged.

I remained in the tub for awhile then I slowly eased myself out. Robert called when I was sipping on a cup of tea.

"Hi Christine how was your shift?"

"It was challenging but satisfying."

"Good!" He paused and narrowed his eyes slightly. "You look and sound different, maybe more relaxed than the last time I saw you."

"As a matter of fact I am and there is a good reason for it. I gave them my notice. I am no longer an employee of the University Hospital."

There was a look of shock on Robert's face. "That's a drastic step. You hadn't mentioned anything to me."

I nodded. "I know but I have been thinking about it off and on for a long time."

"I would like to ask you what your plans are now that you're one of the unemployed. I would also like to talk about other things. Maybe we could see each other this weekend. I know that you are upset about our relationship and have every reason to be." When I didn't answer right away he became worried that I would say no. "Have you already made plans?" he asked nervously.

"No. In fact I was wondering if you would like to stay here at my place." I smiled. "We could relax and pretend that we are an old married couple."

Feeling relieved Robert grinned from ear to ear. "Does that mean that you may develop a headache?"

"I would like you to know sir that I have never had a headache in my entire life."

"Mm, what a healthy young lady you are."

"Yes and I am also a cheap drunk, almost a perfect housewife."

We both laughed.

"All kidding aside, I'll have supper ready by seven on Friday?"

"It sounds great. I can hardly wait. See you then."

We threw each other a kiss and disconnected.

Chapter Seventeen

The only thing that I could think of when I rolled out in bed on Thursday morning was the upcoming court case. Determined to remove any pangs of guilt that I was feeling I phoned Lara around eleven.

"Hi, I was wondering if you were up to having some company today. If you're still not in the mood I'll certainly understand."

"No, no. As a matter of fact I was just thinking about you. Your company is just what I need. Why don't you come over and join us for lunch."

While I was entering the circular driveway in front of the house I was filled with nervous apprehension. I had no idea what I was going to say in regard to Robert's participation in the trial, and as far as Becky was concerned I was unsure just how fragile she was at the present time.

When Lara answered the door she still had that worn and drained look about her. After giving each other a hug we walked arm in arm into the living room.

"How's Becky?" I asked anxiously while sitting in a forward position on the couch.

"She's upstairs resting but she'll be down shortly," Lara answered as she sank her body wearily into the adjacent chair.

There was an eerie feeling in the house resembling what might be found in a home after a death in the family. As though respecting our feelings all noises gave the illusion of stillness, including the grandfather clock that made little or no sound, while in the kitchen the clatter of dishes seemed softened as the maid prepared lunch. I had nursed many similar patients in a structured setting, however when placed in a personal atmosphere the rules seemed to have changed.

"Is there anything that I should do, or not do, Lara? I feel so lost."

Lara smiled warmly at me. "Just be natural Hon, just love her."

While waiting for lunch to be served I filled Lara in about my resignation from the hospital. Her jaw literally dropped in reaction to the news.

"But you love nursing, Chrissy! I can't believe that you have actually quit!"

"I know, but lately every time I have to work I feel that it's an effort. I don't seem to find it enjoyable anymore."

"Won't you end up with a lot of spare time on your hands?"

"Perhaps I will."

Just then we heard a commotion on the stairway as Becky and her nurse was slowly descending the final steps. Filled with embarrassment and humiliation Becky's eyes were fixated on the floor, and when I walked up to her she had to force herself to make eye contact with me. The moment I wrapped my arms around her frail body it began to tremble and soft muffled sobs could be heard coming from her face that was buried in my shoulder. I stroked her back while making soft hushing sounds.

"I feel so awful, Chrissy, so awful."

"I know honey, I know." By now all eyes were watering. "We're all so sorry and we love you so much."

The awkward silence was broken by the nurse who spoke with a definite Norwegian accent. "Vell I don't know about you guys but I know that I am really hungry."

There was a relieved laugh as we headed for the dining room. On the way Lara made the introductions. The nurse's name was Hilda. She informed us that she had specialized in psychiatry ever since she had graduated thirty years ago. Lunch was more relaxed than I had anticipated however I still felt that everyone was walking on eggs due to Becky's fragile state of mind.

Lara looked up from her plate to her daughter, her fork poised in the air with a piece of lettuce on it. "Guess what, Becky? Christine has resigned from the hospital."

Becky's reaction was ever so slight but still detectable to me. The word 'hospital' with its recent memories had sent a slight jolt through Becky's system. This would be an ongoing effect that would follow her for a long time. Certain words, specific smells, particular shapes and colors, would touch a raw nerve in her memory bank triggering a brief flash of pain.

Hilda turned and stared at me with wide inquiring eyes. "Oh, you are a nurse too?" She was quite impressed that she was sitting next to a colleague. "Vat area did you vork in?"

"I'm…. I mean I was on a float team." It pained me to use the past tense for the first time. "I was assigned to all areas except, of course, to the more critical care units."

"I have vorked on the psychiatric units for so long that I vould be afraid to vork anywhere else. Just to think of it sends chills up and down my spine and makes my hair stand on end."

We all laughed as we envisioned such a picture. Even Becky smiled. When Hilda brought Becky upstairs for an afternoon nap Lara informed the maid that the two of us would clean up the kitchen.

"Maybe we'll see more of you from now on," Lara commented.

I raised my eyebrows giving her a sidelong glance. "That is until you get back to work and are swamped with sales."

"I don't know, Chrissy. Since this thing happened to Becky life suddenly seems too short and unpredictable to waste."

As I looked at my friend and realized just how much I loved her I once again felt the pangs of guilt due to Robert's participation in the defense. How was I ever going to give Lara and the rest of the family the support that they needed and deserved?

"Lara I hope that we will always be friends and that nothing will ever come between us."

Lara looked at me with a puzzled expression. "Of course we will, silly. You look so serious."

I went up to her and gave her a warm hug.

I left without telling her. It wasn't the proper time. Tomorrow I promised myself, tomorrow!

Early on Friday morning I went to the hospital in order to deliver my letter of resignation then afterwards I spent the remainder of the day preparing for Robert's arrival. When I moved into his waiting arms it seemed like an eternity since we had held each other, however the instant our bodies touched memories came flooding back making it seem as though it always was.

"Mmmm, you feel so good Princess. I really missed you." He moved his upper body back so that he could have better eye contact with me. "After last weekend I had some fears that you would never want to see me again."

When I didn't answer him immediately he suddenly became distracted by an odor in the room. Raising his head in the air he sniffed like an animal scenting its prey. "Mmmm, something smells good."

"Looking rather proud I answered. "I hope you like Italian."

Arm in arm we walked into the living room where the powerful but effortless voice of Pavarotti filled the area. I gave the command and the volume turned down.

"Would you like a drink, Robert?"

"Why don't you let me serve you? What would you like?"

"I'd like some red wine, please."

Robert was only slightly familiar with my bar but he soon had two drinks poured. Sitting beside me on the couch he reached over and we touched glasses.

"Here's to a very enjoyable weekend."

After taking a sip I sat back and gazed at him with an open-eyed look. "Well dear, how was your day at the office." Although my face remained serious he knew that I was deliberately being stereotyped.

He smiled comfortably at me. "I guess that is what it would be like if we were married. It sounds rather nice. To answer your question the office is quite busy right now. I think that perhaps we have too many cases on the burner and not only that there is also a heavy back log."

"Then why don't you hire another lawyer for the firm?"

"That's not where the problem lies. It's the legal system. Another lawyer won't speed up the courts."

"That's interesting but also discomforting. By the way, how is the action in which the woman shot her husband in self defense?"

"Oh, that one is scheduled for court next week. Actually it got pushed ahead. Since the evidence is overwhelming in her favor I'm sure that we won't have a problem with it."

Concerned that I might bring up Becky's case, which would undoubtedly create a confrontation, he quickly changed the subject.

"So what is this I hear of you resigning from the hospital?"

"Well I brought my letter of resignation in this morning."

"How do you feel about it?"

"Actually, I feel good."

He smiled with approval and raised his glass. "Here's to a new lifestyle." Tapping them together we took a sip. "So where do you plan to go from here?"

"I have several options. I'm fortunate that money isn't an issue. I've been tossing around the idea of expanding my real-estate investments, perhaps buying another building."

He looked at me with admiration. "It sounds interesting and very enterprising."

"Right now I'm going to take a rest and perhaps spend more time with my friends." I shrugged. "I might even take a vacation."

"Sounds very nice," he agreed.

"Well, anyway, enough of that. Are you hungry?"

The dining room looked elegant. My best china and crystal were carefully placed on an heirloom lace tablecloth and antique, baroque, candelabras stood at each end. In the center was a beautiful, high colored, floral arrangement that had been delivered fresh from the florist that day. Pavarotti's voice continued to serenade us as background music which added to the romantic setting of the candlelight.

After a salad that was garnished with my own Italian dressing I served a dish of spaghetti. Both the pasta and sauce was made from scratch from an old recipe that I had received from an Italian girl friend of mine many years ago. As Robert wound his fork against the spoon for the second time he commented on the flavor of the meal.

"This is delicious, Christine! And I find it charming that you made it yourself."

Deciding to pass up on the dessert, due to the heaviness of the meal, we carried our coffee that was laced with liqueur into the living room. The next couple of hours were spent in a game of Five-Hundred Rummy. Our skills being evenly matched resulted in a one-to-one tie. After watching the night news we strolled hand in hand to the dimly lit bedroom where the covers on the bed were invitingly turned down.

Sometimes we enjoyed sex with more passion than with love but tonight our love prevailed. Slowly we moved to the bed, where, lying side by side, we continued to enjoy the heightened senses of sight and touch. When passion caught up and he entered me, my hips rose in eager acceptance as I attempted to pull him deeper into me. The world outside faded away as we rode higher and higher to the top of the cliff, then in a rappelling sensation we floated back down to the physical plane. Contented we fell asleep in each other's arms.

The mood did not change but continued for the remainder of the weekend. We temporarily parted company on Saturday afternoon, Robert going to his office and me paying a visit to my apartments where I received an update from Larry. That evening we ate out and afterwards we saw a late show at one of the cinemas. It turned out to be a rather erotic movie thus heightening our eagerness when we returned to the condo.

After depositing our coats in the front hall closet I turned to Robert. "Would you care for a Jacuzzi?"

"Mmmm, that sounds nice."

"Could you do me a favor? Would you pour a couple of drinks while I fill the tub? "

While he was busy I turned the taps on full power and lit the several candles that were strategically placed on the marble ledges. I had just enough time to remove my clothing in the bedroom before he returned with the glasses.

"Here give them to me and I'll meet you in the Jacuzzi."

When he walked into the en suite a few minutes later he quickly sucked in his breath. I lay stretched out in the soft gauze-like illumination with the bubbly water kissing and caressing my skin. As Robert slowly sank into the opposite end facing me, we talked, caressed, and laughed as we sipped on our wine. Playfully picking up one of my feet he sensually nibbled on my toes while I ran the other foot along the length of his thigh. Unable to wait any longer we moved to the bed where with great expectation we became lost in another world. After exhausting our energy we fell into a satisfied sleep.

Sunday was a quiet day. We woke late, enjoyed a leisurely breakfast, then taking advantage of the warm sunny afternoon we took a long walk through the park. We both expressed how we had never been happier and how the last few days had been as close to perfection as any human being is permitted in this world.

Regretfully on Sunday evening we had to say our good-byes.

He looked down at me tenderly. "Any happier and I would burst. I love you so much. You are the best thing that has ever happened to me."

With one last loving embrace he left.

Closing the door behind me I slowly turned and rested my back against it. Looking up I thanked my God for giving me this miracle of love. Little did I know that it would be a long time before I would once again experience the joy and gratification of a totally uninterrupted weekend!

Chapter Eighteen

The moment I awoke on Monday morning I was filled with a determination to get my life back in order. Not only did I have my bizarre dreams to contend with, there was also the added stress of possibly having a distorted relationship between Robert, his children, and myself. Lastly but most importantly was the matter that was tearing me apart and putting a strain on my sense of loyalty----the upcoming trial. First I concentrated on the short-term goal of cleaning my apartment and by Thursday evening the place was spotless. Feeling exhausted, but contented, I took a shower and washed my hair then flopped down on the couch.

It is curious how hard work improves one's mental outlook on life. Years ago while nursing on an extremely busy unit the charge nurse, a woman for whom I had a great deal of affection and respect for, had looked at me dog-tired and said. "I think that I am going to have a nervous breakdown but I'm too busy today." We both laughed while at the same time we acknowledged the wisdom of the words. I was so deep in thought that I literally jumped when the phone rang. It was Robert. When I looked past him to the background I frowned.

"It looks as though you're still at the office. Don't you ever go home?"

"I have a meeting here shortly but in the mean time I thought I would ask you if you were interested in having lunch with me on Friday."

I quickly agreed. Just as we were about to disconnect I called out his name. "Robert, are you spending the weekend with your children?"

"As a matter of fact I am."

When there was no polite invitation attached to join him I wanted to say more but instead I simply said, "I'll see you tomorrow."

When the image disappeared from the screen I slumped down deeper into the couch feeling more and more left out of the picture, like an uninvited guest, or an unwelcome family member.

"Give it time, Christine" I muttered to myself. "Just give it time."

Suddenly when I remembered the horrible weekend that had occurred two weeks ago I became determined to take more control of my life. The word 'control' triggered another thought. A little voice from somewhere in the back of my mind whispered, "except for the nights when you have no control at all." My spiritual energy took a dive leaving me again with that familiar feeling of total helplessness and despair.

When I met Robert for lunch on Friday his mood was amicable but cool, and when he made no mention of his weekend plans I leaned back in my chair and looked at him analytically.

"The children aren't ready to meet me yet, are they Robert?"

His expression was noncommittal. "No, but I'm working on it. I'm sure that it won't be too long. Please be patient just a little bit longer."

Saying nothing and holding my cup close to my mouth, the remainder of the conversation was trivial and meaningless with Robert promising to call me on Sunday evening.

I think that what had transpired between Robert and me gave me the push that I needed to approach Lara about Robert's involvement with the trial. Arriving home I called Lara and asked her if she could possibly come over on either Friday or Saturday evening emphasizing that I had something of a rather serious nature that I wanted to discuss with her.

Recognizing the same intense tone that she had heard on that previous night when she had tucked me into bed she inquired if it had something to do with my dreams.

"No. Actually it's entirely different but it's too complicated to get into on the phone."

"Well since I have another appointment this evening would Saturday be okay?"

"Certainly and I really appreciate it. I'll see you then."

My hands were shaking when I contemplated the inevitable confrontation.

With renewed energy I turned to my computer and worked on my bookkeeping and banking then I put in an order to replenish my frozen food stock. Generally I preferred to cook from scratch however I also liked to keep a supply of pre-made meals in my meal machine---just in case of an emergency, or for times when I was too exhausted to cook.

When my stomach began to make low growling sounds I was reminded that I had not yet eaten. In my brightly lit kitchen I carefully cut a few slices of chicken and placed them between two pieces of whole wheat bread to which I added lettuce, a touch of mayonnaise, and a sprinkle of salt and pepper. Pouring myself a large glass of milk I carried them to a TV table in the living room then picked out a comedy. Two hours later I was feeling quite relaxed and ready for bed. Pulling the blankets closely over my shoulders and tucking them under my chin I secretly whispered a prayer before drifting off to wherever never-never-land is. "Please God, don't let me dream tonight." He must have been listening because I didn't.

When Lara arrived on Saturday evening she looked and sounded more like her old self, while I on the other hand felt like I had changed places with her. As I was pouring the two of us a drink I nervously and apprehensively called out over my shoulder. "How's Becky?"

"She's getting better every day. Thanks for asking. You know your visit the other day did her a world of good. Up to then she had been so apprehensive at the thought of facing her friends." She gave me a look of warm appreciation. "Actually we have canceled the nurse however either Tom or I is with her at all times. I don't think that there is still a danger of her being suicidal but she still needs to know that someone is there. She is constantly in fear that he will return so she jumps at every sound." Lara gazed gloomily toward the window. "It's all so sad."

It was getting more and more difficult with every spoken word to broach the subject.

"It's really nice to have a friend like you. Tom said to thank you for your help that night." Leaning forward Lara affectionately placed her hand on my knee. "So tell me what your plans are now that you are one of the unemployed?"

"Well I've been tossing around the idea of investing in another multi-unit complex but this time I was thinking more of a row of town houses rather than another high rise building. I might even become more involved in the development of it. So far I've been doing a fair amount of research on architects and contractors. If I do go ahead with the project I thought that perhaps you could help me to select a good real-estate site since I would much rather you get the commission than someone else."

"Thanks so much, I really appreciate it. It will also help me to get back on track as far as my job is concerned. If you get serious about it be sure to give me a call." She paused and looked at me. "Is that what you wanted to talk to me about?"

"No." My answer was hardly audible and my stomach began to twist in a knot.

Lara's face filled with concern. "What is it, Chrissy? You look, and sound so upset."

My mouth was dry as I began to speak.
"It's something that I've known for awhile and should have mentioned to you right away, but with all of the problems that you were having at home I delayed talking to you about it." I gritted my teeth and forced myself to go on. "Before I do tell you I want you to know that the subject had a very heavy impact on me. I needed time to think about it." When there was a slight pause while I carefully attempted to choose my words, Lara stared at me with curiosity.

"I guess that I can presume that there is definitely going to be a court case in regard to what happened to Becky?"

"Of course there will be." Lara looked perplexed.

"Have you spoken to your lawyer about any of the details in connection with the case?"

"I only know that Don has pleaded not guilty however our lawyer explained that it wasn't an uncommon plea. Other than that he has respected our need for privacy. I realize that at the preliminary hearings Becky is going to have to testify, which of course is stressing all of us."

I gazed at Lara with sad painful eyes. "Do you know who the defense lawyer is?"

"No. I haven't given it any thought, I----." She stopped abruptly as though she had suddenly walked into a brick wall. Slowly a look of recognition crept over her face. Immediately she knew. "Robert?" It was barely a whisper. She looked horrified. "Robert is going to represent Don!"

My face was filled with pain. "I'm sorry, Lara. I'm so sorry." The words seemed weak and feeble.

A stunned Lara literally slumped in her chair. "Why? How could he do that to us? After all we are his friends."

"Evidently he also knows Don's parents and has known them for years."

We both sat in silence, both of us at a loss for words. Lara seemed mesmerized by a patch of carpet on the floor in front of her while I couldn't take my eyes off of her face. Without looking up at me she finally spoke in a voice that I hardly recognized.

"Oh Chrissy, all of a sudden the whole picture looks so ugly and dirty. I feel so wretched and angry that I'm afraid I might say something I will later regret. If you don't mind I think I would like to go home. Maybe after a while

I'll be able to find some rationale in all of this and some of the pain will disappear."

"Lara, I am so sorry. I want you to know that I am feeling the same distress that you're feeling."

Lara stared at me for what seemed to be a long period of time then rising slowly from her chair she walked to the front door. Standing with her hand on the knob she said without turning. "Take care, Chrissy."

As the elevator door was closing I once more repeated that I was sorry but I wasn't sure whether she heard me or not. Curling up in the chair by the bay window with my arms wrapped around my legs I sobbed late into the night.

Chapter Nineteen

Waking with a start late Sunday morning I sat bolt upright in bed and leaned forward with my head resting in my trembling hands. My forehead was dotted with perspiration and I was hyperventilating.

"No! No! Not today I'm so tired. Please, not today."

Jumping out of bed I staggered to the bathroom, turned on the cold water and when I shoved my face under the icy torrent its biting pain felt medicinal as it anesthetized my shattered spirit. Leaning my weight on my outstretched arms with my hands pressed flat on the counter for support I looked up into the mirror at a face that I hardly recognized. My skin was pale, my eyes were bloodshot, and my hair hung damp and straggly in disarray. I was desperately cold to the bone and I was shivering uncontrollably.

Reaching over and grabbing my old faithful terry bathrobe off of the hook I wrapped its soft heavy texture close to my body then shoved my feet into my oversized slippers. After shuffling into the kitchen I successfully poured the cold water into the chamber of the coffeepot but cursed under my breath when I accidentally spilled the grounds over the counter and floor. Feeling too weak to clean up the mess I carefully refilled the basket then sat at the table and stared vacantly through the window to the park below while I waited for it to brew. The vision of my dream kept flashing through my mind and each time I gagged with nausea. It was worse than motion sickness. Finally when the coffee was ready I poured myself a large mug full then warmed my icy hands by curling my fingers around the smooth porcelain surface. Later after moving from one room to another, cocooning myself into different spots, I filled the Jacuzzi then sank into it for almost an hour while allowing my mind to examine the incident in detail.

My first recollection: I was standing in a room in a space ship with three or four other companions whose state of mind was like my own. We were all being escorted by an older gentleman to a destination which, at that point, didn't seem to matter. As usual, any power of reasoning or making choices that I normally might have had was completely obliterated. The five of us stood silent and motionless while the two men that were wearing the customary uniform moved about controlling the operation of the vessel.

Suddenly our escort walked up to us and hastily explained that it was necessary for the ship to enter rather quickly. Apologizing for the situation he said that this was an unusual move and that they didn't like to do it when there were non experienced people on board. Emphatic that we were not to look out through the windows he then became concerned over the present situation, turned and walked back to the two staff members. The three of them became very engrossed with whatever task was at hand.

I had always been a very curious child and grew up to be an even more curious adult. That particular quality of inquisitiveness was naturally stimulated while waiting for--whatever. The three men were so preoccupied with their problem that they did not notice me taking the few steps across the room. They were so absorbed in what they were doing that they did not see me peer through the window and they did not observe my violent reaction when I recoiled from what I saw.

Looking through the open span of transparency it was quite obvious that we were located in space. I later repeatedly tried to remember whether the universe should be described as having a blue color or a darker shade, perhaps black, but it was never clear. Conceivably it was variable. There was nothing out there but a void, nothing except a tiny globe that appeared to be no larger than the size of a plum. As I focused on the small circle something happened that sent my sense of perspicacity into a whirlwind of disorientation. In only a second, perhaps even less, I was looking at landmass. The tiny sphere had been hurled towards us at astronomical speed, or rather we towards it. The sudden unexpected and unprepared change left me with a feeling of nausea and a total loss of a frame of reference. I had been immediately thrown into a technology of colossal dimensions without the luxury of desensitization.

Weak and trembling as I took the few steps back to my companions, my eyes didn't seem to be focusing properly and I felt a lump well up in my throat. With the blood draining from my face I wanted so desperately to sit down. In the mean time, satisfied that the craft had been properly stabilized, the gentleman that was our escort returned to our group.

The moment he looked at me and our eyes met he was instantaneously alarmed. "What's the matter Christine? Did you look through the window?"

I stared up at him with sad puppy dog eyes. "Yes."

"Didn't I tell you not to look out of the window?"

"Yes."

He shook his head with disappointment. "You feel awful, don't you?"

"Yes."

"Now do you know why I asked you not to look out through the window?"

"Yes." I was feeling quite penitent.

He looked at each of my companions. "You have just learned a lesson. All of you should listen to what you are told because there is always a reason for our orders."

His demeanor had been firm through the incident but it quickly became gentle and caring as he protectively wrapped his arms around me and assured me that I would be all right.

That was the end of the recall.

Traumatized by the recollection of the incident I went into the kitchen and refilled my cup. Returning to the couch my thoughts would vacillate between the confrontation with Lara and my latest dream. Both scenarios made me feel wretched thus precipitating a fresh flow of tears. In regard to the dream I kept replaying the events over and over again, particularly focusing on that one incredible second when the space ship had hurled towards the earth. Since an indelible imprint had been formed on my mind it was simple to recall the event at any time. Unfortunately due to its clarity it also produced a sudden spasm of nausea.

I looked back to the characters involved in the scenario. The four young people to whom I was connected with had been in the same trance-like state that I had been in, while our escort had been kind and amiable with no apparent intent to harm. The two operators of the ship had gone about their business therefore had not affected us in any negative way. After breaking it down my apprehension and fear diminished while my awe and curiosity of the escalated landing fascinated me more and more. It left me with only regrets, regrets that my mental state had not been more sophisticated and my tolerance to the scene more appropriate with their times. I had to face facts. If full awareness had been permitted I would have been shattered mentally and emotionally.

The incident did leave me with a hundred questions as did all of the other adventures. Who were they? Where had I been before entering this spaceship? Why had they chosen me? Did everyone share similar experiences? What was their purpose in taking me? All of these mysteries, as well as others, still haunted me night and day. I was still deep in thought when Robert called.

"Hi Christine, you're still in your housecoat and you look awful. What's the matter?" He looked genuinely concerned.

"It's nothing to worry about. I had a touch of the flu today so I have been sort of babying myself." It seemed that lately I was constantly lying in order to cover things up.

"I'm sorry! Is there anything that I can do for you?"

"No, no. The worst is over." I quickly changed the subject. "How was your week end with the children?"

"Good. Thanks for asking."

After a short silence I impulsively blurted out. "I told Lara last evening." I regretted the comment the moment it left my lips because I really didn't want to get into the topic on the phone.

"I beg your pardon. You told her what?"

It was one of those moments when you presume that the other person is reading your mind and therefore on the same track.

"I'm sorry. I told her that you were defending Don."

Robert looked surprised. "You mean that she didn't know."

"No, she didn't before but she sure does now."

"How did she take it?"

"Not well. She was really hurt and I can't blame her."

"I'm really sorry Christine. You must realize that I never meant to hurt you, or her. If I mixed my social and business life together I wouldn't have any clients. It's a rule that I made for myself a long time ago and there is no room for compromise."

I could feel the color rising on my face. "I, on the other hand, cannot compromise my principles either."

Like opponents we glared at each other until Robert broke the silence.

"This week is going to be very busy for me. I'm not only referring to the office but also to the fact that the divorce is on docket for Friday."

"Oh Robert, I knew that it was soon but I never did ask you for the specific date. How do you feel about it?"

"I just want to get it over with." He suddenly looked weary. "Would I be presumptuous if I asked you whether I could spend the weekend with you? I sure would appreciate your company on Friday evening."

"Mi casa es su casa, and if you need me for anything during the week don't hesitate to call."

"Thanks."

I wished him luck then we disconnected.

Chapter Twenty

It didn't take any great talent or a gifted supernatural ability to realize who was calling me on Tuesday morning. Hillary was a rather attractive woman who possessed the typical classical features of a straight nose and high cheekbones. The color of her dark, wide-set eyes matched her hair that was pulled back in a severe bun with not a strand out of place. Both her clothes and jewelry depicted wealth and good taste but there was something about the total picture that diminished the image of beauty. Instead of softness her cold and calculating eyes were void of compassion, or love. Instead of sensuality her full lips seemed to thin in an unrelenting, self-serving line. As she looked at me from the screen they parted in a wide friendly smile but her eyes remained hard.

"Hello, Christine. Let me introduce myself to you. I'm Robert's wife, Hillary. I'm sure that you're surprised to suddenly hear from me but there's a reason why I called. Since you are going to be involved with Robert, as well as with my children, I thought that it might be nice for us to get acquainted with each other." She raised her eyebrows. "In fact I thought it would be nice if we had lunch together today."

Since I wasn't prepared for this sudden event my reaction was one of confusion and disorientation. Even though my sixth sense told me to back off Hillary's persistence caused me to hesitate.

"It will be a quiet luncheon and you can pick the time and place." When I didn't answer immediately, she quickly added in an almost condescending tone of voice.

"Surely you don't feel threatened by me?" Without realizing how she had done it she had skillfully manipulated me into a defensive position.

"No, of course I don't feel threatened." Even to me my voice didn't sound too convincing.

"Well then?" She pushed at the issue.

By then my reflexes weren't quick enough to defend myself therefore the whole event was out of my hands. After quickly agreeing on the time and the restaurant the image on the screen vanished.

When I hung up I grabbed a fistful of hair with each hand. "Shit! Why in the hell did I agree to meet her today?" Quickly placing a call to Robert's office his secretary informed me that he would be in court all day. I roughly hung up, "double shit!"

Glancing at my watch I realized that I had a little over an hour to shower, dress, and get to the restaurant on time. On my way to my bedroom I kept muttering derogatory words to myself. If only I had taken control of the situation instead of being such a wimp. Carefully I selected my most appealing suit then I took great pains putting on my makeup. After vacillating back and fourth I decided to wear my hair down.

Since I wasn't familiar with personal confrontations the probability of facing one generated both nervousness and apprehension in me. I made a point of arriving ten minutes early in order to establish a home ground however Hillary had out-maneuvered me and was already in an advantageous position. She had selected a table for two choosing to face the room leaving me with only a blank partition to look at. Since I could feel any movement that took place behind me I always felt a little claustrophobic with this type of seating arrangement. As I was advancing to the table Hillary's cold callous stare pierced any protection that might be surrounding me leaving me feeling uncomfortable and vulnerable.

"So this is Christine." Hillary's voice was polite but cool. "How lovely it is to finally meet you."

Neither of us extended a hand. Positions were already being established.

As I sat down I had a distinct feeling that I was in enemy territory, and during a period of silence the two of us simply stared at each other like two animals sizing up their opponent.

"I must say that Robert still has good taste in his choice of women."
This time there was no doubt about her patronizing attitude. I could feel my face flush with anger and I was finding it very difficult to keep myself in check. When the waitress appeared, thus preventing me from saying something nasty, I asked for a coffee and stated that I would like more time to look at the menu.

After she left Hillary dramatically placed both hands flat in front of her as though she was in the process of conducting a business meeting. "Now that we are together Christine I think that we should put our cards on the table." Glaring at me with narrowed probing eyes she said without hesitation. "Exactly what are your intentions?"

I was stunned. "I beg your pardon? What are my intentions?"

"Oh come on now Christine, don't act so coy."

I shook my head in confusion. "I don't understand."

Hillary stared at me. There was a tone of arrogance and impatience as she continued. "Well then if you insist let us start with my intentions. As you are probably aware the divorce is to be finalized on Friday." Her eyes were hard and her stare was direct. "Christine I want you to talk Robert out of it."

When my mouth fell open in bewilderment Hillary held up her hand. "Please Christine let's be practical. It is not going to be beneficial to anyone to break up the marriage, especially to the children. They need him in their home to function as their father and I'm afraid of what they might do with him gone." She sighed and rolled her eyes in disgust. "I also think that he is going through a period of male menopause because his conduct in the last while has been totally out of character." She paused long enough to scrutinize me. "You're young and can get any man you want. Why are you picking on my husband, a married man with two lovely children? Find yourself someone else. We need him at home."

I couldn't believe my ears. Dumbfounded I stared at the woman that sat across from me. Is that what Robert had been tolerating for the last twenty odd years. No wonder it was so easy to please him. I was furious.

Leaning forward I held one hand up in the air as though stopping traffic. "Just hold on right now lady." I shook my head in disbelief. "I can't believe that you really meant what you just said.

"First of all, since I do not make it a habit of trying to control people I definitely have no intentions of telling Robert anything. Robert is a mature adult, who by the way is definitely not in any menopause, and I do not make his decisions for him."

"Secondly, you talk about our relationship as though you are discussing buying a car, or a dress. Robert and I have a bond a kind of a rapport that I think would be missed in your thinking processes. Since you will not be able to comprehend it I will not explain it to you."

With the adrenaline pumping through my system I was a little breathless.

"Thirdly, whatever problems you have with the children has nothing to do with me. I don't even know them. Any complication that exists has been created long before I came into the picture without any help from me. I'm sorry but you can't load that crock of guilt on my lap, so don't try." I leaned towards her. "Obviously Hillary we have nothing further to discuss." I stood up and made a move to leave.

"Christine!"

I turned.

"You haven't heard the last from me." Her voice was menacing and the hatred was frozen in her eyes.

Unruffled I leaned forward a little more and placed both of my hands on the table. My eyes that were positioned parallel with Hillary's were as hard as hers. My voice was as icy cold. "Hillary don't you dare threaten me!" With that warning I turned and left the restaurant.

I sat in the car for several minutes in order to collect my thoughts as well as to regain my composure. My hands were trembling and I felt as though I was hyperventilating. I had learned something about myself today, something I had always wondered about. Would I be able to stand up to a personal confrontation? Well now I knew. What a bitch!

Chapter Twenty-one

On Friday the divorce went through as scheduled. When I opened the door that evening an exhausted Robert was resting his weight against the door jam. Without saying a word I reached for his hand, guided him into the apartment and helped him off with his coat. Taking his briefcase I placed them both on the hall chair then escorted him into the living room. After maneuvering him over to the reclining chair I carefully helped him off with his suit jacket while at the same time I gently nudged him into a sitting position. Kneeling in front of him in servile style, I removed his shoes one after the other then placed them beside me on the floor. With a sensual smile I seductively sat down on his lap, removed his tie, and undid the top two buttons of his shirt.

"Does that feel better?" My voice was husky.

He embraced me lovingly. "Much," he had difficulty speaking.

Two hours later we were enjoying a picnic lunch on the middle of my bedroom floor. After spreading out a blanket I arranged an assortment of dishes of aromatic and tasty food along with a couple of bottles of expensive wine. Eating in Tom Jones style we used our hands to consume the assortment of cooked meat and fresh fruit and vegetables. For dessert we covered strawberries in dark chocolate sauce and thick whipped cream then reaching over he touched each nipple of my bare breasts with the rich foods. We were drinking heavily perhaps in an attempt to forget our own personal nightmare. After emptying the second bottle and carelessly tossing it aside we made love to each other with no holds barred. With all inhibitions vanished we entered into a new realm of imagination doing things that we had only fantasized about, experimenting with bizarre and exotic creations in complete abandonment.

The next morning we awoke with hangovers to beat all hangovers. It was painful to open my eyes but it felt even worse to speak, or to move my head.

I moaned. "Oh, I feel awful." Within seconds I struggled out of bed and raced to the bathroom where the retching and gagging didn't do much to help Robert's queasy stomach. As quickly as I could I staggered back to the bed where I gratefully rested my spinning head down on the pillow.

"I just looked into the mirror and I could swear that I was green," I muttered. Even talking was agonizing.

"That's okay. I like green." Robert's position remained fixed. His eyes remained closed.

"But it will clash with my lipstick." My voice was whiny."

"Then don't wear any."

Two hours later we were sitting at the breakfast nook, with Robert leaning forward and holding his head in his hands and me resting my forehead on the table. For half an hour we argued over the best remedy for a hangover.

"I told you that I was a cheap drunk." I painfully turned my head in his direction. "Didn't I?"

He rolled his eyes up and agonizingly grinned at me. "That you did but you also don't get headaches."

At noon, still feeling weak, Robert left for the office. In parting we leaned forward but our lips just barely touched.

By dinner things were pretty well back to normal. After him giving me a brief account of the divorce proceedings, I informed Robert of my so-called luncheon date with Hillary.

"You did what?" He appeared not only shocked but also horrified.

"On Tuesday morning she called and invited me out to lunch. When she suggested that we get to know each other I agreed to see her against my better judgment. I think that when I tossed it about in my mind I asked myself how bad could it be anyway? I called your office immediately to get your opinion but your secretary informed me that you were in court all day."

Placing his fork and knife down on his plate Robert ceased eating while he listened to my story. "Hmm, so that was why Hillary was so curious about my schedule that day. My secretary mentioned that she had called and wanted to discuss something of importance with me, but when I called back later that evening she said that the problem had resolved itself. She knew that if you spoke to me I would have advised you against the two of you meeting like that." He looked at me apologetically. "Was she just unpleasant, or downright vicious?"

"Both."

"I'm sorry."

"Robert you aren't accountable for her behavior."

"I know but I still feel responsible."

We moved to the living room where we enjoyed our after dinner coffee. Switching to the newspaper channel we discussed some of the articles for that day. Problems in the world were still escalating and tensions seemed to be stretched to the breaking point. "It's a sad world out there, Robert."

Just then the phone rang. I turned the sound down on the TV and flipped on the telescreen.

"Oh my God," Robert gasped as he stared at Sara's distraught face.

"Daddy, please come and get us because Mommy's been drinking and we're scared." In the background the shrill voice of Hillary cursing, and using abusive language, all directed towards me, could be heard.

Sara began sobbing louder. "Please, Daddy, please!"

Robert held out his hand motioning for Sara to stop crying. "Listen Kitten Daddy will be right over. I want the two of you to go into the bathroom and lock the door. Don't open it for anyone but me. Do you understand?"

"Yes, but please hurry. We're so scared."

Before the set was even turned off Robert had grabbed his suit jacket that was on the chair and was rushing to the front door. While he was putting on his shoes and boots I retrieved his overcoat and held it up for him. Just as the elevator door was closing I hollered out for him to phone me. After closing the door then walking over to the bay window in the living room I spread the curtains slightly with my hand. Soon I saw Robert's Mercedes rushing out of the parkade. Sitting down in a slumped position on the chair I realized that the picture was much worse than I had anticipated.

As Robert was rushing up to the house he could hear Hillary's drunken shrill voice. Letting himself in through the unlocked door of his former home the scene that confronted him was vicious. In the past the few times that she had indulged herself with alcohol her low tolerance to the substance had resulted in a flood of tears and a barrage of paranoid accusations. The doctor had severely warned her to avoid it at all costs.

From his position in the hallway Robert could see her sitting on the middle of the living room floor surrounded by picture albums and torn photographs. With a pair of scissors she was slicing away at a piece of paper that she was holding in her hand, all the while spewing out obscenities. There was a glass half-filled with red wine beside her as well as an empty bottle lying on its side.

Since his main concern was his children he turned and dashed up the stairs then hurried down the hall to the bathroom. Tapping lightly on the door he called out softly. "Open up kids, its Daddy." Two terrified children rushed into his arms.

"Oh Daddy I'm so scared." Sara sobbed. Tears were streaming down both their faces.

"Listen I'm taking you with me to my place. Don't worry everything will be okay."

The three of them hurried down the stairs. As they passed by the archway to the living room Robert was unable to completely prevent his children from glancing in and witnessing Hillary while she was engrossed in one of her tirades of hate. She on the other hand was oblivious to their presence or departure. After settling the children safely in their seat belts he climbed into the driver's side. As he drove away he turned on the audio portion of his car phone and called his ex-wife. Ten rings later she answered. It took everything that he had to keep his voice under control.

"Hillary I'm informing you that I have the children in the car and that I'm taking them with me to stay at my place overnight. When she began to object he snapped. "Don't say anything. I'm calling your sister to ask her to go over and stay with you tonight. I'm not going to lecture you now but I will talk to you later." He quickly hung up before she could respond. The children had already been exposed to enough trauma for one night.

When he arrived at his apartment he instructed them to go to their bedrooms to change into their pajamas, then, after they left the room he scanned through his personal phone numbers. Finding Hillary's sister's name he put a call through to her house and sighed with relief when she answered.

"Betty I'm so glad that you're home."

"What is it Robert? You look upset."

"It's Hillary. If I'm not interrupting anything I was wondering if you could go over to the house. I just came from there and she's in a bad way. I think that she has consumed a whole bottle of wine so perhaps she might even require some medical attention. You know how low her tolerance is to the substance."

Betty anxiously asked where the children were.

"I have them here with me at my place so they're okay; a little upset of course but they will be all right. Did you want me to call Hillary's doctor?"

"No you have your hands full already." She paused. "You know Robert this whole matter of the divorce has me very upset."

"I understand."

"Well I had better get over there right away. Thank you for calling."

"Thanks for your help and please call me and let me know how she is." He then made sure that she had his new number.

After disconnecting he called me. "Hi, I can't talk to you for very long because I have the children with me. Hillary is really intoxicated so I called her sister Betty and she's on her way there as we speak. I'll call you back later after the kids are in bed." When he heard some commotion in the hall he quickly disconnected.

After making them some hot chocolate the three sat in the kitchen nook. Their father explained that their mother was not well and that the alcohol had affected her the way it did. He explained that alcohol is like a drug and was responsible for the things that she was doing and saying. He assured them that she would see a doctor and that an episode like the one that they had just witnessed would be avoided in the future. They were emotionally drained when he tucked the two of them into their beds. He assured them that they were very much loved by both him and their Mom and that the love was not only with them now but would always be in their hearts.

After I spoke to Robert for the second time and listened as he described what had happened in more detail I wished them well. Turning off the system I sat looking at my big empty apartment. "What a mess," I muttered to myself. Scanning through my library of books I pulled out one that I had not yet read, then, taking it and a cup of warm tea to the bedroom I propped up the pillows and made myself comfortable. The aroma of Robert and our lovemaking lingered on the sheets inducing emotional nostalgia, mental loneliness, and physical warmth and excitement. After reading for about an hour I set the book aside, turned off the light and curled up on my side. I was sleeping in seconds.

Chapter Twenty-two

It was the beginning of December which meant that Christmas was quickly approaching. Stores had already been decked out with commercially seasoned strings of lights, and Christmas music was filtering through the sound systems. Outside, the city had its first snowfall.

I loved winter. I delighted with the first sight of freshly fallen white flakes as it spread a blanket over the hard gray concrete world, and I enjoyed the crunching sound of firmly packed snow under my boots. It was cold necessitating the act of bundling up in clothing that would protectively insulate the wearer from the freezing temperatures. It was cold. It was winter.

Hillary's therapist had reached her in regard to her coping skills as far as the divorce was concerned, and in regard to the consumption of alcohol she sincerely agreed to avoid the beverage at any cost. Robert had hired a temporary Nanny so that the children could stay at his place therefore I only saw him for short periods over lunches and coffee breaks. Because it was such a fragile time for Robert's family I said nothing more about the prospect of me meeting Sara and Johnny.

In the mean time by my taking the initiative Lara and I healed our injured relationship. When I called to arrange a meeting with her she hesitated, but when I stubbornly persevered she agreed to visit me at my home where we could discuss the present dilemma. The atmosphere in the apartment was tense as we sat stiffly with grim faces in our chairs.

"I know that you're angry with me as well as with Robert," I began. "I can appreciate what you are going through and I'm really sorry for what has happened however I don't think that you can imagine how devastating it has been for me. If we value our friendship, and I know that I do, I think that we have to talk about it and tell each other how we feel. If we shut each other out all of the years that we have been together will be for nothing."

"I'm angry with you Chrissy. You're my friend, my very best friend, and yet I keep feeling that you have deserted me by conspiring with the enemy. Now every time that I look at you I see and think of you with Robert, a man who is going to rip my Becky apart on the stand. That same night you will be lying in bed with him and you will make love to him. I feel that you are betraying me." There was anger and bitterness in her eyes.

We sat swallowed up in sadness, our spirits broken. At first the pain was so great that I couldn't speak so Lara continued.

"Of course I'm angry with him but at the same time I realize that Tom and I are more like acquaintances than we are like friends. I also realize that he is very close to Don's parents. I can understand what he is doing, and why he is doing it----but not what he is doing to you." She looked hard into my eyes emphasizing each word. "He is supposed to love you. Surely he is aware of the ramifications as far as we are concerned. He must realize how your loyalties will be strained. If he loves you he sure has a poor way of showing it."

During the next few moments there was an awkward silence. Since I had so much invested in my relationship with Robert acceptance of what she had just said was a difficult expectation for me. Finally I spoke.

"Lara, please be patient with me because I feel that I am a victim along with you and your family in this whole mess. Please believe me when I say that I was painfully torn into two pieces when Robert informed me that he was defending Becky's rapist. Yes, I feel wounded by him," I paused in order to choose my words carefully, "but not enough to give him an ultimatum. Robert and I have so much more between us that I can't give him up without making an attempt to heal the problem. Besides I cannot dictate to him in matters concerning his profession just as I wouldn't appreciate him telling me what to do in mine. Please bear with me while I work my way through all of this because it is really paining me and putting a strain on my sense of right and wrong." My lips began to quiver slightly and my eyes moistened. "I don't know what I'll do when the trial comes up. You must realize that since I won't be able to go to the court with you I won't be there when you need me the most." I sighed and looked desperately at my friend. "Oh, Lara, for the first time in my life I feel so confused. Please don't ask me to make choices at this point."

Lara sat for a long time painfully watching my torment then making a decision she moved over and put her arms around me and held me close. Pulling back Lara firmly gripped both of my upper arms.

"Chrissy we're going to get through this one way or another. One thing that I am sure of is that we will never desert each other. I realize now that you're also hurting and that your choice will not come easy but whatever that choice ends up being I will accept it." She looked pensive for a minute. "I guess that I would find it impossible to leave Tom because of one indiscretion. There are just too many other good things between us to give up."

I looked at Lara with a sad expression. "I don't want to hurt you and I certainly don't want to lose your friendship."

"One day at a time Honey. One day at a time."

Chapter Twenty-three

It had been two weeks after the tragic weekend that Robert's children were once again placed back into Hillary's care which allowed him to spend time with me. I felt like a teenager as I waited for him in my condo on Friday evening. When I opened the door and encountered a thinner and much older looking man it was obvious to me that the experience had had its toll on him.

As he protectively wrapped his arms around me and held me close he sighed into my ear. "I've missed you so much Christine. It feels so nice to hold you again."

"I missed you too Sweetheart."

We went out for dinner choosing a restaurant that had a leisurely atmosphere where the food was excellent and the service was appropriately paced. As we sipped slowly on our 'before dinner' drink, the conversation was light and frivolous, and by totally centering our attention on each other everything and everyone else became inconsequential. It all had a healing and rejuvenating effect on us.

That evening the lovemaking was needy but slow. Filled with a feeling of satisfaction we fell into a deep and contented sleep.

Saturday we slept in then lounged around the apartment like an old married couple. Since the day was unusually warm we made our way across the street to the park. With our coats wide open we strolled hand in hand along the dry sun-warmed sidewalk then finding our familiar park bench we sat down. Robert leaned back with his legs extended and crossed at the ankles, while I sat up straight with my head tilted back to the sun and both arms extended along the back of the frame. We didn't speak for a long time but instead we listened to the chirping and squawking of birds and the distant sounds of children at play.

"Tell me about the trial, Robert."
The unexpected question took him off guard. "Christine I've already told you that I'm not allowed to discuss the case with you." Neither one of us had changed our position on the bench.

"No, I mean the generalities. Explain the system to me. What has taken place so far?"

While his face took on a silent look of consternation he appeared to be absorbed with a rabbit that was hopping between two tall trees, then, focusing on a patch of ground between his legs he changed his position by leaning forward resting his elbows on his knees.

"Don was taken from the house by the authorities to the police station where he was charged under section 271 of the criminal code. Translating it in layman's terms he was charged with sexual assault. Due to the report of a routine sexual assault procedure that was done in the Emergency department at the hospital there was no additional indictment of causing bodily harm. He's lucky because that is a much more serious accusation. In the morning after he had sobered up he was taken in front of the Justice of Peace where he was charged and then released. Do you understand so far?" he inquired as he sat up straight.

"Yes, but they just let him go? Why didn't they keep him in jail?" I was appalled.

"They would have if they had felt that there was a possibility that he might re-offend, or that there was a chance that he wouldn't show up for the trial. My associate pointed out to the court that this was his first offense and that he was a well established citizen within the community."

I sat musing over what he had just said. "When did Don first call you?"

"He called my office on Sunday as soon as he sobered up." He glanced at me. "You were aware that his parents were out of town at the time and that I was the logical person for him to get in touch with since his father and I have been good friends for years. I didn't find out about his call until Sunday evening." He turned and peered at me from under his eyebrows. "Remember we were away in Banff that weekend."

"Did you have any hesitation in taking the case?"

"No. At first I was unaware who the victim was so that there was no indecision on my part. Later when I was enlightened it certainly did produce some vacillation on my part."

"Why was Lara and Tom not informed that you were representing Don? I mean there must be some procedure that would have given them some clue as to who the defense lawyer would be."

"Not really. Ethically a lawyer doesn't advertise the names of his clients. The next day there was a docket appearance in the provincial court at which time the prosecutor and one of the lawyers from my office was present. Neither the victim or the victim's family is obligated to attend." There was a pause as he looked at me. "I'm sure that Lara and Tom were so involved with Becky that no one bothered to inform them."

"What happens at this so called docket appearance?"

"Firstly it is a formality at which time they announce the advocate for the defense, and secondly it is when they set a date for the preliminary hearing. Unfortunately there is always a backlog of cases and right now there is an approximate six month waiting period."

"Six months! So the criminal is allowed to walk the streets for that length of time."

He turned and looked at me from under his eyebrows, "Alleged criminal."

I looked at him quizzically, "Pardon?"

He repeated himself, "Alleged."

I gave him a disgusted look. "Robert he is obviously guilty."

"No comment."

I sighed. "I'm not familiar with court cases except for the ones that I see on television and in the movies. Will he be tried in front of a jury?"

"Since this is an indictable offense the accused gets an election of three choices." He looked at me. "Are you sure that you want me to get into all of this?"

"Yes I am really interested. It also may help me to be of some assistance to Lara and her family."

He leaned back getting more comfortable. "Okay. First option he can be tried by a provincial judge using the same level of court. Secondly he can be tried in a court of Queen's Bench without a jury. With that method a judge collects all of the information presented at the trial and on that basis makes a ruling. The third choice is a court of Queen's Bench with a jury. This is the more dramatic and costly procedure and is usually the one depicted by the entertainment media."

"Which way have you chosen for Becky's case?"

"Sorry. I will let you know after the preliminary hearing. Now where was I? Oh yes. At the hearing the crown runs the evidence in front of the judge to see whether there is sufficient ground for a case. If he decides that there's not then the accused will be discharged. However if there is sufficient evidence then the accused will be charged and a date is set for the trial."

"Not another delay? How long will that take?"

"Oh probably it will take another six months, again due to the backlog of cases."

"So that's a total of a year from the time that the crime is committed to the time that the case is heard in court."

Robert opened his mouth to speak but before he could I interjected. "Pardon me the alleged crime." I made a face. "So when is the preliminary hearing booked for? "In this case the date was moved up a bit and will be heard in the middle of February."

Because I dreaded the answer I hesitated to ask the next question. "Robert, will Becky have to testify at the preliminary hearing?"

He looked at me with a painful expression. "I'm afraid so, Christine."

"Oh how awful for poor Becky!"

We sat watching a flock of birds gathering around an elderly gentleman who was throwing what looked like breadcrumbs on the ground in front of him.

"Robert." My voice was subdued. Without saying anything he turned his head and looked at me.

"I'm really disappointed in you for taking this case because it's causing so much upheaval in my life. Didn't you realize how badly it would affect my relationship with Lara? After all, she is my best friend?"

It took him a few seconds to answer. "Yes it did. I already explained all of this to you Christine. First of all I had already committed myself to my friends. Secondly I have a very strict rule not to let," in unison I repeated the last phrase with Robert, "personal relationships to interfere with my profession." Upset with my sarcasm he gave me a wide-eyed look. "I'm sorry to repeat myself but I have never deviated from that standard."

I looked off in the distance. "I think that you could have made an exception in this case, for my sake."

"I'm sorry, Christine."

I studied him for a moment. "Are you sorry that you hurt me, or are you sorry that you won't change your mind?"

He shrugged his shoulders. "I guess that I'm sorry for both reasons."

We dropped the subject but it put a pall over the remainder of the day.

Later at dinner we ate our meal focusing more on the cuisine than on the conversation. I left part of my food untouched and we both declined on the desert. Over our coffee Robert informed me that he had a lot of work to catch up on therefore he would have to get an early start in the morning." He took a sip then placed his cup down. "By the way the legal offices are having their Christmas party in two weeks and I was wondering if you would like to go with me. It would give you a chance to meet a lot of my friends and acquaintances. I would really like it if you would say yes."

My face lit up. "I'd love to go. What night would that be?"

"Saturday night. Cocktails are at six, dinner is at seven followed by a dance."

"How formal will it be?"

"It's a black tie event."

It had been a long time since I had been to such a formal affair so the idea excited me.

"Speaking of parties I thought that I'd invite a group of friends over to my place. It would give you a chance to meet **my** friends and acquaintances."

"Splendid! I've been looking forward to it."

Feeling as though the gap between us had shortened I walked over to his chair and snuggled into his arms. "It will be nice getting back on track with each other. I do love you and I'm the most happy when I'm with you."

As he wrapped his arms around me he said in a husky voice. "Christine you're the greatest thing that has ever happened to me. I love you so much."

Since the evening was too young to be going to bed we selected a movie then sat back and enjoyed the entertainment for the next two hours. It was a category that involved participation by the viewer leaving us very intellectually stimulated when it was over.

Robert gave my hand a squeeze. "That was really exciting. I think that we make a pretty good team but now I'm so keyed up that I don't know if I can sleep." He then excused himself and headed toward the bathroom.

When he came out the apartment was dark except for a faint unusual light coming from my bedroom. Approaching the open doorway he stepped over the threshold and quickly inhaled. The strange illumination was coming from numerous red candles that I had placed strategically throughout the room. As I lay naked on the crimson satin sheet my hair was fanned out on the pillow and my scarlet lips were moist and filled with passion. Slowly opening my eyes they took on an eerie luminosity, tantalizing and enticing him to have his way with me. The submissive expression on my face excited him more than he anticipated, or understood. Driven to unbelievable heights of passion he made love to me in a rough demanding manner, while I reciprocated with masochistic pleasure. Any discomfort became pleasure, and pleasure dominated the pain. The gratification went on and on while our climaxes seemed to last forever. With his strength sapped from his body he awkwardly rolled off of me. Our skin glistened in the candle light and our chests heaved with exhaustion. He stared wide-eyed at the ceiling.

"Oh my God," he moaned. "Never have I felt anything like that." Suddenly feeling uneasy he turned to me. "Princess, are you all right? Did I hurt you?" There was such an expression of concern on his face.

Turning to him I gasped for air. "Don't worry. I'm fine but it sure was different." Even though I sounded blasé I was quite concerned over what had just transpired.

Satisfied and exhausted we fell asleep in each other's arms.

The next morning there was evidence of our love making from the previous evening. When he witnessed what he had done Robert closed his eyes in disgust. "Oh Christine I'm so sorry. I'll never do that again."

"Robert I'm as much to blame as you are." I chuckled. "Besides I think that you look worse than I do." I took one of his hands. "Come on let's take a shower and then we will tend to our wounds."

Later I made him a quick breakfast of half a grapefruit, two boiled eggs, and some whole-wheat toast;

all of which he gobbled up rather quickly then washed it down with a cup of hot coffee. At the door we hugged.

"I'll call you this evening." Looking at me with affection he added, "This is a weekend that I will never forget."

When he left the apartment there was a giddy Cheshire grin on his face which remained for the balance of the day.

Still dressed in my housecoat I sat at the kitchen table staring out over the park. Life as I knew it had suddenly changed, or at least I was having a new perspective of it. I was genuinely surprised that I had been capable of being part of a rather violent lovemaking session. The more I thought about it the more I realized that it was not the act itself that was objectionable but rather the intent. When I thought of Becky and the traumatic and heinous scenario that had been forced upon her I realized that the two incidents were slightly similar in action but totally different in principle.

Of course there must be consent, consent that is given freely without duress, coercion, badgering, or any use of force or trickery. I remembered an incident in which I had finally given in to a gentleman after undue pressure. Afterwards any recollections of the event made me feel uncomfortable. I had fulfillment during the intercourse, a physical response, but the intellectual memory was repugnant.

In an unsatisfied relationship as long as the victim enjoys the act the perpetrator feels justified. Because the victim is the one who usually accepts the blame and responsibility it is he, or she, who is left burdened with feelings of guilt and regret.

My thoughts brought to mind a patient that I had been in charge of while working on a psychiatric unit. My client, a man who was in his forties, had been repeatedly sexually molested by his father when he was a child. This activity lasted for several years. It was damaging enough to him that every time his father entered the room my patient had to endure his advances but he compounded his son's feelings of guilt by telling him to indicate when to stop. The father always made sure that he asked his son while his son was having extreme pleasurable feelings. By doing this he made his son feel that he was in control and therefore was responsible for the performance; the poor innocent child, the poor ignorant man. Thankful that I had never had to experience such trauma I wrapped my arms around myself holding the spiritual child within me. I felt so fortunate to have Robert as a lover as well as a friend because he made me feel loved but never ever used.

Suddenly I was reminded of my dreams and realized that in reality I had been used many times. I was also aware that I hadn't had a visit for awhile. Perhaps they had forgotten me----perhaps.

Chapter Twenty-four

When I had lunch with Lara on Monday she was slightly preoccupied during the meal.

"Will you be seeing Robert this coming weekend Chrissy?"

"No he'll be spending it with his children."

"In that case I have a big favor to ask you but if you don't want to do it, for any reason, please don't hesitate to say so."

"Of course, what is it?"

"I was wondering if we could leave Becky with you for the weekend. I know that it's a lot to ask of you but Tom's business is sponsoring a trip for his staff and it's compulsory that he attend. I would really like to go with him but there's Becky to consider. Her usual nurse has another assignment and I don't want to leave her with someone new."

"Of course I wouldn't mind." Raising my eyebrows I stared across the table. "What does Becky say about it?"

"I hope you don't mind that I spoke to her first. Actually she's eagerly looking forward to it."

"Do you want me to stay at your house or would you prefer to have Becky come over to my place?"

"Perhaps it would be better if you discussed that with her."

When Becky decided to spend the time at my place I felt that she had made a wise choice as it would give her an excellent opportunity to initiate a change of scenery. Lara briefed me on Becky's most recent status then gave me a few phone numbers in case of an emergency. On Friday evening they anxiously arrived at my door.

"Sorry that we can't stay too long. We don't want to miss the flight."

They then turned to their daughter. "Remember Becky. Call us at the lodge any time night or day if you need to talk to us, okay Sweetheart." After giving her a long affectionate hug they finally relinquished her to me.

The moment the door closed the apartment suddenly seemed morphed into a quiet empty void. Seeing that Becky was feeling uncomfortable with the strangeness of her surroundings I attempted to direct her attention to something more positive.

"Why don't you go in and unpack your clothes. Meanwhile I'll be in the living room with a cup of coffee. By the way, would you like me to pour you one?"

"No if you don't mind I'd like to help myself."
I watched her as she disappeared down the hall with her suitcase and it wasn't long before I heard a commotion in the kitchen. A few minutes later a nervous and subdued young woman entered the room. Sitting on the other end of the couch she curled her legs under herself in a protective position.

"I guess it's been quite awhile since you were here last."

As her gaze moved slowly around the room she simply responded with a quiet yes. "Your place is really nice but then I've always admired your taste."

"Thank you but I can't take the credit. Most of the pieces here belonged to my parents."

"I know but you have a way of arranging them in the room and picking out the right colors. That's very important."

There was an awkward silence.

"Becky I haven't made any plans for us for the weekend because I thought that we could do that together.

Again there was no sign of interest. "Oh, I don't know. I haven't been going out very much." Her lips formed a crooked sarcastic smile. "In fact I haven't been out at all."

As the climate in the room became awkward I was more determined to change it. "There's a lovely park across the street. Perhaps tomorrow we could take a walk in it. Actually they have forecasted good weather."

"I'll see." There was a total lack of enthusiasm in her response.

I sat back and sadly gazed at a broken girl whose vital spark for life had gone out. This definitely wasn't the same girl that I once knew.
"Honey I want you to know that if you ever need someone to talk to I'm here for you. I love you very much and I think that you are one of the sweetest and kindest people that I have ever known."

Becky's shoulders suddenly hunched over and her hands began to twist in an involuntarily constant washing motion. When she finally spoke her voice sounded hollow and broken. "I don't feel like a kind and sweet person."

As I watched her reaction I could feel her pain. "I know that you don't and it makes me feel so sad."

Without warning an unexpected surge of emotions began flowing through Becky. "Chrissy I don't like myself, in fact I hate myself. I hate my body. I hate what he did to me." She began sobbing.

"Becky, listen to me. Listen. One day when you have healed yourself you will realize that there is a part of you that no one can touch or destroy unless you allow it to happen. That is a piece of you that belongs to you, and only you. It is the essence that makes you beautiful. It is the fragment that some people call the spirit. Hold on to it, nurture, love, and protect it, because no amount of torture, rape or degradation can destroy what is yours unless you let it."

"Oh Chrissy, I just wish that I felt that way now." She covered her face and continued to sob.

When I walked over and sat beside her in an attempt to comfort her Becky stiffened. I withdrew far enough to give her some space then waited until the tears had subsided and she had blown her nose.

"Becky, do you think that it will make you feel better if you talk to me about it?"

At first Becky wrapped her arms protectively around herself and stared across the room. "If you knew what happened to me that night you wouldn't think as well of me afterwards. Yes I feel embarrassed about it but what's more important I also feel so guilty and dirty."

Reaching over I cautiously took her hand. "I know that you feel these things Honey and it's perfectly natural. I would be surprised if you didn't have these sentiments. Staring silently into the crackling fire her mind seemed miles away. Suddenly she yanked her hand from mine as though she had once more shifted into herself for protection.

"They took me to the emergency department at the hospital afterwards. It was so embarrassing. I felt as though someone else was violating me only this time it was the good guys. Oh the nurses and doctors were really nice to me but when they began to examine me all over I just wanted to run and hide, to crawl into a corner." She paused. "I think that I made my mind go numb and pretended that it was happening to someone else. It was the only way that I could stop myself from screaming."

Suddenly her face twisted into a grimace. "I was covered with blood and'...." Unable to finish the sentence she shuddered and sobbed wretchedly.

Instead of reaching over and holding her I handed her a few more tissues. We both sat for a long time mesmerized by the tongues of fire in the hearth that were leaping as though they were in some strange tribal dance. When she finely spoke her eyes hadn't moved from the flames and her voice was soft and calm, almost as though she was talking to herself. "I was a virgin you know."

"Yes your mother told me that you were."

Without warning Becky burst into a barrage of anger, her voice sounding full of resentment and rage.

"I always tried to do the right thing. All of my friends had sex with guys in fact they had sex many times, but not me, oh no not me. I was special. I was saving it for the right time and the right person. It was going to be perfect and beautiful. There was going to be love and tenderness and all that crap. Well, it wasn't pure, or special, or wonderful. He stole all of that from me and nothing can ever bring it back. He stole the most beautiful gift that I had to give to a man, the man that I will someday love. It's gone, gone, gone." She pounded the couch on each side with her fists. "I hate him! I hate him so much! Oh, how I wish that it had never happened!" She began rocking back and forth and sobbing bitterly.

When her tears finally stopped the only sound that could be heard was the crackling of the firewood in the hearth and the soft ticking of the tireless, ancient clock. Standing up I announced that I was getting myself a drink of wine and returned with one for Becky as well. We sat for a long time sipping in silence.

"Mom and Dad were worried about diseases and pregnancy but I was lucky because nothing showed up in the tests." She shuddered. "I don't even want to think of how I would feel if something like that had happened."

"Yes, that would have been terrible," I answered.

"In the hospital they said that it was fortunate that I hadn't washed myself, but later at home when I finally did get into a shower I stayed in it until the hot water turned cold. I scrubbed and scrubbed but I couldn't seem to get rid of the feeling that I was dirty. Mom was anxiously keeping an eye on me while at the same time desperately coaxing me to get out but I couldn't." She paused and looked over at me. "Chrissy I have never felt so dirty in my life. My psychiatrist said that some girls even use varsol and other caustic cleaners to try to remove that awful feeling."

"Becky if that had happened to me I don't know if I would be as brave as you are. I probably would have hated my body so much and felt so dirty that I would have liked to slip out of it and gone far, far away."

Becky looked at me pensively for a minute. "Yes I guess I felt that way too. It would have been nice if I could have done that but I'm afraid that if I did I might never have come back."

"That's right, Becky. There are things that we can't run away from, things that have to be faced and dealt with."

Our glasses were empty so I stood up to refill mine and asked Becky if she wanted more.
"Sure. It's helping me to relax." She kept on talking as I walked over to the bar.

"You know what is really bothering me Chrissy? I keep feeling guilty as though I might have caused it to happen, or else maybe I could have prevented it from happening."

"And how do you figure that?"

"Well maybe I shouldn't have allowed us to be alone together, or maybe I should have have seen it coming and left with the others. Maybe I was dressed wrong or made a gesture that encouraged him."

"Or maybe it was your mother's fault," I responded quickly as I handed her the glass.

"What? Becky was stunned by my sudden unexpected response. "How can you say that, Chrissy?"

"Well maybe she shouldn't have let you go to the party and maybe she should have come to pick you up when it was over."

Becky stared at me in horror.

"You see Becky it's no more your fault than it is your mother's. There is no way that we can anticipate or predict what is going to happen so we live our lives for the moment. When we cross the street there is the possibility a car might hit us but that doesn't stop us from crossing the street. Every day we face risks. That's what life is all about."

"Besides that you are only responsible for your own actions and Don was responsible for his. You did not make poor choices, you did not ask for it to happen, and you did not encourage it to happen. Even when it is the victim's fault it still remains the responsibility of the perpetrator to have control over his own actions. Don't carry around his guilt for him because he isn't worth it. You did nothing wrong."

Becky was becoming a little tipsy. "Yeah, he's a vile snake in the grass."

"That he is." I slowly nodded my head in agreement.

"I still wish that it hadn't happened. I wish that so much."

"I know, I know. Honey once you embrace the real Becky within you and place the blame where it belongs the pain **will** disappear. You will be the master once again and he will be pushed out of your life. You'll find an inner peace and love yourself even more than you did before. You will be the victor and he will be the loser and that is the way it should be."

Becky stood up, moved over to me and curled up in my arms. I love you so much Chrissy."

"And I love you too Becky."

We sat talking for a long time about Becky's plan for a career and for her future. She had a desire to become a renowned sculptress. She wanted to meet a man, get married, and have two or three children. We exchanged views on fashion and music but we also avoided any discussion about Robert. That would be another conversation.

When our energy finally died, as did the fire in the hearth, we turned off the lights and walked down the hall together.

"Goodnight Honey. Sleep with angels."

I had just settled into bed and was about to pull the blankets under my chin when I heard a sound at the door. "Becky! What is it Hon?"

"Do you think that I could sleep with you tonight? I don't want to be alone."

"Sure. Come on," I said as I pulled the blankets aside. Becky climbed in and moved close to me while I wrapped one arm around her in a protective gesture. Soon the two of us were breathing deeply in a cocoon of love.

Chapter Twenty-Five

We slept in until noon the next morning, probably due to the wine that we had consumed the night before. From the breakfast nook we sat gazing down on several joggers that were eagerly persisting along the path in the park. Other people were enjoying a casual stroll. I broke the silence.

"I thought it might be nice to go shopping today Becky?"

At first she paused while she thought about it then to my relief she agreed.

As I was pulling out of the parkade I turned to her, "Boutique alley?"

Becky grinned, "Why not?" We giggled like two schoolgirls.

While browsing through the shops I was pleased to see that the spark of animation had returned, and
when she admired a sweater I insisted on buying it for her.

"No Chrissy it's too expensive."

I quickly convinced her that it was my inalienable right to buy my niece a gift once in awhile.

After arriving back at the apartment we kicked off our boots in the vestibule, hung our coats up in the closet and after entering into the living room flopped down on both couches. Shortly Becky announced that she was going to her room to call her parents then afterwards she wanted to have a nap. Would you call me later?"

As Becky started down the hall I looked over my shoulder from the couch. "Say hello to your mom and dad for me."

With an exhausted sigh I stretched out then gave a verbal command for some quiet soothing music. As I pondered over potential plans for the evening I clearly knew that I didn't want to push Becky too far, too fast because I knew that there would be many things that could trigger off an unwanted response. It could be as simple as an association with a color, an odor, a word, or it could be as serious as bumping into a look-a-like or even Don himself. Until she was able to transfer the incident from the emotional part of the brain to the intellectual section it would always trouble her. I knew that when it was in the latter part the incident would appear at arm's length where one is capable of analyzing it objectively, putting it on its proper shelf then getting on with one's life. That is the point when one is truly back in control.

While Becky was sleeping I scanned through the movies in the theaters and finally selected a comedy that I felt would be enjoyable and produce no jolts. I also reserved a table at one of the better restaurants for dinner. When the evening went well with no unfavorable incidents we returned shortly after midnight to the apartment.

"Thanks for a wonderful day Chrissy and thanks for the sweater. If you don't mind I think that I will crash because I'm really pooped." She took a few steps then turned. "Oh by the way I'll sleep in the guest room tonight."

"Of course, I'll see you in the morning."

Since I had been feeling Becky's pain I was also completely exhausted. Climbing between the sheets I closed my eyes, sighed, and slept.

The next day while the two of us sat on the same park bench that Robert and I had occupied a short time ago the dreaded subject of the trial was broached. The day was cold, the skies were overcast, and the weather bureau forecasted snow. After being touched by frost and by freezing temperatures the ground was hard and the trees were bare having already surrendered their leaves to the winter season. An occasional rabbit with its fur still brown hopped cautiously across the dried up dead-looking grass while the winter species of birds scavenged for nourishment.

I could not think of a gentle way to approach the subject. "Becky I don't know when we will get a chance to see each other again like this so I wondered if you would like to talk about Robert."

Any positive mood that Becky was in immediately evaporated as her shoulders slumped and an aura of sadness surrounded her.

"I just thought it might be a good time to clear up any questions that you might have and also give you a chance to talk about anything that is bothering you. If you don't want to we will drop the subject and discuss it some other time."

Becky slowly shook her head. "No, no it's okay."

She sat staring across the park for what seemed like a long time then she said. "I'm really frightened, Chrissy. I get scared every time I think about the trial and I get sick to my stomach when I think about what is going to happen."

"I'm scared too Becky, and so is your mom and dad."

Becky gazed around her taking in all of nature's beauty. There was a strange look on her face like she was experiencing a mixture of feelings. The next words that came out of her mouth shocked and surprised me because they were not the ones that I was expecting to hear.

"I know that you love Robert very much so this whole mess must be very hard on you. It must be difficult for Robert too and I'm so sorry about that." She looked down at her hands that were now clasped on her lap. "I know that it is going to be his professional duty to break me down on the stand and that it's probably going to get really ugly." She turned to look at me. "Chrissy I know that the whole thing will be too difficult for you to watch so I will certainly understand if you should decide not to be there. Mom and Dad understand it too. I guess that it must hurt you a lot." She looked at me sadly. "Again I'm so sorry."

I was unable to speak. I was so overwhelmed with emotion.

"Don't feel badly about being with Robert since your relationship has nothing to do with my situation." She looked at me earnestly. "I certainly don't want the two of you breaking up because of me."

My eyes became moist with tears. "You know Becky I'm not worried about you anymore. I'm positive that you will find the strength to get through the ordeal and get on with your life. You are a very mature and wise little lady."

The skies were getting darker and the winds were increasing as we headed back to the apartment. A storm was imminent.

Lara and Tom picked Becky up later that night and thanked me profusely. Becky and I assured the two of them that we had had a very pleasant time. When Becky and I embraced each other we exchanged a meaningful personal message.

After they were gone I sat in my living room for a long time feeling melancholy but also grateful that a heavy burden had been lifted from my shoulders. I also thought about my dreams.

Chapter Twenty-six

As Robert and I paused in the entranceway of the anteroom most eyes focused in our direction while those who had their back to us turned when they realized that they had lost the attention of their audience. Alcoholic beverages were flowing freely from a counter that ran along the length of one wall, and each individual was keeping one guarded eye on their companion and one on the crowd. Robert skillfully maneuvered me around the mass of people pausing on several occasions to say hello to some of his friends and colleagues. Finally reaching our destination six people greeted us eagerly, five of them warmly.

"Robert! We were getting worried that you might not show up," exclaimed one of the women.

After excited hugs from two of the females, and a dramatic hug from the third one, all eyes turned in my direction. Robert wrapped his arm protectively around my waist and introduced me to his friends.

"Christine I'd like you to meet Harold and Cynthia Snowden, Helen and William Smyth, and Annalyn Ferguson and Stanley Spielman. Everyone this is Christine Anderson."

Harold and Cynthia were the oldest of the groups, perhaps in their early sixties, while Helen and William appeared to be in their late forties. Annalyn and Stanley I guessed to be approximately the same age as myself. Reaching out and grasping my hand William's handshake was firm.

"I've been looking forward to meeting the amazing woman who has successfully torn Robert away from his office for a little R and R. I'm very pleased to meet you Christine."

As soon as he relinquished my hand his wife Helen took it in hers, however the pressure was more gentle. "I'm so glad that you could come."

Harold and Cynthia greeted me warmly and Stanley enthusiastically shook my hand but Annalyn stood back guardedly while giving me a weak smile of acknowledgment.

As the room began to fill with people the noise level increased proportionately, however any nervous tension that might have existed earlier had been eliminated by the continuous flow of drinks. The sparkle and glitter of colorful designer gowns were contrasted by the display of dignified but monotonous black tuxedos. Periodically several of Robert's associates stopped for a little shoptalk as well as to wish him the season's greetings. Finally a melodious bell sounded. After depositing glasses on the nearest hard surface there was a mass movement to the next room.

The ballroom was exquisite. Light refracted from the pieces of crystal and silverware that dotted the tables, while colorful floral centerpieces depicted a Christmas theme. Strings of coruscating lights, along with pine-scented boughs, were generously arranged around the room. All of this paid homage to a large Christmas tree that was typically decorated with a definite color motif. Our table for eight was ideally located far enough from the band podium but close enough to the dance floor.

Immediately I felt accepted by the group thus experiencing one of those rare occasions when one feels that one had always been a part of their life. However there was one exception, Annalyn. From the very beginning I felt alienation along with resentment simply because of my presence. Several times I caught her staring at me with her cold green eyes sending icy chills up my spine.

When Annalyn first greeted Robert she had pressed her body just a little too close, and the kiss that she had planted on his lips was a little too long. She had rudely whispered something in his ear then with a toss of her long, silky, blond hair had relinquished him back to us. Her conduct seemed to embarrass the others but apparently did not surprise them. Robert, who of course was aware of Annalyn's inappropriate behavior, occasionally squeezed my hand or rubbed my back in order to reassure me that everything was okay.

During the course of the conversation I learned that Cynthia and Harold had known my parents since before their death. At the mention of their names a wave of sadness washed over me. Noticing my reaction Cynthia reached across the table. "I'm so sorry. Your mother and father were both wonderful people and were loved by everyone who knew them."

The conversation was light as the group reminisced over the past. As they teased and joked I sat back enjoying the insight that I was gaining into Robert's life through the little anecdotes. In the middle of one of his narration's Harold gently placed a hand on mine. "I'm so sorry. Since you have no idea what we're talking about you must find this to be completely boring."

"On the contrary actually I'm fascinated. Please, do go on."

As the conversation resumed my attention was unexpectedly interrupted by a cold draft that sent shivers through me causing goose bumps to form on my arms. My first thought was that someone had opened an exterior door thus letting in the cold night air but I quickly realized that the reason was much more ominous. Focusing across the table to the source of the manifestation I locked eyes with one of the most heartless hateful pair that I had ever witnessed. Where the spirit should have been there was a cold deep empty space like two black bottomless holes. I had never felt such a feeling of nothingness. To most people the image would have sent them praying to their own personal God but for some reason I was not afraid. Instead, unflinching, I stared back showing no fear, no retreat, no surprise. Eventually with an indifferent shrug Anallyn turned her head away.

I was left with confusion but also with a feeling of strength. I had just conquered another hallway, another pinpoint of light.

Finally after five delicious courses the tinkling sound of metal against glass slowly eliminated the hum of voices. From the head table a distinguished gentleman introduced himself as being the chairman of the organizing committee after which he gave a general welcome to the guests. He announced that there would be dancing and drinks until two a.m. then cautioned everyone about driving. He warned us that if anyone had consumed an excessive amount of alcohol he suggested that they use a taxi service rather than becoming a statistic thus giving one of their colleagues some business. There was a ripple of laughter throughout the room.

While the servers removed the last of the china and silverware from the tables a five-piece band, along with a female vocalist, entered through a side door. Quickly taking their place on the podium the lights dimmed and soft music filled the room. Robert turned to me. "Shall we?"

After finding a spot on the floor we turned and moved into each other's arms, then as we swayed slowly to the music I could feel the firmness of his physique as he pressed his body against mine. Not wanting the magic of the moment to end we held on for a few extra seconds after the song faded.

"Whew! I'd better watch myself or I might get thrown off of the dance floor."

I smiled. "That's one advantage women have over men."

The tempo of the music was much faster when it resumed. As we eagerly began gyrating with the rest of the crowd my eyebrows raised in surprised approval when I watched Robert move with rhythmic co-ordination. After a few more songs Robert put an arm around my waist, directed me back to the table and assisted me into my chair. As I was sitting down I noticed a hand on his arm in my peripheral vision.

"Come on Robert let's dance for old time sake." Her voice was musically seductive, her eyes flirtatious. With cat-like movements she wrapped her arm through his while walking to the dance floor.

I knew better than to watch them and I was right. In the corner of my eye I could see Annalyn moving her body seductively, using all of her feminine wiles with touches, smiles, and manipulative gestures. As she pressed her body against his she kept her eyes on me. The others were absent from the table except for Harold and Cynthia who silently watching the spectacle. Cynthia reached over and touched my forearm.

"I'm sorry. Her behavior is anything but subtle, or discreet."

I smiled. "That's all right, he's a big boy."

Cynthia tilted her head. "So how long have you known Robert, Christine?"

"We met in September. Actually it was a short time before his divorce was finalized."

"He seems to be very fond of you. He often speaks of you."

I smiled. "That's nice to hear." There was a pause. "I guess that you find it strange having me here instead of Hillary. After all they were married for quite a long time."

"Yes." Her face took on a reflective look. "However things didn't seem to work out for them. I don't think that either one of them was ever happy." She smiled sincerely. "I do wish the best for both of you."

I gave her an appreciative look. "Thank you so much for those words. They mean a lot to me."

When Stanley came back with two drinks he spotted his date on the dance floor and immediately noted her conspicuous behavior thus embarrassing him. When I asked if he would care to dance, in an effort to help him, he forced enthusiasm by roughly pushing his chair back.Stanley was approximately five feet nine inches tall and a little overweight and balding. What he lacked in good looks he compensated for with a terrific sense of humor and an amazing wit. On the dance floor he proved to be light on his feet and was an excellent dancer.

Four dances later laughing and exhausted we returned to the table.

Robert was deep in conversation with the others but Annalyn was sitting back in her chair looking sullen, and if it was at all possible looking even more furious.

Robert leaned over and gave me a short kiss on the lips. "Love you," he said fondly.

"Love you too."

I wondered why there was such a strong reaction to the kiss from the group, well except for Annalyn, until I learned later that Robert and Hillary had never been demonstrative in public. There never seemed to be any warmth or affection between them.

The evening went well. We had all arrived by cab but when the party ended a limousine was waiting for us at the curb. Standing at attention the uniformed chauffeur held the door open for us while a cold blast of wind sent us scurrying into the vehicle. Huddled together in couples we all agreed that this year's affair had been successful. As expected, Annalyn pouted in a corner next to Stanley. One by one they were dropped off until only William and Helen were left with Robert and me. When we were in front of my condo and the chauffeur was about to close the car door William held it open with his hand and looked up at Robert.

"Don't forget to ask her."

"I won't." Robert smiled reassuringly.

As we rushed up the sidewalk then hurried into the lobby the comment puzzled me. "What was that all about?"

"We'll discuss it when we get upstairs."

The first thing that I did when we entered my living quarters was to ignite the starter log in order to take the chill out of air. Sitting on the couch I snuggled into his arms, partly for affection and partly for warmth.

"Tell me. I'm dying of curiosity. What did William mean by that statement?"

He squeezed my shoulders and grinned. "What are you doing during the New Year holiday?"

"Nothing really, why do you ask?"

"There are reservations for six at one of the lodges in Banff and two of them are mine. Would you like to join me?"

I sat up straight and looked at him. "Of course I would! You said six. Who are the other four?"

"There is Helen and William, and Harold and Cynthia."

"What about Annalyn and Stanley?"

"They really aren't a part of the group that I see on a regular basis."

"I see." I looked at him fondly. "I really like your friends Robert."

"I'm glad and I'm sorry about Annalyn. She gave you a hard time."

"Hmmm, I nodded in agreement. "What's her problem? She obviously has very strong feelings for you."

"After I left Hillary I took her out a few times. It never developed into anything serious but she's been on my case ever since. It's strictly one sided."

"How did she happen to be included this evening?"

He chuckled. "Oh she worked on poor Stanley and convinced him to ask us if he could be included at our table. We never realized that he was bringing Annalyn."

I suddenly felt sad. "Poor Stanley," then, "poor Annalyn."

Suddenly with a great deal of acting ability Robert stretched and feigned a yawn. "I don't know about you but I'm exhausted."

I slyly imitated his actions then laughing we walked arm in arm to the bedroom where our mood seriously changed. The nice part of being out together is the anticipation of what lies ahead when one gets home. After spending a beautiful evening the most enjoyable part is still waiting, like the icing on the cake. That night the dessert was exquisite.

Chapter Twenty-seven

Since Robert had no plans to return to his office the next day, and there were no complaints from Larry in regard to the buildings, I decided that it would be a good time to discuss our plans for the remainder of the Christmas season. I broached the subject while we were sitting in the living room with some reading material. He continued reading for a few seconds before looking up from the novel.

"Of course, what would you like to talk about?"

"Well, Christmas eve, Christmas day, and Boxing day."

At first he sat in silence then inhaling deeply he said. "Christine I hope you realize that I have to consider the children."

"Of course I realize that. For heaven's sake I'm not insensitive." When he didn't answer me right away I impatiently repeated my question.

He turned his head and stared directly at me after deliberately putting his book down on the table. "Christine I've promised to spend Christmas day with the children."

My mouth dropped open in disbelief. "All day, please don't tell me that you're going to spend the whole day with them?"

Feeling uncomfortable he looked down at his lap. "I'm sorry Christine but I've already told them that I would."

Suddenly the room became abnormally quiet and even the clock seemed to have stopped its ticking. All of a sudden a horrible thought occurred to me. "Are you going to be spending the day at your house, or at Hillary's?"

There was a long agonizing pause. "We'll be at Hillary's. We thought that it would be the least upsetting for the children."

"What about the next day, Boxing Day?"

"Since it's been a custom of ours for years we're already expected over to my side of the family for dinner. I'm sorry Christine."

"You're sorry! You're sorry!" I closed my eyes and shook my head. "Robert, why does it have to be the whole day? Couldn't we get together during the morning, afternoon, or evening? Can't you see that Christmas day is also important to me?"

Feeling pressured Robert became more defensive. "I'm sorry but I've already promised the children that I would be there in the morning and Hillary has made arrangements for her family to join us for dinner. It would be rather awkward to get away."

I stared in disbelief. It was like a nightmare. "What about later in the evening. Surely you aren't sleeping there."

There was an uncomfortable moment of silence.

"Since we'll all be going over to my uncle's house the next day the children have been promised that they could spend the night at my place."

"No, no. All of this is not acceptable. It may be fine for the children but what about me. Don't I count?"

"Of course you count."

I felt as though all of my energies had been horribly twisted and wrung from my body.

"What about Christmas Eve?

"I have no plans." Guilt was plainly written all over his face.

"Well isn't that nice," I said sarcastically.

I was hurt and furious. Why had I not asserted myself earlier and insisted on meeting the children and was there not a special bond between Robert and me?

"Sometimes I wonder just exactly what I mean to you. One day I feel that I am someone special in your life then the following day I feel like a third class citizen. First of all it seems that I come in second to your work. Next I feel like I am not good enough for your children and now," I threw up my arms, "I feel that you're more concerned with Hillary's welfare than you are with how I am going to be spending the holiday."

"I'm sorry Christine." He was clearly feeling very uncomfortable.

My face turned red with anger. "Hillary did this, didn't she? She made all those plans just to keep the two of us apart."

Robert said nothing but his jaw tightened as he stared at me.

Suddenly feeling as though something precious was slowly slipping away from me, my shoulders slumped in defeat and I seemed to sink further into the seat. "Please don't do this to us, Robert."

"Don't do what?"

When he was obviously insensitive to my needs, as well as to my pain, I stared at him in disbelief? Didn't he recognize what he was doing to me?
"Hillary, I mean Christine." His face reddened.

I gave him a penetrating look of disdain and my voice was cut with sarcasm. "My, that was a Freudian slip." I walked out of the room and returned a few moments later with my coat and boots on. As I wrapped a long wool scarf several times around my neck I announced that I was going out for a walk. "I need time to think."

As I marched briskly down the path the cool crisp air felt refreshing on my face. At first I viciously kicked at the snow with the tips of my boots while muttering angry derogatory remarks under my breath then my pace eventually slowed and resentment and disappointment replaced my anger. Brushing the snow off of one of the benches and sitting down on it, I allowed myself the infrequent luxury of indulging in self-pity. Tears began to well in my eyes.

How could he do this to me without at least discussing it with me first? Since my parents had passed away I had always found Christmas to be a lonely time even though Lara and Tom welcomed me into their home as one of the family. For some reason I always felt like a third wheel. I had actually grown to dislike the holiday that was supposed to bring good will and happiness to all. When Robert came into my life I thought that all of that would change. This year I thought that Christmas would be special and I would be with the man that I loved. As I let out a deep sigh I closed my eyes and tilted my head back to the sun.

Just then I heard the crunching sound of approaching footsteps. Without moving my head I covertly opened one eye as Robert sat down beside me. There was a long period of silence.

"I'm sorry, Christine. I should have discussed it with you before I made my plans."

I looked at him sideways with a sour expression that said, 'that's an understatement.'

"One day when I went to see Hillary she informed me in front of the children, of course, of the plans that she had made. I looked into their faces. Christine I couldn't disappoint them by refusing. I felt that I had hurt them so much already. I'm really sorry."

Feeling totally exhausted and empty I stared blankly towards the trees in the distance. "Things have to change Robert because I can't take any more of this treatment but more important I don't deserve it."

"I know you don't."

"I want to meet your children. I want to be a part of your life. I know that they don't want to meet me but the longer that you put it off the more difficult it's going to be." I reached over and placed a hand on one of his. "You have to take control Robert. Right now I'm not sure whether the control is in your children's hands, or in Hillary's."

We sat for awhile in silence, then, emotionally drained we walked back to the apartment.

Later while we were warming up with a cup of hot chocolate at the kitchen table Robert studied me with concern.

"Do you think that you'll be spending Christmas day with Lara and Tom? I don't want you to be alone."

I shrugged my shoulders. "She's always invited me in the past so I guess that she will invite me again this year."

Later that afternoon we made love. It was a healing process, an attempt to reclaim the lost trust, to mend the hurts, to regenerate our affection. That night while I was lying alone in bed the last stanza of a poem that I had written in high school came back to me, haunting me.

Oh that the cinders of love may not be wet
But flame up soon again, and yet,
I weep and sigh with bitter tears
For I am human with human fears.
Oh God in heaven to Thee I plea,
Grant me the strength to face eternity.

I called Lara several times that week and was greeted either by the answering machine or by the housekeeper. When Lara finally answered the phone I asked her why she hadn't returned my calls. She simply explained that she had been busy with last minute Christmas shopping. She also casually informed me that she would not be attending my Christmas party the following weekend. Evidently the entire family had decided to spend three weeks in Switzerland.

I was surprised and disappointed. "I'm sorry to hear that you won't be here for the holiday. I'll miss you very much." My eyes narrowed with suspicion. "You must have decided rather quickly because Becky didn't mention it when she was staying with me."

"Yes. As a matter of fact we decided that it would do us all a world of good to get away from everything."

"What about Bill? Will he be going with you?"

"Bill will only be spending a few days with us because of his studies."

"Lara, is there anything wrong? You sound so strange."

"I'm just tired Chrissy." She rubbed her forehead as though she had a headache. "I don't know if I will see you before we go since we'll be leaving this Friday after Tom locks up the office for the weekend."

"I feel bad that we won't be spending some time together on Christmas. It almost feels as though it's become a tradition."

"Well at least I know that you will have Robert."

I felt a stab of pain. "Yes. I'll be with Robert." Not wanting my friend to worry nothing was said about his plans to be with his family. "Well have a good holiday and wish the others a merry Christmas for me. Call me when you get home."

"You have a nice Christmas too." The phone went dead.

I sat puzzled for a long time after the image disappeared from the screen.

Chapter Twenty-eight

I had been experiencing unusual episodes throughout the years, some inconsequential but others that had a lasting effect. One specific event that had taken place many years ago was to be refreshed within my memory in the next few hours. I would recall it as though it had happened only yesterday.

* * *

The Past Experience: After falling asleep I found myself in a room that was about the size of a small bedroom. Since the floor was covered from wall to wall with mattresses I had logically dubbed it 'the mattress room'. You see I had been in a similar room before. This wasn't the first time. As the happening began filtering into my then-conscious-mind I became aware that I was not alone. Peering beside me through the fog I focused on a man, a handsome man who possessed an evenly featured oval face and thick dark blond hair. Not only was I aware that I felt a great deal of affection towards him, his presence also sexually stimulated me. When I attempted to gratify him by giving him oral sex he hesitated and unsuccessfully attempted to stop me claiming that he had never experienced it before. When it was over he thanked me profusely and professed his undying love for me. Finding him to be sensitive and caring, as well as attractive, I told him that I loved him too.

I became confused and disoriented when I realized that he was directing his conversation not to me but to someone else in the room. In a slow motion I peered to my left in an attempt to see who it was while at the same time I tried to focus on my friend's conversation. He was telling a second person how wonderful it was to have sex with me and instructed him to do so likewise. Now this did not compute with my sensitivities nor did it settle well with the second man who attempted, with much difficulty, to refuse the request. He seemed to be having the same problem that I was having, that of being out of control of his actions. Naturally, because of the discipline that we were under we soon became intimate.

As I stoically suffered through the procedure my lack of interest puzzled the first man. "Why are you not enjoying it, Christine?"

"I don't want to do it because I don't love him. I love you but I don't love him."

The traveler frowned and tilted his head. "What does love have to do with it?"

"Without love I don't feel like doing it."

After a few seconds of deep thought he suddenly leaned over and began kissing me sensually on the lips. This stimulated my passions, which of course encouraged me to have intercourse with the other man.

There was a blank space of time.

I remembered being led by the hand down a hall into a room that was cluttered with technological equipment where an older austere man was apparently waiting for us. Still stimulated by the memory of our lovemaking the traveler excitedly described what had transpired while we were having sex. The second man simply answered, "Yes, they do that here." My brows furrowed. Were we not all alike in the universe?Thinking that the issue had been put to rest the older man ordered the younger one to put me on the pad so that they could send me back. He then promptly turned and became preoccupied with a panel of instruments.

Instead of doing so the younger man paused and hesitated. "Can I take her with me?" He looked and sounded full of hopeful expectation.

The older man stopped what he was doing, turned, and frowned at him. "Of course you can't."

"Why? I love her very much."

I will never forget the sad look on my companion's face.

The older man didn't become angry, as I thought he would, but instead he turned from the panel and deliberately walked up to my friend. There was not only compassion but also a sense of pure logic on his face. "If we take her with us she'll have to remain as she is for the rest of her life. Do you want that for yourself? Do you want that for her?"

Understanding the rational of the statement my friend's enthusiasm quickly disappeared. Before placing me in the chamber he took both of my hands in his. "Christine I love you now, and I always will. Whenever you think of me know that I will see your face and will be thinking of you. No matter how far I travel or no matter how many light years away that I might be we will never lose touch with each other."

Placing me on the pad he made one last hopeful attempt to see me one more time.

"Will we be coming back this way again?"

By now the older man was losing his patience. "Of course we won't. You know that we never take the same path twice."

My lover sadly stood back and the recall ended.

The following day: The next day after that episode I had gone into the business section of the city to do some shopping. The streets were busy and the pedestrian traffic was heavy. As I walked along the sidewalk, deep in thought, my head suddenly snapped up while my vision projected about thirty feet directly ahead of me focusing on a man that was walking towards me. I quickly inhaled. It was the traveler.

In one spontaneous moment my face became radiant at the mere sight of him while my heart overflowed with happiness and love. Realizing that I had recognized him his sad expression changed to one of surprise then total elation. For that one moment in time our two souls met on the same level pouring fourth a pure, spiritual love.

Suddenly becoming aware of the two realities my mind screamed in sheer panic. Mentally pulling away and distancing me from the alien anomaly the connection between us strangely vanished as quickly as it had been created---like a puff of smoke. The moment that the light faded and died from my eyes it instantaneously died from his. He once again had to accept the sad reality, the undeniable fact that we could not be. The last thing that I saw as I walked past him was his sadness then I stared blankly into space.

It was not until I arrived home that I allowed myself the luxury of tears.

Present Day: On a bitterly cold day before my party I decided to do some Christmas shopping. As warm air jetted out of their exhaust systems great clouds of condensation formed around the cars. The same crystallization manifested itself around the pedestrians as they exhaled. The vapor would hang for a fraction of a second as though frozen solid in mid air then it disappeared only to be replaced with a similar cloud. Streets and stores had been decked out with lines of twinkling lights that were twisted around trees and posts while age old Christmas carols were channeling through sound systems. Santa impostors, some of them pretty scraggy looking, stood on street corners shaking their bells as they continuously danced from one foot to the other in an attempt to keep warm.

I had just purchased a beautiful hand knit sweater for Robert as well as a handcrafted wallet in one of the men's specialty shops. The spirit of 'Christmas Commercial' was in full force.

I was probably half way through the store when I sensed it. It was an awareness that was truer than true leaving no doubt in my mind. I knew that the man would be standing on the other side of the six-foot counter waiting for me, waiting for me to confront him. As though in a trance and unable to stop myself my body carried me along the ten feet to the end of the isle then around the end of the counter. Standing before me, his face filled with recognition and pain, was the second man that I had been with in the mattress room. The torment and confusion that was indisputable in his eyes saddened me beyond the perimeters that I could ever imagine as being possible. I desperately wanted to take him in my arms, to comfort him, to assure him that everything was all right. What was he thinking? What emotions were unearthed by his preternatural memories?

I wanted to approach him but fear gripped my mind causing me to hesitate. Would the reality induce him to break down therefore to generate an irreparable scene one that I would never find an acceptable explanation for? Would it even push him over the edge into madness? We stared at each other for what felt like a long time with recognition undeniable, recollection painfully obvious.

After several seconds his shoulders sagged and with downcast eyes he turned and slowly walked away. With total helplessness I stood and watched as he disappeared around a corner and out of my life. Feeling drained I was unable to find the strength to move. When I did I felt that I undoubtedly resembled the figure that had just disappeared from my sight.

"The poor man, the poor man," I muttered to myself as I shuffled towards the exit of the store.

The crowds were a blur of faceless people as I wandered aimlessly through the mall. Bumped and jarred by passersby's I was too drained to care and too exhausted to find the energy to get out of their way. Without remembering how I got there I found myself out in the cold bitter air. I felt nothing. Somehow finding my way to my car my unconscious mind once more carried me safely through the traffic across town.

Wanting to get away from the stress of driving I turned into the parking lot of a coffee shop. I was unaware of walking across the expanse of asphalt and of entering the building. Suddenly confused and embarrassed I found myself looking up into the quizzical expression of a young girl behind the counter. Taking my cup I selected a corner table and with my back to the wall sat deep in thought oblivious of the curious on-lookers. At this particular moment they were of no importance to me. Since I had difficulty in assimilating the pain of others I was only concerned for the man that I had just left behind in the mall.

A blond-haired slimly built waitress with energy to spare moved swiftly around the room cleaning tables from previous customers. Occasionally she glanced at me with curiosity and perhaps a little apprehension.

Over and over again I replayed the sequence of events marveling at what had happened. I knew that his face would be indelibly imprinted in my memory forever.Slowly a very significant thought formulated in my mind. Why had I not thought of it earlier and why was the obvious truth always so difficult to see? Today I had come face to face with an entity like myself therefore I wasn't alone. Smiling I sat up in my chair and took in a deep breath. It was a thought to bathe in, it was a realization to saturate my senses with, and it was so refreshing. I was not alone. I had let him slip through my fingers but in hindsight I knew that I had no other choice.

As I was leaving the shop the waitresses pleasantly called out. "Come again."

Startled I turned and looked at the blond woman. "Thank you. I will."

Suddenly the world looked much brighter.

Chapter Twenty-nine

I had decorated my apartment with typical poinsettias and other floral arrangements all selectively placed on various tables. Stretched along the mantel of the fireplace a fresh garland filled the room with just a hint of fresh pine scent. For background music I selected some Christmas songs then programmed them into the sound system. As a final touch the conventional sprigs of mistletoe were strategically placed over doorways.

When Robert arrived he gave me a soft kiss on my cheek, handed me a bottle of champagne then stood back and carefully eyed me up and down with obvious approval. "Mmmm, I think I'll call off the party and keep you all to myself. I do love you Christine.

Arrangements had been made with security to allow anyone with an invitation automatic use of the elevator. My guests soon began arriving.Later in the evening while I was talking to Robert I suddenly realized that I had lost his attention. Following his line of vision to the door I saw Crystal entering the room with Armand. When he realized how blatant his reaction had been he quickly glanced in my direction for fear that he had offended me but when he became aware that I had found it to be quite amusing his cheeks flushed with embarrassment.

"She is beautiful, isn't she?" I remarked as I linked my arm in his.

Nodding his head he raised his eyebrows. "That's quite an understatement."

"Come on. I'll introduce you to her."

The moment Crystal saw me her arms came up for a generous hug and I barely had time to give Armand the conventional, continental two-cheek kiss before my friend turned to Robert. "My, my, this must be the man that I have been hearing so much about."

I possessively hooked my arm through Robert's and smiled proudly. "Crystal and Armand I would like you to meet Robert. Robert this is my very dear friend Crystal and her companion Armand."

Crystal graciously extended her hand. "It's so nice to finally meet you Robert. Chrissy has told me so many nice things about you."

Robert reached over and accepted her hand in a firm handshake. "I'm pleased to meet you too Crystal. Christine has often spoken of your friendship."

Then to Robert's unexpected surprise Crystal linked her arm firmly in his. "Come on Robert. Let's wander over and get me a little ol' drink then I want to know every little thing there is to know about you."

With a quick awkward handshake with Armand, and a helpless glance towards me, Robert headed to the bar with Crystal.

Most of my guests were nurses, doctors, and interns, all of them associated with the hospital. There was more than enough food and drinks including my special lethal eggnog that was served with a dash of nutmeg and ornamented with a stick of cinnamon. One of the interns from the hospital, who had volunteered to act as a bartender for the evening, found himself quite busy working from the well stocked bar. As the food and liquor were consumed the constant hum of voices got louder and at midnight the tinkling of bells and the deep-throated jovial laughter could be heard coming from the area of the elevator. It was Santa Claus!

Santa did his job well so much so that by the end of the evening no one had guessed who he was, even though I swore that they all knew him. He thoroughly enjoyed his anonymity until late in the night when one of the girls, in a ploy to plant a kiss, pulled off the beard. They were all shocked to discover that it was one of their own interns. By one the music was slower creating a much more romantic mood. With arms wrapped amorously around each other and feet planted firmly on the floor Robert and I barely swayed to the rhythm of the music.

"If it wasn't your place I would carry you off to one of those bedrooms. God I need you right now." His voice was deep and sexy as he ran his hands over the full length of my back.

At four the guests, who were obviously feeling no pain, departed in a few prearranged limousines. Since Crystal and Armand was the last to leave the apartment there were kisses and promises for us to get together soon. After putting the food that might spoil into cold storage then checking the place for potential fires the two of us retired to my bedroom.

As I laid my head down I wrinkled my nose. "Robert I think that I can smell someone's after shave lotion on the pillow."

He pulled me close to him sensually wrapping his arms around me. "Well I hope that they had a fraction of the pleasure that we are going to have."

Due to the sedative effect of the alcohol our lovemaking may have been intense and our climaxes fulfilling but it was as though there was a gauze-like quality surrounding the act. As I drifted off to sleep my mind reflected on past memories, vague sensations, and blurred realities, all remnants of times past.

On Christmas Eve Robert arrived late in the afternoon. Most offices closed at noon but because of the responsibilities that were associated with owning a business it was necessary that he finish off a few loose ends before locking up. The mouth-watering aromas of turkey and minced meat and apple pies pleasantly greeted him when he stepped off of the elevator. That along with the magical strains of Christmas music awakened childhood memories filling him with nostalgia.

When he arrived I reached over and gave him a warm kiss on the lips. "Merry Christmas Robert how was your day?"

After throwing his coat and briefcase on the chair he reached over and placing his arm around my waist we walked toward the living room. "Oh the office was a little crazy. Someone spiked the water cooler with vodka."

"Really," I commented as I looked up at him.

"Really," he answered. "I had a small bar set up and some hors d'oeuvres so I think that he, or she, did it as a practical joke."

"What did you do about it?"

"Oh I ignored it. We closed at two although almost everyone didn't leave until after four."

Outside it had been pitch black since five o'clock while inside the Christmas tree looked beautiful with its multitude of miniature lights and assortment of colorful baubles. The bottle of champagne and two glasses sat invitingly on the coffee table. "Would you like a glass or have you had too much to drink already?"

"No, actually other than one drink at the office I saved it for tonight."

Reaching over for the bottle he removed the cork then smelled it for that offensive corky smell. Satisfied with its freshness he poured the sparkling liquid.

"Here's to you Princess and to the evening ahead of us."

"Here's to our first Christmas together." At the realization that we wouldn't be with each other for the next two days I felt a twinge of sadness.

Carrying the bottle and glasses to the dining room table we ate by the romantic glow of candlelight then afterwards we retired to the living room for an exchange of gifts.

"This is really nice Christine," he said as he removed the Armani sweater from its box. "I love the color."

Pleased with his reaction I urged him to try it on.

Awkwardly he pulled it over his head then quickly he ran his hands through his hair. "Well?"

"It really looks good on you, Robert. I mean it. You look very handsome."

Reaching under the Christmas tree I then handed him a smaller parcel. Opening it he discovered a billfold made of Spanish leather with his initials engraved in gold. After thanking me he disappeared into the hallway and returned with a small box in his hand. Bending over he kissed me lightly on my lips. "Merry Christmas, Sweetheart." When I stared silently at the gift he cocked his head with curiosity. "Well, aren't you going to open it?"

Undoing the ribbon and removing the paper I discovered a deep blue velvet jewelry case. After first glancing with apprehension towards Robert I slowly took the lid off and gasped.

"Do you like it?"

"Robert it's beautiful!" Resting in its groove was an emerald ring bordered with two circles of cut diamonds.

Taking the box from my hands he removed the piece of jewelry and placed it on the ring finger of my right hand. "Christine the next one will be for your left hand."

"Thank you so much Robert. I will always cherish this...always."

With a feeling of contentment I rested in his arms for the remainder of the evening. We spoke of many things avoiding any unpleasant issues that might spoil our mood. At midnight our kiss seemed to unite us into a single entity, but at three the spell was broken when Robert reluctantly left after promising to call me when he had the opportunity.

I didn't fall asleep immediately but when I did I had the ring held preciously against my cheek.

I was immediately aware of the large empty bed the moment I awoke on Christmas morning. Without turning my head I gave the verbal command "time".

'The correct time is 0800,' Came a well-toned masculine response from the system.

Groaning I rolled over and plunged one of the pillows over my head in an attempt to blot out the world and the long empty day that loomed ahead of me. After lying for a while in an attempt to induce sleep I reluctantly struggled out of bed. Walking into the en suite bathroom I confronting myself in the full-length mirror and gave myself a disgusted look, however my mood became more optimistic after a long refreshing shower.

Activating some soothing classical selections by Vladimir Horowitz I was soon able to focus on the positives. After admitting to myself that I was actually happy that Robert and the children were together my concern for myself slowly evaporated and in its place I found an inner peace. Towards noon I threw on a pair of warm slacks and a Nordic sweater, piled my hair up with one hand, and then pulled a toque over my head with the other.

It was a beautiful day. The sun was high and the sky was clear. A soft blanket of white snow covered the drab grays and browns of the empty street as well as the park that stretched out before me. The same covering blanketed the branches of the trees turning the area into a virtual fairyland. The beauty was awesome. A few of nature's wildlife could be seen and heard but other than that I was alone. I walked for a long time feeling one with nature and when I gazed up into the blue skies I also felt a connection with the universe. I had been looking for so many answers from outside of me but perhaps, if I was to be honest with myself, they had to come from within.

On the return trip I stopped and brushed the snow from the now familiar bench. Sitting quietly I suddenly didn't feel alone. I didn't feel abandoned. Instead I was filled with an overwhelming sense of love. It was only then during that very special moment that I could truly accept the fact that what was to be, would be.

Chapter Thirty

While I was waiting for Robert to pick me up for the trip I made a quick last minute inspection of my apartment by systematically checking any electrical equipment then making sure that all windows were securely locked. I was in the process of making a mental inventory of the contents of my luggage when I heard the elevator approaching. By the time Robert stepped off I had my coat and boots on and was standing in my vestibule with my bag sitting on the floor beside me.

The ride to Banff was pleasant. We had pre-arranged plans to meet the others for lunch then afterwards Robert and I would check in at the main desk. Months ago when they were making the reservations they were unable to reserve a chalet large enough to accommodate all six of them, but since Robert wasn't sure whom he would be going with he had offered to stay in a second adjacent unit. The moment we drove into the small village the festive spirit was evident by the throngs of people packing the sidewalks. After pulling into the driveway of the lodge, and parking the car into one of the slots, we left the luggage in the trunk and walked hand in hand to the lobby.

William called out as we were coming through the doorway. "Hey, I thought you guys were never going to get here."

There were hugs and excited greetings then over lunch in the dining room we discussed plans for the next three days. Although everyone had preferred a chalet for sleeping accommodations there had been a consensus to spend the New Years Eve party at the Banff Springs

Hotel.Early in the evening, dressed in formal attire, we huddled together in the crowded taxi. As the vehicle wound its way up the hill along the twisting road to the building that stood majestically on a higher level, the ominous gigantic mountains that loomed behind it could only be felt but not seen due to the pitch darkness. Knowing that they were there hovering like an ominous predator made the whole scene even more overpowering and frightening.

The lobby was alive with activity and the extent of the lavishness of the affair was blatantly obvious. Women were adorned in sparkling ostentatious evening gowns, while men wore various styled shirtfronts and cummerbunds in an attempt to break the monotony of their stark black tuxedos. Eye catching jewelry, some removed earlier from the hotel's security, refracted light from thousands of facets contained in the hundreds of precious stones.

The evening was a blur of succulent food, tasteful music, and brilliant charming company. As we slowly but continuously ate and drank the noise in the room escalated. When I sat back and looked at the total picture I was amazed and in awe at the close relationship that I had with Robert's friends. I had never felt so comfortable or had such a sense of acceptance in such a short period of time. At the end of the evening, feeling exhausted, we crawled back into a cab. After retracing our path back to the Chalets we said our brief goodnights in front of the building. I barely remembered climbing into bed with Robert and in the morning I had to ask if we had made love.

After sleeping in then having a leisurely breakfast we headed for the ski hills. When we saw the length of the lineups at the towlines we moaned with disappointment, however after getting into our gear and taking our places the time literally flew. Before we knew it we were seated on the swinging chairs as they carried us up the side of the mountain. Once we reached the top we stood for a few moments appreciating the view while pointing out several spots with our ski poles. As we weaved back and forth on our way down the trail at breakneck speed, the air whipped at our faces and the sun's rays burned our skin creating the typical skiers tan. We continued the runs for the remainder of the afternoon then exhausted we relaxed with a hot drink in the chalet.

That evening we once more dined in the Banff Spring Hotel where the cuisine was superb. After a bowl of cold vichyssoise we enjoyed the antics of the waiter as he tossed together a delectable Caesar salad. In a democratic system the six of us put our heads together for a consultation then with a consensus we eliminated the anchovies. Robert and I shared a chateaubriand that was cooked to perfection and after the main course I managed to find enough room for my favorite dessert, crème caramel. The custard was rich and creamy and the sauce had that slightly burnt flavor to it. I had thrown my calorie counter out for the holiday so I added a touch of Bailey's to my coffee. When the evening was over it was necessary to wait for an available cab but eventually we were dropped off at our chalets.

Since the temperature outside had dropped considerably the larger suite had cooled down. There were loud blustery sounds as the wind howled through the trees and brushed against the sides of the building but after adding a few logs to the fireplace the room was soon cozy and warm. So far there had been no snow but some was forecasted overnight.

Harold was stretched out on one of the couches with his head resting on Cynthia's lap while Helen sat on the floor with her back leaning against William's legs as he sat in one of the chairs. I discretely watched them from time to time as they made body contact with a stroke, a caress, or a touching of hands. It was obvious that the couples were still very much in love. One by one each of us moaned with pain when a particular movement aggravated the over-strained muscles from the day's activities.

Suddenly William jumped up and said. "You know what I think we need in order to soothe our tortured bodies?" They all looked in his direction and shouted in unison, "a hot tub!" William began shedding his clothes even before he left the room then slowly one by one the others followed, although not with his agility. Soon the rush of the water and an occasional moan of relief could be heard coming from the tub room.

Robert looked at me shyly. "We do it Finnish style."

Even though my upbringing had been rather conservative I only hesitated for a second. "Why not, I questioned with a toss of my head.

My initial reaction at my sudden liberation in front of people that I hardly knew was that of embarrassment, however as I quickly climbed into the steamy bubbly waters I realized that they hadn't paid any particular attention to me. Within minutes I was enjoying the sensation of no longer feeling like an assortment of body parts but like a total person. As I sat 'au natural' beside Robert and the others I surprisingly found it to be quite relaxing.

Helen sighed. "Oh this feels so good." She turned to her husband with a teasing look on her face. "It's almost as enjoyable as Jock."

William scowled but somehow I knew that it wasn't sincere. "One day I'm going to have to meet this Jock," he said in a rather stern voice.

Helen and Cynthia gave each other a meaningful look.

I looked from one to the other hoping to gain some understanding as to what was going on. "Who is this Jock or should I ask?" It was obviously a private joke.

Cynthia answered. "Oh he's the 'gentleman,' she smiled as she looked slyly at her husband, "that gives us our massages at the spa."

Harold playfully splashed his wife.

Suddenly Robert stood up and announced. "We forgot something. Would anyone like a drink?" He took orders then returned shortly with the glasses, big glasses.

Later, waterlogged and feeling no pain, we decided to call it a night. As we staggered along the sidewalk to our chalet Robert and I held on to each other for warmth as well as support while the light falling snow swirled and pirouetted around us. Once inside we shed our clothes and snuggled together under the blankets. Our heads had hardly hit the pillow when we fell into a deep sleep.

Chapter Thirty-one

Awakened with uncontrollable hysterics I threw off the blankets, bolted out of bed then rushed into the bathroom where I knelt in front of the toilet and shoved my head over the bowl. Between the wrenching and gagging I kept mumbling an incoherent, "no, no!"

Awakened by the commotion a frantic Robert stumbled out of the bed and quickly bolted into the bathroom. "My God Christine, what's wrong?" When he reached out, to touch my arm, I responded as though I was about to be branded by a hot red iron rather than by a hand whose intention was to give me solace.

Without answering I shoved him aside then rushed into the shower stall where I received a sudden blast of cold water. Alarmed, Robert opened the door in hopes of putting his arms around me in order to give me some comfort however he was totally surprised when I reciprocated his touch with flailing arms and fists.

"Don't touch me! Don't touch me! Get away!" I was sobbing.

Robert immediately began withdrawing until his back touched the opposite bathroom wall. Taking a few steps he stood in the middle of the room naked, dripping with water, and feeling utterly helpless and bewildered. Painfully he listened to the sobs that were coming from the enclosure.

To Robert it seemed forever before I appeared at the bedroom door. My eyes were red and my hair hung limp and wet around my face while the heavy terry robe that was securely wrapped around me seemed to dwarf my small frame. Robert was sitting on the bed leaning forward with his elbows resting on his knees and both hands hanging limply in front of him. Instead of going over to him I moved towards one of the straight back chairs and sat stiffly on its edge. We were quiet for a long time before Robert broke the silence. When I didn't immediately answer he waited, knowing better than to push me, and when I did speak my voice was hollow and there was an unnatural weariness in the tone.

"I suppose that I should have discussed this with you a long time ago but at the time I was afraid of what your reaction was going to be. You see I was worried that I might lose you. I thought that if you grew to love me first I would have a better chance of you not leaving. I realize now that I wasn't being fair to you, and I wasn't being fair to myself. If you couldn't accept me then, you won't accept me now."

"Accept what Christine?"

Defeated and feeling helpless I carefully attempted to explain the issue that I had been avoiding for such a long time.

"All of my life I've had things happen to me, different unusual things. I can remember that even at an early age there were strange occurrences. At first they were just memories so I assumed that they were probably only dreams but as I got older I thought that they were memories carried in my RNA. Eventually I realized that it was actually happening and that it was I in the sequences. I looked off in the distance as though I was still trying to figure out the puzzle. "But the time frame still eluded me." There was a pause as though I was attempting to organize my thoughts. "Gradually, as though guided by a hand, my dream-like mode became connected with my conscious state, a state in which I systematically received proof of the validity of what was happening. As the characters from my fantasies began making an appearance into my everyday life I became convinced beyond any doubt that it was not my imagination but rather a reality."

Slowly I began to see the signals in Robert's eyes, the signal that in the past had prevented me from sharing my experiences with anyone. From time to time I had tested the waters with others but when I acknowledged their disbelief, the patronization, and the ridicule that was manifested on each face, I changed my mind. However this time I was devastated. This was not just anyone but was the man that I loved, the man that I wanted to share the rest of my life with.

My voice caught in my throat and I was unable to continue.

Robert had an incredulous look on his face. "What were you so upset about in the bathroom? What made you so hysterical? Was it one of those dreams?"

"Yes."

He sat staring at me shaking his head.

I felt as though I had disappointed him in some astronomical way. Feeling defeated and humiliated I looked away experiencing more pain and disillusionment than I thought was possible. All of my energy seemed to drain out of me.

"Have you seen a doctor about this?"

I let out a dry chuckle. "You mean a psychiatrist?"

"Yes. " Robert answered.

My jaw tightened as I slowly shook my head in the negative.

Robert then spoke to me like a father to a child. "Christine things like that cannot happen. They are not possible. When we get back we will make an appointment with a friend of mine." When I said nothing he stood up, walked over, and cautiously knelt in front of my chair. Slowly he reached out and took my hand. "Come on back to bed Sweetheart. We'll talk about it in the morning."

Obediently I allowed myself to be led, and submissively I lay down beside him. Lying on my side facing the door I remained mute while Robert curled himself around me and was soon breathing deeply in sleep. I lay awake with my mind spinning with thoughts. The more I thought about the whole thing the more restless I became. Eventually I eased myself out of Robert's hold and slipped out of bed. I put on my housecoat then tip toed out of the room and down the stairs where the area had become quite cold. Shivering I gathered some paper and kindling wood, lit a match, and when the fire was burning brightly I placed two more logs on the grate then curled up in one of the chairs.

Each time I attempted to remember the last dream a shudder would pass through me and nausea would well up in my throat. There was no one to talk to, no one to turn to, and no one from whom I could receive solace and comfort. Angry with myself for telling Robert in the first place I solemnly vowed that I would never make the same mistake again. I had tried it with Lara and now I had attempted to reach Robert and in both cases I had failed. I was alone, so alone.

Robert like so many others was a black and white person. There were no grays. He only believed in what he could see, hear, touch and smell. The intangibles didn't exist for him. The others didn't really matter but if I wanted to spend the rest of my life with him I needed Robert's support. When I looked ahead through Robert's eyes all I could see was the tunnel vision and a hard impregnable wall.

The fire was dying when I finally drifted off to sleep.

Upstairs towards morning Robert's hand reached over only to find an empty pillow. Alarmed, fearing that I might have done something foolish he jumped out of bed, grabbed his housecoat and put it on as he dashed down the stairs. His steps slowed when he caught sight of me curled up in the chair. Cautiously he walked over then knelt down on the floor. Frightened because of his love for me he stared down at my sleeping face. With moist eyes he kissed me lightly on the slightly parted lips then whispered my name.Startled, I woke up.

"Good morning Princess."

I looked at him with affection. "Good morning Robert."

"Why are you sleeping in an uncomfortable chair and in such a cold room?" His voice had become strained with emotion.

"I couldn't sleep."

As he sadly looked at me he saw a helpless misdirected girl who needed guidance but little did he realize that the opposite was true. It was at this moment of time that with added inner strength I was determined to face the future alone.

"Would you like a cup of hot coffee?"

Feeling quite subdued I nodded my head. When it was ready he handed me a mug then sat down facing me on the couch.

"You know Sweetheart dreams can be very misleading." Filled with a feeling of painful sadness I glanced up at him as he continued. "I once had a client whose wife accused him of controlling her through her dreams by placing thoughts into her mind while she was sleeping. Evidently she was close to having a nervous breakdown and was suing her husband for divorce on those grounds. Can you imagine that?"

I smiled. "Who won?"

"Why, my client of course. No one can do such a bizarre and odious thing." Robert looked as though someone had told him that the world was the center of the universe. When I realized how difficult it is to convince people of various new theories, or realities, I suddenly felt sympathy pain for Christopher Columbus.

Robert continued to talk but I was hardly paying attention since my mind was elsewhere. I was recalling a patient that I had cared for a long time ago when I was a student working on a psychiatric unit in the hospital. A girlfriend of this middle-aged native gentleman had accused him of invading her mind while she slept, telling her to do horrible things. It had become so tiresome and out of control that she had gone to a psychiatrist with her story, who, in turn, approached the man. In this case the perpetrator admitted to the crime and claimed that he was able to control people when they slept. The man had also voluntarily allowed himself to be admitted to the psychiatric ward for assessment and evaluation although I always thought that it was probably an order from the courts.I had sat in several group sessions where he was present. What concerned me was that on various occasions while sitting in the room with the man I had felt an invasion into my own mind. Each time I looked up I would see him staring at me with a satisfied smile, almost a smirk, on his face.

One day when I found him sitting alone in the hospital lounge I walked over to him and sat in one of the chairs. As we were talking I could once more feel the 'fingers' moving through my head. Upset I turned to him.

"You know I can tell when someone is entering my mind."

"I know."

"You just did it to me again."

"I know."

"Why are you doing it?"

"I'm doing it because I can."

I stared at him with an overwhelming feeling of disgust and sadness. "You're doing it because you can." I slowly shook my head. "You know some day you are going to do it to the wrong person and then you will be very sorry."

With a look of alarm he snapped his head in my direction. "What do you mean by saying I'll be sorry."

"You're not the only one out there who can do this. If one day you happen to chose one of the others as your subject it may result in them becoming very upset and the retaliation won't be pleasant."

The man's mouth dropped in astonishment at the revelation. Once the patient had acknowledged his gift he came to terms with his reality and was discharged the next week. I often wondered how he had chosen to use his power. Everyone controls their own destiny by the choices they make in life.

Chapter Thirty-two

Since we were to meet the others for breakfast the next morning I paid more attention to my morning care while at the same time Robert was busy discussing business matters with the staff from his office. When he was finished he turned and gave me a strange stare, then, walking over to me he took me in his arms to give me comfort but all that I could feel was patronization.

During the meal I sometimes had difficulty concentrating on the conversation however no one seemed to notice, probably attributing my attitude to fatigue. Afterwards we headed back to the chalets where standing in front of the building in the newly fallen snow we said our good-byes. Cynthia and Harold gave me a hug and Helen and William stood for a few seconds each holding one of my hands.

"It has really been a wonderful few days Christine. We can see why Robert loves you. Thanks for helping us to make this a happy holiday season."

I choked up with emotion as each one gave me a hug.

After the two of us finished packing I sat in one of the chairs while Robert set the bags by the door. Walking over and taking me by the hand he led me to the couch then sitting down he wrapped his arms protectively around me.

"Are you still upset Christine?" He kissed the tip of my nose. "Did you have a good time?"

"Yes it was really nice Robert and your friends are kind and a lot of fun. I'm sorry to have spoiled the vacation with my outburst last night but please don't worry about me. As you said it was probably just a nightmare."

Taking me in his arms he held me close to him. "If only we could stop time right now. If only we could ignore the rest of the world and just enjoy the feelings that we have for each other."

A tear trickled down my cheek.

When Robert felt the wetness on the side of his face he turned to me in surprise. "Christine, why are you crying?"

I gazed at him with a feeling of extreme sadness and loneliness. "It's because I love you so much."

Robert whipped it away with his thumb and held me tighter.

It was mid afternoon when we headed back to the city. Due to the road conditions from the storm the night before Robert had to concentrate on his driving, and since I was preoccupied with my own thoughts the two of us spoke very little. Because of the fact that we had stopped for something to eat, as well as the fact that the drive was slow, it was around nine in the evening when the two of us said our good-byes inside my door. He took both of my hands in his.

"I want to thank you for a wonderful three days."

"I enjoyed them too. I guess that I won't see you for the next two weeks."

"Yes I'll be quite busy in the office but if I can I'll call you for lunch." He sighed. "I want you to know how proud I am of you."

Frowning I pulled my head back and looked up at him quizzically.

"I appreciate the way that you accepted Helen and William. I was unsure just how you would react to them."

I shook my head in confusion.Since he was unaware of my reaction Robert kept on talking.   "There wasn't a flicker of animosity."

Suddenly my heart stopped, my blood turned to ice and I found it difficult to talk. "What did you meanwhen you said that it was as if I didn't know?"

"Well that they were Don's----." He stopped. I jerked away from him as though he was a hot flame and horror filled my eyes.

"That they were Don's parents." He had to force each word from his lips.

There was a full moment of silence while the truth settled in. Throwing my head back my hands flew up to my face as an inhuman cry of agony poured out from my throat. "Oh, my God please say that it isn't true Robert!"

His hands hung limp at his side as he stared at me. "You didn't know?"

"I didn't know! I didn't know! Why didn't you tell me?" I moaned.

His voice was quiet and defeated. "I thought that you knew."

The tears were now pouring from my eyes. "I never knew Don's last name. I never thought that it would be important to know his last name." I let out a low painful groan. "Oh Robert I feel so horrible!"

He cradled me in his arms. As he picked me up and carried me into the bedroom I was too weak to resist, and too drained to care. After removing all of my clothing, except my underpants, he gently placed me between the sheets and tucked the comforter under my chin. Lying beside me he held me until my weeping stopped and I succumbed to sleep. He remained for a long time staring into space. A tear trickled from his eye and ran down his cheek dropping onto the pillow. As he carefully got out of bed I stirred slightly and moaned in my sleep. After writing a brief message he placed the note on my bedside table then letting himself out closed the door soundlessly behind him.

I woke up crying. It is strange but children do the same thing in the operating room. If they go under the anesthetic crying they wake up crying, and vice versa. As memories came flooding back, thus intensifying my tears, the emotional seesaw was becoming unbearable.

A sudden thought caused me to let out a low moan. Now I understood my friend's attitude during the last couple of weeks and comprehended the reason for the sudden trip to Switzerland for the holidays. "Oh my God, was I the reason why they took the trip?" All of a sudden the pieces fell into place: Lara's odd behavior concerning the phone calls and the strange silent attitude when I spoke to her. She must have known of my association with Helen and William since the Christmas dance for the bar association.

I sobbed into my pillow feeling loathsome like a traitor to my best friend. Lara and the family had been suffering enough emotional traumas without me adding more. What must they be thinking of me?

It was then that I saw the note on the table. The message was simple.'It seems that I am always apologizing, love Robert.'

Chapter Thirty-three

It is unimaginable how the body is able to keep on functioning when the spirit is dead. It amazes me how some people manage to live with the unbearable emotions of self-condemnation and guilt. I spent the following day on the living room couch and probably would have remained there forever if the phone hadn't rung. Startled by the sudden piercing sound I activated the audio after five or six rings. It was Robert.

"Christine?" It was more like a question than like a statement.

"Hello, Robert."

"Christine. Please turn the screen on."

My voice was dry and void of emotion. "Not now Robert."

"Please. I'm so worried about you."

I sighed heavily. "Well don't be. I'm just a little tired right now so if you don't mind I'll call you later."

"I'm sorry, Christine. I do love you."

"I know." I disconnected before he could say anything more.

I called security to inform him that I didn't want to be disturbed then I disconnected the phone service. At nine PM, feeling emotionally exhausted, I put one of my faithful pills in my mouth and within fifteen minutes I was fast asleep.

I hardly recognized the next few days as they came and went. I wasn't worried about Robert because I knew that he would be with his children and I assumed that Lara was still out of the country. When I called her home the following Tuesday Becky answered.

"Hi Becky I see that you're back. Did you have a good time in Switzerland?"

The instant change in Becky's demeanor created a sudden heaviness in my heart.

Her answer was a simple, "Yes."

"Becky, could I please speak to your mother?"

There was uneasiness in her response. "Just a moment and I'll see if she's busy." The phone went dead and was replaced with holding music. Several unnerving moments later Lara's face appeared on the screen.

"Lara. Thanks for talking to me."

"What do you want?" The indifferent tone in her voice made me feel as though I was talking to a stranger.

"I want to see you Lara. There are things that we have to discuss."

"I don't think that we have anything to say to each other."

"Yes there is. It's not what you think. Please at least let me talk to you."

She stared at me for a long moment, inhaled deeply, and then slowly exhaled. "Come over this evening at eight."

"Thanks." With so little energy left in me it was difficult to take the next breath. When we disconnected my hands were shaking and there was a deep sick feeling in my heart.

When I arrived at their place at eight sharp Tom answered the door. He escorted me into the living room where Lara was sitting rigidly in a chair with her back to us and presumably staring into the fire.

"Honey Christine is here." When she didn't move I thought for a moment that our relationship was going to be irreconcilable, but when she finally did turn the pain and anger was blatantly obvious on her face.

It was difficult to bare the humiliation that I was feeling. "Lara where is Becky?"

"She's upstairs. Why?" Her voice was cold and unforgiving.

"Could she come down? What I have to say has to be said to her as well as to the two of you."

Lara and Tom glanced at each other then without a spoken word Tom turned and went upstairs to get Becky. Meanwhile, since I was having difficulty holding myself in an upright position, I gratefully slumped down on one of the chairs. The feeling of doom and gloom saturated the room. After Becky and Tom arrived all eyes avoided contact with me as I began to talk.

"I've known the three of you for the last fifteen years. During that time we were close, in fact I always felt that you had replaced my parents that had passed away. I grew to love you as my family and I feel that you loved me in return."

I paused for a few seconds while I attempted to regain some composure. It was difficult even painful for me to speak.

"One day a man called Robert Power came into my life. I thought then that I had everything, friends and a wonderful man to love. Unfortunately something horrible happened that was out of my control and my secure world was turned upside down. However even though our relationship was suddenly threatened we somehow managed to save it. As Christmas season began to approach and festive plans were being made I was excited at the thought that Robert was finally going to meet my friends and I was going to meet his."

At this point I leaned forward and looked directly into their eyes. I emphasized each word. "You must believe me when I say that I did not know that Helen and William were Don's parents. I never knew his last name."

Tom and Laura stared at each other in shocked disbelief and it was Tom who asked the question. "Do you mean to tell us that he never warned you, that he never even mentioned it to you?"

"He thought that I knew. It was all a misunderstanding. I certainly wouldn't have gone with them if I had known who they were."

There was a long silent pause in the room. Tom was beginning to dislike my friend more and more with each passing minute and when he spoke his voice was icy with anger.

"When did you find out?"

"Not until we'd returned from the three days in Banff. When I realized what I had done to your family I was devastated." Sadly I looked into their faces one by one. "I'm so sorry, so sorry." I began to weep.

At first the three of them sat looking from one to another all wanting to thrash Robert for being so inconsiderate and insensitive. Tom was the first one to make a move. Sitting beside me he put his arm around my shoulder. "Don't cry Christine. It wasn't your fault." Becky moved over and knelt on the floor in front of me while Lara was the last to approach me since it was she who had been hurt the most by the situation. She was the one who was having the most difficult time to transfer her traumatized feelings into one of acceptance.

"I missed you so much on Christmas day Lara." I took a tissue out of my pocket and blew my nose.

"Where did the two of you spend it Sis?" Tom was gently rubbing my back.

"I spent it alone. Robert was with his children."

Tom's hand stopped. "What!" Robert and Lara both exclaimed at the same time. Furious Tom jumped up and began pacing back and forth. "That bastard, how could he do that to you?"

"It wasn't his fault." I was quick to defend him.

"Then whose fault was it?" Tom's voice was filled with sarcasm.

"It's a long explanation and it's also a little confusing."

Tom and Lara exchanged glances then Lara leaned forward. "Don't you see Honey? In the first place it was in bad taste to bring the four of you together without first discussing it with you. It was also thoughtless and insensitive to leave you alone at Christmas." When she saw how miserable I was feeling she continued in a more gentle voice. "Honey, I know that you are going through some difficult times right now so that all we can ask you to do is to keep a clear perspective of the situation. We also want you to remember that we will always be here for you. If you ever feel overwhelmed please don't hesitate to call us, or to come over."

Looking through tears I asked in a contrite tone. "You didn't go to Switzerland just because of me did you?"

"No Sweetie. We all felt that since the last few months have been very difficult for all of us we all needed a change of scenery."

Tom got up and when he returned he was carrying a tray containing four glasses and a bottle of champagne.

After he popped the cork and filled the goblets he passed one out to each of us then holding his up he made a toast. "Here's to our friendship! It may get bumped around a bit but it will always survive."

Chapter Thirty-four

During the next few days I did a lot of soul searching. Robert discretely left me alone knowing, or perhaps hoping that I would call him when I was ready. When the weather was agreeable I spent hours sitting on the familiar bench in the park remembering what Lara had said to me. "Keep your perspective." However, when one feels something precious slipping away it becomes so easy to rationalize and to make excuses.

For long periods of time I curled up in the chair by the bay window or else I stretched out on the couch and simply stared at the ceiling while trying to find an easy answer. There was none. Was Robert insensitive to me or had there just been a lack of communication? Of course I preferred the latter explanation because it was repairable. The first was not.

With my mind made up by Thursday evening I gave a verbal command on Robert's phone. Since he wasn't at home the call was automatically transferred after two rings to his office. Being deeply engrossed in his work he activated the system with a verbal command. Startled by the sound of my voice his hands stopped in mid-air over the keyboard then he slowly rested them on the desk.

"Christine! I've been worried about you. I'm so glad that you called."

"How are you Robert?" I glanced at the background. "I see that you're still in your office?"

"Yes." He looked anxious. "I'm fine. It's you that I am worried about."

As I looked at his painful expression I had second thoughts about blaming him for the incident. I realized how easy it could have been for him to presume that I knew Don's last name however he still should have spoken to me about it. I also recognized that the real issue lay deeper than that.

"Robert the reason why I called was to see if you would like to get together with me sometime this weekend. I think that once again there are a lot of things that we have to discuss."

"Of course and I agree with you one hundred percent."

"Are you free tomorrow evening?"

"Yes."

"I'll expect you at the usual time."

Linked into a natural familiar groove the words felt like music to our ears.

All of my good intentions of keeping an open mind disappeared the moment I saw him standing in the doorway. When he put his arms around me I momentarily put a pause mode in my thinking process and instead enjoyed the luxury of feeling with my heart.

Inside the living room the blazing fire was giving additional warmth to the room while outside the wind was howling in the black night. Drifting snow was piling up against buildings and fences until some of the shorter structures had partially disappeared from view. During the last several hours long fingers of the white stuff had stretched dangerously across roads and highways resulting in warnings being broadcasted to avoid driving unless it was absolutely necessary. When he arrived a few flakes of snow still remained on his hair while his face was slightly reddened from the raw wind.

"Would you like a drink, Robert?"

"I'd love something warm. It's freezing out there."

After making him a hot toddy I curled up into the cushions at the end of the couch.

"So did you have a hard day? You look tired."

"Actually I had a hard week." We simply stared at each other feeling but not speaking then with a grimace he spoke. "Do you mind if I suggest something Christine?"

"No go ahead."

"Perhaps we can both express how we feel and then we can take it from there." When he nodded his head in my direction and asked me if I would like to go first I admired his diplomacy, but quickly I realized that in his profession this was just a natural common procedure. I agreed then sat for a moment while I contemplated what to say.

"All of my life I have always felt in control of myself. There were never any extreme downs but then in hindsight there were never any exceptional highs either. I always knew that I was doing the right thing and I never had to question my motives. When I met you I imagined that my life had become perfect, especially when I felt heights of happiness that I never dreamed were possible. Unfortunately I also began experiencing other emotions, disturbing ones."

"I felt alienation and rejection, sentiments that I found to be extremely painful. In all of my dealings with people I had always been accepted as well as liked by everyone but suddenly my self-esteem was being challenged and my self-worth bruised. The world seemed to be rotating around me without any consultation from me. I seemed to have little or no say in the decision making and at the same time I was confronted with one surprise after another." I glared at him. "Robert, not only do you not discuss things with me first you don't even warn me when it's about to happen."

For a moment I stared into the dancing flames of the fire then I continued. "For the first time in my life I also became torn between two loyalties." I shuddered at the thought. "The feelings of guilt that resulted were so ugly and revolting. What a horrible destroying force that is. You know Robert I am not attempting to control your activities where your profession is concerned, and if you asked your peers you'd probably get a divided pole as far as your choice of defending Don. However I feel that it would have been nice if this one time you had put my welfare ahead of your rigid professional rule. Personally I think that it had more to do with you helping an old friend. At the same time you have to realize that it has caused extreme havoc in my life where **my** friends are concerned."

"Robert, in regard to your children I feel that you have been walking on a fence. The longer you delay in arranging for us to meet the stronger Hillary's position will be in influencing their attitude and behavior. You are the adult. You should be in control." I looked at him sadly. "I never should have had to spend Christmas alone."

His eyes flew open. "But I thought that you spent the day with Lara and her family."

"No I didn't. They went to Switzerland for three weeks."

He looked miserable. "Oh Christine I'm so sorry. I never meant that you should be alone on Christmas."

"Well what is past is past but things have to change. For one thing I must become a part of your life with the children. I don't mind you worrying about Hillary's welfare, after all you spent many years together, but I don't want you sacrificing my welfare in order to protect hers.

And Robert, please talk to me about everything. I'm not Hillary. Discuss any plans that you make because I'm never prepared for all of the new revelations that pop up. And don't surprise me Robert because I don't like surprises." I sat back and dramatically waved my right arm in a circle as though I was giving him access to the podium. "I guess that I'm finished."

Robert's voice was clear and well modulated. After all this was his forte.

"Perhaps my defense, my only defense, is the fact that during my life with Hillary a definite pattern had been established. Our relationship began to deteriorate shortly after the children arrived. She resented both my work as well as my independence from the moment I stepped out of the front door until I returned home in the evening feeling exhausted and needing a listening ear. She quickly let me know that she wasn't interested in anything related to the office or to my business friends. Slowly I began to withdraw, to hold everything to myself, while at the same time I left all household decisions up to her and simply went along with whatever she decided. After awhile it became a way of life."

"I'm sorry that I have sprung so many things on you without discussing it with you first. I guess that my mind was so absorbed with business and personal problems that I never gave the issue enough thought and consideration." He looked at me apologetically. "Old habits die hard. I guess that I have given you a difficult time. I'm so sorry"

I stared hard into his eyes as I gave one brief nod with my head. "Apology accepted." For awhile we sat looking at each other then at his request I moved over into his arms. We remained for a long time listening to the romantic lyrics of Barry Manilow as the fire crackled in the hearth while outside the winds became more intense as the storm escalated.

"Well Princess would you like to meet Sara and Johnny?"

I turned slowly to him. "Do you really mean that Robert?"

"Yes. No more procrastinating."

I gave him a hug. "Oh Robert, thank you so much."

As our mood improved we were soon anxiously making plans to rectify the past mistakes. Picking me up in his arms and carrying me into the bedroom he gave verbal commands to extinguish both light and sound behind us. Placing me down on the bed he slowly began undoing the buttons on my blouse then bending over he kissed first one breast then the other. Moving down he pulled my slacks over my hips exposing a pair of delicate lace panties. As he kissed the light fabric his lips could feel the softness of the mound of hair and his nose could smell the faint bouquet of perfume and sweet personal musk. I was hurled into a state of ecstasy as our lovemaking lingered long into the night.

Chapter Thirty-five

While Robert was working on Monday morning, his thoughts kept shifting to the unavoidable and disagreeable task of approaching his children about me. He knew that he was going to meet resistance so he definitely was not looking forward to it. When he placed a call to his former home that evening Hillary talked on and on about matters and situations that he was no longer interested in. When he finally did speak to Sara and Johnny he clearly stressed that he would pick them up at seven sharp on Friday. As he was hanging up he had a distinct feeling that Hillary was eavesdropping.

After the long talk that Robert and I had the bond between he and I was firmly reinforced. As far as Lara and I were concerned, in order to preserve the trust that had been gained between us I kept her updated about any decisions that I made.

"Just be careful. I don't want you to get hurt anymore than you have been."

"Don't worry I will and thanks for caring."

"And let me know what happens when you see the kids this weekend. I don't know how anyone could not love you, Sweetie."

"Thanks for the vote of confidence. It's too bad that you weren't their mother."

"I'm sure that everything will turn out all right."

Robert picked the children up as planned. Once they were settled in the apartment the three of them eagerly challenged each other in participation games on their virtual reality program. Because he was having difficulty keeping up with the two youngsters the sweat soon formed on both his forehead and armpits. When Johnny made a move on his character and zapped him Robert cursed under his breath. "Damn!"

"What did you say, Dad?" Johnny asked through a broad victorious grin.

"Darn."

It was becoming more and more difficult to keep up with the upcoming generation. Any new advances in technology created large gaps, spaces that left you far behind if you didn't persistently update. During the evening while the children were sipping on a cup of hot chocolate Robert decided to bring up the subject of meeting me.

"Do either of you have any plans other than the hockey practice and ringette game tomorrow?"

They both answered in the negative.

"Good. I've asked Christine to come over for dinner, in fact she should be here by the time we get back from the arena."

He didn't anticipate the degree of emotion that instantly poured out of his children. Sara screamed viciously. "No! I don't want to meet that bitch! I'll go home if she comes here!" She glared at her father while at the same time Johnny cringed with fear in his chair.

Stunned by her unexpected outburst Robert quickly remembered my warning. As he stared at her he felt that he was looking at a mirror image of Hillary.

"Sara you haven't even met her yet. And how can you say such nasty things about anyone?"

"Because she's selfish and she just wants you because you're a lawyer. She doesn't give a damn about Johnny and me. She's a cruel and evil woman."

"Oh my God," his words were barely audible. "Honey daddy would never love a woman who was as awful as you describe."

Sara looked horrified. "You love her!" She spit out the words as though it was something vile and odious.

"Yes I love her. She's a lovely person. You will see for yourself when you meet her tomorrow."

"I will never meet her! Standing up with fists clenched Sara's face was distorted with hate." She began to sob. "I want to go home." By now Johnny was shaking with fear.

Robert sat silently looking at the picture in front of him and seeing for the first time the damage that their divorce had done. He didn't blame the divorce but instead he blamed the poor way that he and Hillary had handled it.

"Come here both of you." Taking each one by their hand the three of them walked over to the couch and sat down. Johnny was the first to sit beside Robert snuggling protectively into his arm then Sara reluctantly followed on the other side. Robert soothed them with words of comfort in an attempt to ease their pain.

When the crying stopped Robert glanced down at his son and noted that he had fallen asleep. Putting his finger to his lips for silence he nudged Sara then he carefully picked Johnny up and carried him into the bedroom. After tucking in the blankets, and brushing a few strands of hair from his forehead, he bent down and kissed him lightly on the cheek. Quietly he left the room.

Sara was sitting at the same spot on the couch with both her arms stubbornly crossed in front of her and she glared at him belligerently when he entered the room. Picking up a light chair Robert positioned it in front of his daughter and sat down facing her. "Sweetheart I think that we have to have a little talk."

Avoiding his eyes she blurted out. "Well I don't want to talk."

"Well I do. And I want to make it clear that there will be no yelling because your brother is sleeping, and there will also be no profanity in this house. Do you understand?"

"Yes." She pursed her lips together and narrowed her eyes.

With determination Robert cautiously began. "When your mummy and I met we fell in love and out of that love we had you and Johnny. We were very glad that we had the two of you and for a long time we were all very happy. For reasons that had **nothing** to do with the two of you your mother's feelings and my feelings began to change. We began to argue a lot and that made you and Johnny very unhappy. You remember that don't you, Sweetheart?"

She simply nodded her head.

"Soon there was more anger and bitterness between your mummy and me than there was happiness. That was when we decided to try living apart." Robert paused. He reached over and tilting Sara's chin looked directly into her eyes. "Even though our feelings have changed for each other they have never changed towards you and Johnny. You're my little girl and you always will be. No one will ever take your place."

There was another pause while Robert allowed the message to sink in. "Yes I love Christine but in a different way than the way that I love you." At the last statement a flash of anger once again flared in her eyes. Wincing with disappointment Robert realized that it wasn't going to be that easy to repair the damage that had already been done.

Picking up both of her hands and holding them between his he asked her if she believed him when he said that he loved her and her brother Johnny. Reluctantly she nodded that she did.

"Sara you would make your daddy so happy if you would just meet Christine." When she opened her mouth to object he held up his hand to silence her. "You must never make a choice or a decision until you have all of the facts, all of the correct facts. A wrong decision can lead you down a destructive path in life and sometimes the choice is irreparable. Do you know what irreparable means?"

"Yes, that it can't be fixed."

"That's right. So when you meet Christine tomorrow you'll have a chance to see and judge for yourself."

"Okay, but I know that I won't like her."

Even though Robert was flooded with a feeling of relief it was overshadowed with a sense of foreboding. He knew that the task tomorrow was not going to be an easy one for any of them. Long after he tucked his daughter into bed he sat with a drink of scotch in his hand sadly wondering what unknown path he was sending himself down and where it would all end.

Chapter Thirty-six

The next day when I entered Robert's apartment I was unaware of what had transpired the previous evening other than the fact that Sara had agreed to the meeting with some reluctance. While they were at their hockey and ringette games I was busy preparing the food, and when they arrived at four o'clock everyone was nervous including Robert. As introductions were being made Sara refused to look at me although I caught her peeking several times when she thought that no one was noticing. Johnny was much more malleable and we were soon conversing comfortably with **him** initiating the conversation. Sara, who was having a difficult time concentrating due to her vigilance over her younger brother sat back in her chair sulking.

When I questioned Robert about the children's favorite meal he had told me that they loved hamburgers, French fries and chocolate cake. That morning I made the cake from scratch and the potatoes were cut and soaking in a container of cold water in the fridge. Lastly there was a platter of molded patties of meat. As I headed into the kitchen I called out for a couple of volunteers to set the table in the dining room then I turned to Johnny and asked him if he would like to give me a hand. Looking quite pleased he followed me while Sara remained in the living room like an unbendable block of steel. When Robert offered her services to help set the table she reluctantly separated herself from the chair and sullenly followed him into the dining area. After they had finished Robert joined Christine and Johnny in the kitchen while Sara quickly returned to her fortress-like position in the chair in front of the television.

"Mm, something smells good." While I was concentrating on flipping the meat patties on the barbecue grill Robert put his arms around my waist. Because he could not remember back to the days when his father and mother had been openly affectionate Johnny stared openmouthed his eyes wide with wonder. Even though it confused him it also gave him a warm feeling somewhere deep inside.

Noticing his confusion I winked at Robert. "Is the table set?"

"Yes. Sara and I did an excellent job."

I removed the fries from the boiling olive oil and drained them well on several layers of paper towels. I then placed the meat between the buns and arranged them on a platter. Lastly I took a crisp colorful nutritious salad from the fridge and placed it beside the other dishes on the table.

"TV off," Robert called out to Sara. When the noise continued he walked into the living room and repeated his instructions. Looking at him with narrowed eyes and mouth she reached over, turned the mechanism off then grudgingly followed him to the table.

The meal went fairly well regardless of Sara's attempts to sabotage the day. Johnny and Robert showed their appreciation for the meal but Sara only nibbled and complained that the hamburgers were overcooked and the fries were undercooked. "My mother never uses grease when she makes her fries. She said grease is bad for you so she always buys the frozen ones and cooks them in the oven."

I smiled. "That's correct Sara however there are good fats and bad fats. I used good fats. It is also true too much fat is not good for you but I thought that as a treat I would deep fry them because I feel that it gives them a better flavor."

"If fat is not good for you then why did you cook them in oil? Do you want us to get sick and die?" Her accusation was filled with hate.

"Sara!" Robert scolded.

I quickly interjected. "Sara, everyone has their own method of doing things and you won't always agree with them. It doesn't make the other person wrong only different."

Sara's eyes blazed with anger when she realized that she had lost in her attempt to belittle me. "You are so stupid!" In a fit of temper she pushed back her chair and stomped out of the room.

Robert stood up, threw his napkin on the table and began to follow her. When I called out to him he turned and glared at me with a face flushed with anger and with eyes filled with humiliation and rage.

Anxiously peering at him I pleaded, "Please----" The word hung in the air as he stormed into the living room. Suddenly I remembered little Johnny who had been forgotten in all of the confusion and my heart ached when I saw that the little tike was pathetically hunched over in his chair and shaking with fear. Going over to him I knelt down and placed a hand over his clenched fist.

"Sweetie I'm sorry that you had to see this. It must be very hard for you when people get upset and start yelling." Without looking up he shyly nodded his head while a large tear trickled down one of his pale cheeks. The muffled sound of raised angry voices could still be heard coming from one of the distant bedrooms.

"Come on Sweetheart let's go and sit in the living room where it's more comfortable." When I took him by his tiny hand and led him to the couch I cautiously put my arms around him after we were sitting down. At first all I could sense was his awkward discomfort but as he began to gulp out sobs he slowly tolerated my attempt to comfort him.

The disturbing yelling finally stopped and there was silence in the other room. By the time that Robert appeared in the doorway Johnny had calmed down considerably while Robert looked like a doomed man. Walking up to his son and picking him up in his arms he protectively hugged him. "I love you, soldier." Johnny desperately clung to him.

I looked at them sadly. "Robert I think that I should leave. There are two people who need you very much right now."

"I'm sorry, Christine. She really is a sweet little girl."

"I know. It's not her fault."

Robert instantly looked guilty.

At the front door I said good-bye to Johnny and told him that I thought that he was a very nice little boy and that I was very pleased that I had a chance to meet him. I told him that he had a very special daddy who loved him more than anything or anyone else in the world. Reaching up I gave Robert a soft kiss on the cheek. "Call me later."

Robert was exhausted when he spoke to me after the children were asleep. "I can't believe how deep rooted their feelings and attitudes are. What am I going to do Christine? I must have been blind not to see this coming. You warned me but I thought that you were overreacting."

"Robert, Hillary has had a long time to implant the ideas of hate. Sadly hate turns and begins to destroy its master thus becoming the master. You won't change it overnight."

"How can anyone use sweet innocent children to attain an end? They have nothing to do with what's happening between Hillary and me and at the way that we handled the divorce."

"Robert, how could you possibly have changed Hillary? She is what she is. I am the one who should step out of the picture. It seems that I'm the catalyst."

"Don't even say that Christine. Don't ever leave me. I need you to be there for me." His eyes were filled with pain and sadness. "Please don't ever leave me."

Chapter Thirty-seven

Early in the week when Crystal called and asked me to join her for lunch I gratefully and enthusiastically accepted the invitation.

"You sound as though I'm rescuing you from a fate worse than death, Chrissy."

I made a wry face. "Pretty close." The tone of my voice matched my face.

We met at our usual place. While we were enjoying the meal our conversation remained light but later while sipping on our coffee the dialogue became more serious.

"So when are you and Armand going to tie the knot? I asked.

"Oh, we like the arrangement the way it is now."

"But what if the two of you decide to have children?"

"Actually, that would be the only reason to get married because the truth is our society would force us to. I don't mind criticism as far as I'm concerned but I don't want my children to be affected by it."

"Yes, I agree with you." I reflected for a moment or two. "You know, seeing how some kids are being raised by their parents I also think that one day the government will become more involved in their upbringing. True, children belong to the biological parent but they also belong to society. I think that too many little ones are being raised by parents who never should have had them in the first place."

"I second that motion." Crystal nodded.

"You know everyone has the right to be happy and to be loved."

Crystal nodded her head in agreement. "While we are speaking of being happy, as well as being loved, what are your plans as far as Robert is concerned?"

I simply shrugged my shoulders. "I don't know Crystal, I really don't know."

"Hey. I was going to nominate the two of you for the most perfect-couple-award-of-the year. What's wrong Chrissy?"

"You know I really don't feel like talking about it here. Let's go over to my place where it's a little more comfortable."

Twenty minutes later Crystal fluffed up the pillow on her chair and wiggled into a better position. At first she slowly looked around the room then she stared over at me.

"It's been awhile."

"Yes. I guess we've both been so involved in our own worlds." Standing up I disappeared into the kitchen then returned shortly with two mugs of herbal tea.

"So what has you so upset Chrissy? You don't look like the girl that I saw before Christmas."

"I'm not!" After making myself comfortable at one end of the couch I stared at her with pursed lips and narrowed eyes. "Crystal, give me your opinion. You know that in the past the few relationships that I had lasted a fair length of time and were uncomplicated."

Agreeably she shrugged her shoulders. "Yes, I would say that from what you always told me you were fairly happy."

"Well with Robert everything's so different. Granted our love for each other is very strong," I rolled my eyes, "and the sex is fantastic. We are also socially and intellectually very compatible."

"Sounds like the ingredients of a perfect match so what's the problem?"

"His family is the problem."

"Ooh, that can be serious."

"It is!" I then filled Crystal in on the fiasco that had transpired during the weekend and of my unsuccessful attempt to endear myself to the children.

"It sounds like his wife is a real dilly."

"Why do you automatically assume that his wife is responsible?"

"Who else could it be?" She gave me a knowing look.

"Crystal she's really hateful. She has no pride or self respect what-so-ever."

"So what was Robert's reaction to his children's behavior?"

"Until then I don't think that he realized just how out of control the situation had become. He really does feel badly about it though. Actually Sara is his biggest problem but as long as she keeps returning to the same environment I don't think that her disposition or attitude will ever change. If Robert and I are to have any future together it's really imperative that there's a good relationship between his kids and me. It's a must because they are very important to him, and rightly so. The last thing that I want to happen to him is for him to lose one or both of the children," I shuddered, "especially because of me. It would break my heart as well as his."

Crystal studied me for at least five or six seconds. "You know, I believe that if it came to that you would definitely give him up."

"Love is not a destroying or consuming force Crystal."

She looked at me sadly. "Not too many people realize that Sweetie."

We talked for the remainder of the afternoon.

Later when hunger produced low rumbling sounds we went into the kitchen to the meal machine. Reading through the selection of frozen foods on the screen we both chose an entree of Chinese food. The containers dropped from their slots then were automatically ladled into the microwave section and within minutes we were removing two steaming platters of aromatic oriental cuisine.

"Grab the chop sticks from the middle drawer in the buffet for me," I requested as I began setting the table.

After the meal we carried our cups of green tea into the living room. Placing mine on the table beside me I made myself comfortable on the love-seat. At first I hesitated whether to bring up an issue that had troubled me ever since it had taken place in Banff during the New Year Holiday, but as I reflected over the situation I knew that she was the only person that I could talk to about the subject.

"Crystal? You once said that you had taken part in a sex orgy."

"That's right."

"By that, did you mean that several of you were---lying together---doing things to each other?"

She chuckled. "Yes, I guess you could describe it that way."

"Did you enjoy it?" Feeling rather uncomfortable with the memory I cringed inwardly.

There was a long silence. "Why are you asking these questions? What's bothering you?"

"I told you that I was in Banff with Robert on New Years Eve."

She nodded.

"Well, on one of the nights that I was there I had a very disturbing dream. Actually it was awful. I guess you could say that I was in an orgy. It was so real that when I woke up I had a rather violent reaction."

"Oh my goodness and Robert witnessed this reaction?"

"Phew, did he ever witness it. The poor man didn't know what to think."

"What happened in your dream Chrissy?"

The act of recalling the incident induced me to protectively wrap my arms around myself for comfort.

"I first remember being in a small room. There was no furniture and the floor was covered from wall to wall with a mattress. There were other people in the room with me, around ten or twelve of them, and we were all naked. I remember that I was very upset and that I didn't understand what was happening around me. While meshed together on the floor the others began poking and prodding and doing things that were actually stimulating but at the same time totally repugnant to me. I felt so confused and so violated." I had to pause because the recall was so traumatic.

"Eventually I did succumb to the irresistible passions that were saturating the room and I found myself on a roller coaster ride of lust and desire." I sarcastically peered sideways at her and asked for her forgiveness because of the dramatic use of words. "Finally exhausted the others fell asleep one by one."

"The man who had brought me there had his arm affectionately around me. 'Well wasn't that nice?' By that time my original feeling of fear and anger had returned so I answered with a firm, 'no'. He looked confused. 'But you enjoyed it.' He didn't seem to understand that the whole thing was not appreciated because they didn't have my consent, but then on the other hand I didn't understand him either. Suddenly a man wearing a uniform appeared in the doorway, woke everyone up and informed us that we had to leave immediately."

"Again in my dream I was very disoriented and ignorant of where I was and what was happening so I naturally panicked. "Where's the war?" I yelled. "I was really frightened."
"They all looked at me with curiosity. "What war?""

"The war, the war, where is it?" I was so exasperated at their ignorance."

"Why do you think that there was a war?" one of the men asked."

"There's a war because of the soldiers and because we all had to sleep together." It all seemed so logical to me." I looked sideways at Crystal. "I'm not proud of the lack of intelligence and intellect that I possessed at the time." The group rolled their eyes at each other but my friend patiently explained to me. "Christine there is no war."

"Of course I didn't believe him especially when the so-called soldier herded us 'en masse' from the room stating that we had to move quickly. I don't remember anything after that."

"Wow, sounds like good material for a movie."

"Yah, Nightmare on Planet X-rated." I snorted.
"Anyway, when I woke up beside Robert in a frantic frenzy

I ran to the bathroom and rushed into the shower. When Robert tried to console me I hit him with my fists."

Crystal laughed. "Remind me not to go to any orgy with you." Her demeanor then became more serious. "Sounds like a typical rape-trauma reaction to me Chrissy." We sat in silence for a few minutes.

"Crystal, how would you have felt if you had had that dream?"

"I probably would have been upset that I had to wake up."

"Really," I looked at her with curiosity. "Intellectually I can accept it but emotionally I find it very distasteful probably due to the years of indoctrination from our society." I paused. "No on second thought I think that it's the control that I object to. I could perform that way but only with people that I want to be with and with my consent. It's not the act but the method that I find odious and objectionable."

"There is one more thing Crystal." I paused as I wondered if I was pushing my luck too far. Crystal's eyes opened wider in question.

"I feel that it really happened, that it wasn't just a dream."

Crystal's expression showed no evidence of ridicule but only curiosity. "Mmmm that's a very interesting theory. Well if you really believe it then go for it and if you ever find the answer I would appreciate you sharing it with me."

"Then you don't think that I'm crazy?"

Crystal leaned forward and stared into my eyes. "Honey there is no one else in the world that I think has their head screwed on better than you do."

Feeling relieved a weight was instantaneously removed from my shoulders. "Oh Crystal thank you so much. You have no idea how much I appreciate what you've just said."

When I lay in my bed that night I realized that I had been lacking in one thing, faith in myself and belief in my convictions. Crystal stayed overnight and left shortly after we woke up in the morning.

Chapter Thirty-eight

They say that one should live each moment as though it was their last. If a person literally put that theory into practice they would be obsessed with the constant thought of their imminent demise, which would prove to be stressful and tiring. When the last moment does come it usually comes with some regrets.

* * *

After we mended our relationship Robert seemed to be more relaxed about sharing his feelings with me. Unfortunately the atmosphere in his former home wasn't as fortunate. When he had dropped the children off on the Sunday evening they had immediately retired to their bedrooms with almost no conversation with their mother. However while they were having dinner on Monday Hillary began to interrogate them. Since they were only too familiar with the terrorizing reaction that my name generated the children avoided any mention of it. Everything went well until during the conversation Johnny made a slip by inadvertently mentioning his father's girlfriend's name.

Hillary sat motionless at the head of the table, her face drained of color, her eyes flashing with disbelief, then just as quickly as the color disappeared it returned to a deep crimson shade. With fists tightly clenched she shrieked. "Did you say that bitch was there in the apartment with the two of you?"

Johnny began to shake with fear and Sara wished that she were dead or so far away that no one would ever find her.

"Answer me!" Hillary's voice became even shriller. Johnny, totally frightened, curled up in a ball and immediately began to whimper.

"Sara, tell me. Was that whore there with you?"

Sara's answer was no more than a whisper. "Yes."

Hillary went wild. With one hand she swiped the dishes in front of her off of the table sending China and crystal crashing across the room and bits of food flying everywhere. Sara bolted out of her chair and ran to Johnny where she protectively put her arms around him. By now both of the children were sobbing

"I told the two of you to leave if that bitch ever came there. Why didn't you call me?"

Sara screamed frantically. "She was only in the apartment for a few hours."

"I don't care. I told you to call me."

As quickly as it began the outburst of rage disappeared. Drained and totally defeated Hillary collapsed in her chair, subdued and exhausted she told them to go to their rooms immediately. As they frantically scampered up the stairs they could hear the wretched sobs coming from their mother in the dining room.

Barricaded behind closed doors the children's minds were tormented with feelings of fragmented loyalties and guilt. Johnny quickly succumbed to sleep but Sara lay awake for hours staring at the ceiling. The tortured wailing of her mother eventually stopped and was followed with dead silence. Sara had never felt so unloved, so alone, with so little desire to live as she did that night.

"Why did God do this to me? I guess that he doesn't love me either."

Just before the sun reappeared over the horizon she finally closed her aching eyes and slept.

As the days went by Sara became sullen and withdrawn neglecting to do her homework and losing track of the school curriculum. When she arrived home each day she went directly to her bedroom coming out only when coaxed to have dinner. At the same time Hillary also became withdrawn but for a different reason. She was over-sedating herself with tranquilizers and antidepressants. No one spoke and the only sound was soft anguished sobbing as well as the muffled din of the TV that was coming from behind closed bedroom doors. The house was like a morgue, like a time bomb ready to explode.

On Friday night all of this was unbeknown to both Robert and me as he stepped across the threshold and took me into his arms.

"Nothing, nothing has ever felt this good," he murmured in my ear.

After snuggling my face affectionately into his neck I stood back and held out my arms. "Here let me take your coat and briefcase. You look exhausted."

"Thanks. It's been a hard week." Suddenly he lifted his head and sniffed the air. "Mm, something smells good."

"I hope you like Cornish hens."

After making ourselves comfortable in the living room Robert ventilated some of his frustrations from work while I informed him of a recent problem that had just come up with one of my buildings. After dinner we moved to our previous positions where we watched the news and then a documentary. Turning the set off, I nestled comfortably into his arms. We sat for a long time saying nothing, simply enjoying each other's company.

Later in the bedroom we leisurely undressed each other embracing each delightful sight. As he removed my blouse he kissed my bare shoulders then moved his lips to my neck tasting the fragrance of my flesh. Eagerly I opened his shirt and kissed each nipple, teasing them with my fingertips. When my skirt fell casually to the floor his hands moved over my delicate lace panties feeling my warmth through the flimsy fabric that was covering my mound. When all obstructions were gone and we had moved to the bed he entered me. For a long time afterwards our contact was unbroken as our skin touched along the length of our legs like an umbilical cord.

I lay motionless staring at the ceiling. "My darling I have never loved you as much as I do tonight. I love you so much that I'm really frightened."

"Frightened? He raised his head and looked over at me. "Frightened of what Princess?"

"For the first time in my life I'm afraid that I am going to lose what I love the most in the world. I feel that uncertainty, that instability, that sacrifice that our very existence often demands from you."

Turning his body towards me he pulled me to him, holding me protectively, attempting to insulate me from whatever unfounded fears were threatening me. "Hush, don't be frightened. I will never leave you."

When we fell asleep in each other's arms my heart was overwhelmed with such an ominous prophecy of what was to come.

Chapter Thirty-nine

The following morning while Robert was transferring some documents into his computer I was filling the apartment with the mouth-watering aroma of old fashioned baking. Entering the den at noon, I walked up behind him, leaned over and seductively kissed his neck and ear.

"It's time for a break. Lunch is ready."

Stretching his arms behind him he wrapped them around me and pulled my lips down to his. "Great. I hope I get to taste whatever it is that smells so good."

"Yes. It's ground ham and pickle sandwiches on freshly baked bread and a fresh fruit salad for dessert."

After washing the meal down with a cup of coffee we decided to take a walk through the park. Bundled up in warm coats and boots we crossed the empty street and made our way along the path. As we did Robert indifferently bent over, picked up a handful of the cold, sticky snow then proceeded to roll it in a nice compact ball between his hands. While I was suspiciously eyeing his movements in my peripheral vision I also bent down and nonchalantly grabbed a handful. The tension built as we casually discussed the scenery and at the same time our devious minds were busy planning our strategies.

Suddenly the war was on. Once the first snowball was catapulted there was a continuous volley of fresh reinforced artillery. Missiles flew everywhere until the two of us were covered with the results of the battle. Exhausted and weak from our laughter and expended energy we collapsed in a heap on the ground rolling over and over until he overpowered me and had me helpless and at his mercy.

"How long has it been since you had your face washed with snow?" He was enjoying his position of dominance.

"No Robert don't you dare put that on my face." Immediately realizing that I had totally lost the upper hand I quickly changed my tactics. "Please Robert. I don't like to have my face washed with snow." My bottom lip pouted and I looked painfully upset so much so that he immediately took pity on me and released his hold. Instead he kissed me tenderly while I strategically maneuvered him onto his back.

When I was assured that his guard was down I attacked. As soon as I had released the handful of the cold snow on his unsuspecting face I jumped up and catapulted down the path as fast as I could. It took him a second or two to realize what had happened but when he did he jumped up and raced after me. Since I hate to be chased, as it always provoked a panic reaction within me, I squealed with fear as though the devil himself was after me. After only a few strides with his long legs he caught up and tackled my body causing me to fall headfirst into a snow bank.

"You are a little deceitful monkey!" This time, impervious to my plea for help, he filled his gloved hand with the cold stuff and with great satisfaction placed it royally on my imploring countenance. With our faces only inches apart he slowly kissed my eyes and cheeks then sensually removed some of the snow from my face with his mouth and tongue. Our lips crushed together.

"Would you like to go home?"

"Yes," I panted.

That evening we ate out returning to the first restaurant that we had gone to several months ago. After Mark greeted us enthusiastically he directed us to the same table that we had occupied on that magical night. With a feeling of contentment the two of us sat for several minutes soaking up the ambiance of the room. At the same time we saturated ourselves with previous memories. As I looked about me I felt as though I was glowing.

"Robert doesn't this feel strange to you? To me it feels like 'deja vu'."As I spoke my voice seemed to slow down in the middle of the sentence and my smile dissolved from my face while I continued to talk at a gelatinous pace."It's like we have gone full circle."

Unaware of the change that had come over me Robert continued to study the menu. "Yes, now that you mention it I guess it does."

My mind suddenly froze while my eyes stared straight ahead of me losing their focus on the room. Instead they turned to another scene one that had a gauze-like quality to it.

In it I was standing with Robert and holding his hand when suddenly out of nowhere his daughter, completely dressed in black and wearing a face that was painted a deadly chock-white color, appeared behind us. Robert slowly turned and painfully stared at Sara then in a leaden deliberate motion he rotated back to me. When I saw the sadness and despair that was in every pore on his face my heart ached and bled for him. At that point his daughter, with the same gelatinous-like movement, twisted her body around and ran away from us her black robe flowing behind her. For a few brief seconds Robert painfully vacillated between Sara and me then reluctantly after giving me one last tormented look released my outstretched hand and ran after his child.

The vision had taken only a few seconds but the result was plainly written on my face. Deliberately focusing on Robert my voice was clear and true.
"Robert something has happened to Sara."

Of course being naturally puzzled he shook his head in confusion.
"What are you talking about?"

I glanced at my watch. It was twenty after seven. By now my hands were shaking and clammy. I repeated myself.

"Something has happened to Sara." I desperately reached over and grabbed his forearm. "Robert, please call home. Please."

As though my very touch was distasteful to him he quickly yanked his arm away.

"This is ridiculous Christine. How could you possibly know that something has happened to Sara?"

"I know. Please believe me. I know. Call the house just to appease me. Please Robert."

While he was curiously studying me he was at the same time strangely threatened by my overwhelming fear. Feeling a little foolish he reluctantly pushed his chair back and headed for the lobby. With the memories of the dreaded vision flashing vividly through my mind I slumped back in the chair in defeat.When he reappeared in the doorway after approximately ten minutes it was obvious by the look of total incredibility on his face that the news was not good. Walking up to the table he collapsed into the chair and stared at me with bewilderment.

"How in the hell did you know Christine?"

"What happened to her Robert?"

"She took an overdose of pills. She tried to kill herself. "He shook his head in order to re-arrange his thinking processes. It was as though the reality of the situation was too difficult for him to assimilate.

"Hillary said that there were several containers of empty pills beside Sara and that she was barely conscious. My God Christine, if you hadn't said anything she wouldn't have been discovered until tomorrow morning." At the mere thought of it he put both hands up to his face and shuddered. "We hung up and I called 911. Hillary was hysterical when I called back. The ambulance had just arrived. They are taking Sara to the hospital right now. I have to go. I'm so sorry." His thoughts and conversation seemed to be confused and disjointed.

As he hurried to the door I called out, "Robert please call me later," but I wasn't sure whether he heard me or not. I sat for a long time feeling numb for there is no greater sadness than that of the spirit. Eventually I informed the waiter that the table was canceled and asked him to call me a cab. After leaving a considerable tip I rose from my chair and with a great deal of effort put on my coat. As I took each step to the waiting car gravity seemed to be working against me and when I entered my apartment I had no memory of my trip across town.

Curled up in a chair I had no problem envisioning what was transpiring at the hospital since I had previously gone through the same scenario with several of my patients. I knew of the desperate panic that was filling their hearts and the saturation of guilt and self-recrimination that was consuming them. I also understood the pleading and the bargaining to one's personal god that even an atheist succumbs to whenever he or she is confronted with a desperate situation. I remained in the chair until the phone rang. It was Robert looking rumpled and tired.

"How is Sara?"

"They're pretty sure that she'll be all right. They pumped her stomach out on time. "He looked at me as though he still could not believe what had happened. "Christine I don't know how I can ever thank you enough. If you hadn't warned me—"

"I know. I'm only glad that I could help."

"I'm going to stay here until morning. They had to sedate Hillary and she's been admitted overnight. Her sister has taken Johnny over to her house. I'm so sorry that I had to leave you at the restaurant. Was everything okay?"

"Everything was fine."

Robert sighed. "Well Christine, I think that I had better get back to Sara. I'll call you later in the week, after I get everything settled."

"Robert. Please look after yourself, and don't be concerned about me. You have enough to worry about."

"Christine?"

"Yes?"

"I love you."

"I love you too Robert." The words choked over the lump in my throat.

Chapter Forty

I didn't hear from Robert for almost a week. Between his responsibilities at work and the hours that he spent at the hospital he barely had time to eat let alone to give me a call. There was also the added pressure of treating Hillary who was also under the care of the psychiatrist and having daily sessions with him in his office.

In the mean time I kept myself busy with my buildings. I also paid frequent visits to Lara and Crystal, that is when Crystal wasn't working or with Armand. I was surprised when on the following Sunday evening security called to say that Robert was waiting in the lobby to see me. When I opened the door Robert looked so awful that it took my breath away. His clothes hung a size too big for his shrunken frame and his eyes were empty on a gaunt and pale face. We said nothing but went immediately into each other's arms. When we finally pulled away I asked if he could stay for awhile.

"Yes, but I can't stay for too long."

After settling into the living room I asked him how Sara was. He simply shrugged his shoulders and when he spoke his voice was empty. "What can I say? She'll be discharged tomorrow but she's going to need extensive therapy." He stared into my eyes with such a sad haunting look. "How have you been Christine?"

"I've been keeping busy."

We were silent. I knew that he had something to say but I was too angry, too hurt, to help him.

"I've had several conversations with Sara's psychiatrist who by the way is also Hillary's doctor. In discussing the problem I voiced a desire to have the children move in with me." He looked directly at me. "I want to apply for custody of them." He spoke as though he was reporting the weather and I responded as though he was talking about strangers. "The apartment that I have is far too small so I've been looking around for a larger one. Actually I found a place that will soon be available. I've also gone to an agency in order to hire a responsible Nanny for the children."

I said nothing.

"I'm sure that you realize that this isn't the right time for you to move in. The children are too upset....but perhaps at some future time...." During a long pause the room felt as though it was closing in on me.

Finally Robert continued. "We can still see each other for lunches but I won't be able to stay overnight, at least not for awhile.

I sat in silence feeling as though I was sitting in a time warp, an empty painful one, and I didn't have the energy to move out of it.

"Princess you haven't said anything. I have to know how you're feeling." His face was a mask of anguish and helplessness.

"Empty," I answered. The word was barely audible.

There was a space of heavy silence during which time the ticking of the clock seemed to be reverberating off of the walls. The stillness was unexpectedly broken by the sound of soft muffled sobs. Looking up I was surprised to see Robert sitting forward with both of his hands covering his face. I was so taken unaware that for a moment I didn't know what to do or what to say.

"Christine I'm so sorry." He let out a soft moan. "I'm hurting you so much but don't you see that my hands are tied? There is nothing else that I can do. Sara is my daughter and Johnny is my son. They are also hurting."

Abruptly aware of the depth of Robert's suffering and grief my pain suddenly shifted from myself. Men don't express themselves as openly as women do and this absence is often interpreted as indifference. Of course Robert was hurting. Our pleasures and happiness had been shared between the two of us and he needed and wanted me as much as I did him. Quickly walking over and sitting beside him I wrapped my arms around his body and held him tenderly. "Oh, Robert, I'm so sorry." Desperately embracing each other tears flowed with unconditional love.

We sat for a long time clinging to each moment consciously knowing that very shortly he would walk through the door and perhaps out of my life. The hour was late when we moved to the front foyer. At the elevator we embraced each other hoping to supersaturate ourselves with an overabundance of devotion that would nurture us for the remainder of our days.

"I'll call you. We'll keep in touch. Perhaps we could have lunch sometime later this week."

With one last kiss he forced himself away and the door closed. I waited and listened to the sound of the elevator descending then unable to take a step or to even support my body I slowly sunk to the floor. When the tears finally stopped I somehow found my way to my bedroom. Curling up into a fetal position I cried myself to sleep.

Over the next few weeks we kept in contact with each other either over lunch or else during a coffee break; that is whenever his schedule permitted us to. At first we said our goodbyes at the cars but soon found the process to be too painful. Slowly, ever so slowly like a lingering death a unique part of our relationship was slipping away.

At one point I was tempted to use anything to keep him with me. I knew that by using his weakness, his need and love for me, I could persuade him to forfeit his children and remain with me. I knew that if I really wanted to I could convince him to stay. One day when the temptation was great and I was feeling weak, a time when I was actually going to put it into action a voice spoke to me. Not a physical voice but more a mental utterance. The message was clear. "If you take him away he will lose his children." The meaning burned deeply into my soul and my spirit gave an agonizing cry of pain. There would never be any way that I could bring him such grief. I also knew that if I took the easy way out and convinced him to come to me the quality of the love that we felt for each other would slowly be destroyed. My decision was absolute. One cannot build ones happiness on someone else's sorrow.

I felt as though I was dead even though my body kept on functioning. Every morning I forced myself out of bed then went through the repetitious motion of hygienic care. With considerable effort I would throw on a pair of jeans and a sweater no longer caring how I looked. After buying a newspaper I drove to the coffee shop where I absentmindedly made an attempt to read. Finding it difficult to concentrate on world affairs when my own world felt as though it had been destroyed, I simply stared out through the window. Although I spent more time at my three apartment complexes I accomplished less. Afterwards exhausted I would flee to the refuge of my home where I would sit for hours staring into space. Catnaps were frequent but long periods of sleep had totally disappeared.

Visits with Robert became further and further apart while I spent more and more time with Lara. It was during the third week of March that Lara reminded me that the preliminary hearing was scheduled on the following Friday. The news sent a wave of nausea through me pushing me into deeper feelings of depression. I looked painfully at Lara.

"I hope you don't mind if I don't go with you."

"Oh Sweetie I didn't expect that you would."

My mind wandered to the day in the park when Robert had patiently explained the legal system. I remembered later lying in his strong gentle arms and feeling his warm lips on mine. Suddenly I was aware of Lara's curious gaze. I smiled weakly.

"I was just thinking of Robert. We had our problems but there were also so many good moments." Looking helpless I began to cry. "What am I going to do Lara? I can't get him out of my mind. I can't seem to function as a normal person. Sometimes I wonder if I even want to live."

"I think that you are acting like a normal person Chrissy." She gazed at me for a few moments. "Why don't you get away from here for awhile? Right now this city is filled with memories and they're hurting you so much. Larry will take care of your buildings for you and I can keep a check on your apartment."

I shook my head in despair. "I'm going to have to do something because I can't keep going on like this. I'll think about it."

Later that day I sat alone in the park. I often returned to the same bench, a place that had become almost a haven for me even though it generated a bittersweet reaction. Today I thought about what Lara had suggested. Where could I go and even more concerning whom could I go with? In this day and age everyone was so busy with his or her own personal life.

No matter how hard I tried to resist my thoughts kept turning back to Robert. Sitting on our bench I spent the next half-hour visualizing a holiday with him, a vacation that I had anticipated since the first day that we met. As I looked about me the scenery seemed to have been transformed from the three dimensional beauty that it always was when I was with Robert into a flat plane. Everything seemed to have lost its allure. With an effort I got up and headed back to my apartment.

That night, feeling exhausted, I retired to my bedroom and to my large empty bed. When I climbed between the cold sheets I wondered if I would ever be happy again.

Chapter Forty-one

With the most important person in my life gone I felt empty void of any positive emotion. Each night I prayed that I could cut the cord that was binding me to this frivolous existence with all of its illusions so that I could soar away to a painless dimension. However I knew that my reality was here and must be faced.

The next day I contacted Crystal and we made plans to meet for lunch. The moment that she saw me walking into the restaurant she was shocked and speechless over my deteriorated appearance. As well any movement that I made was slow and without enthusiasm, or passion. I waited until after the meal before I made my request.

"I have a big favor to ask you, Crystal."

"What is it, Chrissy?"

"My breakup with Robert has had a devastating effect on me." I gave a dry laugh. "But then I guess that it is quite obvious. I'm sorry to be such bad company."

"Hon don't even think that way."

"Anyway Lara suggested that I take a trip somewhere but I don't want to go alone." Desperately I glanced over to my friend. "I was wondering if you could possibly come with me."

First Crystal smiled then she began to chuckle. Feeling wounded I glared at her from across the table.

"Why are you laughing? Did I say something funny?"

"No Chrissy, it's just such a coincidence. Armand and I have already planned on taking a trip in April. We haven't decided where we're going yet but if you want to come along with us you're certainly welcome, that is if you don't mind having some extra company."

"But wouldn't Armand mind me tagging along?"

"Of course not in fact I think that he would really enjoy it. He really likes you, Chrissy."

"Oh Crystal you don't know how much I appreciate this. Like you said what a coincidence."

My mood took an abrupt turn for the better. Eagerly we began tossing around preferences for the trip. Feeling a little awkward we decided to get together with Armand so that he could have an equal input into the plans. When we said our good-byes I once again felt that I had a future.

The last Friday of the month was the date of the preliminary hearings. By manipulating some shifts with his colleges Bill managed to get the day off. Since Becky's doctor wanted her rested but also alert for the hearing he prescribed a minimal dose of an anti-anxiety medication the night before. That morning as Lara and her family prepared to leave for the courthouse the anxiety level in the Johnson home was critical. Finally the hour came for their departure. They collectively hugged each other at the door while making reassuring utterances then they headed out to the car.

Later that day I called Lara after dinner. She sounded exhausted and indicated that she would prefer to discuss the events after a good nights sleep.

"Why don't you come over for lunch tomorrow?"

"Are you sure?"

"I'm sure."

I arrived just before noon to an unusually quiet house. Becky was nowhere to be seen and Bill, of course, was at the hospital. I sat with Lara and Tom in the large living room while the maid was busy preparing their lunch in the kitchen.

"Becky has had a setback." Lara once more looked drained. "She's required further sedation and is resting up in her room."

Tom reached over and took his wife's hand. "Christine I don't think that we are ready to talk about it just now."

I slowly nodded my head.

Suddenly Lara thought of something. "You will probably be interested to know that Robert wasn't in the court room. He had one of his associates go instead."

For a brief moment my eyes opened wide with hope.

"Mr. Crawford, our lawyer, explained that it wasn't an unusual procedure. Robert will still be there for the court case."

Once again my shoulders drooped in defeat. We sat in silence each with our own private thoughts. While we ate our lunch conversation was minimal and afterwards at the front door we warmly hugged each other. When I left I brought some of the sadness home with me.

Crystal and Armand met at my apartment one evening so that we could put our ideas together for the trip. Unanimously we decided that we would drive to Jasper then head over the mountains by way of the Coquihalla Trail to Vancouver. From there we would take the ferry to Vancouver Island, stay for a few nights and then take a second ferry to Seattle. We would probably remain in Seattle for two or three days before heading back up north.

The day before our departure for the mountains I decided to take a drive to break in my new car. I had attended the short compulsory driving course in order to acquaint myself with the new technology however I still felt a little uncomfortable with the changes and innovations that had been made in the design and operation of the vehicle. The seats were now slanted back slightly so that one was in a semi-prone position with their feet extended out in front of them. Although there was an illusion that one was looking directly in front in actuality they were looking at a reflected image. The government was finding that there were fewer head injuries using this design. Most of the functions were computerized and the panel and the screen were easily accessible.

No longer were seat belts optional. One was assessed for size and height then automatically wrapped with a protection. Even though there were radar detectors built into the system in order to avoid collisions, some of the main highways were converting to the hookup system. With this technology the government was finding that there was a reduction in stress as well as an elimination of traffic accidents that were becoming more and more devastating due to the complexity of the transportation picture. There was also a marked increase in the mass transit systems.

Flitters, a vehicle that had the capacity of taking off in a perpendicular direction were also now available. Realizing that it was still in its infancy stage, as well as being very expensive, I opted to remain on terra firma--- mostly due to my fear of heights. I didn't really trust the system anyway.

Somehow I found myself on Robert's street, perhaps with only a partial conscious intention of being there. Pulling over within a short viewing distance of his building I turned off the lights then sat in silence. A solitary window was casting its light into the dark night, and from the memories of his apartment I knew that it was coming from his den. The feeling of his nearness sent waves of pain through me but at the same time it provided me with a peaceful comfort.

"Oh, Robert I miss you so much." Suddenly in my mind I could see him clearly as though I was in the room with him. He was sitting at his desk with his hands dangling in mid air over the keyboard while on his face there was a shocked painful expression.

"Christine!" His voice was barely a whisper.

We sat each in our own space, each feeling the intense nearness of the other, each sensing our undying love.

"Christine, I love you." Robert had never experienced such a bizarre happening nor felt such a depth of the emotion.

Sensing his words as though he was gently whispering them into my ear I let out a long sigh. "I love you too my darling."

The impression lasted for perhaps a minute then it slowly faded and disappeared leaving me once more in the cold world. With moist eyes Robert returned to his work while I put my car in gear and slowly drove home.

Chapter Forty-two

The next two weeks were filled with sun and above seasonable temperatures. While we were cruising north along the highway towards Jasper the three of us belted out, in a rather discordant harmony, to the music that was blaring through the speakers. Because of Crystal and Armand's infectious attitude I was enjoying myself for the first time since the breakup. When we reached Jasper we decided to stop at one of the restaurants. We were escorted to a table with a picturesque view of a colorful garden as well as a shallow brook that wound its way under a quaint wooden bridge. After washing the meal down with two cups of coffee we were once more on the main road.

With the sun shining brightly in a cloudless sky, and Mozart's sonatas caressing us with his melodic melodies, we sailed along the Coquihalla Trail with its breathtaking view. Each time that I was reminded of the painful loneliness of the composer's life I was filled with such sadness. To be a genius, to be unique, but to have no one to share your dreams with must have been devastating. It was enough to send one into madness. No wonder he appeared odd to others. What a terrible joke to play on someone.

As I gazed at the seemingly endless mountain range and looked up into the infinite universe I said.

"I think that I'm in heaven."

"Well we're closer to it." Armand chuckled with his sense of humor.

The first night we found a reasonable motel in Kamloops where we rented two rooms. The next day when we reached Vancouver we weren't as lucky due to a major convention that was in the city. The desk clerk discreetly eyed us up and down then obtained a cancellation in another hotel via his computerized system.

"I must warn you that the room will be very expensive."

Without hesitation all three of us eagerly responded in unison. "We'll take it." In fact we were lucky enough to get it for two nights.

When we entered the room we were delightfully surprised by the spaciousness of the accommodation. It had two generous king sized beds, a large sitting room area, and a bathroom containing a shower stall and a four person Jacuzzi. Moving outside onto the balcony we were thrilled by the excellent view of the magnificent ocean. Leaning on the rail we saturated our senses with the spectacular panoramic scene while the refreshing breeze cooled our hot bodies. Once we were back in the room Crystal sat on one of the beds testing its resiliency then stretching back into a supine position she spread her arms out at her sides.

"Isn't this fantastic? The beds are so big we could have an orgy in them."

For a split second I felt a fleeting sensation of panic.

After we unpacked we went down to the main floor where the lobby was jammed with people, many of them displaying name-tags that indicated their connection with a convention. There were lineups at both the coffee shop and the dining room resulting in a twenty-minute wait for a table and another twenty-minute for our meal. Since it was as noisy as it was busy it felt so soothing when we stepped out onto the relatively quiet sidewalk.

After strolling through the city for several hours we discovered a quaint restaurant that overlooked the water.

Enjoying the catch of the day, while sitting on the open patio, we were serenaded by the rhythmic sound of endless waves as they lapped up on the shore. One could smell the water and barely feel its mist on our faces. That evening we did some bar hopping then exhausted, but relaxed, we returned to our room. Armand had some difficulty in getting the card into the slot correctly however after a few tries we heard the familiar click.

The night remained hot and humid. When I came out of the bathroom I found Armand and Crystal completely nude and relaxing on the couch. My first reaction was surprise but oddly no feelings of embarrassment. Crystal stretched her body and arms out and casually ran her hands through her thick blond hair while tiny damp curls framed her unusually beautiful face. She reminded me of perfection, of a piece of art, a picture that should be hanging in one of the museums.

"For heaven's sake Chrissy you look so uncomfortable. Just looking at you makes me feel so hot."

Since it is the nature of the beast to conform I obediently shed my light cotton dress and bra but kept my panties on.

Crystal threw each arm out over the cushions of the couch and let her head fall backwards. "It's so nice to know that I don't have to work tomorrow."

"Work, what is that?" asked Armand with his slight French accent.

We sat sipping on our drinks in silence long enough for Robert to squeeze into my thoughts. Feeling maudlin a tear trickled down my cheek.

"What's the matter, Chrissy?" Crystal asked. "Are you thinking of Robert?"

I nodded my head in frustration. "Why can't I get him out of my mind?" I quickly sniffed through my nose while my bottom lip protruded and quivered into a pout. "I think that I'm going to become an old maid."

Armand glanced over sideways and scanned me up and down in a quick appraisal.
"I would bet my money that you won't become an old maid. You are a very lovely and desirable woman Christine. Some lucky man out there is waiting just for you." His expression turned to one of sympathy and understanding. "Give it time Chrissy."

I sighed deeply. "Love can be so beautiful when one is preoccupied with it but if it's taken away it becomes so painful."

Crystal stared at me as though she was giving it some thought then leaning forward in her chair she said. "Maybe if you think about it, and you are really being honest with yourself, perhaps it just wasn't meant to be."

As I allowed the negatives of my relationship with Roberts to flood into my mind I looked over at her with sad puppy dog eyes. The first thing that came into my thoughts was his lack of acceptance in regard to my strange dreams. The loss of that support was a very important issue to me and I knew that it would undoubtedly give rise to some serious problems in the future. It was a very painful loss. Also the problems with Hillary and his children seemed insurmountable. I quickly chugged down the rest of my drink and asked for a second one.
"You know, Lara and Tom didn't like him very much, especially Tom, at least not for me.

Crystal nodded her head. "Sometimes it's wise to have an outside opinion. Only time will tell if you did the right thing but I have a pretty good idea that you did. You are a very smart lady and I've never seen you make a wrong decision yet."

After we finished our last drink Crystal and Armand excused themselves then climbed dog-tired into their bed. Feeling dejected and a little tipsy I awkwardly slipped between my own sheets. With alcohol as a catalyst tears began to flow and soft choking sounds escaped from my throat. Suddenly feeling someone pulling the blankets off of me I looked up and saw Crystal standing beside my bed with her hand stretched out towards me.

"Come on Chrissy. You're going to sleep with us tonight."

Now since any moral judgment had been softened by the alcohol, and inhibitions had become nonexistent, I allowed myself to be led to their bed. Armand moved over and I was directed to lie down then Crystal climbed in on the other side. There I received the hugs that I so desperately needed and within seconds we were all breathing heavily in sleep.

Waking late in the morning it took a few seconds for me to orient myself and when I did I realized that an alien arm was resting across my chest. Lifting my head slightly I was relieved when I saw that the arm belonged to Crystal. Elevating my head slightly higher I saw Armand stretched out on the other bed. I remained on my back for a moment then gently lifting Crystal's arm I cautiously slipped out and grabbed some fresh clothing on the way to the bathroom.

After shoving my hair into a shower cap I stepped into the stall and programmed the several shower heads to full power. Finally turning off the flow and completing the drying process I stepped out and finished my morning care by carefully applying a light covering of makeup on my face. Pulling my long hair back into a ponytail I secured it with a colorful scarf then I quickly put on my skirt and blouse. They were still sleeping when I re-entered the bedroom. Slipping into my sandals I reached over for the pad of paper that was on the desk, wrote a brief note then quietly closed the door.

When I stepped through the threshold of the coffee shop I immediately noticed the degree of static energy that saturated the room. Making my way to a table on the far side my eyes locked with several people all who appeared to be wearing the same odd sympathetic expression. After the waitress filled my cup with a deep savory liquid I picked it up and used it as a so-called protection while I inquisitively scanned the room. The heavy bombardment of energy that persisted was puzzling.

"The restaurant is quite busy, don't you think?" Startled I glanced at an elderly gentleman who was sitting at the next table and when I looked closer I noticed that he had a peculiar knowing and compassionate smile.

"Most of the people here are with the convention that I am attending. Actually we just arrived this morning." His smile widened. "We belong to a Psychic Society."

I inhaled deeply and nodded my head. "Ah, that explains everything."

The gentleman's eyes twinkled. "It must have been very confusing for you."

Now there is one advantage of having psychic abilities. First of all one is sensitive enough to automatically recognize the capability in others. Secondly, with the so-called sensitivities there are no secrets. The more developed the gift is the deeper that one can see into another's soul and into his or her most intimate moments and personal thoughts. However there is no judgment, no condemnation since everything is natural and nothing is wrong. Each person is in one's own individual space and every experience that they have has its purpose. Without that involvement there is no advancement. Sometimes the person who appears to be at the short end of an ordeal is actually the benefactor of the happening. Sometimes the observer is aware of it, sometimes not. Sometimes the receiver is aware of it, sometimes not.

We exchanged first names and chatted until it was time for the group in the room to leave. Standing up and extending his hand there was an exchange of positive energy when our skin touched. The man stared deeply into my eyes pushing away the layers of superficial thought.

"I just want you to know that I am very proud to have known you." As he said it his eyes narrowed and the corners of his mouth turned up slightly as though there was a hidden message.

As I stared into two knowledgeable eyes I somehow knew that someday I would realize the full implication of his statement. After he left I gazed out through the window looking at the fathomless ocean and the endless skies.

Chapter Forty-three

That evening we took in a stage production in one of the theaters and later when we returned to the room Armand quickly found a favorable position on the couch. Crystal moved over to him, carefully raised his head and positioned it on her lap. As she began running her fingers through his hair I curled up comfortably in the plush chair that I was in.

"How's Becky Christine?"

"She was doing well until the preliminary hearings. I guess that when they questioned her about the details of the rape the pressures were so great that it created a setback."

"That's too bad," she said sadly.

"Robert wasn't there. He sent one of his colleagues."

Armand looked from Crystal to me then back to Crystal. "I think that I'm missing something here."

"I didn't tell him." Crystal's comment was directed towards me.

When I began to explain the incident and to describe the details Armand was unusually quiet, while at the same time Crystal appeared to be studying him through the entire narration. When I finished there was an awkward silence so that it was now my turn to feel in the dark.

Before I could ask any question Armand bluntly explained. "I was once raped."

My mouth dropped open in shocked disbelief. "I---I never think of a man as being raped. Was---was it done by a man or a woman?"

"It was done by a woman."

When I tried to visualize how a woman could overpower a man sufficiently to rape him I felt really confused. I naturally assumed that he would have to be tied down although I couldn't bring myself to ask the question. Armand looked straight ahead and his eyes had a faraway look in them as though he was reliving the incident.

"Several years ago I had also been at a party and like your friend I had remained behind to talk to the hostess, a woman that I had known for a few years. She was taller and stronger than I was but in no way did I anticipate what would happen. Before I knew it she had me pinned down on the couch, undid my zipper and began fondling me. I warned her emphatically. "I do not want to do this." Even though I had become very upset she ignored my reaction. Instead she simply answered me with those three dangerous words. Well I do."

When I looked at Armand's face I saw not only embarrassment but also humiliation.

"Of course being a man I could not help that I had an erection---so she mounted me and we had intercourse." At this point Armand was beginning to look a little pale.

"You know men fantasize and have great expectations about something like that happening to them but believe me it's not as attractive as it seems to be. Ever since that day whenever I think of it I feel ill. It is not a pleasant memory." He looked directly at me. "I can sympathize and empathize with women who have been raped because it is a very traumatic experience."

"I'm very sorry, Armand. I guess that I never gave much thought to the fact that a man could be as sensitive as women are in that area. I guess I always thought that a man was always a ready and willing partner and that women were not aggressive."

"Christine, it is not the sexual aspect that is destructive it is the total loss of control that is devastating. Under different circumstances I would have been a willing partner."

I sat thinking over what he had just said and compared it with Becky's situation and with my dreams.

"You know Armand I think that women experience an added loss."

"What do you mean Christine?" He looked at me quizzically.

"From day one women and men are orientated to the social-sexual world in a different way. Often men are not selective and society does not expect them to be." I looked at each of them. "You understand that I'm speaking generally and the rules do not apply to everyone because there are always the exceptions." I repositioned myself on the chair. "Where they put their penis is not judged by society in fact they are often applauded for their actions by their peers. With a woman the rules are entirely different. They must be selective where they place their vagina since the world is waiting and judging her every move. Also women and young girls are taught by the church that the vagina is almost a holy place. They're warned that it's imperative that it be guarded and cherished at all times so that there's more of a loss than just personal control when someone enters the so-called 'hallowed grounds'. In Becky's case something very precious was taken away from her, the hymen." I gave a dry laugh. "It's too bad that men don't have them although I think I remember someone saying that they do."

Crystal and Armand smiled slightly as they nodded their heads in agreement.

"The bottom line is that we are a product of our society. What has been taught to us and ingrained within our nature results in a natural response."

I directed my next comment to Crystal.

"Crystal, you have a non-conforming and emancipated attitude towards sex. What would your reaction be towards a rape?"

"She chuckled as she said, "I certainly don't think of my vagina as being a holy ground. I think that I would mostly feel that my power of control had been taken away from me therefore it's probably more similar to a man's view."

We sat in silence for a long time, each with our own thoughts.

I sighed. "What a sad world this is."

Armand stretched his arms over his head and looked lovingly at Crystal. "I think that I would like to pack it in."

That night lying on my side and staring at the wall I listened to Crystal and Armand as they made love in the next bed. I had never wanted someone to hold me in his arms as badly as I did that night.

The remainder of the trip was enjoyable. On the ferry to the island we walked around the deck feeling the cool salt air on our faces. Later while sitting on the chairs with the sun warming our skin we were lulled by the constant motion of the ocean water. As we approached the city of Victoria with its New England architectural motif the view was charming as always. Here on the Island the temperatures were more constant throughout the year and it was a place that seldom saw snow. Flowers bloomed everywhere and large trees cast their shade onto well-groomed lawns. Frequently the clip clop of horse's hooves could be heard on the pavement as the animals, straining at their harnesses, pulled sightseers along the streets and through the scenic park.

We stayed in Victoria overnight then spent four days exploring the island. "It's no wonder people want to retire here. It's so beautiful, so peaceful," I said wistfully.

The ferry ride from the island to Seattle was a longer one lasting for three hours. In the gambling casino the slot machines gobbled up money as fast as the people could put it in and gave back just enough to feed their expectation. The dining lounge was huge and the entertainment consisted of a live musical group.

While relaxing after the meal the music was slow pulling at my heartstrings creating disturbing questions in my mind. What was he doing at this moment? Did he still miss me? How were his children? At the next thought my breath caught in my throat. Had he found someone new? Suddenly I felt their eyes searching me. I looked from Crystal to Armand.

"Sorry about that.

Armand reached over and gently placed his hand over mine. "Mon Cherie, don't ever apologize for loving someone."

Within a couple of miles from Seattle the waters became dotted with large military ships. While leaning on the rails on the upper deck I was filled with the alarming sensation of military power and of the consciousness of war and devastation.

"What terrible things we do to each other." Armand's voice was filled with sadness.

We enjoyed the city for two days consuming as much of the freshly caught fish of the day as we could. With the steep grade of the hills from the ocean still unnerving me, I could swear that the car was going to lose its traction on the road and we would topple end-over-end all the way down into the water. After a few days we packed our suitcases, placed them into the car, and headed north. Re-entering Canada the terrain in the Okanagan Valley became relatively flat with rolling hills and farmland but soon we were once again on mountainous terrain.

As I mentioned before my phobia was heights. Up to now I had felt quite safe on the mountain's highways due to the fact that the roads were sufficiently wide and were protected along the edge with intermittent barriers. Not so while traversing through Rogers Pass. The road was cut out of the side of the mountain, two lanes only, and periodically signs of, 'watch for falling rocks', and, 'exit for failing breaks', were displayed. With the cracks on the asphalt running the length of the highway, rather than across it, the explanation was that the pavement was moving towards the edge of the cliff. At one point a huge piece of the road had fallen away plummeting down hundreds of feet to the green forest below. Repairs were now being done and traffic was being directed around the construction site. I always wondered if the piece of asphalt had claimed some victims.

When we stopped at one of the lookout stations Armand and Crystal stepped over the low security fence that brandished a sign, 'do not go beyond this point', and taking the few more steps stood at the edge of the precipice. I almost had a fit.

"If you guys don't step back I'm driving away and leaving the two of you here." I was pacing back and forth with an uncontrollable fear. "Don't you know that the ground could give way under you?"

To appease me they moved back to the safe area.

The last few days of our trip was spent in Banff where we rented a chalet that boasted a hot tub and a fireplace. During the trip the three of us had become much closer, a bond that would last for the rest of our lives.

"What do you think you'll do once we get back to the city?" Crystal asked.

Sitting in one of the chairs that was situated in front of a crackling fire with my legs curled comfortably under me I gazed into the flames and sighed.

"You know all good things come to an end and when it does we once again have to face reality. Just the thought of being back home fills me with feelings of loss and loneliness. I know that I have to work through the problem and that I can't run away from it but I still wish that there was something else that I could focus my energies on." I looked over in their direction. "My real estate isn't enough."

Armand looked at me with curiosity. "Do you think that you and Robert will one day recover what you once had? His children might change their attitudes. If not they will eventually grow up and move away from their house in order to make a life of their own."

"No Armand. Too much has been lost. Besides I have no intention of putting my life on hold for him or for anyone. Even if we eventually did rekindle our relationship his children would never really accept me due to the many painful memories that they are carrying. If I really do love Robert I have to let him go so that he can find a more acceptable path." I shook my head. "I will not delude myself with impossible fantasies."

Later after we filled the hot tub we carried our drinks and placed them on the ledges while we sank into the hot steamy waters. Armand put his arm around Crystal's shoulder and looked fondly from her to me.

"I think that right now I am the luckiest man in the world."

Raising our eyebrows we looked at him.

"I have the pleasure of being with the two most beautiful women that God has ever created. Not only are they so pleasing to the eye but they also have the most beautiful hearts."

Embarrassed, we playfully splashed water on him.

"I think it's the booze that's talking."

"The poor gentleman is hallucinating."

"We are really old hags in disguise, demons of the devil."

Soon water was flying everywhere.

Before retiring to our own bedrooms, Armand and Crystal hugged me. With much hesitation Armand said. "You know Christine I wish that we could all make love together."

My eyes opened a little wider in fear.

"No, no, do not misunderstand me. It is because we love you so much. I know that you don't feel that way so please don't think of it as an insult."

"I don't Armand. It's just that I'm not ready for that."

"We know. Please always know that we love you."

That night I stared up through the sky light at the millions of stars in the universe and silently whispered to myself. "I have so far to go." Suddenly my future seemed to spread out before me and I could clearly see what lay ahead. With a deep sigh I repeated myself. "I have so far to go."

Chapter Forty-four

The moment I stepped into my apartment I was overwhelmed with a sudden rush of old familiarities. By running away I hadn't changed anything but had just put everything on hold. There were several messages on my answering machine, most of them from Robert. For the first week he had tried several times each day but for the second week, as though resigned that there would be no response, there were fewer attempts. Since it was late in the evening I decided to call him the following morning.

Around nine o'clock I programmed a selection of classical music on the system then curled up in my favorite chair with a book. Finding it difficult to concentrate on the story line I reluctantly went to my bedroom where I climbed between the cold hard sheets and was soon fast asleep.

When I called Robert the next day he was in court so I left a message with his secretary. Having better luck with Lara she greeted me with enthusiasm and asked me over for dinner. While we were relaxing before the meal in their living room I gave the family a full detailed report of the trip excluding, of course, the nudity and sexual episodes. Later when I returned home I listened to a message from Robert requesting that I call him at his office immediately after I got in. Before I did I had to steel myself against any reaction that I might have at the sound of his voice, or at the sight of his face on the screen.

The moment he heard and saw mine he blurted out. "Christine, where have you been? I tried calling you every day."

"I took a trip through the mountains and to the Island with Crystal and Armand. I'm sorry I should have called you but you've been so busy with your work lately that I, well, anyway, I'm really sorry."

"Sweetheart I was so worried. I thought that perhaps you had left town for good. Please promise me that you won't do that to me again."

After promising, without much enthusiasm, we simply stared at each other for several seconds.

"I still love you, Christine." The pain was obvious in his eyes. "Perhaps we could have lunch one day this week."

Since I didn't want to fan the flames anymore than I had to I hesitated for a second before agreeing. "That would be nice."

"My appointment book is solid but I will clear some time. On second thought perhaps we could have dinner. Maybe we could go to our special place."

"Robert!"

When he searched my face my expression told him not to go in that direction. "I know. It's not practical or realistic."

"No it isn't."

"But it's all right if I call you one day for lunch?"

"Yes." At the precise moment that we disconnected the room appropriately darkened as a cloud passed over the sun. In my mind I had already formulated a plan that would ultimately severe my ties with Robert forever.

Due to the fact that the noon rush was over there was only a quiet murmuring of conversation when I entered into the room. When I approached him we didn't dare touch, or hug each other, however after sitting down Robert's hand slowly moved across the table and covered mine.

"I missed you so much Princess."

I smiled at the familiar use of my name and his hand felt so warm, so large and so comforting. "I missed you too Robert." As I searched his eyes I recognized the pain that he was feeling. "How are the children?"

"They are much better. Sara is still in therapy." He looked down at his cup. "We also have Johnny seeing the psychiatrist. I guess that we really made a mess of everything."

I winced.

His eyes shot up. "I mean Hillary and me."

"Sweetheart in hindsight everything always looks so much clearer."

There was another long moment of silence.

"So Christine, tell me about your trip. Did you have a nice time?"

"Yes it was very enjoyable." As I began giving him a brief outline all of the old familiarities came flooding through as though time itself had bent backward. Unfortunately the sensation was not to last. Feeling ill to my stomach I attempted to brace myself for what I was about to say.

"Robert there is something that I have to tell you." My eyes were cold and empty, my voice was blunt and to the point as I stared across the table. "I'm going to move away for awhile."

The painful shock was clearly visible on Robert's face while at the same time his eyes desperately tried to read mine in order to find some kind of explanation for the insanity.

"My father and mother left me a cottage in the Muskoka Lakes area in Ontario. It's just north of Toronto. Actually when my parents were living we used to go there every summer. Up to now my uncle has been living in it and as a favor to me he has been looking after the grounds as well as the building. While I'm away Larry will take care of my properties and Crystal and Armand will live in my condo."

Robert looked as though his very being had sunk into a deep, tortuous, bottomless, hole, and when he spoke the voice didn't sound like his. "How long will you be gone?"

"I'm not sure. My decision will be made one day at a time."

For a few long moments we sat in silence. It's strange how the world around us has a chameleon-like effect by changing to match the events of ones life. There was no longer that dimensional depth, those vivid colors, or the aura of well being that at one time had exuded from every detail around me. Instead the world had become dull, flat and indifferent. Robert wanted to beg me to stay however his love for me prevented him from doing so. I could see that his next words were difficult for him to say.

"It sounds like a good idea," he gave a valiant smile, "and I do envy you. I wish that I could spend a lazy summer lying on a lawn chair beside a cool lake."

Realizing that we were both putting up a valiant front I felt miserable.

"When will you be leaving?" He dreaded my answer.

"Probably I'll leave as soon as I can, possibly within the next month."

"You will be leaving that soon!"

Just then the waitress came with our meal. We nibbled on the food but since we both found it difficult to swallow we left most of it untouched on our plates. Finally pushing our chairs back we began walking to the parking lot and to my car.

"Will I see you before you leave Christine?"

"I don't know Robert. It's so painful."

"I know."

Suddenly we were in each other's arms, clinging desperately, crushing ourselves together. His familiar smell was intoxicating and the feeling of the contours of his body was overpowering. As our tears flowed he whispered in my ear. "I will always love you Princess."

"I will always love you too. Oh Robert I love you so much. Life is not fair." I turned my face towards his and with painful tenderness our lips met in a long, farewell kiss. Breaking away I opened my car door and quickly climbed in behind the wheel. Without looking back I pressed on the accelerator and drove out of the lot while he stood where I had left him watching a part of himself disappear out of sight.

I spent the next two weeks packing my personal belongings and spending as much time as I could with my friends but on the last evening in the city I preferred to be alone. My bags were packed waiting at the doorway while the other items had been sent on ahead.

It was a beautiful evening. Because the days were longer and the park was well lit I decided to take a walk along its path. As I did the memories were overwhelming and the nostalgia powerful. Every young blade of grass, every new leaf seemed to remind me of my love for Robert. When I came to the familiar bench I sat down and began recalling the times that we had spent on it together. The air was heavy with his presence but strangely I felt too sad to cry. Finally with one last look I said good bye to my past and slowly walked back to the condo.

Crystal and Armand were announced by the security system early the next morning. I was all wound up at the prospect of driving alone for over 1500 kilometers, or in other words 2,000 miles, while Crystal and Armand were excited at the thought of living in such opulence for awhile.

"Are you sure that you won't accept some rent Christine?"

"No, just pay the condo fees and water the plants. Actually you guys are doing me a favor."

When it was time to leave I promised to call them each week. "Who knows perhaps one day I will come back."

Leaving a precious part of me behind tears filled my eyes as I drove out of the city. Suddenly there was a distinct jolt to both my body and my mind as though a physical wall had formed behind me. Startled I looked ahead and with optimism realized that it was not just the sun that was shining brightly in the East.

BOOK TWO

Chapter One

As I turned off the main highway I decreased the speed of my car in order to negotiate the two-lane road that twisted through the countryside. Due to my nervous anticipation of what lay ahead, the closer I got to the cottage the tighter my hands clutched at the wheel. Sadly I longed for the comfort and security of things that were familiar to me: my favorite chair, my comfortable bed. Not only was I anxious at the prospect of starting a brand new life, I also had qualms over renewing the brief relationship with my father's younger brother, an uncle that I hadn't seen since my parent's funeral fourteen years ago. After their burial I had made arrangements with my uncle that he continued to live in the cottage in Ontario and in exchange he would maintain the grounds and the building for me. I chose not to return to the area for two reasons. One because of my education and two because it held too many memories of time spent with my mother and father.

The moment I rounded the bend in the road and saw the familiar mailbox with the shingle containing the words 'The Anderson's' hanging above it, I quickly inhaled and a lump formed in my throat. Each letter was neatly burnt into the piece of oak wood. After driving halfway around the circular driveway I parked at the back door, turned off the motor, then sat for a few moments in complete stillness while attempting to reinforce my memories of the place I had loved for so many years.

The sun was low in the sky and the building cast shadows over the entire back yard giving the illusion of coolness therefore it took me by surprise when an unsuspected wall of stifling heat assaulted me the moment I stepped out of the car. Feeling cramped from the long day of driving I stretched my arms and therapeutically arched my back before walking up to the door. When I knocked no one answered, and when I attempted to turn the knob I discovered that it was locked.

Leaving my luggage in the car I walked around the outside of the building to the front yard where I made my way down the stone path that led to the lake. Immediately I was impressed at how immaculately my uncle had kept up the grounds. Neatly trimmed grass stretched from the cottage down to the shore and fully grown ash and maples trees, that I remembered being planted when I was a child, were growing randomly over the two acres of land. Reaching the shoreline I called out, waited for a moment, then turned to the right and advanced to the boathouse. When I tried the main door it opened easily and when I glanced inside I discovered that the cabin cruiser was safely in its stall. Feeling puzzled I climbed the stairs on the proximal side of the building, opened the door to the change room and steam bath, and peaked in. Both were empty. Suddenly I became concerned that there had been a mix up in the date as well as the approximate time of my arrival.

Once outside and standing at the water's edge I inhaled the intoxicating fresh scent of pine while appreciating the panoramic view. Advancing down the length of the dock I kicked off my sandals, sat down and cautiously swung my bare legs over the rough wood dipping my feet into the cold water. The lake glistened with the reflection of the setting hazy sun while the sky was a spectrum of oranges and reds. The clear sounds of our feather friends communicating back and forth was like a soothing melody. As I soaked in the all-embracing beauty that surrounded me I sighed. "What an unbelievably exquisite world we live in." Time passed and the sun quickly sunk even lower until a piece of it had disappeared over the horizon.

Suddenly I cocked my head. I could distinctly discern the faint put-put sound of an outboard motor however it took me a few moments to determine its location. As the noise became louder I turned to the left. Placing my hands protectively over my eyes I focused on a small outcropping of land. Finally the bow of a small boat poked its head from behind the trees and soon the entire dinghy could be seen along with a solitary figure sitting at its stern. As I watched it slowly change direction then head closer and closer towards my property the man's features became clearer. It was my uncle.

Scrambling to my feet I gave assistance by grabbing the line that he threw to me. As I expertly tied it to the post he pulled in his line of fish, threw them on to the wooden platform, and easily hopped up with surprising agility. His smile was broad and sincere. When I looked into his open honest eyes I knew that we would be friends.

"Christine."

"Hello Uncle Arthur."

I was about to offer my hand when he reached over, wrapped his arms around me, and gave me a firm hug. Pulling back he held me out at arm's length.

"I almost didn't recognize you. You have grown up Christine."

I smiled shyly. "Yes after all it's been fourteen years since we last saw each other and before that you were hardly ever around. If I remember correctly you were always abroad."

There was a moment of awkward silence before he spoke. "Well come on up to the cottage. You must be exhausted. I'll make a pot of herbal tea and you can settle in." As we were proceeding up the path he asked me where my bags were. When I answered that they were still in the car he informed me that he would get rid of the fish then he would bring in my luggage.

As I stepped over the threshold I suddenly stopped dead in my tracks causing my uncle to bump into me. The unexpected smells and familiar sights brought back a flood of precious memories thus producing a few tears. Feeling embarrassed I turned to him. "I'm sorry Uncle Arthur. I didn't mean to get so sentimental."

There was a long pause while he studied me. "My dear don't ever apologize for natural feelings." Suddenly becoming sentimental himself he motioned to the fish. "Pardon me while I get rid of these."

As I slowly advanced into the living room I was amazed to see that everything was just as we had left it fourteen years ago. Every stick of furniture was in its place. Nothing had been moved or changed. As I approached the large picture window and gazed out at the panoramic view there was still sufficient light to clearly see the still water of the lake. An occasional loon cried out plaintively shortly to be answered by another one. My peaceful revelry was interrupted when I became aware that my uncle had re-entered the room.

"Everything is just as I remember it Uncle Arthur; the cottage, the lake, the smells, the sounds." I continued to stare with amazement through the glass.

He smiled with affection and said, "Christine I'll put your bags into your old room. By the way have you had dinner?"

"I almost forgot about food but now that you mention it I'm starving."

"Well while you freshen up I'll cook up one of the fish that I just caught and I have a salad in the fridge. I picked some strawberries from the garden earlier which you can top with fresh cream that I bought from one of the local farmers." He chuckled. "Does that tickle your pallet?"

I looked at him fondly. "It sounds absolutely delicious."

As he grinned with satisfaction and pride I followed him to the bedroom.

When I was alone in the room with the door closed I was filled with a tremendous feeling of nostalgia. It was as though I had passed through a time warp, as though fourteen years ago was only yesterday. The room remained a sea of white eyelet and lace while my stuffed animals sat propped on the bed staring with their glassy button eyes and their stitched-mouths turned up in a grin as though they had been waiting for me. A vase of freshly picked flowers sat on the dresser beside the framed pictures of me and my mom and dad. My uncle's thoughtfulness touched my heart.

It took me about half an hour to unpack, wash my face, and run a brush through my hair. When I opened my door I was immediately aware of the aroma of fish cooking. When I entered into the kitchen my uncle was quietly whistling as he carefully turned the trout over on the grill.

The table was set for two and I noticed that another bouquet of flowers was sitting as a centerpiece.

"Sit down Christine. The fish will be ready in a minute."

I could not remember when I had enjoyed a meal so much. The rainbow trout was garnished with a homemade herbal lemon sauce while the salad was fresh having been picked from the garden a few hours ago. After I placed the last strawberry that was covered with thick cream into my mouth I leaned back patting my stomach.

"Uncle Arthur this relationship could prove to be deadly."

With an overwhelming feeling of happiness Arthur threw his head back and laughed heartily.

After a short silence I set my teacup down in the saucer and my tone became more serious. "Uncle Arthur I can't express how grateful I am to you for taking such good care of the place. If it hadn't been for you I would have had to sell it."

He sat back smiling at me, his eyes seemingly taking an appraisal of the woman sitting in front of him. Finally he spoke.

"Christine if you don't mind I would like to get a few things straight with you. In the first place would you mind calling me Arthur, the uncle part seems so formal. Secondly there is no need to thank me because favors were done both ways and that is the way it should be."

I stared solemnly into his deep twinkling eyes. "Yes, that is the way it should be."

We sat for a long time at the table reminiscing over the past, me with my parents and he with fascinating stories of his travels. He proved to be an interesting man who seemed to have seen the whole world during his lifetime.

"You actually went to an embassy party while you were in Russia?"

"Yes I did."

"And you saw a ballet performed by the Bolshevik Ballet Company?"

"Yes."

"Oh how I envy you. It must have been wonderful! Imagine seeing the world's best ballet performers."

"You must realize though that my first visit to Russia was made during times of stress between our country and theirs. They carefully assigned each one of us with a guide and mine just happened to be a lovely young lady."

"Mmmm, it sounds romantic."

He simply smiled while the color on his face deepened.

"And you have been to China, Africa, British Isles, and several other countries in Europe and Asia."

"Yes I've been to a few places."

"When was your last trip?"

"Around two years ago. I had a friend look after this place while I was gone."

"Do you plan to go away again?"

He looked introspectively. "Perhaps," there was a pause, "perhaps."

After cleaning up the kitchen we walked into the living room then out into the adjacent porch. The night outside was pitch black and through the screens a melody of cricket sounds took precedence in the night while an occasional unidentified ominous sound reminded them that there was life out in the dark forbidding world.

"Well Christine I'm going to turn in now."

"I am too. It's been a long day for me. Thank you for making my welcome so warm." Reaching over I gave him an affectionate kiss on his cheek.

"Goodnight, Christine." His voice cracked ever so slightly.

I waited for a moment or two while I took one last look at the lake then I walked through the living room, turned right and down the short hall to my bedroom suite. In the direction of the other hall, to the left, there was silence so I assumed that Arthur had retired quickly. I lay in my bed for a long time with my mind swimming with sentimental thoughts of my past as well as uncertain ones of my future.

Chapter Two

When I awoke the following morning there were a few seconds of disorientation, and when orientation set in I was immediately filled with an unwanted sensation of homesickness. It was another hot humid day and already the sheets were sticking to me. Tossing them off I appreciated the cool hard surface of the hardwood floors under my feet while walking over to my dresser. After finding my bathing suit in one of the drawers I quickly donned a black, spandex, one-piece garment then on my way out I grabbed a white towel. Quietly, so as not to disturb my uncle, I exited through the front door.

At the end of the dock I casually dropped the piece of terry cloth, stretched my arms above my head, tucked my chin in then dived off into the cold water kicking my legs up in perfect form. I stopped around fifty feet out, pausing for a few seconds in order to catch my breath. Quickly turning and swimming back to the dock I stepped off of the ladder onto the wooden surface then walked over to the shoreline. There I sat down on the cool grass with my legs stretched out in front of me. As I gazed out over the still water I contemplated over my future, as well as on my emotional past. While I was advancing up the path towards the cottage I began to vigorously rub my hair. Wrapping the towel snuggly around my hips I entered the front door. My nostrils were immediately confronted with a tantalizing odor, one that I quickly identified as being yeast.

"Good morning, Christine." My uncle was bent over curiously checking the two pans of bread that he had placed in the oven. "I see that you've already had a swim."

"Yes. The water's very refreshing first thing in the morning. Actually it's a habit that I had when I was growing up." I looked at him quizzically. "Unc..., pardon me, Arthur how long have you been up?"

"Oh I'm an early riser; get up at five, five thirty every morning. Best part of the day I always say. Can I get you some breakfast Christine?"

Walking over to him I touched his arm. "Arthur, let **me** get **you** some breakfast."

Without hesitation he said. "Pleased if you would. I would like sausages well cooked, eggs done over easy, and two pieces of toast. There is some fresh orange juice in the fridge and the coffee is already made. I'll be back in fifteen minutes." With that said he was gone.

8I chuckled to myself as I began preparing the food. "Now that's what I call a no-nonsense man."

We had just finished eating and were clearing the table when he informed me that he had a few errands to do that day.

"Will you be all right by yourself? I probably won't be back until late tonight so don't hold dinner for me."

Even though I assured him that I would be fine there was a hidden disappointment behind my smile. I missed him already. Within five minutes he was in his pickup truck heading towards the highway, sending a cloud of dust in his wake, while I stood at the window watching him as he disappeared from sight.

Suddenly I felt extremely alone and vulnerable. After placing a c.d. in the slot I poured myself a cup of coffee and headed over to an outcropping of rock that formed part of the shoreline. I found a comfortable spot, sat down and looked out over the lake as Mozart's composition filtered through the air. The mellifluous melody floated over the water blending with the constant splashing notes of the waves as they washed against the rocks. In this isolated moment of reality life was so serene. Unfortunately at the same time another reality reared its head bringing with it pain and emptiness. How could such sorrowful heartache and incredible contentment exist side by side? As involuntary tears began to flow I let out a heavy sigh. I was so tired of crying.

Angry with myself I placed the empty cup down on the rock and ran across the lawn towards the dock. After dashing down the length of it I dug my toes into the rough surface of the wood lunging into the air. Ignoring the coldness of the water I swam out with a strenuous over-stroke not stopping until I felt my fatigue. Breathing heavily I turned towards the shore, immediately becoming alarmed when I realized that I had swam out farther than I had anticipated. While I floated on my back I took several deep breaths until my strength had returned, then with clean even strokes I headed back to the beach.

I was approximately fifty feet from the dock when I first felt the excruciating pain. As the muscle of my right calf seized my immediate reaction was to attempt to release it with manual manipulation, but since the cold water was preventing its relaxation I soon realized the futility of this decision. Removing my focus off of the leg I centered my thoughts on my stroke. 'Concentrate, Christine, concentrate.' Within twenty feet from the dock the muscles twisted even harder and the tears were tears of physical pain. Burying my face in the water I pulled as hard as I could with my arms, digging frantically with my cupped hands.

It seemed forever before the welcomed feel of the bottom rung of the ladder was in my grip. Using both my arms and shoulders I pulled myself up on the dock where, moaning with pain, and freezing from the cold water, I curled up in a ball while attempting to squeeze out the spasm. Grabbing my toes I pulled them in an upward position towards my ankle. Finally the muscle relaxed and the pain disappeared.

Feeling both exhausted and frightened, stretching out on my back I stared up at the white puffy clouds and the blue sky. A shudder went through my body when I realized that it had been foolish of me to disregard even the basic rules of the water. From now on I would be more careful.

That afternoon I decided to take a long walk along the country road in order to inspect my surroundings. I stood for a moment pondering which direction to go in then after a short deliberation I turned west. After walking a hundred feet or so I stopped at the first driveway, cautiously peering down the length of it. It was strange. There were no cars in the driveway. Also the windows were protected with drawn curtains giving the illusion of abandonment, not emptiness. Hesitating for only a moment I approached the back door knocked and waited. The answer was dead silence. As I knocked again I moved my ear closer to the door straining to hear even the faintest sound from within but the result was the same, silence.

Circling the building to the front yard I made my way down to the beach. As I did I noticed that the grounds were as well kept as my own even though there still hung that aura of vacancy. Filled with curiosity I slowly paced back and fourth across the lawn admiring the attractive architecture. Sitting on the edge of the cool grass I stretched my legs out in front of me while gazing out over the calm blue water. Suddenly, like a warm flow of liquid washing through my body I was filled with a consciousness of complete contentment and happiness. As I bathed in this overwhelming sensation an enlightened smile spread over my face. "I know," I uttered aloud as I let out a deep sigh. During this special moment my body and mind were at total peace.

For the next two hours I investigated the west portion of the shoreline. Whenever I came across one of my neighbors introductions were made with invitations extended for future socializing. That evening after a simple meal of cold meats and vegetables, topped off with some fresh fruit for dessert, I selected a movie from the video library then settled into a comfortable chair with a glass of Perrier water with a slice of lime. When the movie was over I moved into the porch to enjoy the fresh evening air. It wasn't long before I heard the welcoming muffled sound of the truck's motor as the vehicle turned into the driveway. A few moments later Arthur appeared in the doorway.

"Christine, you're still up. How was your day?"

"It was fine. I took a walk down the road and met some of our neighbors."

"Good. I'm sure that you'll like them."

"Arthur, I was wondering. I noticed that the float is tied up near the boathouse. Is there anyway that you could anchor it out on the water for me?"

"Of course I could. I'll do it first thing tomorrow morning." His answer was simple and brief. He didn't mention where he had been during the day and I didn't ask him. I was soon to discover that my uncle was a very private man who spoke very little of his activities.

"Goodnight Christine. I'll see you in the morning." He turned to leave.

"Oh wait Arthur." He looked back to me with curiosity. "Who lives next door to our left?" Suddenly realizing that it depended on which way you were facing I added. "Sorry I mean that way." I pointed in the appropriate direction.

"It's a gentleman by the name of Stephen Stewart. He's an archeologist."

"The place looks closed up."

"He's away on a dig. He's been gone for a year and probably won't be back for another. When he goes on those expeditions he's usually gone for at least two."

"Who looks after the place? It looks as well kept and manicured as this one."

Arthur smiled. "There is a logical reason. You're looking at its gardener."

I cocked my head gazing at him with curiosity. Quickly I realized that there was much to know, or at least to wonder about my mysterious uncle. "Good night Arthur."

"Goodnight Christine."
A few minutes after he had disappeared into the living room I stood up and walked down the hall to my room.

Chapter Three

With the fresh country air having a relaxing effect on me I slept until eight the following morning. When I stepped out through the front door the first thing that I noticed was that Arthur had already secured the float in place. Upon hearing some commotion in the boathouse I poked my head through the doorway to see my uncle standing at the far side of the room with his back to me.

"Thank you so much for putting the float out on the water for me Arthur."

As he turned he continued to rub his palms and fingers with a dirty rag. "I told you I would. Let me know if it's out far enough for you."

At the lake I made a shallow dive into the cool waters then swimming out to the wooden structure I reached up, grasped a rung of the ladder and hoisted myself onto the platform. I first walked around the perimeter checking the water to see if there were any possible hazards. When satisfied I climbed up on the diving board, moving out to its edge, where I bounced up and down a few times to test its resiliency then I did a clean dive into the water. When I returned to the shore twenty minutes later I found my uncle throwing some boxes into the back of the truck.

"Once more I'll be gone for the day. The family next door, on our right, usually arrives for the weekend around seven. I'm sure that when they realize that you're here they'll be over to introduce themselves to you. They're very friendly so I hope you don't mind." With a grunt he threw in the last box.

"No, in fact thanks for warning me."

Arthur climbed into his truck and once more was gone in a cloud of dust.

While I was enjoying an after dinner cup of tea on my porch I heard a commotion next door to my left. Since the property lines were filled with trees and shrubbery the only thing visible was a flash of color or a hint of movement between the branches. Perhaps an hour later when there was an expected knock on the back door, I anxiously opened it to find myself looking into the eyes of a beautiful unusually tall Hispanic woman. She gave me a warm friendly smile while extending her hand.

"Hi. You must be Christine. I'm your next door neighbor Carlotta. Arthur said that you'd be arriving from the west today so when I saw your car in the driveway I thought that I would drop in to say hello."

"That was very nice of you. Would you like to come in."

"Since we're still unpacking why don't you drop over, oh say, around nine? That way you can meet my husband Paul as well."

When I closed the door I instinctively knew that I was going to like my new neighbor.

Before leaving the cottage I left a note on the refrigerator for Arthur then I grabbed a bottle of wine and shoved it into a gift bag. After a hesitation at Charlotte's cottage door I took in a deep breath, lifted the knocker and rapped twice.

"Would you get that Hon?" I could hear Carlotta's voice coming faintly through the screen.

Through life it had never ceased to amaze me how unlikely is the appropriate match up of partners.

Supporting this theory Paul was nothing what I expected him to be. He was perhaps fifteen years Carlotta's senior and an inch shorter than his wife's five ten structure. His body was lean and in fairly good shape but his hair had thinned and his eyes appeared hard and guarded. Contrary to the intense lack of softness that emanated from his eyes he welcomed me with an expansive smile and a hearty greeting.

"You must be Christine. My name is Paul. Please come in. It's so nice to finally meet you. Your uncle has mentioned your name several times." He called out over his shoulder. "It's Christine, Sweetheart."

I was led into a spacious living room that had a similar view of the lake as mine did but its décor was completely different.

"Sit down. Sit down. Can I get you a drink?" He was already heading for the bar.

"Yes I'll have a white wine please."

"Would you like it sweet or dry?"

"A zero if you have it." As he was pouring it he topped his own off with some Crown Royal. Suddenly I realized that I was still holding the bottle that I had brought with me.

As he was walking across the room with the two glasses in his hands Paul's eyes scrutinized me intensely without discretion or shame. His smile hadn't changed and somehow I felt that it never did. Accepting one of the glasses I handed him the bag which he casually placed on the table then he sat down in a chair facing me.

"So how was your trip from the west?"

"Long, although I found it very interesting. Canada's a big country but I don't think that one realizes it until one drives across it."

"A little boring through the Prairie Provinces, don't you think?"

I shrugged. "Oh I don't know. I took my time and stopped to do some sight- seeing in the few major cities. Between listening to my tapes and appreciating the beauty and uniqueness of the landscape the time went by rather quickly."

Just then Carlotta entered the room. "Christine it's so nice that you're here. Paul was so pleased when he heard that you were coming over."

After we were settled in our chairs I glanced about me quickly sizing up the room. Everything in it seemed so unique. It was as though I could spend the whole evening studying individual items and still discover something new the next day. It was, however, not cluttered since each exquisite item was delicately arranged throughout the area.

"You have a very nice place Carlotta." My eyes settled on an unusual lamp. "That's beautiful and so different. Where did you buy it?"

With a slight show of modesty Carlotta informed me that she had made it.

"You made it! That's so remarkable."

Paul spoke up. "Carlotta has made almost everything in this room." It was obvious by his response that he was very proud of his wife's accomplishments.

I looked at Carlotta with admiration. "You're so talented."

Paul continued. "Carlotta has a shop in Toronto in Yorkville where she's often commissioned to make one of her creations."

I listened to Paul but I did not divert my eyes from Carlotta. "I'd love to see the store some time."

"Drop by one day during the week and we'll have lunch. By the way, now that I think of it we were wondering if you would like to join us tomorrow for a strip party."

Since I wasn't sure whether I'd heard her correctly my eyes opened wider and my mouth dropped open in shock. "What did you say?"

Carlotta laughed. "Don't worry it's nothing naughty. We're referring to a land strip. Every weekend we get together with several of our neighbors and spend the day on a booze cruiser; that is if the weather is permitting. We take turns supplying the food and the liquor, but since tomorrow you will be a guest just bring your bathing suit and your appetite. However, if one day you should decide to join the club then it will be your turn to be the hostess."

"I'd love to come. Thanks for inviting me."

The evening went well. Three hours and two glasses of wine later I made my departure after promising to attend the party. As I made my way up the driveway I noticed Arthur's truck sitting in its usual spot but I also saw that the cottage was in darkness so I naturally assumed that he was already in bed. Feeling a little restless and deciding that sleep would not come easily, I walked out onto the screened-in porch and made myself comfortable in one of the chairs. As I tilted my head back the cool refreshing breeze caressed the soft strands of hair that framed my face.

While I was appreciating the sounds and smells of the night I suddenly caught the site of a light in my peripheral vision. Turning my head in the direction of the guesthouse I noticed that one of the rooms was dimly lit behind the heavy drapery. Alarmed I jumped up and quickly moved through the living room and down the opposite wing from mine where I presumed that Arthur had his bedroom. The doors of the guest rooms were gaping wide-open and all three of them were empty. Feeling confused, since I had assumed that my uncle had been occupying one of them, I paused for a moment. There was no doubt that it had to be Arthur that was in the guesthouse.

Returning to the same spot on the porch I stared out at the lit window. Had my uncle felt obliged to move to more cramped quarters because of my presence? The thought made me feel terrible. Later as I lay in bed I promised myself that I would insist that he move his things back into the main building. In minutes I drifted off to sleep.

Since I had set my mental clock for seven the sun was already shedding light into the room when I awoke. Dressing quickly I went directly to the kitchen only to find it empty; then I checked through the house and the grounds but Arthur was nowhere in sight. Standing in the middle of the front yard with my hands on my hips I looked in one direction then the other. I was certain that he had to be around somewhere because his pick-up truck was still parked in the driveway.

Suddenly from behind the vacant cottage next door I heard what seemed to be a chopping sound. Deciding to investigate I crossed my property, waded through the shrubbery that bordered the two lots then rounded the building to the West Side. Standing with his back to me clad in jeans and a pair of work boots Arthur was hacking away with long powerful blows on a rather dead looking tree. Completely surprised by his strength and fitness I stood very still while my gaze was transfixed on the lean muscular body. Suddenly, like an animal sensing my presence, he wheeled around with legs spread and the ax held up in a defensive stance. Shocked by his sudden action I gasped in fear. When he saw that it was only I he slowly lowered the hatchet and his body relaxed.

"Sorry Christine you startled me."

My face was pale. "I didn't mean to frighten you. I just came out to tell you that I wanted to have a talk with you but it can wait until later."

"I'll be over shortly." Without another word he turned to resume his work.

Just as I was about to make my way through the bushes I thought of something that puzzled me. "Arthur what would you like for breakfast?"

"It's all right. I've already eaten. Thank you."

As I headed back to the house the vision of the untouched kitchen and the absence of cooking odors flashed through my mind. Was he also eating in the guesthouse?

After breakfast I curled up in the chair on the verandah with a cup of tea. Arthur walked in shortly and made his self comfortable on the couch by leaning back against the cushions, crossing his legs in a manly style, and placing each arm along its back. "It's going to be another nice day." He gazed out over the lake.

As I studied my uncle with curiosity I attempted to decipher this strange man that was sitting across from me. "Why are you living in the guest house Arthur?"

Appearing unruffled by my question he answered in an off-hand manner. "Probably it's because I prefer to live there."

"Did you move out of the main building because of me?"

He turned and looked at me. "Is that what you think? No. Actually I have been living there all along."

Frown lines appeared on my forehead as I stared at him with incredibility. "Why? Why would you live in such cramped quarters when you could be living here with all of its luxuries?"

"I do because I have everything that I need in the guest house."

Even though the reason and rationale eluded me it was quite obvious that everything was completely logical to him.

"But there is a fully equipped kitchen here and everything that you might need."

"I have a hot plate, a fridge and a miniature oven."

"There is a fireplace for cold winter nights."

"I have electric heaters."

I shook my head as I stared at him in confusion. Apparently understanding my sentiments he simply smiled.

"Uncle Arthur I feel awful that you are living out there like that."

"No need to."

"You won't consider moving into the main house?"

"No. Truly I am quite comfortable where I am."

As I was attempting to understand the whole situation he suddenly slapped his knee and stood up. "Well, I have a few more chores to do so if you don't mind I'll be off."

Just as he was leaving the porch I remembered something. "Oh Arthur," he turned, "I've been invited on a booze cruise party this afternoon. Are you coming?"

"No I'm not going today Christine."

"Do you usually go?"

"It depends. Sometimes I do."

When Arthur disappeared through the doorway I was filled with an overwhelming frustration that the two of us were leaving a trail of blanks and unfilled spaces behind us. Gazing out over the water I sat with my cup of tea and my unsatisfied curiosity.

Chapter Four

The booze cruiser comfortably accommodated approximately thirty people, all ranging between the ages of eighteen and seventy-four. Even though there was a partial overhead covering that protected us from the hot sun, we occasionally stopped so that those who wished to take a dip in the cool water could. Music was being piped through speakers from a ghetto blaster and there was a never-ending supply of food and drinks. Everyone welcomed me with open arms treating me as though I had always belonged while two unattached males soon showed signs of optimism. By using delicacy and diplomacy I returned their advances with polite rejection. When I was dropped off, along with Carlotta and Paul, the night was black.

"Would you like to come in Christine?"

"No thanks I'm exhausted. I'm going home to crash." I turned to Carlotta and gave her a warm hug. "Thanks. I really enjoyed the day."

As I turned Paul was standing only inches away and without warning I was in his arms. When I tried to pull away he held me even tighter making me helpless in his grip while Carlotta stood only a few feet away. Finally breaking out of his clutch I glared into his eyes, eyes that seemed amused at my resistance. Overwhelmed with revulsion I turned, ran up their driveway then down my own to the back door. Quickly locking it I nervously leaned my back against the cold hard surface while I gulped for air. For reasons known only beyond my conscious mind I was filled with fear.

I didn't awaken until around noon. Glancing at the clock I blinked my eyes to make sure that they were in focus. Swinging my legs over the side I sat for awhile to regenerate then slowly I shuffled off to the kitchen. After making myself toast and tea I sat slumped over the food, eating slowly.

Arthur, concerned with my obvious fatigue, studied me carefully from across the table. "What's the matter Christine?"

"I don't know." I shook my head. "I feel like a rag. I find it an effort to even breathe."

The lips on Arthur's face thinned with concern. "Does it happen often?"

"Not really. It only happens occasionally, however sometimes I'm more tired than other times. I went to the doctor and had tests done but nothing showed up. He said that it was just exhaustion but so often there is no reason to be feeling the way I do. It just doesn't seem normal."

"I see. Did you have a nice time at the party?"

"Yes."

"How did you like Carlotta and Paul?"

I pushed my hair back from my face. "Carlotta is really nice as well as very talented. I think that the two of us will be good friends."

"And what do you think about Paul?" I failed to notice the gravity of his tone.

I sat up straight once more running my hands through my hair. "Seriously," I looked directly into his eyes, "Arthur I don't like him."

"Oh?"

"There's something about him that makes my skin crawl. I just can't imagine the two of them together." I paused for a second, looked off in the distance then turned back to my uncle. "You know I never did ask you what he does for a living."

"He's a doctor."

"He's a doctor? Does he have a specialty?"

"Yes in Obstetrics."

I shuddered. "Well he gives me the willies." There was a pause while I let out a long sigh. "Anyway, I'm really exhausted so I think that I will lie down in the porch with a book."

Arthur watched me until I disappeared from view, his face deadly serious.

Later that day I saw my uncle having a heated discussion with Paul on Paul's lot by the shore. They were out of earshot but the sign language left nothing to the imagination. Before he left Arthur pointed his finger threateningly at Paul who simply tossed his head with indifference. Arthur went directly to his cabin and remained there for the night. In the morning I asked if there was a problem.

"It's a personal matter." His voice was firm and cold.

We never spoke of the incident again.

It wasn't until the following Thursday that Carlotta and I could meet for lunch in Toronto. For convenience I parked my car in one of the parking lots on the perimeter of the city and took one of the mass transit cars to Yorkville. Since the size and sophistication of the metropolis intimidated me somewhat, I was happy to discover that Carlotta was already seated at the table when I arrived at the restaurant. Once we were eating I began to relax and to feel a part of the ambiance of the room.

After we finished our meal it was only a short walk to Carlotta's shop. From the outside it appeared to be small but when we entered I realized that what it lacked in width it made up for in length. I was immediately impressed with the exquisite selections of 'objects d'art', so much so that it took me a long time to decide to purchase a vase that was actually very pricey. When she insisted that it would be a gift from her I argued but without success. She promised to deliver it to my cottage that weekend.

"Why don't you stay in the city with us tonight? We have plenty of room in our condo."

My stomach gave a lurch. "No, sorry I can't. Arthur's expecting me. He said that he was cooking something special for dinner so perhaps another time would be better."

Once in the subway I stared vacantly out through the window. One thing that I had learned in my life was that I should always go with my gut feelings and right now my gut feeling was warning me to stay away from Paul.

The weeks slipped by. The relationship between Carlotta and I blossomed while the one between Paul and me remained the same, or worsened. Whenever I was in his presence a guarded wall went up and my behavior became cordial but distant. It aggravated me, even appalled me that his level of confidence never wavered while at the same time his smile mocked me as though there was a secret that he would not share. Carlotta never suspected, or at least I thought that she never suspected, until the day that she confronted me while we were having a cool drink on the front porch.

"You don't like Paul do you, Chrissy?"

I had difficulty swallowing the mouthful of Perrier water. "Why do you say that?" I was embarrassed.

"I'm not stupid, Chrissy. You have a very classy way of covering up but I feel it."

"Has Paul said anything to you?" I asked.

"No Paul's ego is too big for that." We stared at each other for a moment before I answered.

"Carlotta I feel very uncomfortable around Paul. It certainly isn't because he treats me badly, or says anything rude to me; it's just the way I feel when I'm around him." After another pause I added. "But I love you Carlotta. You are one of the few fine people that I have met during my lifetime."

"I love you too, Chrissy."

We never spoke of the matter again.

Chapter Five

Up to now my relationship with Arthur had been rather awkward. It could be compared to having an interesting book, one in which you were allowed to read the first few pages but nothing more. He never permitted me to get close to him and his activities were all so elusive. At the same time he was consistently kind, never invaded my freedom to be myself, never condemned or criticized me, and lastly never offended me or anyone else other than that one episode with Paul. It wasn't until the occurrence of an act of nature that a door opened thus allowing each of us to touch below the surface, to become more intimate and to understand each other in a richer more personal way.

It occurred in the middle of the week when most of the residents around the lake were in the city. A terrible storm was brewing outside in the ebony black night and the only illumination was coming from frequent flashes of lightening. At the same time the temperatures had taken a nosedive. Arthur remained in the main cottage after dinner perhaps for my sake perhaps due to his own concern. He built a generous fire in the hearth in order to take the chill out of the air while I, at the same time, turned off anything electrical and pulled out all wall plugs. With the erratic illumination coming from the fire and the intense phosphorescence coming from the lightning, which was quickly followed by loud crashes of thunder, a perfect setting for a psychotic thriller was created.

When I suggested a drink he poured himself a heavy one of scotch with a dash of water then a screwdriver for me. As the storm increased in strength the numbing effect of the alcohol was appreciated. At first the conversation was rather formal but slowly it became more personal.

"You've never married, Christine?"

The question stimulated nostalgia which in turn created sadness. Unable to speak for a few seconds I slowly nodded my head in the positive.

"That's too bad." His face was serious.

"What about you Arthur?" I glanced at him with curiosity.

He answered with a tone of indifference. "Yes. I was once married then divorced." He was obviously uncomfortable with the subject thus he quickly changed it. "Have you never met someone that you wanted to marry, or someone that you loved, Christine?" he asked with curiosity.

Feeling rather maudlin due to the effect of the alcohol tears quickly filled my eyes. The leaping flames of the fire reflected off of their shiny surfaces.

"Yes I once loved a man and wanted to marry him."

Arthur seemed well aware of my depth of pain. "So why didn't you marry him Christine?"

"It's a long story."

"Well we have all night." He stared out through the window at the downpour of rain. "And I doubt there is anywhere else that we can go."

And so I told Arthur about Robert and our love for each other, about the turmoil with his ex-wife and the rejection by his two children. I informed him of his dedication to his profession and of the devastation that resulted. During the talk we replenished our glasses, Arthur's more than once. By the time I had finished mine I was feeling even more sentimental than I wanted to be, and he had become overly protective. When I began to sob he moved over and wrapped his arms around me. Gratefully I rested my head on his shoulder.

"Oh Arthur, when will the pain stop? When will I forget him?"

"You will never forget him my dear. He will always be a part of your life but the pain will disappear I promise you that." We sat in silence while he soothingly ran his hand up and down my arm. "Sweetheart a great sacrifice was made when you decided to leave because of your unselfish love for Robert. During our lives we often have to make choices. In making these choices we usually have to sacrifice something that means as much to us as our own existence does. That is the test. That is what life is all about. When we accept the sacrifice, not selfishly for ourselves but for others, we move forward. The greater the sacrifice the greater is the gift that one receives. Remember, when one door closes, another one opens."

"I will receive a gift?" I turned to face him. "What do you mean, Arthur?"

Arthur stared across the room. "Tell me Christine, do you not know deep in your heart that something wonderful is going to happen to you one day?"

I sniffled and blew my nose. "You know now that you mention it I do. I never said anything to anyone but I do feel that there is someone, or something, very special waiting for me."

He held me in his arms for a long time while we gazed into the fire. "What about you Arthur?" I turned and faced him. "Who was the woman that you were married to and what happened?"

My uncle opened up a book that had remained closed for years.

"When I was a young man I married a very pretty very intelligent young lady. Actually she was a teacher. We had been married for only three years when she found someone else which resulted in us getting a divorce." He smiled sadly at the recollection. "I can't blame her though. I was very ambitious then so I wasn't around very much."

"What did you do," I felt uncomfortable asking, "I mean for a living?"

"I was a structural engineer and I wanted to make money fast."

I looked sadly at my uncle. "Do you still love her?"

"I guess I do Sweetheart. I guess I do."

"Arthur if I am being too inquisitive please just let me know but what do you do now?" My words were slurred due to the effect of the alcohol.

His speech was even worse. "I oversee my real estate and I dabble with the stock market."

I looked at him with surprise. "Oh just like me, the real estate I mean. What do you own?"

"Some high rises and an office building."

"Wow, really? Where are they?"

"The high rises are in Toronto and Barrie and the office building is also in Toronto."

I sat up straight and stared at him with incredibility. "Uncle Arthur you're rich."

"I guess you could say that I'm rich." He looked unimpressed.

"Then why are you living in my guest house and doing all of those menial jobs?"

"Because I want to and because that's all that I need."

For awhile I sat trying to focus on a picture on the wall.

"Uncle Arthur you are very peculiar."

There was a moment of heavy silence after which he threw his head back and roared with laughter. The two of us were laughing so hard that tears were streaming from our eyes and I had to hold onto my painful stomach. Finally exhausted I curled up at one end of the couch while Arthur stretched out his legs in front of him and rested his head on the cushion behind him. Soon the two of us were fast asleep.

Chapter Six

I had become quite lazy during the warm summer months but with winter approaching I was determined to do something that would make me feel productive. It was on one of my walks along the road that bordered the lake that I unexpectedly noticed a rather run-down estate. After I made my way through the heavy foliage and the trees both the dilapidated state of the building and the unkempt condition of the yard were apparent. Obviously no one had lived in it for years. While I paced around the outside of the building for the next half-hour I checked for signs of decay and deterioration. Afterwards I made my way through the tall grass then stepped out onto an outcropping of rock. After sitting by the water for some time I finally made a decision.

Jumping up I returned to my cottage with a quicker pace and a lighter step. For the next few hours I attempted to keep busy while waiting for Arthur to return home. When he opened the car door I was waiting for him.

"Arthur, how do I go about finding out who owns a piece of property?"

"Do you mean in this area?"

"Yes."

"Well I know that there is a registrar's office in Barrie although there is possibly a closer place."

"Is the information available to the public?"

"Yes, why do you want to know?" He frowned as he scrutinized me. Something had definitely inspired my enthusiasm.

"I'll let you know after I check on a few things."

I was up before Arthur the next morning. I had just gulped down a glass of orange juice, a bran muffin and a cup of coffee when he walked through the back door. I could see that his curiosity was peeked but he diplomatically kept quiet until we were about to climb into our vehicles.

"Christine I'll be in Barrie all day. Would you like to have lunch with me?"

I eagerly nodded my head. "That would be really nice."

He gave me the name of the restaurant along with its address.

"Are you sure that you will be able to find your way around the city? Even though it's not that big the layout is slightly different and confusing."

"When in doubt ask, n'est pas?" With a smile I waved then accelerated out of the driveway and down the road.

At the registrar's office it didn't take me long to discover who owned the property and even less time to contact him on my cell phone.

"Mr. Graham? My name is Christine Anderson. I'm fairly new in the area and I'm interested in purchasing a piece of lakeside property. I understand that you own one and I was wondering if you were interested in selling it." When there was a pause at the other end of the phone I held my breath.

"As a matter of fact I do own a piece of prime land," emphasizing prime, "and I might be persuaded to put it up for sell."

"Could we meet at your convenience to discuss the matter?" There was another pause.

"Let me see. I'm looking at my schedule. Would Thursday at ten be okay?"

"That would be excellent." As we disconnected I gave the air a short punch with my fists. "Yes!"

When I met Arthur for lunch I was so excited that I couldn't stop talking about it. Over the meal I described my plans in detail while he sat back smiling with eyes filled with admiration and love.

"It sounds as though you will be busy for several months."

"If we can agree on a price," I reminded him.

Arthur smiled warmly and nodded with confidence. "I'm sure that you will work something out."

"You should see it, Arthur." I was leaning over the table towards him. "It has so much potential. From the outside it looks sturdy, well constructed, and the foundation looks solid but I will have to wait until I examine the inside before I will know for sure. The shoreline is good except for some boulders and muck that can be easily cleared away while the shrubbery and grass are out of control but that's no problem either. Oh Arthur I hope that the inside isn't going to be a disappointment."

He smiled with affection. "I have a feeling that it won't be."

On Thursday morning I threw on a pair of jeans and a T-shirt and was five minutes early for my appointment. At ten after ten I was admitted into a rather disorganized office where an equally disorganized looking middle-aged-man sat behind a desk that was piled high with papers. He stood up eagerly and with a warm sweaty hand reached out and shook mine.

"Mr. Graham? My name is Christine Anderson."

"Yes, please sit down." Leaning back in his chair he appraised me with a discerning eye. "So you are interested in buying my cottage."

"Yes."

"Well if the price is right I certainly would be interested in selling it. You see I actually just inherited it from my father who recently passed away. It has been in my family for years but with business and everything I haven't been able to spend much time there."

"I understand."

"Do you live in the area? You were saying that you just moved here."

Yes. I'm living with my uncle several cottages down from your property."

"I see." He rubbed his chin while once more studying this apparently non-threatening young woman who was sitting in front of him. "Well since I don't have the time to go out to the cottage myself I can arrange to have someone else show you the inside of the building."

"That would be fine."

"Perhaps you could be on the site tomorrow at two and a Mr. Butler will let you in. He will also have the blue prints with him."

"Thank you so much, Mr. Graham." I stood up and once more extended my hand.

"If after seeing it, you are still interested in buying it, we can talk about the terms." As I left the office he turned on the communication system to call his brother-in-law. After all why should he lose money on a commission with a real estate agent?

When I walked through the doorway of the badly maintained building I was confronted with the accumulation of ten to fifteen years of dust and dirt. Looking through the debris I studied the wooden structure, eyeballing the floors for any signs of a sinking foundation. When I carefully peeled back the corners of a cheap dirty rug that covered the entire area I was delighted to see hardwood floors underneath. The kitchen cupboards would have to go along with the sink but the old-fashioned bathtub and wash stand in the bathroom I would definitely keep. When I recognized that some of the light fixtures were the original ones from the forties I had a difficult time containing myself.

The living room featured a cathedral ceiling as well as a large stone fireplace that covered most of one wall. After examining the floor plan I decided that by tearing down one or two non-supporting partitions a much more spacious concept could be achieved. Outside I discovered that there were no cracks in the foundation but that the chimney needed either replacement, or restoration.

"Well I've seen enough for now." I looked up at the building with skepticism. "It certainly will need a lot of repairs. Please tell Mr. Graham that I'll call him in a couple of days." After thanking Mr. Butler for his trouble I climbed into the ten-year-old half-ton pickup that I had traded with my uncle for the day.

Patiently waiting in the driveway for Arthur's arrival I was unable to contain my excitement. When he pulled up and stepped out of the car I threw my arms around him and gave him a firm hug. Linking my arm in his, we walked to the cottage door.

"It's so beautiful, or at least it has the potential to be beautiful. I have to have it Arthur." He smiled broadly as he listened to this woman who had brought happiness into his private life of solitude.

Since Mr. Graham's business hadn't been doing so well lately he was in need of some capital to cover his debts and expenses. He was therefore even more anxious to unload what he considered to be a white elephant. To him the building was beyond repair and would have to be completely torn down. He never did suspect my cash flow and with the final agreed price he believed that he was taking advantage of a naive foolish woman. In the presence of my lawyer and an attorney, who by the way was another relative of Mr. Graham's, we signed the final papers and the finesse was completed. That evening Arthur and I opened a bottle of good wine and toasted to my success.

"You look radiant Christine. I'm so proud of you. You are the most beautiful and intelligent woman that I have ever had the pleasure to know."

Overwhelmed by the generosity of the compliment I swelled up with pride. The words coming from him meant so much to me. "Arthur I have never felt towards anyone else the way that I feel towards you. I love you Arthur." I stopped for a second while I looked intently at my uncle. "Sometimes that love makes me feel uncomfortable."

Arthur believed that it was important for him to say the right thing so it took him several seconds to respond. "Christine when we are put on this planet our positions are sometimes awkward due to the dictates of our society therefore we are limited by our social, sexual, and/or racial boundaries. Away from this world we are all free spirits, and as free spirits all of our learned prejudices disappear and loving fills us to completion. There is nothing shameful in loving. I love you too Christine."

As I reflected on my true feelings I narrowed my eyes and gazed into his.
"I sense that we have known each other before, like you have always been a part of me. I feel we'll always touch each other's lives."

"I know that we will." He seemed so serene and sure of himself.

We sat for the next few hours talking, never running out of things to say. The one thing that I especially appreciated was our ability to laugh, to break down the pain and sadness in life, and to find the humor in the simple act of existing.

Chapter Seven

During the following two months I concentrated on the exterior of the building leaving the inside for the upcoming long cold winter. A crew came out to strip, stain, and varnish the log siding then to re-caulk the wood to ensure a good seal against the weather. Meanwhile the roofers were redoing the shingles on the roof. After carefully examining the chimney the workmen agreed that it could be either rebuilt or pointed. In order to maintain the original motif I chose to have it pointed. While they set to work with the task another crew scrapped the dock and built a larger sturdier one in its place. At the same time the grounds as well as the beach was cleared. The cold weather was upon us by the middle of November and soon after that we had our first light snow fall. Now I could concentrate on the interior.

An excited Carlotta promised to give me a hand in restoring the light fixtures to their original condition and when necessary to locate some new ones. We spent a great deal of the time together but I never did spend a night in Toronto with her and Paul. My association with him remained aloof. Whenever we were in each other's company I kept my guard up making sure that we were at arm's length both physically and mentally, however he never wavered in his egotistical attitude towards me. His eyes seemed to taunt me as though he was laughing at some great colossal joke. Knowing that since my ammunition was all so circumstantial and intangible I would undoubtedly lose any argument that resulted, it took all of my effort to ignore him and to stop myself from having a confrontation with him. How could Carlotta love such a hateful man?

One day I broached the subject with Arthur. "Why don't you like Paul, Arthur?"

Once again he took time to select the right words. "He treats Carlotta well but he doesn't behave the same way towards other women nor does he have the same respect for them."

"You mean to say that he goes out with other women?" I looked disgusted.

"You could say that," he paused to examine his answer, "yes you could say that, and when he does he plays some pretty rough games." He regarded me rather seriously. "I hope you realize that this information is not to go any further."

"Of course I realize that. Does Carlotta know?"

"No."

"How ugly the whole thing is." I thought for a moment. "I guess he really doesn't like women, I mean to treat them that way."

"I could agree with you. The bottom line is that he is consumed with a need to have control over them." He regarded me sadly. "There is also another quality that he admires," he paused for a minute, "perhaps worships would be a better word and that is pain. He loves to inflict suffering, to play cruel games with them, to torment them mentally, emotionally and physically."

"But he's a doctor!"

"I know."

"Don't the women object?"

"At the time they do but," he shrugged his shoulders, "afterwards he always finds a way to quell any accusations or charges. Just watch yourself around him and hope that he gets bored with you."

As I remembered his arms around me on that day after the booze cruise icy fingers crept up and down my spine. "Thanks for the warning."

As always the Christmas Season brought both joy and sadness. I was grateful for my friends and my new career but there were holes, voids in my life, which created a certain melancholy. It was the time of the year when I most missed my parents but this year there was an additional ache in my heart----Robert.

With Arthur's help we wound dozens of strands of tiny white lights around the trees thus transforming the cottage into a winter wonderland then collectively we selected a huge pine tree for the living room. It was a project and a half getting it through the front door and a challenge to anchor it securely in place in front of one of the windows. After hanging my prized decorations, the ones that I had taken with me from the west, I stood back while Arthur turned on the lights. I drew in my breath.

"Oh Arthur it's beautiful."

Arthur stood back gazing with admiration at our artistic endeavor. The look of awe on his face reminded me of the expression of a young boy's innocent discovery of beauty. "It's the nicest tree that I have ever seen."

I had sent out invitations to the neighbors asking them to drop in for a customary Yuletide drink and to my delight almost all of them showed up. When the last guest had left I called Lara and Crystal. While I spoke to each one there were a few tears and promises to visit each other in the near future. Later my uncle and I sat alone in the living room. With the hundreds of sparkling lights outside and the splendor of the huge decorated Christmas tree inside, the loving strains of Christmas carols gave the final touch to the Yuletide scene. All of my troubles seemed to have temporarily disappeared.

"I wish that time could stop right now. I'm so happy." I murmured.

Arthur smiled. "I feel that way too Christine." Rising he excused himself only to return with a small gift-wrapped box in his hands. Walking over to me he leaned down, kissed me lightly on the lips and said, "Merry Christmas, Christine."

Because I really hadn't expected a present from this diamond-in-the-rough I stared back in surprise. Taking the wrapping off, I then removed a deep blue velvet case from the box. Holding it protectively in my hands my breath caught in my throat when I opened the lid. "Oh Arthur it's gorgeous." An elongated figure eight turned sideways hung on a fine gold chain. The figure eight was made of the same gold and was dotted with small cut diamonds.

"Do you know what that symbol means Christine?"

"I'm not sure."

"It's the sign for eternity."

"I thought that it was open at one end."

"No. That way it can't go on forever."

"It's so beautiful. I'll never take it off."

"I'm glad that you like it." Filled with pride he helped me to put it on.

After giving him a tight hug of appreciation I walked over to the tree. Reaching down I picked up a large box that was decorated with bows and holly. "This is for you."

Because he rarely received gifts it was his turn to be surprised. I held my breath as he awkwardly pushed away the colorful tissue paper. Peering inside with the curiosity of a child he discovered a leather jacket with a fur lining. Excitedly he pulled it out of the box and tried it on. It was a perfect fit.

I felt uncomfortable when he didn't say anything so I nervously explained that the lining was removable just in case he found it to be too hot. Still he was silent. "It's practical." My voice rose at the end. "You're out in the cold, raw wind so many times that I thought it might keep you warm."

When he did speak his voice cracked with emotion. "I've never received anything so nice. Thank you, Christine." He slowly walked over to a full-length mirror where he strutted back and forth turning his body one way then the other so he could see himself from all angles. As I watched his peacock-like movements I saw a touch of vanity that probably eluded everyone else. It softened my heart.

"It really looks nice on you, Arthur."

With his chin held high he continued to appreciate the view. "Yes it does."

It was the nicest Christmas that I had ever spent. I felt no emotional turmoil, no third wheel insecurities, and above all I liked myself more than ever.

New Year's Eve was spent at a gala in Toronto, one that had been organized by friends of Carlotta and Paul. It took severe persuasion to get Arthur, who resisted by using the excuse that he didn't own a tux, to go with me. With relentless perseverance on my part he finally agreed to rent one. Carlotta had suggested a blind date with one of Paul's friends but remembering Arthur's words of caution I declined the idea. Besides I would feel much more comfortable in the company of my uncle rather than with a complete stranger.

During the evening another surprise awaited me on the dance floor. Arthur was an excellent dancer.

"Don't tell me. You learned to dance in some exotic country."

Holding his head up and mimicking George C. Scott he answered, "In several of them my dear, in several of them."

Chapter eight

On the last day of January a blizzard hit both southern Ontario and the North Eastern States. With the cottage area crippled roads were impassable until the fourth day. I worked on my project through the cold months sometimes until midnight. As the cottage took shape it developed a unique style, a blend of the old along with the new. By the middle of April I was ready to sell. Because of the unusual warm weather that year the snow had disappeared early allowing me to execute the last touches. A warm blanket of green sod completed the picture.

I decided to sell privately. After a flood of advertising on the Internet an open house was held during the last weekend in April. There was a continual flow of people, some just on-lookers but many of them interested in buying. The bidding went up on Monday and soon a deal was made with a Toronto couple who was tired of living in a concrete jungle. Two weeks later I was sitting in the lawyer's office signing papers and receiving a substantial check.

When I arrived home that evening several bouquets of flowers as well as bottles of good wine were sitting on tables throughout the living room, all tokens of congratulations from neighbors and friends. Arthur had made a scrumptious meal beginning with a Caesar salad followed by crab legs in garlic butter, brown rice, asparagus and miniature carrots, the last two cooked to perfection--- just slightly crisp.

"I'm so proud of you, Christine." He held up his glass of wine.

"Thank you." As I touched my glass with his, my face beamed with gratification. "I am too."

After our meal I felt excited and restless. "Why don't you light up the steam bath Arthur? I'm sure I won't be able to sleep tonight."

Agreeing with me he headed down to the building while I put on one of my bathing suits. As I was passing through the dining room I picked up the bottle of wine along with two glasses and carried them to the sauna with me. When I entered the room the coals were just beginning to warm up.

"It'll take a few minutes before they're really hot." As though to validate his opinion he picked up a ladle and threw a small amount of water on the coals causing a weak puff of steam to waft into the air.

"That's okay. In the mean time would you like another glass of wine?" I indicated the bottle that was in my hand.

"Thank you. Don't mind if I do."

Taking our glasses with us we climbed up to the top bench in order to receive the maximum effect of the heat. I leaned back extending my bent legs and resting my feet on the rail in front of us. With the only illumination coming through a small window from the adjacent area we relaxed in the dimly lit room. Within fifteen minutes the water sputtered on the hot coals sending up searing clouds of hot steam. It burned the skin and when we inhaled the warm wet air breathing became difficult.

For a couple of minutes Arthur stared with open-eyed innocence at the ceiling. "You know the proper way to have a steam bath is 'au natural'. In all of the countries that I have been in this is the only one where people cover up."

I sat for a moment deep in thought. Suddenly without hesitation I slipped both straps off of my shoulders, pulled the bathing suit down then raising my hips discarded the garment on the floor. He looked surprised then quickly removed his. "Ahhh, finally out of bondage." With a flourish he tossed his beside mine. Picking up the bar of soap I began to generously lather my body then turning to Arthur I asked him to wash my back.

After he finished and was scrubbing his own body he casually asked with a twinkle in his eye. "Now how do you suggest we rinse it off?"

Turning my head I looked at him with a puzzled expression. "We can rinse it off in the shower in the next room of course. Why?"

He slowly shook his head. "That is not the traditional way to do it and it certainly isn't very adventuresome."

I cocked my head and stared at him. "What do **you** propose that we do?"

"Jump into the lake of course."

I gasped. "Not at this time of the year. The water hasn't had time to warm up."

"Oh I've jumped through a hole in the ice in the middle of winter. It's really very invigorating."

Of course I loved a challenge so I hesitated for only a second. "You're on." Bounding off of the bench I raced through the change room and opened the exterior door. When a rush of cool wind brushed against my steaming hot skin it was totally unrecognizable. Running down the stairs and dashing down the length of the dock I held my nose then jumped out over the dark water. Arthur followed in seconds. Surprisingly it actually felt warm. Coming to the surface the two of us burst into laughter as we splashed water on each other's face but that only lasted for a fraction of a minute. Very quickly our bodies began to lose heat and the cold frigid waters clamped to our skin.

"Oh God it's so cold!" I shouted. With a few frantic strokes we reached the short ladder then shivering we scampered into the sanction of the steam bath. We repeated the process two more times before opting to call it a night. Feeling perfectly sober, cleansed, and rejuvenated I wrapped a towel around myself and raced up to the cottage while Arthur stayed behind to put out the coals and to lock up.

When he entered through the front door, a short time later, there was only a towel wrapped around his waist. I was sitting on the couch in the living room hand drying my hair. I looked up. Arthur stood staring at me motionless as though he was rooted to the spot. He said not a word but he didn't have to. I knew. We looked at each other for a long time before I finally spoke. My voice was faint.

"Arthur I wish so much that you weren't my uncle."

He looked at me sadly. "No more than I." He studied me for a few seconds then he turned and left through the door that he had just entered.

That night I cried myself to sleep and we never did repeat the liberated unconventional behavior again, at least not alone.

Chapter Nine

Shortly after I sold the cottage I coaxed Arthur, by using all of my powers of persuasion, to go out with me for dinner and a show. He stubbornly insisted that he only appreciated the live theater and found movies to be boring and common. Finally giving in we went to a documentary that was dated from the late seventies about the probability of extra terrestrial life existing in our universe. Since it was a complement of information that had been gathered from scientists, astrologers and archeologists I was curious about its content.

At the theater I took the lead choosing two aisle seats about five rows from the back. Almost immediately the lights dimmed and the movie began with a composite drawing of the universe on the screen. I found it to be rather strange because the scientific world had actual living images of the space beyond. The gentleman who was sitting to my right found it to be even more ridiculous and totally amusing thus he reacted with a loud guffaw of laughter. Cringing with embarrassment I pulled my shoulders in, not because of the man but because of the child-like depiction that was on the screen. His two companions, a woman and a man, turned and gave him a reprimanding glare.

Suddenly like a light going on the situation was crystal clear to me. Filled with anger and humiliation my words were only thoughts. 'The people on this planet are not that stupid. We do realize that it's only a composite drawing. We know what the universe really looks like.' Simultaneously the man and I turned and glared at each other while his companions acknowledged our interaction then all heads once more turned toward the screen.

After watching the movie intently for about half an hour I became disappointed with its content. Feeling restless I turned to Arthur only to find him breathing deeply in sleep. Since I was also bored with the presentation I turned my head slightly transferring my attention to the trio that was sitting beside me.

The man that was the nearest to me was in his mid thirty's and had a slight build and evenly proportioned facial features. Sitting to his right the woman appeared approximately the same age, height, and build, and wore little or no make-up on her unremarkable face. The third person, another man, was very similar to the first. Realizing that they were being scrutinized the three turned their heads in unison towards me then after a few seconds they exchanged glances with each other. It was only then that I noticed that both of the men sported an unusual mustache, an image that was not one of my favorites. When I suddenly realized that they had been reading my feelings I was overwhelmed with embarrassment. I sighed and turned back to the screen.

I felt very calm. 'I know who you are. You don't live in this world. You're travelers.' Once again all three heads turned in unison in my direction. I glanced at them briefly then looked back at the screen. 'I can always tell when someone has come from another place.' Reaction! Curiosity!

'I can always sense them in the room.' Reaction was a question mark.

I went on. 'Well, there are the three of you here and there is that gentleman in the back row.' With amazing speed my head spun around and with a sudden force my eyes locked with a startled inconspicuous looking man. He stared at me with amazement, unable to believe what he had just witnessed.

I turned and faced the screen and continued, 'and Arthur.' I mentally nodded to my uncle beside me.

There was an immediate consensus from the trio. 'No he isn't from another planet.'

Being surprised I inquired, 'he isn't?'

The trio, 'no-- a pause--but you are.'

Now the world and all of its old beliefs abruptly came to a stop. The emotional elation that overwhelmed me surpassed the act of winning a lottery, receiving an academy award, or a Pulitzer Prize. My eyes flew wide open as I sat up straighter in my chair. 'I am? I'm from another planet?'

When they realized that I was unaware of that fact an immediate concern generated from my three friends. Fruitlessly they attempted to delete their previous statement. 'No, you aren't.'

Now often there is one complication that arises when minds can be read. It is not limited to thoughts but also includes feelings and emotions therefore it is almost impossible to lie, deceive, or conceal information. The result was that it was too late for them to take their statement back. 'I am? I'm from another planet?' I was having difficulty in believing what I'd just heard while they, on the other hand, obviously did not want to discuss the matter any further therefore their answer was silence.

The four of us continued to watch the movie but I wanted to talk--rather think--to the strangers. 'You people are so lucky to be traveling in space. You're so fortunate to be living on a different planet.'

Their answer, 'Oh this world is all right.'

Disgusted that they should try to deceive me I snorted. 'Would you change places with me? Would you stay here and let me live the life that you are living?' The answer once again was silence.

'I thought so. This is not one of the more favorable planets in the universe, what with all of its pain and misery.' More silence.

Now all of this could be rationalized and with time I probably would have chalked the whole thing down to a possibility but what happened next gave total credence to my original analysis.

Approximately two-thirds through the movie my heart sank as the trio stood up to leave. I was disappointed because I had been enjoying the uniqueness of their company. The first gentleman took two steps to his left, stopped directly in front of me, rotated one hundred and eighty degrees facing me and stared down into my upturned eyes. I froze. After several seconds, which by the way felt like an eternity, he turned back the one hundred and eighty degrees and moved out into the aisle. The second person, the woman, repeated the movements of the first also focusing directly into my eyes. By the time the third person duplicated the scenario I was weak with fear. Within seconds the three of them walked up the aisle and disappeared through the door.

I sat for a long time frozen in my chair, staring ahead at nothing, my mind playing the scene over and over again. Finally reaching over I shook my uncle's arm. "Arthur let's go."

His eyes snapped open. "I'm so sorry Christine. I must have fallen asleep."

"That's okay. Let's get a coffee.

Jaywalking we dodged a few cars and entered a restaurant that was located directly opposite from the theater. Once again I sat in my favorite position with my back against the wall and facing the front door.

My uncle studied me closely. "What's wrong? You look so pale and jittery?"

I had never broached the subject with Arthur and I sure wasn't going to do so now.

"It's all right I just feel a little weak. Maybe it's something I ate."

As we sipped on our coffee Arthur continued to study me with concern. "Maybe we should go home."

I shook my head. "No if you don't mind I'd rather sit for awhile."

Gazing out of the window my mind replayed over and over again what had just happened. While I was staring vacantly at the people hurrying by something caught my eye in my peripheral vision. Slowly I moved my eyes in the direction of the doorway then carefully and cautiously I lowered the cup while I still had control of it. There walking through the door and sitting at the booth by the entranceway, facing me, was one of the men with the strange mustache. My heart began to pound.

The man watched me intensely, calculating my every reaction, never removing his eyes from my face. As the two of us stared at each other I frantically tried to think of something intelligent to say, or rather think, but what do you say to a person who could cure all the ills of the world? Do you ask how to eliminate the deadly diseases, stop famine and wars, or do you inquire if there really is a God? The only thing that I could think of was my intense curiosity concerning everything about this man.

Arthur was becoming anxious after he had asked me a question three times before the remark registered in my mind. I couldn't think of anything else except the strange man who was sitting across the room and what his thoughts were about me. Did he know who I was, what I was, where I had been and where I was going? Just then after several people came into the restaurant and blocked my view I suddenly realized that I had lost sight of him. When the crowd cleared I was filled with disappointment. The table was empty.

"What's wrong Christine?" Arthur asked with concern.

"Sorry my mind must be a million miles away," I grinned cynically, "probably more."

Chapter Ten

In early June I received a call from my friend Crystal. Her voice had an unusually happy ring to it and her smile appeared to be camouflaging a secret.

"Hi stranger what's new?"

I looked at her suspiciously. "No—thing what's new with you?"

"Are you up to going on a trip?"

"Going on a trip? What are you talking about?"

"Chrissy. Hold onto your hat. How would you like to be my maid of honor?"

"What!" I jumped up. "I can't believe it. You're getting married?" Suddenly an alarming thought struck me. "To Armand, I hope."

"Yes of course." Crystal laughed. "Your place must have some magical quality about it because we have been so happy living here. Anyway, one day we sat down and carefully examined our lives and when we did we realized that now was the right time to have a child. At the same time we also agreed that we definitely wanted to give him, or her, a good home which meant that we had to get married."

"When and what day have you decided on?"

"Well if you can get here next week… There will be just you, Armand's friend and the two of us in the wedding party. We'll be married at city hall---just to make it legal."

"What about a honeymoon?"

"We thought that for now we'd have a short one then later on we'll take a trip to Montreal to visit his parents and to Alabama to visit my family."

"Oh Crystal I'm so happy for you. I presume that I'll be staying at the apartment."

"Well of course you will. It'll be so nice to see you again Chrissy because we really miss you here in the west."

We chatted briefly then disconnected.

Later that evening when I related the good news to Arthur he seemed very pleased however there was a hint of concern. I was not only going back to my old home I was also going back to the place where Robert lived. For the next couple of days I was busy getting my clothes ready for the trip then I reserved a seat on an early flight Tuesday morning. I left a message on Crystal's service of my T.O.A. and immediately afterwards I called Lara to let her know of my plans.

Early on the morning of my trip Arthur drove me out to the airport in Toronto. With luggage deposited and boarding pass in hand I stood nervously beside him at the gate. Looking down at my face he fondly reached over and took each of my hands in his.

"Be careful, Christine."

Grasping his hands a little tighter than normal I looked up with worried eyes. "I'm afraid, Arthur."

His smile was reassuring. "I know but I also know that you will do the right thing. Call me if at any time you want to talk, do you understand?"

I reached up and kissed him. "I love you Arthur."

Once belted in my seat my stomach tightened as the plane's motors revved up for the take off. While gazing out through the window my thoughts were of Robert.

Immediately after landing at the airport I rented a car then headed for the city. As I drove up the familiar street and parked in my usual spot everything was recognizable but there was also an intangible difference. When it was necessary for me to knock at the door rather than to use my key I felt rather foolish. When Crystal answered she greeted me with open arms.

"Your room is just as you left it Chrissy."

Standing in the middle of my familiar bedroom I slowly set the suitcase down while I scanned the room and scrutinized each object with a lump in my throat. When my eyes painfully rested on the pillow where Robert had rested his head, and on the side of the bed where he had slept a physical pain wrenched through my heart. After unpacking I joined Crystal in the kitchen.

She looked at me with her usual sensitivity. "Feel like a coffee?"

"Thanks." I nodded.

As she sat across from me on one of the chairs in the kitchenette alcove Crystal studied my face. "Well how does it feel to be back home Chrissy?"

It took a few seconds before I could answer her. "It's strange. I almost feel like a visitor, which of course is what I really am."

"Please don't say that. This is your home whether you're in it or not."

"I'm not too sure about that Crystal."

We spent the rest of the day confirming the arrangements for the wedding dinner as well as the appointment with the justice of peace. She had made reservations at a rather posh penthouse restaurant that was located in one of the hotels. There was to be only one other guest, the best man's girlfriend.

"Is there anyone you'd like to invite as your escort, Chrissy?"

My mouth curled up in a crooked smile as I peered at Crystal. "You're referring to Robert aren't you?"

"We'd be only too happy to include him."

"Thanks for your thoughtfulness but it would only open up old wounds."

On Wednesday afternoon the wedding went off without any problems. The day was sunny and the weather was warm. Crystal looked radiant as she and Armand repeated their wedding vows in front of a magistrate that turned out to be a pleasant elderly gentleman who brought personal warmth into the brief ceremony. Later we ate under hundreds of tiny white lights that gave us the allusion of sitting under the stars, while a vocalist serenaded us with a selection of older romantic tunes.

The following morning Crystal and Armand took off for Banff leaving me alone in my condo. During the next two days my choices would once more be tested.

Chapter Eleven

There is a belief that one should never look backwards in life only forward since nothing ever remains the same. I was soon to discover the validity of this statement.

* * *

When I arrived at Lara's she greeted me with open arms.

"I can't believe it. You're really here. God I missed you and your complicated world Sweetie. Everything has seemed so damn dull and ordinary ever since you left." She held me out at arm's length. "You look so different so refreshed almost rejuvenated."

After making ourselves comfortable in the living room I painted a picture of my life in my cottage in Ontario as well as the project that I had successfully taken on. I spoke once more about the wonderful qualities of my uncle and described my friendship with Carlotta but I neglected to mention the discord with Paul. At Lara's request I gave an account of Crystals wedding.

Since we were both having difficulty in approaching a certain subject when there was a sudden heavy lull in the conversation I brought it up. "I guess you're glad that the trial's over Lara."

Lara slowly nodded her head.

"I really wish that I could have been there for you."

"You know Christine it would only cause one more problem for all of us, and besides afterwards we needed some time to be alone."

My voice was numb. "So they found him innocent."

"Yes. Evidently he had an allergic reaction to the caffeine that was in the chocolates that he ate as well as in the numerous sodas that he drank." Lara gave a sarcastic snicker. "Who would believe that such a simple thing as caffeine could make a person become psychotic?"

I simply nodded my head while remembering an occurrence that had happened a long time ago. I recalled a slight frail-looking child of ten who had been admitted into the emergency department after trashing the living room at a birthday party. It had taken two policemen, two ambulance attendants, and two nurses to get him into a body restraint. His strength was phenomenal. At the time the doctor explained that he had gotten into a box of chocolates and had consumed several sodas thus producing a psychotic reaction. Evidently he was also sensitive to caffeine.

We sat in silence for a few minutes each absorbed with our own thoughts.

Finally Lara spoke. "You know Chrissy, when it was explained to me I had a difficult time in accepting that there was a logical reason for what had happened to Becky."

I raised my eyebrows. "What do you mean Lara?"

"I suddenly had no one to vent my anger on." Twisting her face into a grimace she said. "Actually I feel sorry for Don. The whole episode must be a terrible weight on his conscience."

"I wouldn't worry Lara. I think that when something, or someone else, is controlling your actions it's very easy to forgive yourself, especially when the act goes against all of your sensitivities. If he had been in complete charge of his intelligence and intellect he never would have committed such a heinous act. I'm sure, though that he was left with an extreme sadness for Becky."

Lara looked thoughtful. "Perhaps you are right, perhaps."

We sat in silence each with our own thoughts. When I finally spoke it took all of my strength to ask the next question. "Was Robert cruel to Becky on the stand?

"Actually, no he wasn't. He had to go through each action that night in order to get his point across but he did it with sensitivity. I think that he was quite sure that he would win because of presidents that had been set in similar previous court cases."

"Well I'm glad that I didn't come."

There was an uncomfortable silence.

"Have you met anyone yet Chrissy?"

"No, but my uncle has become my friend. I'm sure that you will like him when you meet him."

Unable to contain myself any longer I looked wistfully at Lara. "How's Robert. Have you seen him at all?"

There was a slight pause as Lara hesitated. "I've seen him in passing a few times but the two of us haven't spoken since the trial." Feeling uncomfortable she attempted to change the subject. "Listen I have two tickets to the opera for tomorrow night. Why don't we make an evening of it and have dinner first?"

"Sure, sounds good. What opera is it?"

"**Not** Madame Butterfly," she said emphasizing the first word.

We both gave a dry laugh.

I spent that evening alone in my condo appreciating all the niceties that I had missed while I was in the east.

Pouring myself a glass of wine and programming classical selections by Horowitz into my system I lit the fire starter log and settled into my favorite chair. Memories soon came flooding back: recollections of tender moments spent with Robert, of walks in the park, of heated passions spent in my bedroom and of his tender touch afterwards. I longed for the simplest of moments: gazing into his eyes, hearing his laughter, feeling the connecting touch of his hand in mine.

It would be so easy to give in. When choosing the wrong path the descent is much less of a struggle because of gravity's help. Perhaps that is why the right path is always the most difficult one? After contemplating in the dark room for hours I climbed into bed wrapped my arms around the pillow that was lying beside me and was soon fast asleep.

Arriving on Friday evening within minutes of the performance we went directly to our seats. Lara had two season tickets for the front row balcony, a position that provided an excellent uninterrupted view of any presentation while opera glasses accommodated any necessary close-ups. The lights dimmed and I was soon carried away with the music and the story.

At one point whether it was a need for a break of concentration or whether it was a preoccupation with other thoughts, my eyes wandered from the scene on the stage to the backdrops, specifically to the fabric of the curtains and the motif on the walls. As I scrutinized the balconies I wondered why people would want to perch precariously on the individual structures. Picking up my glasses from my lap I began scanning the people below in the orchestra and mezzanine area. As I was studying the crowd I suddenly stopped and backed up my line of vision. In a panic I quickly adjusted the focus while a gigantic wave of vertigo washed through me. There sitting in one of the orchestra seats was Robert. I couldn't take my eyes off of him. The magnification gave the illusion that he was sitting right in front of me thus producing the false image that I could reach out and touch him.

What happened next made me feel as though my heart was being ripped out of my chest. As he turned to his right and smiled he reached out and took her hand. The pain was excruciating. She looked into his eyes and returned his smile then they both looked back at the stage. Literally glued to the scene I was unable to tear my eyes away while all of the energy that I possessed seemed to be viciously sucked out of my body leaving me empty and dead. When the pain suddenly transferred to anger I had an almost uncontrollable urge to stand up and scream in protest. No, No! It's not fair! The hand should be mine! The smile should be ours!

When the heartache became too much to bear I turned away and stared vacantly at the backdrop. Nothing seemed to matter to me anymore. As the curtain began to close and the lights came on for the intermission I slumped back in my chair and held the program up in front of my face. At the same time Lara sat up straight and arched her back.

"Well do you feel like having a...." She stopped when she realized that something had happened. "Chrissy, what's wrong? Are you ill?"

Just then Robert and the woman stood up and began to walk up the aisle. Lara followed the direction of my gaze as I peered over the paper.

"Oh my God Chrissy I'm so sorry!" Lara sat down and stared helplessly at me. "What in heaven's name are you going to do?"

"I'm not doing anything." My voice was dry and brittle.

"You're not doing anything? Don't you want to talk to him?"

"No!" I answered firmly. "Who is she?" My tone had a touch of bitterness as well as pain.

"She's a lawyer who works in his office."

A million images flashed through my mind bringing with it unbearable heartache. It was a few seconds before I was able to speak again.
"Have they been seeing each other for a long time?"

"I'd say for the last couple of months. I should have told you about it last night but I procrastinated. It's so difficult to tell someone bad news. I guess I can now understand how you felt when you had to tell me of Robert's involvement in the trial. Actually I was going to discuss it with you later this evening. I'm so sorry. I didn't want you to find out this way."

I slumped back in my seat. "If you don't mind Lara I'd like to be alone. Please go down and have yourself a drink---or something---please."

"Will you be okay?"

I simply nodded my head.

"Are you sure?"

"Please Lara I just need a few minutes to myself."
After squeezing my arm and taking one last concerned look Lara moved out into the aisle.
I sat motionless feeling as though my life had just ended even though I was still breathing. I knew that I had initiated the breakup but the door never really seemed

closed. I always felt that I could go back at any time and he would be waiting for me. Now I had to face the bitter truth that it was definitely over. Shortly the people began filling the room for the second half of the performance and presently Lara sat down beside me.

"Is everything okay?"

"Yes." Looking down at Robert and his friend as they settled themselves in their seats I allowed myself one more onslaught of pain then for the entire second half I stared at nothing. When the opera was over I insisted on remaining in the theatre until I was sure that Robert was out of the building. Eventually we walked through the almost empty lobby. Apologetically I refused an invitation to join Lara for coffee.

"I'll call you tomorrow."

Curled up at the end of the couch I sat in silence. There were no lights, no music, just the black night. As the shock began to wear off I was slowly able to think about it more rationally and gratefully some of the pain began to fade. I did not doubt that I had made the right decision months earlier so why was I angry with myself now? Was it selfishness? I certainly didn't want Robert to be alone for the rest of his life or to suffer due to the loss of our relationship. I knew that I still loved him and if I really did love him I didn't want him to be unhappy. Suddenly overwhelmed with my unconditional love for him I choked on a sob and let out a painful sigh. For the second time it was necessary for me to let him go.

Letting go is perhaps one of the most difficult things that we have to do if we are ever to go foreword in life. Sometimes we hurt others in doing so, sometimes ourselves. Once I reminded myself of this I actually felt some intangible force leaving my body. It was as though a weight had been lifted leaving me with a feeling of buoyancy within my spirit.

The sun was almost rising when I climbed into bed. This time I turned away from the pillow beside me and hugged myself instead.

On Saturday I spent most of the afternoon at my apartments with Larry. As usual he was doing an excellent job so I rewarded him with a substantial bonus check. When Crystal and Armand arrived home on Sunday evening I announced that I would be returning to Ontario the next day. Crystal had only to look at me to realize that something had happened during the three days that they had been away. When I informed my friend of what had transpired at the theater Crystal wrapped her arms around me.

"I'm so sorry Chrissy. I didn't know or I would have told you."

"I know. I realize now that there is nothing for me here. One can't go backward but only foreword, and my future is in the east."

There were kisses and tears at the airport the next day. When the plane lifted off the ground I closed my eyes and exhaled deeply as I severed the cord for the last time.

Chapter Twelve

The moment I returned to the cottage I immediately buried myself in another project. After driving for endless hours around the shoreline I finally found a property that was ideal for renovations. Even though I was aware that because of its location the profits wouldn't be as lucrative as the last one was, I nevertheless dove into it with an equal amount of enthusiasm. Waking early each morning, sometimes before Arthur, I would pour over my plans and figures on the computer or else I would rush out to the sight. Challenging myself with physical participation I worked until my hands were cut and blistered and many times it was midnight before I packed it in and crawled exhausted into bed. Feeling helpless Arthur could only watch me knowing that I had to work through my grief alone.

When the cottage was ready for sale I had two open house parties before I received the price I wanted but unlike the previous sale this time the celebration afterwards was quiet. Arthur and I went out for dinner then immediately afterwards we returned back to the cottage. Sitting alone in my living room in the darkness of the night I stared out over the black water.

It was during one day at the end of September that my life changed forever. Flowing through me leaving in its wake a pleasant warm consciousness I felt that certain awareness that the time had finally come. Savoring the feeling I slowly stretched my arms over my head and let out a long sigh of contentment. There was no need to hurry because it was inevitable and it wasn't going anywhere. It was waiting for me just as it always had been.

I remained in the shower for a long time enjoying the water as it pelted against my body, as though I was not only cleaning myself I was also wiping away my past. Leisurely I dusted my skin with a soft scented powder then pulled on a pair of khaki colored slacks and a simple white T-shirt. After thoroughly brushing my hair I reached up and tied the thick dark strands back in a ponytail. When I wandered into the kitchen Arthur was sitting at the table with a peculiar smile on his face and as I looked into his eyes I tilted my head slightly to one side while scrutinizing him with curiosity. He silently responded with a simple conspirator's nod. He also knew.

"Christine I'll be going into Toronto today and won't be back until tomorrow."

My eyes narrowed and watered and my heart filled with love. "Oh Arthur, thank you so much."

All was right with the world.

Humming happily I moved about the house doing my morning chores then by mid afternoon I stood on the threshold of the front porch and slowly raised my face up to a cloudless sky. As I made my way down to the beach the sun was shining brightly, the birds were singing sweetly, and the air smelled fresher than ever. With each step the feeling of anticipation became more and more powerful until the air about me was almost static with energy. Standing at the edge of the grass looking out over the calm blue water, the hot sun kissed my skin and the warm breeze ran its fingers through the loose strands of hair that had freed itself from the bondage of the band. Filled with great awareness I turned my head to the left.

He was standing by the water's edge just as I always knew he would be. He was tall and his hands were casually placed in the pockets of his slacks. He stood for a moment looking out over the lake then certain of my presence he tilted his head slightly while rotating his body towards me. Even from that distance I could feel the bond, the enchantment that connected us. Slowly, as though drawn by a magnet, I began walking towards him while he stood rooted to the ground savoring each inch of my face and body as I approached him. Standing in front of him, facing him directly, we stared into each other's eyes with an overwhelming feeling of familiarity. Our smiles were so alike that they strangely felt cloned.

"Hello Christine. Arthur has told me so much about you in his letters. It's so nice to finally meet you."

As our hands touched it was as though the very essence of our beings converged into one. When I looked at him it was as though there was some strange mystical illusion that I was looking at my own image, which confused and overwhelmed me.

"I understand that you've just returned from South America, Stephen."

"Yes that's right. I just arrived yesterday." His voice was rich and masculine.

"Are you planning to stay for awhile?" Our eyes remained magnetized together.

"Yes." His answer was simple but the significance of the message made me feel weak.

Glancing up at the sky he casually commented on the warm day then asked me if I would care for a cool drink. While we were on our way up the path to his cottage I was suddenly aware that I didn't feel the ground beneath my feet. I had once heard that such a phenomenon existed but I never really gave any credence to the statement until now. Passing through the patio doors we entered into a large spacious room.

"Please make yourself comfortable while I get us some iced tea."

When he left I took advantage of his absence to look around quickly deciding that the decor was definitely masculine. The colors were warm but darker than the ones that I usually chose, and each piece of furniture was unusually interesting and appeared to be a collector's item. Returning shortly with two glasses Stephen handed me one then sat directly across from me. As I took a sip I noticed a few crates that were sitting in one of the corners. His eyes followed the direction of my stare.

"Those contain some artifacts that I've gathered throughout my life. Actually I was planning to unpack them shortly. I don't like them here when I'm not around."

My curiosity was sparked. "I'd love to see them when you do. It sounds as though your work is really intriguing."

Pleasantly surprised he raised his eyebrows. "Oh. Are you interested in archeology?"

"Yes, although I don't know too much about it, only what I've seen on the television and in the movies. When I was studying ancient history in high school I always felt that I had a definite connection with that era. Sometimes I wondered if perhaps I had lived in one of their societies a long time ago."

He slowly nodded his head. "That could be very possible."

I couldn't believe that I had said, what I had said, but what was even more shocking was his response, and he didn't laugh.

"Do you really believe that, or are you just humoring me."

"No I believe in reincarnation, don't you?"

"Yes I do, very much so, although in the past I haven't had too much support from my friends."

"That's too bad. It's very difficult to carry a philosophy all by yourself." He smiled broadly and his eyes twinkled. "Now you have an advocate."

I had just met him but I knew him as well as I did myself. Our conversation flowed freely as though we had known each other for several life times and were now catching up on the time of separation. It was as though two pieces of a puzzle had finally been placed together, completing the picture. It was as though it always was. As I looked around the room I once again realized that I didn't see any female influences. "Are you married, Stephen?" I held my breath.

"No, I'm not."

My eyes rested on a selection of framed photographs that were randomly sitting on one of the tables. "Are those your children?" Remembering the tragic experiences that I had had with Robert my fingers were unconsciously crossed.

He glanced over at the pictures. "No, those are my nieces and nephews. I've never been married but I do have a brother and a sister. In fact," he turned in his chair, "the painting on the wall on your left is one of the three of us as children."

As I stared at the young faces Stephen watched me intently. "What about you, Christine. Do you have any siblings?"

"No. I have no brothers or sisters and my mother and father passed away when I was eighteen."

"I'm so sorry. Arthur told me that you were also never married."

"No. I came close to it once but the relationship didn't work out."

The next words that came out of his mouth startled me.

"Christine I'm glad that it didn't," he paused, "because I'm going to marry you."

I looked back at him with complete recognition.

"I know," I whispered.

As we stared with open familiarity into each other's eyes he said. "I've been waiting for you for a long time Christine."

During the next few hours we filled each other in on our lives, and when we shared our interests and goals we were pleasantly surprised how much we thought alike. He told me that he was forty years old, an archeologist, and had worked as a professor in the university since he graduated many years ago. From time to time he had taken leaves of absence in order to accompany some of his colleges on various archeology sites. His mother and father had both passed away, first his mother of cancer then his father a year later.

"I think that he died of a broken heart."

"How sad that is. How old were you?"

"I was thirty. I'm the youngest of my peers. My mother was sixty at the time."

I looked about the room. "How long have you known Arthur?"

"I've known him since I bought this place ten years ago. I don't know whether you know it or not but he was kind enough to look after the cottage while I was gone."

"Yes, he's done the same favor for me." I stared at Stephen then with hesitation I spoke. "He's a very special man Stephen, and I love him very much."

He seemed to understand my awkwardness.

"Christine I love him too."

It was my turn to enlighten Steven about my life. He sat back in his chair allowing me room to feel and have my own space while I briefly described my younger years. When I spoke of my nursing career and my real estate involvement he was filled with admiration.

"My, but you are a very enterprising young woman."

It was all so stimulating, so satisfying, to know that we could savor every little detail about each other. It was like picking up a book that you knew would always be your favorite and to be on the first page with the best yet to come. A short time later, after excusing myself, I went to the bathroom. When I returned to the room Steven was standing in deep thought staring over the lake. Aware of my presence he turned as I walked over to him.

"Would you like to go out for dinner Christine? There's a place not too far from here that opened a couple of years ago. It serves excellent food, has a warm atmosphere, and is also fairly casual." He reached down and gently moved a strand of hair from my face. "I'll pick you up in an hour. Will that give you enough time?"

It felt so natural when he took my hand and walked me to the door.

As I made my way to my cottage I was in a daze. After entering the building I leaned my back against the door, let out a long breath then rushed to my bedroom. In the shower I washed my body, not once but twice, then after drying myself I rummaged through the closet. After scenting myself with my favorite powder, in all the strategic areas, I stepped into my best lace panties and hooked on the matching bra. Lastly I slipped on a simple summer dress. While I ran the brush through my hair and put on a light covering of makeup my hands were shaking. Overwhelmed with anticipation of what lay ahead I spent the last ten minutes pacing back and forth between the living room and the porch. It was the longest hour that I had ever spent. Finally there was a knock on the door. Taking in a deep breath I opened it.

The restaurant was just as he had described it to be. It had a quaint English motif, cordial staff and excellent food. We took our time through the four courses eating slowly while the waitress timed her approaches carefully. Every time I thought of what lay ahead I became dizzy and a pleasant sensation flowed through my body. The sun was beginning to set when he pulled up into my driveway.

Once inside my cottage we stood in the middle of the living room floor. "Have you ever been here with Arthur, Stephen?"

"No, we usually spent the time together over at my place but a couple of times he had me visit him in the smaller building." He looked thoughtful. "I think that he felt more comfortable there." Slowly he cast his eyes around the room stopping at an oil painting that hung over the mantle. "Are both of the people in the picture your parents."

"Yes."

He glanced over at me, with curiosity, then quickly back to the picture. "Your mother was certainly a very beautiful woman." He paused to examine it more intently. "Actually you look a lot like her."

"Thank you. She was even more beautiful than how she is portrayed in the picture, but then I guess it's difficult to capture that inner beauty."

"Yes, but I can see it in her eyes. They're quite mesmerizing. The artist was quite talented "

After moving over to the CD player and picking out a selection of songs I programmed them into the unit then when I turned to face him he began walking towards me. The sun had already sunk below the horizon sending shadows splaying across the room. I reached up and touched his face with my fingertips while he passed his hand down my other arm caressing the skin.

"I love you, Christine. I have always loved you."

"I love you too, Stephen. I always felt you out there---somewhere."

Picking me up, holding my body close to his, I wrapped my arms around his neck and nestled my face into it. There was an overwhelming feeling that I had finally come home.

Once inside the bedroom I reached over and turned on the bedside lamp thus casting a soft illumination over the area. We began to slowly undress each other, feeling no desperation, no need to hurry because we knew that we had the rest of our lives together. When he took me in his arms the passions that had captivated us were obvious.

"My beautiful Christine I love you."

Moving onto the bed we lay together, first running our hands slowly over the surfaces, kissing one spot after another, but soon we could hold back no longer. Our bodies crushed together into a complete coalescence of body, mind, and spirit. I soared to a place that I had never known, a place where time became one with the universe, and when we climaxed it seemed endless, fulfilling every wish, every desire that I had ever hungered for. The familiarity seemed timeless as though we had always been. When we fell asleep we were supremely content that we had finally met our destiny.

Arthur didn't return to the cottage until late the following afternoon, and when he walked in he found us relaxing on the front porch. Discretely he poked his head through the doorway.

"Am I interrupting anything?"

"Arthur my old buddy," Stephen rose and embraced his friend, "it's so good to see you again."

"It's nice to have you back." Arthur smiled. "For some reason you're looking especially good." He then winked his eye at Stephen.

"You're not looking bad yourself." Stephen scrutinized him from head to toe. "Maybe a pound or two heavier. Has someone been feeding you too well?" It was Stephen's turn to wink at me.

"Yes I must admit that I am a spoiled man." As Arthur watched the look that was passing between Stephen and me he beamed with happiness. "I see that the two of you have gotten to know each other."

"Yes." He looked at me fondly. "She's everything that you said she was, and more."

That evening Stephen moved in with me.

Chapter Thirteen

My relationship with Paul changed dramatically after Stephen returned home from the dig in South America. Since Stephen was away when Carlotta and Paul moved into their cottage, introductions were necessary when he returned home. Stephen and Carlotta warmed up to each other however the climate between Paul and him was rather chilly. While Paul continued to behave in his usual boisterous manner by leering at me with his overly confident, egotistical look of self-assured control, Stephen sat back and discretely studied his rude behavior.

Suddenly Stephen began questioning Paul, probing for all sorts of personal information. His unexpected interest obviously upset Paul resulting in Paul's answers becoming more, and more, brief. Carlotta and I were embarrassed with the strange performance which stopped as quickly as it began, then, focusing in a totally unrelated direction Stephen began telling us a few anecdotes in connection with his work in South America. Although Carlotta and I soon put the incident past us, Paul seemed to have become argumentative and impatient after the scenario. Finally Stephen stood up and suggested that, due to the fact that they were to have an early start the next day they should leave. When I glanced at him I thought I detected a smile of confidence on his face.

The next time when we met was at our place for a game of bridge. Arthur showed up and observed us while we finished the last hand. Afterwards, while we were enjoying a small lunch with tea and coffee in the dining room Stephen suddenly remembered something.

"Oh Christine I forgot to tell you. You were sleepwalking last night."

"What! I was sleepwalking." My jaw dropped in shock.

"Actually you woke me up when you were getting out of bed. I called your name but you didn't answer me so I got up and followed you. You left through the front door and proceeded to walk towards Carlotta and Paul's place. Because I knew that it wasn't advisable to wake up a sleepwalker I carefully turned you around and led you back to the bed."

"Oh my God", I exclaimed, "I've never done anything like that before. At least I don't think that I have." When a sudden thought came to me I anxiously turned towards Arthur. "Do you think that sleepwalking could be the reason why I sometimes get so tired?"

Since Stephen was unaware of my history of fatigue I gave him a brief account. As I did Stephen and Arthur kept glancing at each other while Paul's expression became tense, almost aloof and angry. Stephen was the one to answer my question.

"It certainly could be but I wouldn't worry about it Sweetheart because I'm sure that it won't happen again. But if it does we will have to investigate so that we can find out what is causing it, then we will have to put an end to it. You'd be surprised how many people walk in their sleep without realizing that they are doing so."

For some odd reason Paul never did look at me with that egotistical stare again, nor did his eyes laugh in his usual mocking way. I could never decide whether it was coincidental or whether Stephen had spoken to him about it. One day when I asked Stephen's opinion about the matter he simply smiled and said. "I guess I'm bigger than he is."

After that night any socializing that we did was with Carlotta since Paul always seemed to be busy. For a long time Stephen, Arthur and myself were inseparable, spending many evenings together playing cards or just talking, often late into the night. The three of us shared the same sense of humor, similar interests, and lived by an equal code of ethics. It was a unique or at least an unusual relationship.

One evening Stephen and I sat before a warm crackling fire while outside the wind raged and lashed at whatever was lying in its path sending all of Mother Nature's creatures scurrying for cover, including Arthur who had retired early. With the feeling of intimacy that comes with isolation the two of us talked about our more personal feelings from the past.

Stephen began describing his relationship with the woman that he had been involved with. Her name was Melissa. When he spoke of her, mentioning only her good qualities, he also explained that some intangible force was disabling him from consummating their relationship with a marriage. He knew in the back of his mind that somewhere a woman existed, a soul mate, and decided that he could not settle for second best. It would be cruel, not only to him but also to Melissa and any children that might result from the marriage. He mentioned how difficult it was for both of them to let go.

"She must be very special to understand how you felt."

"Yes she is."

I then told him about Robert. As I was mentioning the incompatibilities between the two of us I realized that the differences would only escalate and bring us grief in later years. When I mentioned the children Stephen kissed me lightly on the forehead.

I looked over at him wistfully. "I couldn't stand to see him lose his children. He loves them so much." I paused. "I will always love him Stephen. Not in the same way that I love you, but in a different way."

"Of course you will Sweetheart. There's nothing wrong with loving someone because it doesn't change how we feel towards each other. With each person that we come in contact with we learn to grow but by discarding ones feelings and pretending that they don't exist, or did not exist, we lose what we are supposed to learn. No one has the right to rewrite your past because by doing so they change what you are. He will always be a part of you as Melissa will be of me."

"Do you still love her?"

"Yes as you love Robert."

I snuggled deeper into his arms as the storm raged outside.

Chapter Fourteen

By October Stephen's family was more than anxious to meet the woman that had come into their brother's life, while I remained a little gun shy due to the experience that I had had with Robert. There existed a firm family tradition in Stephen's life to spend Thanksgiving together. One day, in October, his sister called to inform us that we were expected to be at their place on the following Sunday.

On a cool but sunny day while driving through his sister's neighborhood my eyes opened wide in amazement. They weren't houses. They were estates. The further we moved into the subdivision the more elaborate the architecture was, however much of the view was obstructed by walls and tree-lined winding driveways. Finally Stephen turned into a property that was protected by a high limestone wall and a black wrought-iron gate. Rolling down his window he pressed a code on the security system and the gate swung wide open.

"My lord," I gasped, "what does Elizabeth's husband do?"

"He works for the government," Stephen answered.

"What is he, the Prime Minister?" I sputtered.

Both Stephen and Arthur laughed. "No. Actually Sweetheart, since this is the house that I grew up in I'm coming home. When Mom and Dad passed away we didn't want strangers to move in so the three of us decided that Elizabeth would be the best person to take over the place. We also wished to keep it in the family so that we could pass it onto future generations." He turned and smiled at me. "Do you like it?"

"Oh Stephen, it's absolutely beautiful."

Pulling up to the curb, and turning the ignition off, he turned and said. "Well let's see what you think about the inside of the house but more important let's see what you think about my family."

Walking over to the entranceway Stephen pressed the doorbell producing a beautiful melodic chime from within, and after what seemed to be a long wait a rather elderly, refined, slightly-stooped gentleman wearing a tuxedo opened the door.

"Master Stephen. It's so nice to see you." When he and Stephen enthusiastically shook hands then embraced the old man's face lit up, not only with happiness but also with love. Turning to Arthur he eagerly shook his hand. "Mr. Anderson. It's so nice to see you too." His eyes then slowly and deliberately shifted to me. "Ah, and this must be the lovely young lady that I have been hearing so much about." He raised his eyebrows to Stephen. "She is indeed lovely." Grinning with pride Stephen made the introductions. "James I would like you to meet Christine. Christine this is James, a very dear member of the family."

"Welcome my dear." His smile was warm and sincere when he shook my outstretched hand then he quickly turned and motioned for us to follow him. "Well come in, come in. The entire family is waiting to see you."

Once inside the hallway we set our overnight pieces of luggage down on the hard marble surface and at the same time we heard a sudden clatter of running feet coming from one of the back rooms.

"Uncle Stephen, Uncle Stephen." As three young girls from the ages of seven to ten raced into their uncle's open arms. Bending down he embraced them one after the other while planting kisses on their lips. "How are my munchkins?"

Looking up over their heads towards four adults that appeared through the same doorway Stephen smiled widely. Taking the lead, his sister, a lovely dark haired beautifully groomed woman in her early forties quickly crossed the wide expanse of foyer and embraced her brother.

"Oh Stephen it's so nice to see you again. We miss you so much when you're gone on those dreadful digs. Promise us that you will stay home for awhile this time." They kissed and gave each other a warm hug then with anticipation she turned to me.

"Christine. Even though we've seen you on the videophone it's so nice to finally meet you in person. We have been looking forward to your visit." Wrapping her arms around me she first gave me a warm squeeze then with arms still locked she pulled back and smiled. "We welcome you to our home." Suddenly remembering Arthur she repeated the kiss and hug just as the other three adults walked up to us. Stephen's brother Andrew, his wife Linda, and Elizabeth's husband Richard welcomed us with equal enthusiasm.

"Wait, you still haven't met these lovely young ladies." Elizabeth gestured towards the three children, tapping them on top of their heads as she introduced them. "This is Paige, Kayla and Meagan and there are two boys but they are presently being mesmerized in my son's bedroom by modern technology."

Bending down I gave each one of the children a hug while at the same time I expressed how pleased I was to meet them.

"Now that we are all here let's go into the family room," Charles suggested. Elizabeth took the two older children's hands while the youngest one, Meagan, reached up for her father.

I had always thought that I knew the meaning of opulence but I now realized that my perception had been definitely dwarfed. As we were following them, I grabbed Stephen by the arm, tugged at his jacket sleeve and muttered through the corner of my mouth. "You didn't tell me you were a spoiled, rich brat."

"I thought that if I did you might not want me." I looked up at his wide pleased smile.

The day was a memorable one for me. I suddenly found myself with a new loving family who immediately made me feel a welcome part of it. I met the two boys, Corey and Nicholas, aged twelve and thirteen, who at one point during the evening lured me upstairs where they quickly initiated me into their computer games. It took about ten minutes to make me a slave to its spell and less time for the adults to threaten to send me home if I didn't separate myself from the program. It was a little confusing knowing who was who but Meagan and Corey belonged to Elizabeth and Richard while Nicholas, Paige and Kayla were Andrew and Linda's children.

Finally we were summoned into the dining room where a huge antique table with twelve high-backed chairs fit comfortably in the area. The white lace tablecloth was covered with china, silverware and platter after platter of food while ornate candelabras were placed at each end. An arrangement of fruit and flowers depicting the harvest season was artistically displayed as a centerpiece, and an enormous well-basted turkey sat glistening on a cutting board at the head of the table.

After we were seated we all joined hands while Richard led us in a prayer of thanksgiving for all of our blessings. While he carved the bird, two women in maid's uniforms magically appeared from the kitchen to assist the family while James walked about appearing to get in the way, more than being useful. I noticed that his hands were gnarled with arthritis thus making it impossible for him to pick up any of the heavier dishes so instead he concentrated on the children, urging them to eat their meal with some decorum.

After the dessert was finished James took the children into the playroom while we settled into the living room where a fire burned brightly in the fireplace. From a silver tea service one of the maids poured each of us a beverage then disappeared in order to give the other one a hand in the kitchen.

At one point, Meagan, the youngest of the children, wandered into the room and immediately migrated to me. Climbing up on my knee she snuggled herself into my arms.

"Are you tired, Meagan?" She innocently nodded her head then closed her eyes and was soon fast asleep.

Walking over to us Richard grinned down at me. "Thank you." He softly mouthed the words then picked his daughter up and carried her upstairs.

After the other children were tucked into bed Stephen and I decided to take a walk out on the grounds. After taking a short stroll we made ourselves comfortable on a couple of deck chairs that were arranged around the pool.

"Stephen, your family is very precious. I can see why you turned out as well as you did."

He reached over and took hold of my hand giving it a squeeze. "You see. You didn't have to worry about anything. They all love you Christine, just like I do."

"I've always wanted a large family, sisters, brothers, nieces, nephews----"

With his head resting on the back of the chair Stephen continued to gaze up at the constellations. "What about children?"

"Oh, of course I want children. That goes without saying."

He glanced over at me. "How many would you like?"

"I don't know. I guess it would depend on how things went. How many would you like Stephen?"

"I guess I'd like at least two or three."

"But you travel a lot. You certainly couldn't leave on a dig for a couple of years if you had a family."

"No, if I had a family I would choose to live at home but if I decided to go away I would take the children with me." He turned to me. "Does that bother you?"

"No," I shook my head, "not at all."

Smiling with contentment he reached over and took my hand while we sat looking up at the stars that filled the universe. That night our lovemaking was slow and gentle.

The following afternoon we stood beside the car saying good-bye to the whole family.

"Christine we do hope that we will see a lot more of you, and soon," Elizabeth said as she gave me a warm hug.

Taking my hand Andrew looked at me with affection. "It's been a pleasure meeting you Christine. I always knew that my brother had good taste." He teasingly winked at Stephen.

By the time we climbed into the car my heart was filled with a sense of belonging. Facing front and looking ahead at the road I heaved a big sigh.

"You guys right now I'm so happy, happier than I've been in all of my life."

Both Stephen and Arthur grinned with contentment as they gazed at the woman that they loved.

Chapter Fifteen

There was one fundamental aspect of my life that I hadn't shared with Stephen---my dreams. I believed that if he became aware of the strange enigma that had been inflicting me throughout the years I would lose him forever. If I did lose him I know that a great part of me would vanish leaving only a reflected image of myself therefore I kept the bizarre unnatural happenings protectively hidden away from him. I had been with him for only a few months but I felt that I had always lived in him, and he in me.

Of course it was only inevitable that he should find out and when he did, it did not happen by choice. One day while shopping in the city I was unable to find what I was looking for so I decided to go to a mall that was situated a short distance out of town. Keeping to my left, while on the highway, with the intention of turning at the approaching intersection I slowed the car down and stopped for a red light. As I waited at the head of the line my gaze shifted diagonally to the oncoming traffic, specifically to the passengers that were in a now stationary car. Suddenly my personal radar became activated causing my eyes to open just a little wider. When I focused on the driver all three front passengers turned their heads in unison automatically picking up acknowledgment that was not supposed to be. At first they responded with surprise, then with concern.

The driver was a dark haired man, around thirty-five years old, sporting a very distinctive ebony black beard. Each hair was oddly the same length, about a quarter of an inch, with well-defined borders as though it had been painted on with a brush. In the middle sat a woman who appeared to be of the same age but with non-specific features, while on the passenger side another man was also staring at me with curiosity. This one was clean shaven and also had hair that was lighter in color than the first man. The driver turned and said something to the three in the back seat which resulted in all six of them looking in my direction.

My mind froze, my stomach tightened, and I shuddered with alarm. 'My God they're travelers and they know that I'm aware of them! What could they be saying to each other, and what are they thinking?' I felt totally exposed and completely vulnerable with no place to hide.

Suddenly the insistent sound of a horn startled me out of my daze causing my mind to snap back to the traffic and the green arrow in front of me. Quickly pressing on the accelerator I turned the car to the left and moved down the street to the shopping center. By the time I parked in the lot I was visibly shaking however I consoled myself with the thought that the travelers were probably half way into the city by now. When I opened the door and climbed out of the vehicle the event was almost forgotten and shoved aside for future consideration and meditation.

Entering the building I walked directly to the back of the store, specifically to the area where I had seen some plumbing fixtures on one of my previous trips. After searching around for a few minutes I muttered under my breath. "Darn! It's not here anymore." Shaking my head with disappointment I turned to leave.

After rotating a complete half circle my mind and body froze. Standing in front of me, looming directly in my path, stood the man with the black beard. Horrified, I stared at him and was unable to think or to move. He simply returned my frightened stare with a calm smile, however at this point in my moment of fear I didn't think that it was a good smile but more like a grin. Overwhelmed with the realization that he had total control of me, that I was his to do whatever he wanted to do, I felt like a helpless bug at the end of a pin. In panic my mind screamed but no sound came through my trembling lips.

'No, no you don't want me. There are so many other pretty girls. Please don't take me---please!' Again they were only thoughts, not physical words. All the while our eyes never deviated from each other. Suddenly remembering something I looked wildly about me. 'Where is he? Where is he?' Once again it was only a thought.

'Where is who?' He looked perplexed.

'Where is the other man? Where is the man with the light brown hair who was sitting with you in the car?' When the man smiled but said nothing I frantically turned to escape in another direction. I stopped abruptly as though I had hit a brick wall. There he was only four feet away from me, the other man. My legs went weak and I thought that I was going to faint, but instead in a fight or flight reaction I looked the second man square in the eye and walked towards him. Blocking most of the aisle he made no attempt to let me pass so after taking another step and squeezing by him I said out loud. "Excuse me." As I brushed against his body the smell of his musk mixed with perspiration wafted up to my nose. When I felt a wave of passion flow through me my eyes flew open with surprise and disgust. His reaction----he smiled.

Filled with revulsion, as well as panic, I freed myself from the scene of terror and began to rush anywhere, as far as I could go to get away from them. Almost in a run I made my way to the front of the store where breathless, my eyes stinging with tears and body trembling, I found myself among the displays of Kleenex and toilet paper. I looked about me. I was alone.

"Please, please don't take me." Suddenly I gasped as another thought came to me. What if they come looking for me? The concept was enough to induce me to make a quick exit to my car. After slamming the door and locking it I frantically looked around me not knowing what I would do if they did appear. With shaking hands I turned the ignition on and quickly drove out of the lot.

When I arrived back at the cottage Stephen and Arthur were both in the kitchen starting supper. Ignoring them, I roughly pulled off my boots and threw my coat on the hanger then without saying I word I stomped past them on my way to the bathroom. Of course the two of them immediately realized that something was terribly wrong, especially when they heard me slam then lock the door. Sliding to the floor I wrapped my arms around my knees for protection then I began rocking back and forth in a state of post-traumatic shock. Suddenly there was a light knock on the door.

"Is anything wrong, Christine?" Stephen's voice was filled with concern.

"No I just feel a little ill. It must be something that I ate. I'll be right out." After pressing his ear to the door and waiting for a few moments he went back into the kitchen.

Dinner was quiet. I sat deep in thought through most of the meal hardly touching my food, while Arthur and Stephen exchanged glances but said nothing. Later that evening curled up on the couch and staring blankly into the fire, I was unaware of Stephen's approach until I felt him sitting down beside me. Staring at the dancing flames and mesmerized by their bizarre movement I glanced at him briefly. When he wrapped his arms around me he became even more worried when he realized that I was trembling.

"Why don't you tell me what's wrong Sweetheart?" His voice was calm and gentle.

I stared ahead unable to meet his eyes. "Nothing's wrong Stephen," I answered curtly.

He waited then took a deep breath. "You don't want to tell me what's wrong?"

Suddenly pulling away from him I sat forward. "Why do you keep insisting that something is wrong? Nothing's the matter. "When I looked at the hurt that was in his eyes I wished with all my heart that I could take back my words. Exhausted my shoulders slumped.

"Please Stephen. Please don't ask me."

"Christine I don't think that it will go away." His voice was so kind and gentle that in my miserable state of mind his attitude created guilt and regret within me.

My eyes filled with tears. "I know that it won't but if I tell you, if I explain what's wrong, you won't love me anymore. You'll think that I'm strange or even worse you'll think that I'm crazy and then I'll lose you forever."

"Sweetheart you will never lose me. The only thing that will drive me away from you is if you don't love me anymore. Don't you realize how much I care for you Christine?"

"Stephen I love you so much that I can't imagine my life without you."

"Nor can I imagine living without you. I've waited for you for forty years."

Since there is a pivotal point at which all decisions are made I quickly realized that telling him was inevitable.

"I have dreams, strange dreams. Sometimes I have terrible dreams." I stopped.

He said nothing but looked at me and waited.

"This is the weird part." I had to force the words from my mouth. "I don't think that they're dreams. I think that they are really happening to me."

"Ah." He looked off in the distance, nodded his head then urged me to continue.

"I see people then dream of them or dream of them then see them on the streets."

Pursing his lips he looked down at his hands. "And I imagine that this really upsets you?"

"That's putting it mildly. Stephen, many times these people are having sex with me, or else I'm on a space ship with aliens." Now I really expected him to react but instead he just stared with a grim face into the fire.

"Have you ever told anyone else about these dreams?"

"Well I once tried to tell my friend Lara but when I saw that she was really worried about my mental state of health I never brought up the subject again. Then one day I woke up beside Robert after having one of my most disturbing dreams and he suggested that I should see a psychiatrist."

Stephen didn't say anything but just sat there with such a sad look on his face.

My shoulders slumped. "You too, you think that I'm crazy don't you!" I jumped up ready to leave the room but was stopped by his stern voice.

"Christine! Look at me. Look at me!" Slowly I turned my head. "I don't think that you're crazy and I don't think that you need to see a psychiatrist. I think that you are one of the warmest and smartest women that I have ever known."

I was utterly shocked and surprised. "You do!"

"Yes. Come here Sweetheart." He reached over, took my hand and drew me into his arms. "Christine you don't ever have to worry that I won't love you because of anything that you believe in. If you say that it's happening to you, then I believe that it is. Perhaps you're not the one who's demented. Perhaps it's the rest of the world that's crazy. Perhaps you see something that they haven't the ability to see. New ideas are being proven every day." He smiled and his eyes twinkled. "Maybe one day you will look back and say to yourself, hell I wasn't loony after all."

A soft smile curled up the corners of my mouth. "Stephen you don't hate me?"

"Gracious no!"

"You still love me?"

"Of course I still love you."

"You don't know how much I appreciate that you didn't laugh at me."

He pulled me close to him. "Christine you can't keep this all bottled up inside of you. If you ever want to talk about it I want you to know that I'm here, and I'm all ears."

"You're the first person that I've been able to say things to without ending up feeling so sad and so alone, especially so alone." Just then I remembered my conversation with Crystal. "I'm wrong. I did mention one incident to Crystal my friend and she didn't laugh either.

We sat for a long time allowing my emotions to settle. He turned to me and tilted my chin up with his hand. "Would you like to tell me what happened to you today?"

I carefully studied his face, just in case there were any signs of rejection, and when I found none I told him everything in detail.

"So you're afraid that you'll dream tonight and they'll come and take you away?"

"Yes." I shuddered at the prospect.

He ran his fingers up and down the length of my arm. "I think that whatever is happening to you is important. I don't know if I can do anything to change it but I do want you to know that I will be lying next to you when we fall asleep, and I will be there with you when you wake up in the morning." He hesitated then carefully chose his words. "Maybe I'm not supposed to change it. Perhaps if I do I might ruin your destiny."

That night after making love I fell asleep snuggled securely in his arms. I woke up the next morning without any memories but I was never sure that they hadn't come.

My dreams continued from time to time. Each morning I was aware that I had had conversations with people but the details were always a blur. I never felt violated or traumatized so I quietly tolerated them. When we were alone I discussed the dreams with Stephen and after listening, with what appeared to be sincere interest, he simply smiled and hugged me. Even though he couldn't or wouldn't do anything about my dreams I felt protected. Arthur stood outside the picture sensing that something was amiss but in respect for his two friends said nothing.

One morning I awoke with a violent reaction after having a fairly disturbing dream. When Arthur walked in the kitchen I was sitting at the table across from Stephen nervously clutching a cup of hot coffee with both hands. After taking one look at me he could no longer keep quiet.

"What's wrong Christine?" He looked from me to Stephen. Stephen said nothing but turned his eyes in my direction.

Helplessly I looked at Stephen and said. "He'll laugh at me." There was a hopeless look on my face.

Stephen shook his head. "No I don't think that he will."

For a full moment there was dead silence in the room then with a deep accepting sigh I began my story. For the second time within a few weeks I described my unusual tale of events that had been plaguing me for an entire lifetime. Arthur's face remained serious as he listened with interest to every word. By the time I was finished I was trembling. Stephen pushed his chair back, went into the living room and returned with a bottle of rye, then getting a fresh cup he filled it half with coffee and the other half with the liquid in the bottle.

"Here Christine, drink this." With shaking hands I reached for the mug nearly spilling its contents then guiding it to my lips I swallowed a few large mouthfuls. As soon as the warm fluid reached my stomach I became calmer and when I looked up at Arthur he wasn't laughing.

"Do you think that I'm crazy?"

He smiled and answered in his simple direct manner. "No I don't."

I looked from one to the other. "Do both of you really believe that it's happening to me?"

After a pause Arthur answered for the both of them. "Let us put it this way. Whether we believe it, or not, is not important. What is important is what strength there is in your own conviction."

When the idea became clear in my mind I sat up poker straight in my chair as my eyes became wide with determination. "It's happening to me but I don't know why, or exactly what is happening."

"Well, maybe in time all of your questions will be answered."

"In other words I have to be patient."

"Yes."

I sat for a moment mulling over what had been said then with introspection I spoke. "All of my life, whenever I looked at myself, always in a symbolic fashion, I would see myself as a horse pawing viciously on the ground while I was being held back by a set of reins. I felt that if the reins were cut I would run without thought or direction to my destruction, possibly over a cliff, or possibly into a pit where I would be destroyed."

They sat in silence staring at me. When they offered me no advice I gave myself some. "I guess that if I'm to survive I'd better slow down."

"At least be patient," they said in unison.

I slowly nodded my head in acknowledgment of the truth. Those words of wisdom would have to suffice for now.

Chapter Sixteen

Shortly after the mentally and emotionally cleansing episode Stephen proposed to me. We were sitting in front of an open fire where several sparks exploded from the logs that were in the grate then in an erratic pattern they disappeared up the chimney. Outside the branches of the trees were covered with a mantel of soft white virginal snow. When he spoke his remark was simple and to the point.

"Christine tonight I'm going to ask you to marry me."

Not only did I stop breathing for a second but at the same time I could swear that the world momentarily ceased turning on its axis. I had been waiting for this moment ever since I first saw him standing at the edge of the water.

"In the beginning I was planning to ask you to marry me in an extravagant glamorous setting, but the more I thought about it the more I knew that those places were wrong. Instead I wanted to ask you the most important question that would ever come up in my life in a place that already had meaning to us. That was when I realized that this was that place. This is where we met, where we shared our love, and where you made me the happiest man in the world. This is the place that I want to remember always."

Carefully removing his arm from around me he sat foreword, reached into his jacket pocket and pulled out a small velvet box. Opening it he picked up the ring between his forefinger and thumb.

"Christine, will you marry me? Will you share this lifetime with me?"

"Oh Stephen, yes, of course I will marry you. I'll spend this life time with you and any others that follow until you tell me that you don't want me anymore."

After he slipped the ring on my finger I held my hand up in front of me allowing the firelight to refract from the countless facets.

"It was my mother's, and her mother's before her."

As I gazed at him I saw a wonderful admirable quality that only made me love him more. "I will always feel honored to wear it. It will mean as much to me as it does to you."

"Thank you Sweetheart. You have made me unbelievably happy."

Curled up in his arms I stared with fascination into the fire.

"You know, now that I look back I realize that I was always aware of what lay ahead for me. Even when I was with Robert I kept feeling you out there, especially when things weren't going too well. When the world was crashing down around me the thought of you often gave me the strength that I needed. It's so much easier to deal with the past and the present, but the future, when I'm waiting for something nice to happen, sends me into a tailspin. The past I can process and file away then finally cut the strings. The present one takes one moment at a time, but the future, especially when it wraps itself around you can be very distracting, almost destroying." I sighed. "You know looking back I can now see where my relationship with Robert was a process for growth."

He ran his hand up and down my upper arm. "Sweetheart so am I."

My eyes flew open as I turned to him. "You don't mind being a process for growth?"

He gave a slight chuckle. "No. That's the reason for any relationship. We meet in this world in order to learn so that we may pass onto a higher level. If one is with a person who becomes more of a hindrance, than an asset, that person may get in the way of one's goal. It doesn't mean that that person is wrong for you because usually there is something to be learned by all associations." Stephen paused for a second. "One thing that is very important is that you have to know **when** to let go."

"It's like it was for me with Robert."

"Yes."

"Stephen everything is always so simple when I'm with you. I love you so much." We sat for a long time saturated in our happiness.

When Arthur joined us the next morning he found me grinning like a Cheshire cat and flagrantly waving my left hand in the air while preparing the breakfast. He immediately noticed the ring.

"Congratulations to both of you. The next time I'll make certain that I am not related and then I'll give you a run for your money. She's a very special lady."

During breakfast a thought came to me while I was dangling a piece of toast between my forefinger and thumb. "I have an idea, why don't we have the wedding here at the cottage and during the Christmas Season?"

The two of them stopped eating and stared at me. I looked wide-eyed from one to the other.
"Stephen you could invite your immediate family, as well as a few friends, and I could invite my acquaintances from out west. As far as relatives are concerned Arthur is the

only family that I really have. Not only will there be enough sleeping space between your place and mine, it will also be an excellent way for you to meet my friends." With high expectations I grinned from one to the other. "Well?"

"That's not a bad idea. In fact the more I think about it the more I like it. I'm well acquainted with a judge who is also a close friend of the family. Let me talk to him." He pushed his chair back and disappeared into the den only to reappear moments later with a wide grin on his face. "He said that he could fit us in on December the twenty-third."

I jumped up and threw my arms around Stephen. "Oh Stephen, now I really feel that we are getting married."

I could hardly wait for the two-hour time zone difference to pass so that I could call both Lara and Crystal out west. Finally!

"Lara! Hi! How are you?" I had difficulty containing my excitement.

Lara glanced at her watch. "Fiiine....! And how are you." She screwed her face up in obvious confusion.

"Have you made any plans for Christmas?"

"No, I haven't made any yet." She looked as though she was waiting for the punch line.

"Would you like to spend the holidays with us here at the cottage---and be my maid of honor." The last phrase was almost a squeal.

"What? Would you kindly repeat those last words! Am I hearing right? Is my little girl getting married?"

"Yes! Stephen asked me last night. I'm so happy. Lara."

"Oh Chrissy, so am I, so am I. Congratulations! I have a feeling that it's going to be a marriage that is made in heaven."

"So do you think that you and Tom can make it?"

"Of course I'm sure."

"What about Bill and Becky?"

"I'm not sure about Bill but since Becky is already in Ontario I'm sure that she'll love to come. Oh, by the way, I was going to call you the other day to tell you that she's found herself a new boyfriend. They came here last weekend and he's really nice. He understands what Becky has gone through and he is going into therapy with her so he can help her cope with any problems that might come up. Chrissy it takes so long to make everything right again."

"I know." The once familiar pain had become an almost alien emotion to me.

"So what day do you plan to get married?"

"On the twenty-third of December but come early and remain as long as you want. All of you will be staying here at the cottage so you don't have to worry about accommodations."

"I'll talk to Tom and get back to you when I'm more certain of the time frame."

"Oh Lara, this is going to be the best Christmas ever."

Next I called Crystal. I wasn't as optimistic but was pleasantly surprised, first to find her home and secondly to hear her say that she and Armand could come.

"I do have Christmas off this year but I would still be there even if they fired me."

While I was contacting **my** friends Stephen was over at his cottage using his personalized phone list. His family was ecstatic upon hearing the news, not only because they were happy that Stephen was finally getting married, but also because they all loved me. After talking to his brother and sister he called two very close friends who were also happy for his good fortune and promised that they and their wives would be there.

"It will be a real old fashioned Christmas," Stephen promised them, "with chestnuts roasting on the open fire and Jack Frost nipping on your nose."

Returning to the cottage he informed me that one of his friends had invited him for lunch in Toronto but that he would be back by dinner.

"That's nice. Enjoy yourself."

"Thanks Sweetheart." As he turned to leave I called his name.

He looked back at me. "Yes?"

"Do you mind if I ask Carlotta?"

"Of course I don't mind. You don't have to ask my permission."

"I know." I looked troubled.

His face became somber. "Its Paul isn't it Christine?"

I sighed, "I guess I'll have to ask him too."

Stephen gave me an 'unfortunately, yes' look.

I sighed again. "I'll talk to you at dinner."

The moment he left I turned on my phone and dialed Carlotta's number at her shop.

"Of course we'll be there. I'll talk to Paul tonight." Before disconnecting she gave me a meaningful look. "Thanks for asking us Christine." I returned her look and simply nodded.

I spent the time from breakfast to lunch flipping through magazines and making lists of things that had to be done. Everything was checked in an orderly fashion and soon the task seemed less awesome and easier to overcome. I was pouring over some figures when I heard someone coming through the front door and when I looked up Arthur was in the process of removing his boots.

"Hi. I was just going to look for you."

"What is it Christine?"

"Please sit down for a few moments. I have something to ask you."

As I looked at him I suddenly felt sad for this unconventional kind man who had chosen a solitary path in life. After his unfortunate breakup with his wife he had elected to move forward, to advance without a commitment to another soul, until me. Although his smile was broad the light in his eyes seemed to have dimmed a little.

"I'm so sorry Arthur. I do love you."

"I know Christine. I don't want you to think that I'm not happy for you because I am. I guess I've been so content having you here with me for the last several months that I'm going to miss all of that."

"But I'll still be here. The three of us get along so well together and all of that will never change."

His eyes became wistful as he saw more than I did. "Perhaps it won't, anyway, not to worry."

"Arthur, Stephen told me that he was having his brother as best man."

"Yes. That's what I've been told." He looked into my troubled face. "Is something wrong?"

I drew in a deep breath and hesitated before asking him.

"Arthur I want to ask you if you would give me away at the wedding." I studied his reaction and quickly added. "If you don't want to I'll understand."

He reached over and took both of my hands in his. "I would be more than pleased to give you away. I would have been disappointed if you hadn't asked me."

My eyes became moist. "Thank you so much. You are so important to me. I'll tell Stephen when he gets home."

He leaned forward and slapped his knee. "Well I'd better get back to my chores."

As he stood up so did I. Taking the few steps towards him I wrapped my arms around him. We stood holding each other for a long moment then with one last squeeze he put on his boots and disappeared out of the front door.

Chapter Seventeen

With both Christmas and my wedding approaching the days didn't seem to have enough hours in them. Since I planned to have the event catered many of the items would automatically be taken care of except for my wedding dress. Instead of using the yellow pages I turned on the videophone and called Stephen's sister.

"Congratulations Christine! We're so happy that the two of you are getting married. Actually I was going to call you shortly."

"Thanks Elizabeth. "I hate to bother you but I was wondering if I could ask you for some advice."

"Certainly, what can I help you with?"

"I need the name of a reputable catering service as well as a good florist."

"Sure. I'll give you the names of the services that our family always uses. I'm sure they'll be more than satisfactory."

"The last item might prove to be more difficult. I have to get a dress and I realize that I don't have too much time."

Elizabeth thought for a moment. "Let me make a few phone calls and I'll get back to you."

Within half an hour the phone rang. "Are you busy tomorrow?"

"No, why do you ask?"

"I've spoken to the owner of a couturier shop in Toronto and he'll see us after lunch. They're the best in the area."

I was so relieved. "Oh Elizabeth you don't know how much I appreciate what you've done for me."

Elizabeth smiled and said. "Well you're going to be my sister aren't you?"

"My eyes became moist. I've always wanted a sister."

"Christine you have more than a sister you have a whole family, that is if you want us."

After discussing it with Stephen we decided that it would be prudent for me to make one trip to Toronto rather than commuting back and forth each day. Once again Elizabeth came to my rescue by asking me to stay with her at her house. When we had everything arranged by late Friday afternoon I climbed into my car and headed for home.

As I pulled into the driveway a lump formed in my throat. Stephen and Arthur had put up the decorations in the yard making the whole place resemble a Christmas card. The moment I walked through the doorway Stephen took me into his arms creating an immediate sexual response. After helping me off with my coat we walked together into the living room.

Looking out through the front window I gazed at the dozens of trees that were covered with tiny glistening miniature lights. "Thank you so much Stephen. It was so thoughtful of you."

"You'll have to thank Arthur. I was working under his direction."

I smiled as I remembered the previous year. "I thought so."

When Arthur joined us for a late dinner I showed my appreciation with a big hug then later at the table I filled them in on what had transpired in Toronto. Feeling exhausted from the trip, as well as being eager to share my needs with Stephen, I excused myself early and it wasn't long before he entered the room. After quickly shedding his clothes and anxiously creeping in beside me the now familiar touch of our bodies soon enflamed an immediate response.

Finally everything was ready for the wedding and the first of our visitors began to arrive. While standing beside Stephen at the airport I nervously shifted from foot to foot as I strained my eyes towards the arrival doorway. Finally Lara and Tom came into view and in seconds we were in each other's arms.

"It's so good to see you. Oh, Chrissy, we miss you so much."

"Congratulations, Sis." Tom gave me a hug and a kiss.

Turning to Stephen Lara and he embraced with a kiss on the cheek then he eagerly shook hands with Tom.

That evening I sat with my friends enjoying both the old and the new. We talked for hours reminiscing over our lives together, and from time to time we filled Stephen and Arthur in on details. The two of them beamed with pride as they watched me interacting with my old friends.

The next day we went to Toronto and, much to our relief, both gowns fit like a glove. That evening Crystal and Armand arrived in a pre-arranged limousine, and shortly behind them Becky and her new bow Brent showed up at the door. Finally, when Stephen's family arrived, including the children, everyone seemed to be talking at once. Luggage and gifts were misplaced then found and deposited into the correct rooms. By the morning of the wedding there was so much commotion that I had my doubts as to whether it would have been far better to elope, but when the dust settled and Arthur stood beside me in the upstairs hallway everything fell into place.

"Your mom and dad are smiling down at you right now Sweetheart. They're so proud of you, and so am I."

Suddenly my parent's warm presence seemed to surround me. "Yes I can feel them too Arthur. They want to thank you for watching over me. Oh Arthur I can almost see them."

"I can too." Giddy with happiness he looked down at me. "Are you ready?"

Slowly the two of us made our way arm in arm down the stairs to the living room while a man and a woman harmonized together. Standing beside Stephen and amongst the people that I loved my heart couldn't have been fuller. As I looked at Stephen then to the people that filled the room I thanked my God for granting me such a magnitude of happiness.

Gazing into each other's eyes we spoke of our love and made promises to support and give aid, but never to control or destroy each other's dreams. With his authoritative words the magistrate pronounced us as man and wife. Kisses and tears of joy mingled with hugs and wishes for all the best that life had to offer.

My life had been a long road, sometimes twisting and painful, but all of that seemed inconsequential now. By making the right choices, some of them most difficult, I had arrived where I should be. Love and happiness would follow me from this lifetime into the next. I had my family. I had the man of my dreams.

Chapter Eighteen

Some people say that when one thing is given to you in this life, another one is taken away. And so it was on a particular stormy night in February.

Outside the howling wind was beating viciously against the solid brick structure of the condo, while inside Stephen and I were snuggled comfortably in front of the blazing fire. After the global headlines were over the local news came on. The first story was about the snowfall and the resulting accidents that had occurred on the 401, one of the busiest highways in North America. When the faces of Carlotta and Paul suddenly appeared on the screen, along with the mangled mass of metal on the side of the road, we both gasped and leaned forward in our chairs. Apparently Carlotta had been transferred by helicopter with life threatening injuries to the nearest hospital while Paul was examined in Emergency then discharged with only cuts and bruises. Evidently they had been returning from their cottage when the accident had occurred.

I quickly jumped to my feet. "Oh my God, I'm going in to see her."

"Wait a minute. Think about it. Are you sure that they will let you in? Usually only family members are allowed to visit?"

"I don't care. I'll find a way." I was in the process of pulling on my boots when I realized that Stephen was standing beside me and putting on his coat.

"You didn't think that I would let you go alone, did you?"

After inquiring at the desk in the lobby we hurried to the elevator. Just as we were stepping off we nearly collided with Paul who grabbed my arm to avoid falling.

"Sorry. Do you mind if I sit down for a minute? I feel a little weak."

After assisting him over to several chairs that were conveniently placed along the wall he sat down and attempted to collect his self. Directing his comments to me, probably due to the typical nurse-doctor relationship, this is what he said.

"Carlotta has life-threatening injuries. She's unconscious and is ventilated. The M.R.I. shows extensive fractures and the E.K.G. shows no brain activity. Christine it doesn't look good." With his head bent down and with hands covering his face soft muffled sobs could be heard.

After several awkward moments I reached over and rested my hand on his shoulder. "I'm so sorry Paul. Steven and I both love Carlotta too." There was another awkward moment. "Do you think that I could go in for just a minute to see her? I promise you I won't be long."

At first he stared into my eyes with a strange look then he nodded his head once in consent. "I'll arrange it with the nurses." After talking to what appeared to be the charge nurse he turned and gave me a nod.

While I was passing Paul our eyes locked one more time. It felt as though I was looking into a pool of diametrical emotions, a concept that left me with a sick feeling in the pit of my stomach. Quickly I turned and walked through the swinging doors.

Lying on a sea of linen Carlotta's jet black hair had been replaced with a wide white dressing, like some new

Paris fashion. On her chalk-colored face a ventilator tube protruded from her mouth but other than that her face was free of cuts and bruises. Her eyes were closed giving the illusion of a deep calm sleep, while her chest rose in synchrony to the whooshing sound of the respirator as though it was keeping harmony to some colossal tune. As I stood beside her and looked down at her frail body I reached out and took her limp lifeless hand in mine. Feeling weak I pulled a near-by chair over and sat down.

"Oh, Carlotta, why is this happening to you? What did you do to deserve it?"
As I attempted to communicate with my friend I was unaware of the passage of time. Suddenly I realized that someone was standing behind me.

"Would you like to come back tomorrow?" There was no hint of compassion in his voice and his face took on the old familiar hardness while his eyes burned into mine. "I know that it would be what Carlotta would want."

Immediately he had made it clear to me. He certainly wasn't burying the 'hatchet', so to speak, he was doing it for Carlotta. It had nothing to do with our association with each other. Up to then all that I had seen in him was hate, disdain, and cruelty towards others, but he did love her. Bending down I kissed my friend on the forehead then silently left the room.

For the next week I continued to visit the hospital each day and each time there was no improvement in Carlotta's condition. When I was with her I attempted to transfer some of my energies into the wasting body however I knew that it was useless.

One week to the day after I had relieved Paul of his vigilance I knew that the end was near. I could almost smell death as I walked into the room. Sitting in the chair beside the bed tears welled up in my eyes and rolled down my cheeks. Bending over and repressing choking sounds I kissed her cold fingers.

What I experienced next was similar to episodes that I had witnessed with other people but this time it was different. It was happening to me. I first felt Carlotta's hand twinge but ignored it, then I felt the definite tightening of her muscles. Puzzled, I looked up into eyes that were open and staring at me. There was a serene smile and her face as well as a look of total happiness and love.

"Oh Carlotta, I love you so much. I don't want you to go."

The look on her face told me that it wasn't her body that I was looking at but it was her spirit. She showed no sign of pain, or sadness, only peace and tranquility. For five minutes I saturated my senses with her overpowering ethereal beauty then as though she had whispered the words in my ear I realized that there wasn't much time.

"Carlotta would you like me to get Paul for you?"

This time Carlotta slowly closed her eyes in response.

After leaning over and tenderly kissing my friend I hurried to the doorway. There I turned and gazed at her for the final time. For those few prolonged seconds a whole lifetime was said with our last lingering look then I quickly rushed out of the room.

When I entered the waiting room Paul was sitting in a forward position in one of the lounge chairs with his hands dangling in front of him. As he looked up and stared into my eyes he immediately knew. Jumping up he fled through the doorway leaving me alone with my grief. That was when the tears really flowed, tears for Carlotta, for me, and for all of those who would be left behind.

Perhaps fifteen minutes later the nurse came out to inform me that Carlotta had just passed away.

Chapter Ninteen

It was on one of my shopping trips to Barrie when traffic is backed up bumper to bumper that I had my next unusual encounter. Several drivers were displaying their irritation by loudly honking their horn and muttering under their breath as they visibly cursed the world and their God for all their ills.

As I was studying the people who were strolling past my almost stationary vehicle I suddenly stiffened and sat foreword. My eyes instantly became focused on a man whose unusual arrogant posture and demeanor totally captivated my interest. Figuratively speaking he reminded me of a peacock as he strutted in a curious elated fashion, and he appeared to be taking in everything as though he was seeing it for the first time. He was a good-looking man in his thirties, again with unusual features, but his clothes were far from discrete. His sports jacket was rather flashy however the hat on his head was the more curious piece of apparel. It had an unusually large brim for the fashion of the day and sported a flaunting flirtatious feather.

My car had now come to a complete stop in the curb lane. While the man was absorbing everything around him he suddenly seemed to sense my presence. Jerking his head in my direction our eyes met---and locked. The smile on his face seemed to be curious as well as pleased as though he recognized who, or perhaps what, I was. As he did so I was filled with sheer panic of the inevitable. At that precise moment I knew without any doubt that this man was going to have sex with me. I knew it! I knew it!

By now the traffic had come to a stop and my car was positioned directly beside him. While he stood rooted to the spot a luminous energy seemed to radiate around his body. Frozen with horror I attempted to become invisible by shrinking behind the steering wheel while my thoughts screamed out at him. 'Please don't do it', I begged. 'Please, I don't want to do it. I'm not beautiful. Find someone else.'

He returned my request with a satisfied smile.

When I was able to move my car foreword, then past him, I maneuvered in and out of the traffic in a dangerous fashion. Sick to my stomach and with shoulders drooped in defeat I periodically pounded on the steering wheel while cursing under my breath. "Shit!"

Stephen's car was in the driveway when I pulled up to the house. Climbing out I grabbed the parcels off of the seat then slammed and locked the car door behind me. After struggling with my bags I managed to open the cottage door and with one movement I pushed it closed with my foot. Dropping my packages on the kitchen table I kicked off my boots and roughly hung up my coat. I was still angry when I walked into the living room where Stephen was sitting on one of the chairs deeply engrossed in a book. When I reached him I knelt on the floor and rested my head on his lap.

He looked down at me. "Well, well. What is this?"

Without raising my head I answered. "It happened again."

He tilted his head and looked at me sadly. "You saw another traveler?"

"Yes. He's going to have sex with me tonight." My voice was flat with little or no emotion in my words. He stroked my hair. I sighed.

That evening the supper hour was rather silent. As we quietly ate our food Arthur's eyes moved from me to Stephen but he said nothing. Later we programmed a movie on the television. I was having a difficult time to concentrate therefore I simply stared vacantly into space. In bed Stephen gathered me up in his arms and held me tighter than usual.

"Are you all right, Christine?"

"Yes I nodded. Do you think that we should make love before or after he does?"

Anxiously raising his head Stephen examined my face with concern, but when he saw my sarcastic grin he relaxed. "It's up to you, Sweetheart."

After a second, or two, I turned my head and raised my face to his. Kissing him full on the mouth I parted my lips and passionately moved my tongue sensually over his. My hands began wandering over his body, stroking, gently pinching and caressing him. Immediately he responded and we made love with such intensity that it surprised both of us. Afterwards feeling contented I fell asleep in his arms.

Chapter Twenty

The next thing that I was aware of was of me being in a small spaceship along with the man that I had met on the previous day, the Peacock. While in my usual dream-like state of mind my abductor led me by the hand to the area where the table and benches were located, then standing in front of me he pressed my back on the cold hard surface. When he entered I found it slightly painful but I endured the ordeal. Evidently a previous sexual experience did not matter to the traveler.

It was at that point that I began to look about me and realized that we weren't alone. Two uniformed men, whose attention was not entirely directed on their work but more on the activity that was taking place on the table, moved about in front of the controls. Since I was not in the habit of having an audience while having sex, this embarrassed me.

The two men ,who were attired in the usual dark garb ,were also sporting something new. It took a considerable effort to concentrate before I realized what it was. Each man was wearing a metallic strip, actually three of them, one around their forehead, one around each ankle and the third was around their waist or their neck. I wasn't a hundred percent sure but I thought that it was around their waist.

The man who was using me broke my concentration on his two friends. He sounded quite irritated. "You don't seem to be enjoying it?"

"I'm not," I responded honestly.

"Why aren't you?" I felt that he was losing his patience with me.

"Because I don't love you," I answered.

"Love, what does love have to do with it" the stranger spat out the words in disgust.

"I don't like to have sex with anyone unless I love them." I felt frustrated when I realized that he didn't understand me, and I also felt helpless when I knew that there was no way that I could convince him of my view.

"That's so stupid," then he stood up and offered me his hand. The two men in uniform continued to glance our way as they moved about in front of the panels. Whatever possessed me to say the next few words is unexplainable because I really didn't have the slightest idea of their meaning. I looked him square in the eye and defiantly said, "I'm going to tell someone."

He notably bristled while the two men stopped abruptly in their tracks and looked at me with surprise and curiosity.

"What do you mean you're going to tell someone? Who are you going to tell?" When I informed him who I was going to tell the traveler paled as he stared at me in disbelief. "You know one?"

"Yes, and I'm going to tell him." When I saw his reaction I was so pleased with myself. Finally I wasn't so helpless, so much on the receiving end.

As the two workers glared at the peacock there was absolute silence in the room. Eventually one of the workers said. "Didn't we tell you that one day you would pick the wrong person to have sex with? Well, it looks like you finally did."

For a few minutes the man tried to reason with me, almost begging me to reconsider, but I firmly held my ground. "No I'm not going to forget what happened and I'm going to tell him what you did to me."

Obviously feeling quite anxious he announced that he was going to send me back.

Since I was eager to get away I quickly moved towards the exterior door. "Not that door," one of the workers called out. That door goes to the outside. Over there on one of the pads." He pointed to the right in the direction of a metal structure.

Still upset by the ordeal the traveler muttered under his breath. "I would love to send you out through that door."

"Don't you dare," one of the men yelled at him. "You're in enough trouble already."

I was placed on the pad and the next thing that I knew I was waking up in my bed. It was morning. The sun was shining through a slit in the curtains and Stephen was lying beside me breathing heavily in asleep. I lay for a long time reveling in my memories, smiling with satisfaction at the turn of events. I finally had gained a little control. What small pleasures I had.

During that day my mind frequently turned to the most recent episode. I attempted to compute the latest knowledge along with the rest of the already processed information that I had gathered during my lifetime. My life was like a great big puzzle and so far the pieces were totally scattered, but never-the-less falling into place. It always frustrated me that there were no reference books, no educational lectures, no soul with the same story, well except for the one man that I had encountered in the store and then let slip through my fingers. I did though have one advantage. I had two avid listeners. It was while relaxing after dinner that I gave them a play-by-play account of what had happened.

"What bothers you the most about your experiences?" Stephen asked.

I thought about it for awhile before answering. "Without any doubt it is the total feeling of vulnerability and loss of control. They come like a thief in the night and take what they want disregarding any objections that I might have. We all pride ourselves of being the captain of our own ship but suddenly I found myself to be one of the work slaves, having no say, no value, almost as though I don't even exist. It's a very destroying concept. No one ever asks me if I want what is happening to me because they don't need my consent."

"Would you give it if they did ask for it?"

I reflected for a moment. "If I was oriented to the circumstances I would probably consent to some of the situations but I would certainly be selective."

"What else bothers you?" It was Arthur's turn to ask a question.

"I guess the casual way that they have sex. I have a friend who would have no problem with the situation but I'm not prepared for it. It seems to be done publicly and appears to be a practice that is as common as shaking hands. It's probably just a different social-sexual society. Actually we, on this earth, have had similar civilizations and probably still do today. I know that during the reins of the Pharaohs in Egypt people were naked and sex was done openly."

Stephen looked down at his hands. "But it certainly doesn't coincide with the present moral judgments which are the backbone of our country."

"Oh heavens no, any church would automatically think of them as being the spawns of the devil himself." I looked off in the distance. "Who is right? Who is right?"

Steven looked into my eyes. "Perhaps there is no right or wrong. Perhaps each person lives their lives the way their conscience dictates. Codes that are right for one person may not be right for another but we cannot force our beliefs on other people. Maybe all of us are right. Maybe all of us are wrong."

I reflected over what he had just said. "You know when I think back no traveler has ever hurt me. Oh, they all have had sex with me and taken me against my will but they were never cruel. In fact some of them have loved me. I know by our standards taking someone against their will would be looked upon as being barbaric but by their code perhaps it isn't."

"It sounds as though you are defending them," Stephen said, looking at me quizzically.

"No I'm not defending them. I'm just trying to understand how a mind from another society, from another reality, thinks. Perhaps we look strange to them." I let out a deep sigh. "I don't know. I just don't know. There are so many unanswered questions, so many pieces that don't fit."

Stephen looked at me fondly. "Well one thing that you have to admit to is that your life certainly isn't boring."

I chuckled. "No, actually as frustrating as it is I probably would miss it if it ever disappeared."

I sat staring into the fire for a few seconds. "You know, the man that had sex with me last night."

They both nodded.

"Well the next morning while I was lying in bed thinking about him I heard a mental utterance in my head." I looked off to the corner of the room. "It's hard to explain but I know that it was a male voice. Anyway he said that the man must be reprimanded for what he did to me. That really surprised me because in the past I don't ever remembering anyone caring. He then said that the type of punishment would be of my choice."

At this point I made a face as I stared at Stephen, then Arthur. "Now I wanted to be fair so I suggested that someone do the same thing to him that had been done to me. I realized that sex would not be a punishment for him but instead would be a reward so I added that it must be with someone undesirable or else under an awkward situation. It must be distasteful to him." I paused for a second. "You know I really find it uncomfortable being his executioner."

Looking grim the two of them only nodded as they joined me in staring into the fire.

It was exactly a year to the day that I was once again to meet this traveler and it happened while driving on one of the main roads of the city. I was casually listening to some easy listening music when I suddenly became alert. My senses stiffened as it does when a wild animal catches the scent of an intruder. My eyes immediately focused on an oncoming car that was still in miniature in the distance however I already knew who the driver was. In an anticipated preparation a calm feeling came over me.

As it moved closer and closer I squinted in an attempt to see its occupant more clearly. Finally I could make out the form of the solitary person, and within seconds I could see the shape of his face. Our eyes met for only a brief moment but it was as though time itself slowed down. It was as though a prearranged meeting had been planned so that an exchange of thoughts could take place.

It was the peacock. As a consciousness of love flowed between us we both smiled along with the surrendering words of touché, then like a ship that passes in the night he disappeared from view. In the future I always thought of him with great affection.

Chapter Twenty-one

In the past Stephen had resided in a two-bedroom condominium in the city so that once we were married we moved into the building. However we continued to drive to our home on the lake on weekends. With Stephen resuming his work in the University of Toronto I decided to take on a new project in order to avoid boredom. Since the cottage area didn't have any promises I focused on the city and it wasn't long before I found an old home that could be bought at a reasonable price, renovated then sold at a decent profit. Eagerly I plunged into my new undertaking. With conflicting hours our schedules were crazy at times but I loved it. Often either Stephen, or I, didn't arrive home until late in the evening but there was never a night that we had to sleep alone. It was in early March while we were relaxing with some reading material that Stephen casually brought up the subject of our so-called delayed honeymoon.

"I was thinking that it might be nice to take a holiday this summer," the corners of his mouth turned up in a mischievous smile, "and I hear that Europe is quite nice this time of the year."

He now had my undivided attention. "Europe!" I exclaimed. "Can you get the time off?.

"I'm pretty sure that I can but what is more important can you have your project finished by then?"

"Oh yes, my project, I almost forgot about it." Without giving it a second thought I indifferently shrugged my shoulders. "If I don't have it finished by then I'll simply put it off until I get back."

With that settled we spent the remainder of the evening making plans for the upcoming trip.

On the evening before we were to leave, several bags were sitting in the front vestibule and our morning wardrobe was neatly draped over hangers. Exhausted, but filled with the energy of anticipation, Stephen sat on one end of the couch with an arm resting on my shoulder while I had my legs stretched out on a footstool in an attempt to return the circulation to the bottom part of my body.

"Oh I knew that I never should have been a nurse." The legs and the back are always the first to go.

"Would you like me to rub them for you?"

"Thanks Stephen, but I think that I'll fill up the Jacuzzi."

When we stepped into the hot water the jets were on full power. Facing each other our heads rested on the built in supports at either end while our legs crossed randomly over each other.

"This is so nice, so relaxing. Will you grab the soap and wash my feet for me Stephen?"

Picking up the bar he lathered one foot at a time gently squeezing the instep and washing well between each toe. He then moved up the length of the leg concentrating on the back of my knees then the inner part of my thighs. With both eyes closed I moaned as his hand moved gently upward.

Much later when the water had cooled down we stepped out and dried off. After making sure that the wake up alarm was set we climbed into bed and were soon fast asleep.

Chapter Twenty-two

The first country we stopped in was England. Cairns, dolmans, as well as mounds could be found scattered across the grounds of the countryside, but the Roman ruins of Stone Hedge was the most mysterious enigma of all. Both geologists and historians say that the area is probably as old as the pyramids of the Pharaohs in Egypt and many people believe that the structures were created centuries ago by what the scientists now call extra terrestrial beings.

After two weeks of sight-seeing, talking to the people, and taking miles of film, we finally drove onto one of the ferries in Portsmouth and headed for France. Standing at the rail with the cool winds tossing our hair, and whipping at our clothes, we watched the white Cliffs of Dover disappear from sight. From there we visited France and Germany, spending a week in each country. Finally we drove into Switzerland.

I fell in love with the country the moment we crossed the border. After passing through the checkpoint we drove for miles on rolling hills, passed through quaint towns and villages, and crossed over unique ancient bridges. Making our way down through central Switzerland we arrived in late afternoon in the charming ski resort village of Zermatt. This town is nestled at the head of the Nicoli Valley and is located at the most southern tip of the country. Since it is closed to automobiles and can only be reached by train or by shuttle from the village of Tasch, the only means of transportation is by foot, electric taxi, or by using one of their quaint horse-drawn carriages thus eliminating any air contamination.

Zermatt is a village that is 5,315 feet above sea level. The main fascination, the reason for its allure, is the majestic pyramidal structure at the right of the town....the Matterhorn. While we were booking into one of the town's most imposing hotels we were awestruck by the unusual décor of the lobby. Resting on a floor of inlayed flagstones, exotic and grotesque statues and demigods were scattered around the room portraying a rather sinister picture.

Upon entering our suite the valet walked over to the drapes that covered most of one wall, opened them then left after receiving a sizable tip. Slowly I approached the window, and timidly I gazed through the transparency. The unexpected fascination of the view caused me to quickly inhale and wrap my arms around myself for protection. Looming up in front of me the Matterhorn dwarfed the building and the village. I was unaware that Stephen had walked up behind me, and only realized it when he wrapped his arms around my shoulders.

"Beautiful isn't it Sweetheart."

Looking wistfully up at the mountain my eyes became moist as an involuntary shiver ran through my body. At the same time my spirit was suddenly filled with a hallow emptiness.

"What's wrong Christine? You're shivering."

"It looks so alone." I said sadly. "It just looks so alone."

That day we looked around the village. Lying adjacent to a quaint church there was a small graveyard that was dedicated to the men and women who had lost their lives in their attempt to conquer the Matterhorn.

While looking down at the markers I wandered what the last few moments might have been for these fearless adventurous victims, and how terrifying their last thoughts must have been before their death. I sadly wondered if it was all worth, while.

Later we slowly walked beside the dark foreboding lake. Due to my fear of heights I became threatened by whatever might be laying beneath the ominous surface of the still black waters. In contrast, above it, the smell of the fresh mountain air and the feelings of peace and tranquility were intoxicating. Because I was in such a secluded hidden place, and far away from the predators and the disturbing dreams, I felt safe for the first time in a long while. That night after a long Jacuzzi Stephen and I made love with such intensity and passion that it frightened me.

"I love you Stephen."

The last words I heard before falling asleep was, "I love you too Christine."

It was perhaps four a.m. when I awoke with a start. My eyes snapped open and I sat bolt upright in the bed. Fearful that I might awaken Stephen I remained very still for a few moments, then carefully I removed his arm from across my lower hip and climbed out of bed. Taking a blanket from one of the chairs I wrapped it around my shoulders and placed my feet in my slippers. After I opened the door and stepped out into the brisk night air on the balcony I gazed down on the deserted streets of the sleepy mountain village. Above me the full moon shone in the cloudless sky giving the allusion of daylight.

Easing myself into a seat I leaned my head back on a padded cushion then I slowly inhaled thus filling my lungs with fresh mountain air. I sat for a long time with my eyes closed, my mind touching on emotions vacillating from frustration to contentment. Sometimes the acceptance of my memories was very painful for me.

Eventually the sun began to rise towards the horizon and a soft morning light was cast over the mountains. Leisurely I turned my head to the left. The Matterhorn was clearly visible as it stood firmly in its solitary position, its craggy pyramidal shape rising proudly to the sky. As I stared at it I was once more overwhelmed with a feeling of sadness as I paralleled it with my own life.

I had had another dream. With my trip to Europe I had arrogantly thought that by my moving out of their line of vision I had taken control, however to my surprise they had found me in this small isolated village that was tucked in the bosom of the mountains. My lips curled upwards in a bold challenge and I gave a short chuckle. The sarcastic tone held both defeat and defiance.

With a sigh I returned my head to the back of the chair, closed my eyes then opened them again and stared out at the endless universe. As I remembered my dreams and my helplessness my eyes became hard with determination. It would be so easy to give up and to lose myself but instead I must persevere. I must remember the beauty. I must focus on the light. I will survive. I will accept my destiny without looking back, and I will choose to go forward no matter how difficult the path might prove to be. I let out a long deep sigh. After all, there is nowhere to hide.   The end.

www.ingramcontent.com/pod-product-compliance
Lightning Source LLC
Chambersburg PA
CBHW020250030726

47499CB00001B/136